D1557637

THE WOMEN OF *WEIRD TALES*

EVERIL WORRELL was born in Nebraska in 1893. She later settled in Washington, D.C., where she got married and worked for the U.S. Department of the Treasury as a stenographer and secretary. At night, in her free time, she would write weird and supernatural stories, many of which were published in *Weird Tales*, though some also appeared in *Ghost Stories*, and – because Worrell sometimes used pseudonyms – other stories may have appeared elsewhere. At least twenty-four stories have been credited to her, including nineteen in *Weird Tales*, five of which appear in this volume. Her best-known tale, "The Canal" (1927), was adapted for a 1973 episode of *Night Gallery*. She died in 1969.

ELI COLTER was the pen name of May Eliza Frost, born in 1890 in Portland, Oregon. At thirteen she temporarily went blind; after her recovery, she set out to educate herself and began a career as a writer, playing piano and organ in movie theaters to support herself while she followed her dream. Her first story seems to have appeared in 1922 in *Black Mask* magazine; she would go on to publish some fifteen stories in *Weird Tales* and several in *Strange Stories*. Her works also include tales of adventure and Western stories. She died in 1984.

MARY ELIZABETH COUNSELMAN was born in Birmingham, Alabama in 1911. She wrote numerous short stories, many of which appeared in *Weird Tales*, though she also published poetry and stories in mainstream periodicals like the *Saturday Evening Post* and *Good Housekeeping*. Her most famous tale, "The Three Marked Pennies," was reprinted numerous times, translated into at least nine languages, and adapted for both radio and television. She died in 1995.

GREYE LA SPINA was born Fanny Greye Bragg in 1880 in Wakefield, Massachusetts. She is credited with over one hundred short stories, which appeared in *Weird Tales*, *Black Mask*, and many other magazines. Her werewolf novel *Invaders from the Dark*, originally serialized in *Weird Tales* in 1925, was published by Arkham House in 1960. She died in 1969.

MELANIE R. ANDERSON is the Bram Stoker Award and Locus Award winning co-author of *Monster, She Wrote* (Quirk Books, 2019) and the co-host of *The Know Fear Cast* and *Monster, She Wrote* podcasts. She is an assistant professor of English at Delta State University in Cleveland, Mississippi. Her academic publication *Spectrality in the Novels of Toni Morrison* (2013) was a winner of the 2014 South Central MLA Book Prize. She holds a Ph.D. in American literature.

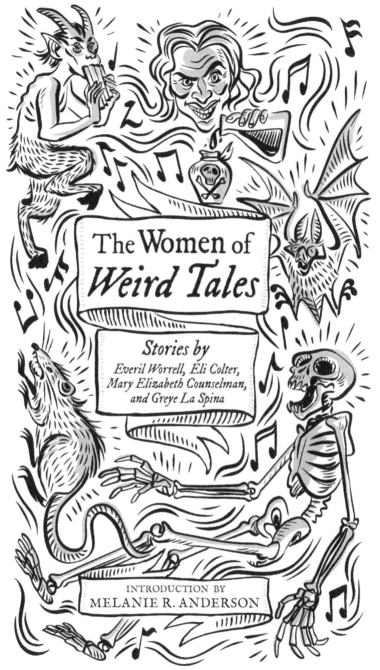

The Women of *Weird Tales*

Stories by

Everil Worrell, Eli Colter,
Mary Elizabeth Counselman,
and Greye La Spina

INTRODUCTION BY
MELANIE R. ANDERSON

VALANCOURT BOOKS

The Women of Weird Tales
First edition 2020

Compilation and artwork © 2020 by Valancourt Books
Introduction copyright © 2020 by Melanie R. Anderson

"Monster, She Wrote" trade dress designed by Andie Reid, copyright
© 2019 Quirk Books. Used under license. All rights reserved.

The stories in this volume all originally appeared in *Weird Tales* magazine
as follows: "The Remorse of Professor Panebianco" (Jan. 1925); "Leonora"
(Jan. 1927); "The Dead-Wagon" (Sept. 1927); "The Canal" (Dec. 1927);
"The Curse of a Song" (March 1928); "Vulture Crag" (Aug. 1928); "The
Rays of the Moon" (Sept. 1928); "The Gray Killer" (Nov. 1929); "The
Black Stone Statue" (Dec. 1937); "The Web of Silence" (Nov. 1939); "The
Deadly Theory" (May 1942); "Great Pan is Here" (Nov. 1943); "The
Antimacassar" (May 1949)

Published by Valancourt Books, Richmond, Virginia
http://www.valancourtbooks.com

All rights reserved. The use of any part of this publication reproduced,
transmitted in any form or by any means, electronic, mechanical,
photocopying, recording, or otherwise, or stored in a retrieval system,
without prior written consent of the publisher, constitutes an infringement
of the copyright law.

ISBN 978-1-948405-75-1 (hardcover)
ISBN 978-1-948405-76-8 (trade paperback)

Also available as an electronic book and an audiobook.

Cover by M. S. Corley
Set in Bembo Book MT Pro

Introduction

LIVE BURIAL, CURSES, THE RISEN DEAD, GHOSTS, women who
turn out to be vampires, mad scientists so obsessed with their
studies that they sacrifice their beautiful wives to the work,
mad artists who create art no matter the cost to the subject, and
townspeople held hostage under bizarre circumstances. Upon
reading this list of plot details, classic horror fans may immediately think of Edgar Allan Poe, Sheridan Le Fanu, Nathaniel
Hawthorne, H. P. Lovecraft, and maybe Rod Serling. These
fictional incidents, however, come from stories by women who
published in the pulp magazine *Weird Tales* from the 1920s to
the 1950s. This is a selection of stories by four of them: Everil
Worrell, Mary Elizabeth Counselman, Eli Colter, and Greye
La Spina.

While these women and their fiction have faded into history,
they were not the only women writing for the first incarna-
tion of *Weird Tales* (1923-1954). They are part of what scholar
Lisa Yaszek calls the "missing link" of women genre writers
between the nineteenth and later twentieth centuries. Women
had been producing these types of stories for hundreds of
years, from Margaret Cavendish in the 1600s to British Gothic
writers like Ann Radcliffe in the 1700s to Mary Shelley and all
the women writing ghost stories in the 1800s. This tradition
of women genre writers continued into the early twentieth
century, when women published fiction and poetry in *Weird
Tales* from its very first issue. According to historian Eric Leif
Davin's count, 114 women authors had work printed in the

magazine before 1933, and these pieces were published in 107 of the 117 issues produced during that time span. In the 1920s and 1930s, three of the women in this collection had stories listed as the most popular with readers: Greye La Spina, Everil Worrell, and Mary Elizabeth Counselman.

In addition to the women submitting work to *Weird Tales*, women were involved in the editorial process and the creation of cover art for the individual issues. In 1938, Dorothy McIlwraith, who had previously served as editor of Doubleday's *Short Stories*, became the associate editor to Farnsworth Wright when the company that employed McIlwraith acquired *Weird Tales*. She became the editor in 1940, and she brought on numerous new writers, like Ray Bradbury, Margaret St. Clair, and Fritz Leiber, to join the already established stable of talent writing for the magazine. In the visual arts, Margaret Brundage was one of the most influential pulp cover artists of the time. Her vibrant, and revealing, portraits of women characters were stunning and sometimes led to controversy. Davin has noted that she created 66 covers for *Weird Tales* in the 1930s alone, 39 of which were consecutive. Her covers included characters such as Robert E. Howard's Conan and C. L. (Catherine Lucille) Moore's Jirel of Joiry, and her work on covers was in demand by readers and writers alike.

The four writers whose stories you are about to read were part of this larger group of women involved in the production of *Weird Tales*. Everil Worrell was talented in writing, music, and painting, and she worked as a stenographer and secretary for the U.S. Department of the Treasury. Her story "The Canal" (1927) was adapted for an episode of Rod Serling's *Night Gallery*. She skillfully subverts the narrative of the "hysterical" woman in "Leonora" (1927) and "The Gray Killer" (1929) by using the Poe-esque convention of presenting a protagonist's journal entries. Mary Elizabeth Counselman was a southern writer of fiction and poetry who taught for many years at what is now Gadsden State Community College in Alabama. Her stories often lie in that area of horror known as the weird where inexplicable happenings transcend human understanding. Eli Colter, the pseudonym of May Eliza Frost, was the one woman included here who regularly used a pen name for her fiction, which ranged from mysteries to horror to Westerns, and sometimes blended all three. In "The Curse of a Song" (1928), we see her turn her hand to a ghost story set in the Pacific Northwest. A young woman finds herself haunted by a particularly mean-spirited apparition who believes he was thwarted in love. An intensely private person, Colter's life is the most shadowed of these four writers. Last, but not least, is Greye La Spina. Born in Massachusetts, she worked in New York City as a photographer and stenographer, and then ended up in a small town in Pennsylvania where she took up weaving as a hobby. She described "The Dead-Wagon" (1927) as one of her most popular stories.

The work of these and other women writers in the pulps has been missing for many reasons, including the dismissal of genre writing in the twentieth century by the academy and some parts of the reading public and the temporary nature of the pulps. These women were publishing stories in paper magazines that were created for cheap and quick consumption. No one was anticipating the need for archival records. After the pulps, if women's work made it into paperback anthologies of genre fiction, these books were not intended as permanent evidence of the era's writing either. These issues, combined with gender discrimination in the larger society, led to what Yaszek calls the myths about women writing for pulp magazines: that they didn't exist at all, or always had to use male pseudonyms, or had to write narratives similar to what men were publishing at the time. While some women did write genre fiction with similar plots, or even, sadly, the same prejudices, as male writers of the time, many produced work that blended multiple genres. They also used the flexibility of fantasy and the weird to write from their perspectives, revise themes, and develop more complex women characters. Their work continued the trajectory of women's horror and speculative fiction from the foremothers of previous centuries to the voices that we read now.

MELANIE ANDERSON
July 2020

CONTENTS

The Remorse of Professor Panebianco

Greye La Spina

"Cielo, what an enormous crystal globe, Filippo!" exclaimed Dottore Giuseppe del Giovine, regarding the great inverted glass bell that hung over the professor's dissecting table. "What's the idea of that?" he added curiously.

The professor's black eyes rested upon the globe with the fondness of a parent. He pushed the table more centrally under the opening at the bell's lower extremity, then pulled on a chain operating a valve at the top.

"The purpose of this globe is to win me such recognition from the world of science as no man has ever enjoyed and no man after me can ever emulate," he responded, with a kind of grim enthusiasm.

"But how?"

The doctor was intensely interested.

"You are aware that Elena and I have long experimented on animals, to ascertain if that thing men call the 'soul' is at all tangible? We have now arrived at a very advanced point in our studies, so advanced that we are at a dead stop because we cannot obtain the necessary subjects for our next experiment."

"One can always find mice—or cats—or monkeys," said the doctor.

The professor shook his head decidedly.

"Such animals are things of the past, *caro amico*. We have seen the soul of a drowning mouse emerge from its body, in a spiral coil of vapor that wreathed its way out of the water to lose itself in the etheric spaces that include all life. We have watched the soul of a dying ape emerge in one long rush of fine, impalpable, smoke-like cloud that wound upward to become invisible as it, too, amalgamated with the invisible forces of the universe about us."

"I myself once saw what I believe might have been the soul of a dying man, as it departed from his body," asseverated the doctor, musingly. "Ah, if one could but detain that fine essence of immortality, what wonders could not one work in time? What mighty secrets would perhaps be discovered!"

"You understand, then, Giuseppe *mio,* what I await with anxiety? The subject for the most tremendous experiment of all! It is futile for me to attempt to make it upon one of the lower animals, since they do not possess the power of reason, and their souls would therefore be by far too tenuous for a successful experiment. I have been trying for months to obtain possession of the person of some criminal condemned to death, that I might subject him to my theory as his dying breath fled, bearing with it his soul—that about which all men theorize, but which none have yet seen or conceived of as have I."

"The idea is tremendous, Filippo. What have the authorities done about it?"

"They refuse to assist me. I cannot tell them all that I desire to do, naturally, or my rivals would try to get ahead of me. Their stupid, petty jealousy! *Quanto è terribile!*"

"Exactly what do you wish to do, and how is this bell to serve you?" inquired the doctor, a puzzled series of lines drawing across his forehead.

"I have observed, *caro mio,* that the vaporous soul of the lower animal is so much lighter than the ether around it that it withstands the pull of gravity and rises, swaying with whatever currents of air are in the atmosphere, always to a higher level, where it dissipates into invisibility.

"I have been trying to possess myself of a living human

being whose life was useless to the world, that his death might be made of transcendent value through my scientific knowledge. I constructed this crystal bell for a wonderful and stupendous purpose. It is intended to hold the tenuous wraith of the subject of my experiment.

"The valve above, open at first, will permit the air to escape at the top of the bell as it becomes displaced by the ascending essence of the dying man's soul. Then, when I pull the chain, thereby closing the valve, the soul would be retained by its own volatile nature within the bell, being unable to seek a lower level."

"Filippo, you astound me!"

There was something more than astonishment in the doctor's face, however, as his eyes searched the countenance of the professor sharply.

"My idea is indeed awe-inspiring, *caro dottore*. Your wonder is very natural," said the professor graciously.

"It must be trying to have to wait so long for a suitable subject for your experiment," ventured the doctor, with a side glance.

"Ah, how I shall love and venerate that human being who furnishes me with such a subject!" cried the professor fervently.

A deep sigh followed closely upon his words. The curtain hanging before the doorway was pushed to one side, as Elena Panebianco walked slowly into the room.

"How you will gaze upon that imprisoned soul!" cried she, with a passionate intensity that startled the doctor anew, as he turned his regard from her husband to her. "If it were a soul that loved you, how happy it would be to know that your entire thoughts were centered upon it, within the crystal bell! To see your eyes always fixed upon it, as it floated there within!"

She leaned weakly against the dissecting table, and her great eyes, dark with melancholic emotion, stared wildly out of her thin, fever-flushed face.

"*Tu sei impossibile!*" cried the professor. "What tragic jealousy is yours, Elena! A jealousy of things that do not as yet exist!"

ELENA did not reply. She loved too deeply, too passionately, too irrevocably. And the only return her husband made was to permit her assistance in his laboratory work. Her eager mind had flown apace with his: not that she loved the work for itself, but that she longed to gain his approbation. To him the alluring loveliness of her splendid body was as nothing to the beauty of the wonderful intellect that gradually unfolded in his behalf.

In private, Filippo complained to the doctor that his wife was too demonstrative. She thought nothing of distracting his attention from important experiments, with pouting lips clamoring for a kiss, and not until he had hastily brushed her lips with his would she return to her work.

"I am obliged to bribe the woman with kisses," cried the professor, despairingly.

Elena had gone so far as to affirm to her husband that she was even jealous of his research, his experiments. That was unwise. No woman can interfere between a man and his chosen life-work. Such things are, as D'Annunzio puts it, *"piu che l'amore"* (greater than love), and prove relentless Juggernauts to those who tactlessly disregard the greater claims.

"He is worn out," said Elena to the doctor. "He has flung himself into his work to such an extent that nothing exists for him but that. He studies all night. He works all day. I have to force him to stop long enough to eat sufficient to maintain life."

"Go on, Elena, go on! When my head swims, I tie cold wet towels about it. When my brain refuses to obey me, I concentrate with inconceivable force of will upon my goal. Oh, Giuseppe *mio,* my very existence is bound up in this last experiment, which, alas! I am unable to complete because the authorities will not permit me to make use of the death of some criminal—a death that must be entirely useless to the scientific world, through their blind stupidity."

The doctor shrugged, with a gesture of his slender brown hands. His eyes sought Elena's face. Since he had been away the Signora Panebianco had altered terribly. She looked too delicate; she had faded visibly. Hectic roses flamed in her cheeks. Her thin hands, too, had been too cold when she touched his in greeting. Her constant cough racked her slender body. It seemed to Giuseppe del Giovine that she had become almost transparent, so slender had she become from loss of flesh. As she went from the room slowly with a gesture of helplessness, he turned to the professor.

"Your wife is a very sick woman," he declared, abruptly.

"I suppose she must be," Filippo responded absently. "She's very nervous, I know. She disturbs me inexcusably with silly demands for kisses and caresses, actually weeping when she thinks I don't see her, because I refuse to humor her foolish whims. I've been obliged, more than once, to drive her away with cold looks and hard words, because she has tried to coax me to stop work, insisting upon my talking with her."

He began adjusting his apparatus with an abstracted air. It was as well that he did not see the expression of indignation and despair that flashed across the mobile face of the physician, who had long loved Elena in secret, but hopelessly, as he very well knew, because she was absolutely indifferent to anybody but her husband.

"Yes, Giuseppe, she interrupts my most particular experiments to caress me ardently, trying to bring my lips down on hers. Often I have reproved her severely for attempting to turn me aside from my life-work. The man whose intellect has driven him to enter the precincts of the great mystery cannot stop to dally with the folly of fools, and love is the greatest folly of all."

"Blind fool, you!" muttered the doctor under his breath. "Love is the very breath of life itself!"

"If Elena is to assist me in my last experiment, the greatest of all, I must get a subject soon, for she is wasting away fast. Oh, yes, I have observed it. Death has his fingers at her throat."

His voice was the voice of the man of science: there was not the slightest intonation that might have indicated other than passing interest in the unhappy Elena.

"What I am afraid of," he resumed, "is that even a human being's spirit will not materialize properly within the bell, unless instructed previously. And how can I expect a criminal to lend himself voluntarily to an experiment that necessitates his death for its success? No, the fool would cling too closely to his miserable life, and might even refuse to listen when I tried to prepare and instruct him. I ought to have for my experiment someone who knows just what I want done: someone who will carry out my wishes faithfully. And where am I to find such a person?" he finished lugubriously.

THE curtains over the doorway swayed to admit Elena. It was only too evident from her expression that she had heard part, if not all, of her husband's words. There was an incomprehensible expression within those dark orbs that shrank not from the glance the professor turned upon the intruder.

"There is but one person in the whole world who could, and would, be able to carry out your ideas," said she deliberately.

Filippo whirled upon Dottore del Giovine, relief and joy flashing over his face. Del Giovine gave a short exclamation and took an involuntary step forward, horror written on his face. The other man turned to Elena, caught her hands in his, and gazed down into those pellucid depths whence came the glow of a fire that burned within her heart for him alone.

"Elena! Can you really mean it? You fill me with the most intense, most vivid gratitude and admiration—and," he added hastily as if with an afterthought, "love."

"My life is burning low," was her quiet reply. "If my death can profit you, it is yours for the asking—if you desire it."

Stiff with incredulous horror, the doctor stood rooted to

the spot. Elena knew what the professor desired; she was ready, willing, to serve as the subject of his experiment. It was for her a final proof of her love for him—and a test of his love for her. She realized that she alone, of all the world, knew the occult foundations of the science that would enable her to carry out successfully the other part of the experiment.

With an access of lofty emotions, Filippo Panebianco gathered her into his arms and kissed her pallid brow. Elena's dark eyes closed ecstatically under this caress; she felt his heart beating high, but knew, alas! it was not for her; it was with renewed hope for the success of the stupendous performance to which he had long been irrevocably pledged.

"Now I shall vindicate myself to those who have called me a visionary, a madman!" Filippo cried in triumph.

His wife clung to him, her eyes seeking his with an appeal that he deliberately refused to recognize. He was only too afraid that Elena might change her mind, might refuse what he desired more than anything else on earth: the accomplishment of his plans.

Hanging eagerly and anxiously on her reply, the professor murmured: "When, Elena? When?"

"When you desire, my husband. The fire of my life is burning very low."

"This is infamous!" cried Giuseppe del Giovine, in an outburst that shook him from head to foot, so intense was his emotion. "Elena, are you, too, insane? Do you realize what you are doing? Cannot you understand that Filippo is quite mad with his visions? Even if what he has dreamed could be possible, do you know that you have offered him your death? Elena, Elena, give me your life! Put yourself into my hands! I will cure you. I know that I can cure you," he begged wildly.

The beautiful young woman looked sadly and understandingly at the impassioned doctor. She shook her head slowly. Then her eyes turned again to her husband. Giuseppe del Giovine realized that his interference was futile; Elena's life, Elena's death, both lay in the hands of the man she loved. And (cruel irony!) it was her death that would mean most to the man she loved.

The professor called a servant and issued hasty instructions; his rivals were to be summoned at once, to see the successful outcome of his experiment. Then he turned to his wife, elation shining from his glowing countenance.

"Help me prepare!" he commanded.

An expression of awful agony passed over Elena's set face, but she motioned the agitated young doctor indifferently from her path, and began to set in position various instruments on the table adjacent to that under the crystal bell.

"What are you intending to do, Filippo?" demanded del Giovine, grasping the exalted dreamer authoritatively by one elbow.

Filippo shook off that restraining hand with impatience.

"Watch, and your patience will be rewarded," was the answer, as he smiled mysteriously.

"But Elena will not die today," said the physician, his hesitating lips forming the words reluctantly.

"She will die today," affirmed the professor, still smiling.

"*Dio mio!* He is absolutely mad!" Del Giovine would have fled for assistance, but the horror of the situation rooted his feet to the spot. Moreover, an imperative gesture from the proud Elena held him frozen there, his questioning eyes on hers.

"When the bell rings, Elena *mia,* I shall free your soul from its earthly shell, on which the hold is already so frail, and let it fly upward into the crystal bell," murmured Filippo, more tenderly than his wife had ever heard him speak to her before.

"I did not believe you could do it," Elena said, strangely. "I thought you really loved me! Have you no soul yourself, my husband, that you can so relentlessly sacrifice a woman who adores you, to add fuel to the fires of your ambition?"

"Elena! No more, I beg you. You surely will not withdraw what you offered freely, of your own will?"

He turned his face from hers, lest unexpected weakness of the flesh might undo his will.

The doctor knew that Elena had risked her all on a single toss of the dice. Womanlike, she believed that Filippo would throw aside the everlasting fame which he hoped would accrue to him, instead of accepting, as he was doing, the sacrifice of herself.

With face still averted, the professor motioned his wife to place herself upon the table under the crystal bell.

She gave one dreadful, tearing sob.

"For me, life has long since lost its value," said she. "I think I may be happier dead!"

She mounted the table and stretched herself upon it.

Footsteps sounded outside the door. Came a knock. The paralyzed del Giovine saw the professor catch up a glittering knife. And then Elena turned her face upward, and gazed so earnestly at the determined and ruthless scientist that he hesitated, weakening. Del Giovine saw the beloved woman of his soul push her lips together for her husband's last kiss.

"Why spoil this last exalted moment?" murmured Filippo harshly.

He dared not risk refusing her whim, for delay would be fatal to his plans; were not his rivals waiting for the work of entrance, behind the closed laboratory door? Leaning over his wife, he hastily brushed his lips against hers. She flung up her arms at once and caught him to her with convulsive strength.

The young doctor heard her whisper, "Farewell, unhappy man!"

Del Giovine struggled to throw off the almost hypnotic spell that bound him.

Furious at the delay, and hearing another knock at the door, Filippo jerked himself away from that passionate embrace. The knife flashed—plunged downward—. Then he stood back, an expression of stupefied amazement on his face as he gazed enchanted at the crystal bell.

"It is her soul! Look! That pale mist of azure cloud that rises from her wounded bosom so lightly! See it sway and drift! Oh, ethereal vapor, now you are entering your crystal tomb! I can almost distinguish her features, Giuseppe. Look, how they change, almost imperceptibly, but surely, as the current of air moves out at the top of the bell to accommodate the entrance of her wraith!

"Why does she look at me so? She is pitying me   me! How can that be, seeing I am to be envied? Have I not attained in this moment to the loftiest pinnacle of my success? My triumph is complete! No—no—I need the envy—the jealous envy—the admiration and astonishment of my fellow-workers, to complete the glory of my success!"

Del Giovine succeeded in throwing off the lethargy of horror that had bound him; a cry burst from the hitherto paralyzed vocal cords of the young doctor.

The door burst open. Into the room rushed the little group of men who were confreres and rivals in science with Professor Filippo Panebianco. Wordlessly the triumphant professor pointed to the crystal bell, all eyes following his guiding finger.

"Dio!" he suddenly screamed, in agony and despair. "I forgot to close the upper valve! See—see—it is wide open! And there—there floats upon the air the last soft, wavering fringes of that wraith that was the spirit of my wife!"

He flung himself upon the lifeless form of the woman who had loved him too well, and beat at her with maddened fury.

"It is your fault, Elena! All your fault!"

Someone uttered a cry: "He has killed his poor wife!"

"Secure him, gentlemen! He has gone utterly mad!" warned the doctor, springing forward.

By sheer united strength they overcame the mad scientist, who fought against them furiously, uttering incoherent phrases as he struggled.

"Why did I stop to give her a silly kiss? Oh, if I had not

stopped, I would have remembered to close the valve, and the wonder of my triumph would have remained to cover with the mantle of success what they are pleased so stupidly to call my crime.

"But alas! I was always a tender fool! Oh, if only I could have remained firm against her, when she desired that fatal kiss! I, who believed I would never experience the emotion of regret, shall suffer remorse for that weakness until I die!"

Leonora

Everil Worrell

I am writing this because I shall not long be able to write it. Why does one long for the understanding and sympathy of his fellow beings—long to have that, even after the worst has befallen and he has gone from this life to that which awaits him? How many bottles laden with last messages float on lonely, unknown ocean surges, or sink to the bottom of the sea?

It will be so with this, my last message. That is, it will be uncredited, unbelieved, uncomprehended, although it will doubtless be read. But I have told my story many times, and heard them say that I am mad. I know they will say that, after I am gone—gone from behind these bars into the horrors of the fate that will overtake my spirit somewhere out in the open spaces and the blackness of night into which it will go. *He* will be there, one of the shadows that lurk in old cemeteries and sweep across lonely roads where the winds moan and wander homeless and hopeless across the waste spaces of the earth from dusk till dawn. Dawn!

But I will tell my story for the last time.

Even now, my years are those of a young girl. I am only seventeen, and they say I have been mad more than a year. When I was sixteen, my eyes were bright and my cheeks red with a color that did not come off when I washed my face. I lived in the country, and I was an old-fashioned girl in many ways. I roamed freely over the countryside, and my wanderings were shared by my only close friend, or else were lonely. The name of my friend was Margaret. Mine was Leonora.

The two of us lived only a quarter of a mile apart, and between us ran a lonely little road crossed by another like it. Our parents believed that it was safe for us, or for any child, to traverse this road between our houses alone at any hour. We had done it from our youngest days. It should have been safe, for we were far from cities, and malefactors of any sort were utterly unknown in our secluded part of the country. There were disadvantages attendant on living in such isolation, but there were advantages, too. Margaret's family were simple farmer folk of sterling worth. My father was a student of some means, who could afford to let the world go by.

On dark or stormy nights, sundown generally found me safe indoors for the night, spending the evening by the open fire. Moonlight nights I loved, and on nights when the moon was bright I often stayed at Margaret's house, taking advantage of my freedom to wander home alone as late as midnight. Sometimes Margaret did this, too, staying late with me and going home without thought of fear; but I was the venturesome one, the one who loved to be abroad in the moonlight. . . .

Do horrors such as come to me march toward one from the hour of birth, so that every trait, every characteristic is inclined to meet them?

Up to my sixteenth birthday, my life had been like a placid stream. It had been without excitement, and almost without incident. Perhaps its very calm had made me ready for adventure.

My sixteenth birthday, Margaret dined at my house and I supped with her. It was our idea of a celebration. It was October, and the night of the full moon. I did not start home until nearly midnight. I would not reach home until a little after that, but that would not matter, because my father would be asleep in bed, and, in any case, not worried about me or interested in the hour of my arrival. The bright colors of autumn leaves, strangely softened and dimmed in the moonlight, rose all around me. Single leaves drifted through the still air and fell at my feet. The moon had reached mid-heaven, and the sky was like purple velvet.

I was happy. It was too beautiful a night to go home. It was a night to enjoy to the fullest—to wander through, going over strange roads, going farther than I had ever gone. I threw out my arms in the moonlight, posing like a picture of a dancing girl which my father had—I had never seen a dancer!—and flitted down the road. As I reached the cross-road, the sound of our clock chiming midnight drifted to my ears, and I stopped.

A beautiful high-powered car stood just at the entrance to our road, its headlights off, its parking lights hardly noticeable in the brilliant moonlight.

I knew it was a fine car, because my father had one, and on rare occasions the fit took him to drive it. When he drove it I went with him, and I noticed cars, for I loved them. I loved their strength and speed, and their fine lines. I loved to rush through the air in my father's car, and was never happier than when I could coax him to drive the twenty miles to the state road, and go fast on the perfect paving. But aside from my father's car, I had never seen a good one on these little back country roads.

I stopped, although I knew I ought to go on. And as I stopped just short of the cross-road, the big car glided softly forward a few feet until it stopped, blocking the road to my father's house. My father's motor was a silent one; but this car actually moved without the slightest sound.

Until now I had not seen the driver. Now I looked at him.

His face was shadowy in the moonlight. Perhaps it did not catch the direct light. There was a suggestion of strong, very sharply cut features, of a smile and a deep-set gaze. . . .

My pen shakes until I can hardly write the words. But I heard the doctor say today that I had nearly reached the end of my strength, and any night with its horrors may be the end. I must control myself and think of the things I am writing down as they seemed to me at the time.

I was just turned sixteen, and this was romance. And so I stopped and talked to him, although we exchanged few words. That night he did not ask me to ride with him, and so I was less afraid. For with the romance was fear—but I answered his questions.

"What is your name?" he asked; and I answered, "Leonora."

"It is music in my ears," he said softly; and again, I felt that this was romance. I felt it again, when he added: "I have been looking for you for a long time."

Of course, I did not dream—I did not think that he meant that. I had read novels, and love stories. I knew how to take a compliment.

"Do you often pass this way as late as this?"

Something made me hesitate. But something about him, something about our meeting alone in the moonlight, fascinated me. If I said "no," perhaps I would never see him again.

"Very often, when the moon is full," I said, and moved to go around the car. In a moment the gloved hand that rested on the wheel had touched the broad brim of his hat; another movement, and the car shot silently ahead and was gone.

I RAN home with a beating heart. My last words had almost made a rendezvous of the night of the next full moon. If I desired, there might be another encounter.

Yet it was two months later when we met again. The very next full moon had been clear, cloudless, frostily cold—and a lovely November night. But that night I was so afraid that I even avoided the full light of the moon when I crossed our yard in the early evening to bring in a book I had left lying outside. At the thought of traversing the road that led to Margaret's house, every instinct within me rebelled. At midnight, I was lying in my bed, with the covers drawn close around me, and my wide-open eyes turned resolutely away from the patch of moonlight that lay, deathly white, beneath my open window. I was like a person in a nervous fit—I, who had never known the meaning of nerves.

But the second month, it was different.

After all, it was a fine thing to have mystery and romance, for the taking, mine. Or were they mine for the taking? Perhaps the man in the long, low car had never come again, would never come again. But his voice had promised something different. Would he be there tonight? Had he been there a month ago? Curiosity began to drive me before it. After all, he had made no move to harm me. And there had been something about him, something that drew and drew me. Surely my childish fears were the height of folly—the product of my loneliness.

I went to Margaret's, and stayed late—almost, as on that other night, until the clock struck 12. At last, with a self-consciousness that was noticeable only to me, I wrapped my heavy coat around me and went out into the night.

The night had changed. It was bitterly cold, and there was a heavy, freezing mist in the air which lay thickly in the hollows. The shadows of the bare trees struck through the dismal vapors like dangling limbs of skeletons. . . .

What am I writing, thinking of? The scream that pierced the night, I could not suppress. I must control myself, or they will come and silence me. And I must finish this tonight. I must finish it before the hour of dawn. That is the hour I fear, worse than the hour of midnight.

It is the hour when Those outside must seek their dreadful homes, the hour when striking fleshless fingers against my window-pane is not enough, but They would take me with Them where They go—where I, but not another living soul, have been before! And whence I never shall escape again.

I walked down, slowly, toward the cross-road. I would not have lingered. I would have been glad to find the cross-road empty. It was not.

There stood the car, black—I had not noticed its color

before—low-hung, spectral fingers of white light from its cowl lights piercing the mist. The cross-road was in the hollow, and the mist lay very heavily there—so heavily that I could hardly breathe.

He was there in the car, his face more indistinct in the shadow of his broad-brimmed hat than it had been before, I thought, his gloved hand resting as before upon the wheel. And again, with a thrill of fear, there went a thrill of fascination through me. He was different!—different from everyone else, I felt. Strangeness, romance—and his manner was that of a lover. In my inexperience, I knew it.

"Will you ride tonight, Leonora?"

It had come—the next advance—the invitation!

But I was not going with him. I had got the thrill I had come for. He had asked me, and that was enough. It was enough, now, if I never saw him again. This was a better stopping-point. (Remember that I was only sixteen.)

A stranger had come out of the night, had been mysteriously attracted to me, and I to him. He had asked me to ride with him.

I do not know what I said. Somehow, I must have communicated to him what I felt—my pleasure in being asked, my refusal.

His gloved hand touched his hat in the farewell gesture I remembered.

"Another night, Leonora. Leonora!"

The car glided forward and was gone. But the echo of his voice was in my ears. His voice—deep, strange, *different*—but the voice of a lover. My inexperience was sure. And already I doubted if, after all, this would be enough for me if I never saw him again. Another time, he would be as punctilious, as little urgent. But he might say—what would he say?

THE January moon we hardly saw, so bitter were the storms of that winter, so unbreaking the heavy clouds that shut us from the sky.

The February full moon was crystal-clear in a sky of icy light. The snow-covered ground sparkled, and the branches of the trees were ice-coated, and burned with white fire. But I clung to the fireside, and again crept early within my blankets, drawing them over my head. I was in the grip of the fear that had visited me before. I was like a person in the grip of a phobia, such as they say that I have now, shunning the moonlight and the open air.

It was March.

Next month would bring the spring, and then would follow summer. The world would be a soft and gentle world again, in which fear would have no place. Yet I began to long for a repetition of the meetings at the crossroad, a repetition that should have the same setting—the rigors of winter, rather than the entirely different surroundings of the season of new buds and new life. My last attack of unreasoning terror had passed away again, and again it seemed as though it left behind it a reaction that urged me more strongly than ever toward adventure.

Had *he* been at the cross-road in the bitter storms of January, and on the sparkling white night which I spent close indoors? Would he be there on the night of the next full moon, the March moon?

There was still no breath of spring in the air on that night. The winter's snow lay in the hollows, no longer whitely sparkling, but spoiled by the cold rains that had come since it had fallen.

The night sky was wild with wind-torn clouds, and the moonlight was now clear and brilliant, now weirdly dim, and again swept away by great, black, sweeping shadows. The air was full of the smell of damp earth and rotted leaves.

I did not go to Margaret's. I sat by the fire, dreaming strange dreams, while the clock ticked the hours slowly by, and the fire sank low. At 11, my father yawned and went up to his room. At a quarter before 12, I took my heavy cloak, and wrapped it around me. A little later, I went out.

I knew that I would find him waiting. There was no doubt of that tonight. It was not curiosity that drove me, but some deeper urge, some urge I know no name for. I was like a swimmer in a dangerous current, caught at last by the undertow.

The car stood in the cross-road, low and dark. Although it was a finely made machine, I was sure, it seemed to me for the first time to be in some way *very* peculiar. But at that moment a cloud swept across the face of the moon, and I lost interest in the matter, with a last vague thought that it must be of foreign make.

Then, suddenly, I was aware that for the first time the stranger had opened the door of the car before me. Indeed, this was the first time I had approached on the side of the vacant seat beside the driver.

"We ride tonight, Leonora. Why not? And what else did you come out for?"

That was true. For the first time I now met him, not on my way home, not on my way anywhere. I had met him, only to meet him. And he expected me to ride. He had never forced, or tried to urge me, but tonight he expected me to ride. Wouldn't it seem silly to have come out only to exchange two or three words and go back, and wouldn't it be better to go with him? A less inexperienced girl might take the trouble to leave her house on a stormy March night for the sake of a real adventure—only a very green country girl would have come out at all for less. I would go.

I had entered the car. I sat beside him, and when the moon shone out brightly I tried to study his face as he started the car down the narrow road. I met with no success. I had become conscious of a burning anxiety to see more clearly what was the manner of this man who had been the subject of so much speculation, the reason of so many dreams. But here beside him I could see no more clearly than I had seen him from the road. The side of his face which was turned toward me, and which was partly exposed between the deep-brimmed hat and the turned-up collar of his cloak, was still deeply shaded by the car itself; so that I had the same elusive impression as before, of strong, sharp features, a deep-set gaze, a smiling expression. . . .

WE DROVE fast, over strange roads. So closely was my attention centered upon my companion, that I did not concern myself with the way we went. Later, I was to become uneasy over the distance we had traversed; but when I did, he reassured me, and I believed that we were then on our way home, and nearly there. I thought he meant by home, my father's house; and had I not thought that, my wildest nightmare could not have whispered to me what it was that *he* called "home"!

He was very silent. I spoke little, and he seldom answered me. That did not alarm me as it might have done, because of my ever-present conviction of my childishness, my crudeness. I blamed myself because my remarks were so stupid that they were not worth a reply, and the taciturnity that so embarrassed me yet added to the fascination that made me sit motionless hour after hour, longing more than anything else in the world to get a good look at the face beside me, to arouse more interest in my companion.

Once only, he spoke of his own accord. He asked me why I was called Leonora.

I asked him if he did not think it was a pretty name, remembering how he had said at our first meeting that it was "music in his ears." But I was disappointed, for he did not compliment my name again.

"Some would say it was an ill-starred name. But, luckily, people are not superstitious as they used to be."

"If that is lucky, you can not call it ill-starred."

I wanted to provoke him into talking more to me. I wanted his attention. But he did not answer me.

I can not go on. I can not finish my story as I intended to do, telling things as they happened, in their right order. There are things I must explain, things that people have said about me that I must deny. And the night is growing late, and the rapping I hear all night long upon my window-pane, between the bars that shut me in but that will soon protect me no longer, is growing louder—as the dawn approaches. The pain in my heart, of which the doctor has said I would die soon, is growing unendurable. And when I come to the end of my story—*to the end, which I will set down*—I do not know what will happen then. But that which I am to write of is so dreadful that I have never dared to think of it. Not of that itself, but of the horrible ending to the story I am telling.

I must finish before the dawn, for it is at the dawn that They must go, and it is then that They would take me—where *he* waits for me, always at dawn.

But to explain first—people say I am mad. You who will read this will doubtless believe them. But tell me this:

Where was I from the time I disappeared from my father's house until I was found, "mad," as they say, and clutching in my frenzied grasp—the finger of a skeleton? In what dread struggle did I tear that finger loose, and from what dreadful hand? And although I, a living woman, could not remain in the abode of death, if I have not been touched by the very finger of death, then tell me this:

Why is my flesh like the flesh of the dead, so that the doctors say it is like leprous flesh, although it is not leprous? Would God it were!

Now, let me go on.

OUR SILENT DRIVE continued through the flying hours. Flying hours, for I was unconscious of the lapse of time, excepting for the once when I vaguely became uneasy at our long journey, and was reassured. Had he who sat behind the wheel refused to answer my questioning then, perhaps I would then have become frantic with terror. But his deep, soothing voice worked a spell on me once more; and in his reply I thought I could detect a real solicitude which comforted me. I was assured that we would shortly reach my father's house; I would slip in before my father could possibly have waked, and avoid questioning.

As the night grew older, it became more dismal. The moon which had swung high overhead sent long shadows scurrying from every tree and shrub, every hill and hummock, as we dashed by. The wind had fallen, but yet blew hard enough to make a moaning, wailing sound which seemed to follow us through the night. The clouds that had swept in great masses across the sky had changed their shapes, and trailed in long, somber, broken streamers like torn black banners. The smell of dank, soggy earth and rotting leaves, of mold and decay, was heavier since the wind had sunk a little. Suddenly, I had a great need for reassurance and comfort. My heart seemed breaking with loneliness, and with a strange, unreasoning despair.

I turned to the silent figure at my side. And it seemed that *he* smelled of the stagnant odor of decay that filled the night—that the smell, and the oppression, were heavier because I had leaned nearer to him!

I looked—with a more intense gaze than I had yet turned on him—not at the face that bent above me now, the face that still eluded and baffled me—but down at the arm next me, at the sleeve of his cloak of heavy, black cloth. For something had caught my eye—something moved—oh, what was this horror, and why was it so horrible?—a slowly moving *worm* upon his sleeve?

I shuddered so that I clashed my teeth together. I must control myself.

AND then, as though my deep alarm were the cue for the hidden event to advance from the future upon me, the car was gliding to a stop. I tore my horrified gaze from the black-clad arm, and looked out of the car. We were gliding *into a cemetery!*

"Not here! Oh, don't stop here!"

I gasped the words, as one gasps in a nightmare.

"Yes. Here."

The deep voice was deeper. It was deep and hollow. There was no comfort in it.

The mask was off my fear, at least. I was face to face with that, though I had not yet seen that other face.

I leaped from the car, and fell fainting beside it. Black, low-hung, and long, and narrow—I had been to but one funeral in my life, but I knew it now. It was the shape of a coffin!

After that, I had no hope. I was with a madman, or——

He dragged me—in gloved hands through which the hard, long fingers bruised my flesh—past graves, past tombstones and marble statues, and I was numb. I saw among the graves, or seemed to see—oh, let me say I saw strange things, for I have seen them since; and I was numb.

He dragged me toward an old, old, sunken grave headed by a time-stained stone that settled to one side, so long it had marked that spot. And suddenly the nightmare dreaminess that had dulled my senses gave way to some keener realization of the truth. I struggled, I fought back with all my little strength, till I tore the glove from his right hand, and the finger of his right hand snapped in my grasp—snapped, and—gave way!

I struggled in the first faint rays of dawn, struggled as I felt the old, old, sunken earth give way beneath my feet. And the sun rose over the edge of the earth, and flamed red into my desperate eyes. I turned for a last time to the inscrutable face, and in those blood-red rays of the dawn I saw at last revealed—the grinning, fleshless jaws, the empty eye-sockets of——

Statement by the Superintendent of St. Margaret's Insane Asylum

THIS DOCUMENT was found in the room of Leonora ——, who was pronounced dead of heart-failure by the resident physician. Attendants who rushed to the room on hearing wild cries, and who found her dead, believe the fatal attack to have been caused by the excitement of writing down her extraordinary narration.

The doctor who had attended her considered her the victim of a strange form of auto-hypnosis. She undoubtedly disappeared from her home on the night of the eighteenth of March, and was found two days later in an old cemetery, three hundred miles away. When found, she was incoherent and hysterical, and *was holding in her hand the finger of a skeleton*. How and where she might have come by this, it was and is impossible to surmise.

It seems, however, that she must have been lured from her home by some stranger, and have escaped, or been abandoned near the cemetery; that she must have read of the legend of Leonora, and that it must have made a morbid impression on her mind which later, following the shock which caused her to lose her reason, dictated the form her insanity was to take.

It is true that her skin, from the time of her discovery in the graveyard, had a peculiar appearance suggestive of the skin of a leprous person, or even more of that of a corpse; and (which she does not mention) it also exuded a peculiar odor.

These peculiar phenomena were among those attributed by the doctor to the effects of auto-hypnosis; his theory being that, just as a hypnotized person may be made to develop a burn on the arm by the mere suggestion without the application of heat, Leonora had suggested to herself that she had been contaminated by the touch of death, and that her physical nature had been affected by the strength of the suggestion.

The Dead-Wagon

Greye La Spina

"Someone's been chalking up the front door." The speaker stepped off the terrace into the library through the open French window.

From his padded armchair Lord Melverson rose with an involuntary exclamation of startled dismay.

"Chalking the great door?" he echoed, an unmistakable tremor in his restrained voice. His aristocratic, clean-shaven old face showed pallid in the soft light of the shaded candles.

"Oh, nothing that can do any harm to the carving. Perhaps I am mistaken—it's coming on dusk—but it seemed to be a great cross in red, chalked high up on the top panel of the door. You know—the Great Plague panel."

"Good God!" ejaculated the older man weakly.

Young Dinsmore met his prospective father-in-law's anxious eyes with a face that betrayed his astonishment. He could not avoid marveling at the reception of what certainly seemed, on the surface, a trifling matter.

To be sure, the wonderfully carved door that, with reinforcements of hand-wrought iron, guarded the entrance to Melverson Abbey was well worth any amount of care. Lord Melverson's ill-concealed agitation would have been excusable had a tourist cut vandal initials on that admirable example of early carving. But to make such a fuss over a bit of red chalk that a servant could wipe off in a moment without injury to the panel—Kenneth felt slightly superior to such anxiety on the part of Arline's father.

Lord Melverson steadied himself with one hand against the library table.

"Was there—did you notice—anything else—besides the cross?"

"Why, I don't think there was anything else. Of course, I didn't look particularly. I had no idea you'd be so—interested," returned the young American.

"I think I'll go out and take a look at it myself. You may have imagined you saw some things, in the dusk," murmured Lord Melverson half to himself.

"May I come?" inquired Dinsmore, vaguely disturbed at the very apparent discomposure of his usually imperturbable host.

Lord Melverson nodded. "I suppose you'll have to hear the whole story sooner or later, anyway," he acquiesced as he led the way.

His words sent Kenneth's heart to beating madly. They meant but one thing; Arline's father was not averse to his suit. As for Arline, no one could be sure of such a little coquette. And yet—the young American could have sworn there was more than ordinary kindness in her eyes the day she smiled a confirmation of her father's invitation to Melverson Abbey. It was that vague promise that had brought Kenneth Dinsmore from New York to England.

A moment later, the American was staring, with straining eyes that registered utter astonishment, at the famous carved door that formed the principal entrance to the abbey. He would have been willing to swear that no one could have approached that door without having been seen from the library windows; yet in the few seconds of time that had elapsed between his first and second observation of the panel, an addition had been made to the chalk marks.

THE Melverson panels are well known in the annals of historic carvings. There is a large lower panel showing the Great Fire of London. Above this are six half-panels portraying important scenes in London's history. And running across the very top is a large panel which shows a London street during the Great Plague of 1664.

This panel shows houses on either side of a narrow street yawning vacantly, great crosses upon their doors. Before one in the foreground is a rude wooden cart drawn by a lean nag and driven by a saturnine individual with leering face. This cart carries a gruesome load; it is piled high with bodies. Accounts vary oddly as to the number of bodies in the cart; earlier descriptions of the panel give a smaller number than the later ones, an item much speculated upon by connoisseurs of old carvings. The *tout ensemble of* the bas-relief greatly resembles the famous Hogarth picture of a similar scene.

Before this great door Kenneth stood, staring at a red-chalked legend traced across the rough surface of the carved figures on the upper panel. "God have mercy upon us!" it read. What did it mean? Who had managed to trace, unseen, those words of despairing supplication upon the old door?

And suddenly the young man's wonderment was rudely disturbed. Lord Melverson lurched away from the great door like a drunken man, a groan forcing its way from between his parched lips. The old man's hands had flown to his face, covering his eyes as though to shut out some horrid and unwelcome sight.

"Kenneth, you have heard the story! This is some thoughtless jest of yours! Tell me it is, boy! Tell me that your hand traced these fatal words!"

Dinsmore's sympathy was keenly aroused by the old nobleman's intense gravity and anxiety but he was forced to deny the pitifully pleading accusation.

"Sorry, sir, but I found the red cross just as I told you. As for the writing below, I must admit——"

"Ah! Then you *did* put *that* there? It was you who did it, then? Thank God! Thank God!"

"No, no, I hadn't finished. I was only wondering how

anyone could have slipped past us and have written this, unseen.
I'm sure," puzzled, "there was nothing here but the red cross
when I told you about it first, sir."

"Then you haven't heard—no one has told you that old
legend? The story of the Melverson curse?"

"This is the first I've heard of it, I assure you."

"And you positively deny writing that, as a bit of a joke?"

"Come, sir, it's not like you to accuse me of such a silly piece
of cheap trickery," Kenneth retorted, somewhat indignantly.

"Forgive me, boy. I—I should not have said that but—I
am—agitated. Will you tell me"—his voice grew tenser—"look
closely, for God's sake, Kenneth!—*how many bodies are there in the
wagon?*"

Dinsmore could not help throwing a keen glance at his
future father-in-law, who now stood with averted face, one
hand shielding his eyes as though he dared not ascertain for
himself that which he asked another in a voice so full of shrinking dread. Then the American stepped closer to the door and
examined the upper panel closely, while the soft dusk closed
down upon it.

"There are eleven bodies," he said finally.

"Kenneth! Look carefully! More depends upon your reply
than you can be aware. Are you sure there are only eleven?"

"There are only eleven, sir. I'm positive of it."

"Don't make a mistake, for pity's sake!"

"Surely my eyesight hasn't been seriously impaired since
this morning, when I bagged my share of birds," laughed the
young man, in a vain effort to throw off the gloomy depression
that seemed to have settled down upon him from the mere pro-
pinquity of the other.

"Thank God! Then there is still time," murmured the
owner of the abbey brokenly, drawing a deep, shivering sigh of
relief. "Let us return to the house, my boy." His voice had lost
its usually light ironical inflection and had acquired a heaviness
foreign to it.

Kenneth contracted his brows at Lord Melverson's dragging steps. One would almost have thought the old man physically affected by what appeared to be a powerful shock.

Once back in the library, Lord Melverson collapsed into the nearest chair, his breath coming in short, forced jerks. Wordlessly he indicated the bell-pull dangling against the wall out of his reach.

Kenneth jerked the cord. After a moment, during which the young man hastily poured a glassful of water and carried it to his host, the butler came into the room.

At sight of his beloved master in such a condition of pitiful collapse, the gray-haired old servitor was galvanized into action. He flew across the room to the desk, opened a drawer, picked up a bottle, shook a tablet out into his hand, flew back.

He administered the medicine to his master, who sipped the water brought by Kenneth with a grateful smile that included his guest and his servant.

Jenning shook his head sadly, compressing his lips, as Lord Melverson leaned back exhausted in his chair, face grayish, lids drooping over weary eyes.

Kenneth touched the old servant's arm to attract his attention. Then he tapped his left breast and lifted his eyebrows questioningly. An affirmative nod was his reply. Heart trouble! Brought on by the old gentleman's agitation over a chalk mark on his front door! There was a mystery somewhere, and the very idea stimulated curiosity. And had not Lord Melverson said, "You will have to know, sooner or later"? Know what? What strange thing lay back of a red cross and a prayer to heaven, chalked upon the great Melverson portal?

2

LORD MELVERSON stirred ever so little and spoke with effort. "Send one of the men out to clean the upper panel of the front door, Jenning," he ordered tonelessly.

Jenning threw up one hand to cover his horrified mouth and stifle an exclamation. His faded blue eyes peered at his master from under pale eyebrows as he stared with dreadful incredulity.

"It isn't the red cross, m'lord? Oh, no, it cannot be the red cross?" he stammered.

The thrill of affection in that cracked old voice told a little something of how much his master meant to the old family retainer.

"It seems to be a cross, chalked in red," admitted Melverson with patent reluctance, raising dull eyes to the staring ones fixed upon him with consternation.

"Oh, m'lord, not the red cross! And—was the warning there? Yes? Did you count them? *How many were there?*"

Terrible foreboding, shrinking reluctance, rang in that inquiry, so utterly strange and incomprehensible. Kenneth felt his blood congeal in his veins with the horrid mystery of it.

Lord Melverson and his retainer exchanged a significant glance that did not escape the young American's attention. The answer to Jenning's question was cryptic but not more so than the inquiry.

"The same as before, Jenning, That is all—*as yet.*"

Kenneth's curiosity flamed up anew. What could that mean? Could Jenning have been inquiring how many bodies were in the cart? There would be eleven, of course. How could there be more, or less, when the wood-carver had made them eleven, for all time?

The old servant retired from the room, dragging one slow foot after the other as though he had suddenly aged more than his fast-whitening hairs warranted.

In his capacious armchair, fingers opening and closing nervously upon the polished leather that upholstered it, Lord Melverson leaned back wearily, his eyes wide open but fixed unseeingly upon the library walls with their great paintings in oil by bygone Melversons.

"Kenneth!" Lord Melverson sought his guest's eyes with an expression of apology on his face that was painfully forced to the surface of the clouded atmosphere of dread and heaviness in which the old nobleman seemed steeped. "I presume you are wondering over the to-do about a chalk mark on my door? It—it made me think—of an old family tradition—and disturbed me a little.

"There's just one thing I want to ask you, my boy. Arline must not know that I had this little attack of heart-failure, I've kept it from her for years and I don't want her disturbed about me. And Kenneth, Arline has never been told the family legend. Don't tell her about the cross—the chalk marks on my door." His voice was intensely grave. "I have your word, my boy? Thank you. Some day I'll tell you the whole story."

"Has it anything to do with the quaint verse in raised gilded letters over the fireplace in the dining-hall?" questioned Kenneth.

He quoted it:

> "Melverson's first-born will die early away;
> Melverson's daughters will wed in gray;
> Melverson's curse must Melverson pay,
> Or Melverson Abbey will ownerless stay."

"Sounds like doggerel, doesn't it, lad? Well, that's the ancient curse. Foolish? Perhaps it is—perhaps it is. Yet—I am a second son myself; my brother Guy died before his majority."

"Coincidence, don't you think, sir?"

Lord Melverson smiled wryly, unutterable weariness in his old eyes. "Possibly—but a chain of coincidences, then. You—you don't believe there could be anything in it, do you, Kenneth? Would you marry the daughter of a house with such a curse upon it, knowing that it was part of your wife's dowry? Knowing that your first-born son must die before his majority?"

The American laughed light-heartedly.

"I don't think I'd care to answer such a suppositious question, sir. I can't admit such a possibility. I'm far too matter-of-fact, you see."

"But would you?" persistently, doggedly.

"I don't believe a word of it," sturdily. "It's just one of those foolish superstitions that people have permitted to influence them from time immemorial. I refuse to credit it."

Did Kenneth imagine it, or did Lord Melverson heave a deep, carefully repressed sigh of relief?

"Hardly worth while to go over the old tradition, is it?" he asked eagerly. "You wouldn't believe it, anyway. And probably it is just superstition, as you say. Ring for Jenning again, will you? Or—do you want to lend me your arm, my boy? I—I feel a bit shaky yet. I rather think bed will be the best place for me."

3

After Kenneth had bidden Lord Melverson good-night, he got out his pipe and sat by his window smoking. Tomorrow, he decided, he would try his fate; if he could only get Arline away where they could be alone. Little witch, how she managed always to have someone else around! Tomorrow he would know from her own lips whether or not he must return to America alone.

The clock struck midnight. Following close upon its cadences, a voice sounded on the still night, a voice raucous, grating, disagreeable. The words were indistinguishable and followed by a hard chuckle that was distinctly not expressive of mirth; far from it, the sound made Kenneth shake back his shoulders quickly, in an instinctive effort to throw off the dismal effect of that laugh.

"Charming music!" observed he to himself, as he leaned from his window.

Wheels began to grate and crunch through the graveled road

that led around the abbey. The full moon threw her clear light upon the space directly under Kenneth's window. He could distinguish every object as distinctly, it seemed to him, as in broad daylight. He listened and watched, a strange tenseness upon him. It was as though he waited for something terrible which yet must be; some unknown peril that threatened vaguely but none the less dreadfully.

The noise of the wheels grew louder. Then came a cautious, scraping sound from the window of a room close at hand. Kenneth decided that it was Lord Melverson's room. His host, hearing the horrid laughter that had been flung dismally upon the soft night air, had removed the screen from his window, the better to view the night visitor with the ugly chuckle.

The grinding of wheels grew louder. And then there slid into the full length of the moon a rude cart drawn by a lean, dappled nag and driven by a hunched-up individual who drew rein as the wagon came directly under Lord Melverson's window.

From the shadow of his room, Kenneth stared, open-eyed. There was something intolerably appalling about that strange equipage and its hunched-up driver, something that set his teeth sharply on edge and lifted his hair stiffly on his head. He did not want to look, but something pushed him forward and he was obliged to.

With a quick motion of his head, the driver turned a saturnine face to the moon's rays, revealing glittering eyes that shone with terrible, concentrated malignancy. The thinly curling lips parted. The cry Kenneth had heard a few minutes earlier rang—or rather, grated—on the American's ear. This time the words were plainer; plainer to the ear, although not to the sense—for what sense could they have? he reasoned as he heard them.

"Bring out your dead! Bring out your dead!"

A stifled groan. That was Lord Melverson, thought Kenneth, straining his eyes to watch the strange scene below.

For suddenly there rose from out the shadow of the abbey's great gray walls two figures bearing between them a burden. They carried it to the cart and with an effort lifted it, to toss it carelessly upon the grisly contents of that horrid wagon—contents that Kenneth now noted for the first time with starting eyes and prickling skin. And as the white face of the body lay upturned to the moon, a terrible cry wailed out from Lord Melverson's apartment, a cry of anguish and despair. For the moon's light picked out the features of that dead so callously tossed upon the gruesome pile.

"Oh, Albert, Albert, my son, my son!"

Kenneth leaned from his window and peered toward that of his host. From above the sill protruded two clasped hands; between them lay the white head of the old man. Had he fainted? Or had he had another attack of heart-failure?

The driver in the roadway below chuckled malignantly, and pulled at his horse's reins. The lean, dappled nag started up patiently in answer, and the cart passed slowly out of sight, wheels biting deep into the road-bed. And as it went out of sight among the deep shadows cast by the thickly wooded park, that harsh chuckle floated back again to the American's ears, thrilling him with horror of that detestable individual.

The hypnotic influence of that malignant glance had so chained Kenneth to the spot that for the moment he could not go to the assistance of Lord Melverson. But he found that he had been anticipated; as he reached his door, Jenning was already disappearing into his host's room. Kenneth retreated, unseen; perhaps he would do better to wait until he was called. It might well be that the drama he had seen enacted was not meant for his eyes and ears.

After all, had he seen or heard anything? Or was he the victim of a nightmare that had awakened him at its end? Kenneth shrugged his shoulders. He would know in the morning. Unless it rained hard in the meantime, the wheels of the cart would have left their mark on the gravel. If he had not dreamed, he would find the ruts made by those broad, ancient-looking wheels.

He could not sleep, however, until he heard Jenning leave his master's room. Opening the door softly, he inquired how Lord Melverson was. The old servitor flung a suspicious glance at him.

"I heard him cry out," explained Kenneth, seeing that the old man was averse to any explanation on his own side. "I hope it is nothing serious?"

"Nothing," replied Jenning restrainedly. But Dinsmore could have sworn that bright tears glittered in the old retainer's faded blue eyes and that the old mouth was compressed as though to hold back an outburst of powerful emotion.

Arline Melverson, her face slightly clouded, reported that her father had slept poorly the night before and would breakfast in his own room. She herself came down in riding-habit and vouchsafed the welcome information that she had ordered a horse saddled for Kenneth, if he cared to ride with her. Despite his desire to be alone with her, the American felt that he ought to remain at the abbey, where he might be of service to Lord Melverson. But inclination overpowered intuition, and after breakfast he got into riding-togs.

"I believe I'm still dreaming," he thought to himself as he rode back to the abbey at lunch-time, his horse crowding against Arline's as he reached happily over to touch her hand every little while. "Only this dream isn't a nightmare."

Instinctively his glance sought the graveled road where the dead-cart of the night before had, under his very eyes, ground its heavy wheels into the ground. The road was smooth and rutless. After all, then, he had dreamed and had undoubtedly been awakened by Lord Melverson's cry as the old man fainted. The dream had been so vivid that Kenneth could hardly believe his eyes when he looked at the smooth roadway, but his new happiness soon chased his bewilderment away.

As the young people dismounted before the door, Jenning appeared upon the threshold. The old man's lined face was turned almost with terror upon his young mistress. His lips worked as though he would speak but could not. His eyes sought the other man's as if in supplication.

"What's the matter, Jenning?"

"Master Albert, Mr. Dinsmore! M'lord's first-born son!"

"What is it?" Arline echoed. "Is my brother here?"

"I can't tell her, sir," the major-domo implored of Kenneth. "Take her to Lord Melverson, sir, I beg of you. He can tell her better than I."

Kenneth did not take Arline to her father. The girl fled across the great hall as if whipped by a thousand fears. Kenneth turned to Jenning with a question in his eyes.

Down the old man's face tears ran freely. His wrinkled hands worked nervously together. "He fell, sir. Something broke on his plane. He died last night, sir, a bit after midnight. The telegram came this morning, just after you and Miss Arline went."

Kenneth, one hand pressed bewildered to his forehead, walked aimlessly through that house of sorrow. Albert Melverson had fallen from his plane and died, the previous night. Had that dream, that nightmare, been a warning? Had it perhaps been so vivid in Lord Melverson's imagination that the scene had been telepathically reproduced before the American's own eyes? Although puzzled and disturbed beyond words, Kenneth realized that the matter must rest in abeyance until Lord Melverson should of his own free will explain it.

In the meantime there would be Arline to comfort, his sweetheart, who had just lost her dearly loved and only brother.

4

Two months had hardly passed after Albert's death before Lord Melverson broached the subject of his daughter's marriage.

"It's this way, my boy. I'm an old man and far from well of

late. I'd like to know that Arline was in safe keeping, Kenneth," and he laid an affectionate hand on the young man's shoulder.

Kenneth was deeply affected. "Thank you, sir. I promise you I shall do my utmost to make her happy."

"I know you will. I want you to speak to Arline about an early wedding. Tell her I want to see her married before— before I have to leave. I have a very powerful reason that I cannot tell you, my boy, for Arline to marry soon. I want to live to see my grandson at her knee, lad. And unless you two marry soon, I shall be powerless to prevent—that is, I shall be unable to do something for you both that has been much in my mind of late. It is vital that you marry soon, Kenneth. More I cannot say."

"You don't need to say more. I'll speak to Arline today. You understand, sir, that my only motive in not urging marriage upon her now has been your recent bereavement?"

"Of course. But Arline is too young, too volatile, to allow even such a loss to weigh permanently upon her spirits. I think she will yield to you, especially if you make it plain that I want it to be so."

Kenneth sought Arline thoughtfully. Lord Melverson's words impressed him almost painfully. There was much behind them, much that he realized he could not yet demand an explanation of. But the strength of Lord Melverson's request made him surer when he asked Arline to set an early date for their marriage.

"I am ready if Father does not consider it disrespectful to Albert's memory, Kenneth. You know, dear, we intended to marry soon, anyway. And I think Albert will be happier to know that I did not let his going matter. You understand, don't you? Besides, I feel that he is here with us in the abbey, with Father and me.

"But there is one thing, dear, that I shall insist upon. I think too much of my brother to lay aside the light mourning that Father permitted me to wear instead of heavy black. So if you want me to marry you soon, dear, you must wed a bride in gray."

Into Kenneth's mind flashed one line of the Melverson curse:

"Melverson's daughters will wed in gray."

Could there be something in it, after all? Common sense answered scornfully: No!

Four months after Albert Melverson had fallen to his death, his sister Arline—gray-clad like a gentle dove—put her hand into that of Kenneth Dinsmore, while Lord Melverson, his lips twitching as he strove to maintain his composure, gave the bride away.

A honeymoon trip that consumed many months took the young people to America as well as to the Continent, as the groom could hardly wait to present his lovely young wife to his family. Then, pursuant to Lord Melverson's wishes, the bridal pair returned to Melverson Abbey, that the future heir might be born under the ancestral roof.

5

LITTLE Albert became the apple of his grandfather's eye. The old gentleman spent hours watching the cradle the first few months of his grandson's life, and then again other hours in fondly guiding the little fellow's first steps.

But always in the background of this apparently ideally happy family lurked a black shadow. Jenning, his pale eyes full of foreboding, was always stealing terrified looks in secret at the panel of the great door. Kenneth grew almost to hate the poor old man, merely because he knew that Jenning believed implicitly in the family curse.

"Confound the man! He'll bring it upon us by thinking about it," growled the young father one morning as he looked out of the window of the breakfast room, where he had been eating a belated meal.

Little Albert, toddling with exaggerated precaution from his mother's outstretched hands to those of his grandfather, happened to look up. He saw his father; laughed and crowed lustily. Dinsmore waved his hand.

"Go to it, young chap. You'll be a great walker some day," he called facetiously.

Lord Melverson looked around, a pleased smile on his face. Plainly, he agreed to the full with his son-in-law's sentiments.

As usual, entered that black-garbed figure, the very presentment of woe: Jenning. Into the center of the happy little circle he came, his eyes seeking the old nobleman's.

"M'lord! Would your lordship please take a look?" stammered Jenning, his roving eyes going from the young father to the young mother, then back to the grandfather again, as if in an agony of uncertainty.

Lord Melverson straightened up slowly and carefully from his bent position over the side of a great wicker chair. He motioned Jenning silently ahead of him. The old butler retraced his footsteps, his master following close upon his heels. They disappeared around the corner of the building.

"Now, what on earth are they up to?" wondered Kenneth. His brow contracted. There had been something vaguely suspicious about Lord Melverson's air. "I've half a mind to follow them."

"Kenneth!" Arline's cry was wrung agonizingly from her.

Kenneth whirled about quickly, but too late to do anything. The baby, toddling to his mother's arms, missed a step, slipped, fell. The tender little head crashed against the granite coping at the edge of the terrace.

And even then Kenneth did not realize what it all meant. It was not until late that night that he suddenly understood that the Melverson curse was not a silly tradition, but a terrible blight upon the happiness of the Melverson family, root and branch.

He had left Arline under the influence of a sleeping-potion. Her nerves had gone back on her after the day's strain and the knowledge that her baby might not live out the night. A competent nurse and a skilled physician had taken over the case. Specialists were coming down from London as fast as a special train would bring them. Kenneth felt that his presence in the sickroom would be more hindrance than help.

He went down to the library where his father-in-law sat grimly, silently, expectantly, a strangely fixed expression of determination on his fine old face. Lord Melverson had drawn a handkerchief from his pocket. And then Kenneth suddenly knew, where before he had only imagined. For the old man's fine cambric kerchief was streaked with red, red that the unhappy young father knew must have been wiped from the upper panel of the great door that very morning. *The baby, Kenneth's first-born son, was doomed.*

"Why didn't you tell me? You hid it from me," he accused his wife's father, bitterly.

"I thought I was doing it for the best, Kenneth," the older man defended himself sadly.

"But if you had told me, I would never have left him alone for a single moment. I would have been beside him to have saved him when he fell."

"You *know* that if he had not fallen, something else would have happened to him, something unforeseen."

"Oh yes, I know, now, when it is too late. My little boy! My Arline's first-born! The first-born of Melverson!" fiercely. "Why didn't you tell me that the Melverson curse would follow my wife? That it would strike down her first-born boy?"

"And would that have deterred you from marrying Arline?" inquired Arline's father, very gently. "You know it wouldn't, Kenneth. I tried to put a hypothetical case to you once, but you replied that you refused to consider the mere possibility. What was I to do? I will confess that I have suffered, thinking that I should have insisted upon your reading the family records before you married Arline—then you could have decided for yourself."

"Does Arline know?"

"No. I've shielded her from the knowledge, Kenneth."

"I can't forgive you for not letting me know. It might have saved Albert's life. If Arline, too, had known——"

"Why should I have told her something that would have cast a shadow over her young life, Kenneth? Are you reproaching me because I have tried to keep her happy?"

"Oh, Father, I didn't mean to reproach you. I'm sorry. You must understand that I'm half mad with the pain of what's happened, not only on account of the little fellow, but for Arline. Oh, if there were only some way of saving him! How I would bless the being who would tell me how to save him!"

Lord Melverson, still with that strange glow in his eyes, rose slowly to his feet.

"There is a way, I believe," said he. "But don't put too much stress on what may be but a groundless hope on my part. I have had an idea for some time that I shall put into expression tonight, Kenneth. I've been thinking it over since I felt that I had wronged you in not pressing home the reality of the Melverson curse. If my idea is a good one, our little Albert is saved. And not only he, but I too shall have broken the curse, rendered it impotent for ever." His eyes shone with fervor.

"Is it anything I can do?" the young father begged.

"Nothing. Unless, perhaps, you want to read the old manuscript in my desk drawer. It tells why we Melversons have been cursed since the days of the Great Plague of 1664.

"Just before midnight, be in little Albert's room. If he is no better when the clock strikes twelve, Kenneth—why, then, my plan will have been a poor one. But I shall have done all I can do; have given all that lies in my power to give, in my attempt to wipe out the wrong I have inadvertently done you."

Kenneth pressed the hand outstretched to him.

"You've been a good husband to my girl, Kenneth, lad. You've made her happy. And, in case anything were to happen to me, will you tell Arline that I am perfectly contented if only our little one recovers? I want no vain regrets," stressed Lord Melverson emphatically, as he released Kenneth's hand and turned to leave the room.

"What could happen?"

"Oh, nothing. That is—you know I've had several severe heart attacks of late," returned Arline's father vaguely.

6

KENNETH, alone, went to his father-in-law's desk and drew out the stained and yellow manuscript. Sitting in a chair before the desk, he laid the ancient sheets before him and pored over the story of the Melverson curse. He thought it might take his mind off the tragedy slowly playing to a close in the hushed room upstairs.

Back in 1664, the then Lord Melverson fell madly in love with the charming daughter of a goldsmith. She was an only child, very lovely to look upon and as good as she was fair, and she dearly loved the rollicking young nobleman. But a Melverson of Melverson Abbey, though he could love, could not wed a child of the people. Charles Melverson pleaded with the lovely girl to elope with him, without the sanction of her church.

But the damsel, being of lofty soul, called her father and related all to him. Then she turned her fair shoulder indifferently upon her astonished and chagrined suitor and left him, while the goldsmith laughed saturninely in the would-be seducer's face.

A Melverson was not one to let such a matter rest quietly, however, especially as he was deeply enamored of the lady. He sent pleading letters, threatening to take his own life. He attempted to force himself into the lady's presence. At last, he met her one day as she returned from church, caught her up, and fled with her on his swift charger.

Still she remained obdurate, although love for him was eating her wounded heart. Receive him she must, but she continued to refuse him so little a favor as a single word.

Despairing of winning her by gentle means, Charles Melverson determined upon foul.

It was the terrible winter of 1664-5. The Black Death, sweeping through London and out into the countryside, was taking dreadful toll of lives. Hundreds of bodies were daily tumbled carelessly into the common trenches by hardened men who dared the horrors of the plague for the big pay offered those who played the part of grave-digger. And at the very moment when Melverson had arrived at his evil decision, the goldsmith staggered into the abbey grounds after a long search for his ravished daughter, to fall under the very window where she had retreated in the last stand for her maiden virtue.

Retainers without shouted at one another to beware the plague-stricken man. Their shouts distracted the maiden. She looked down and beheld her father dying, suffering the last throes of the dreaded pestilence.

Coldly and proudly she demanded freedom to go down to her dying parent. Melverson refused the request; in a flash of insight he knew what she would do with her liberty. She would fling herself desperately beside the dying man; she would hold his blackening body against her own warm young breast; she would deliberately drink in his plague-laden breath with her sweet, fresh lips.

Lifting fast-glazing eyes, the goldsmith saw his daughter, apparently clasped fast in her lover's arms. How was he to have known that her frantic struggles had been in vain? With his last breath he cursed the Melversons, root and branch, lifting discolored hands to the brazen, glowing sky lowering upon him. Then, "And may the demon of the plague grant that I may come back as long as a Melverson draws breath, to steal away his first-born son!" he cried. With a groan, he died.

And then, thanks to the strange heart of woman, Charles Melverson unexpectedly won what he had believed lost to him for ever, for he could not have forced his will upon that orphaned and sorrowful maiden. The goldsmith's daughter turned upon him limpid eyes that wept for him and for her father, too.

"It is too much to ask that you should suffer alone what my poor father has called down upon your house," she said to him, with unexpected gentleness. "He would forgive you, could he know that I have been safe in your keeping. I must ask you, then, to take all I have to give, if by so doing you believe the shadow of the curse will be lightened—for you, at least."

Touched to his very heart by her magnanimity, Charles Melverson released her from his arms, knelt at her feet, kissed her hand, and swore that until he could fetch her from the church, his lawful wedded wife, he would neither eat nor sleep.

But—the curse remained. Down through the centuries it had worked its evil way, and no one seemed to have found a way of eluding it. Upon the last pages of the old manuscript were noted, in differing chirography, the death dates of one Melverson after another, after each the terribly illuminating note: "First-born son. Died before his majority."

And last of all, in the handwriting of Lord Melverson, was written the name of that Albert for whom Kenneth Dinsmore's son had been named. Must another Albert follow that other so soon?

7

KENNETH tossed the stained papers back into the drawer and shut them from sight. There was something sinister about them. He felt as if his very hands had been polluted by their touch. Then he glanced at the clock. It was on the point of striking midnight. He remembered Lord Melverson's request, and ran quickly upstairs to his little dying son's room.

Arline was already at the child's side; she had wakened and would not be denied. Nurse and physician stood in the background, their faces showing plainly the hopelessness of the case.

On his little pillow, the poor baby drew short, painful gasps, little fists clenched against his breast. A few short moments, thought Kenneth, would determine his first-born's life or death. And it would be death, unless Lord Melverson had discovered how to break the potency of the Melverson curse.

Torn between wife and child, the young father dared not hope, for fear his hope might be shattered. As for Arline, he saw that her eyes already registered despair; already she had, in anticipation, given up her child, her baby, her first-born.

What was that? The sound of heavy, broad-rimmed wheels crunching through the gravel of the roadway; the call of a mocking voice that set Kenneth's teeth on edge with impotent fury.

He went unobtrusively to the window and looked out. After all, he could not be expected to stand by the bed, watching his little son die. And he had to see, at all costs, that nightmare dead-cart with its ghastly freight; he had to know whether or not he had dreamed it, or had seen it truly, on the night before Albert Melverson's death.

Coming out of the shadows of the enveloping trees, rumbled the dead-wagon with its hunched-up driver. Kenneth's hair rose with a prickling sensation on his scalp. He turned to glance back into the room. No, he was not dreaming; he had not dreamed before; it was real—as real as such a ghastly thing could well be.

On, on it came. And then the hateful driver lifted his malignant face to the full light of the moon. His challenging glance met the young father's intent gaze with a scoffing, triumphant smile, a smile of satisfied hatred. The thin lips parted, and their grating cry fell another time upon the heavy silence of the night.

"Bring out your dead!"

As that ominous cry pounded against his ears, Kenneth Dinsmore heard yet another sound: it was the sharp explosion of a revolver.

He stared from the window with straining eyes. Useless to return to the baby's bedside; would not those ghostly pall-bearers emerge from the shadows now, bearing with them the tiny body of his first-born?

They came. But they were carrying what seemed to be a heavy burden. That was no child's tiny form they tossed with hideous upward grins upon the dead-cart.

"Kenneth! Come here!"

It was Arline's voice, with a thrilling undertone of thankfulness in it that whirled Kenneth from the window to her side, all else forgotten.

"Look! He is breathing easier. Doctor, look! Tell me, doesn't he seem better?"

Doctor and nurse exchanged mystified, incredulous glances. It was plain that neither had heard or seen anything out of the ordinary that night, but that the baby's sudden turn for the better had astonished them both.

"I consider it little short of a miracle," pronounced the medical man, after a short examination of the sleeping child. "Madam, your child will live, I congratulate you both."

"Oh, I must tell Father, Kenneth. He will be *so* happy. Dear Father!"

The cold hand of certain knowledge squeezed Kenneth's heart. "If anything should happen to me," Lord Melverson had said. What did that revolver shot mean? What had meant that body the ghostly pall-bearers had carried to the dead-wagon?

A light tap came at the door. The nurse opened it, then turned and beckoned to Kenneth.

It was Jenning, frankly unashamed of the tears that were rolling down his wrinkled cheeks. He choked back a sob.

"He's gone, Mr. Dinsmore. Break it to her easy, sir—but it's proud of him she ought to be." His voice trembled, broke. "'Twas not the little master *they* carried away in the accursed dead-cart, thanks to him. I tried to stop him, sir; forgive me, I loved him! But he *would* make the sacrifice; he said it was worth trying. And so—he—did—it. But—*he's broken the curse, sir, he's broken the curse!*"

The Canal

Everil Worrell

PAST the sleeping city the river sweeps; along its left bank the old canal creeps.

I did not intend that to be poetry, although the scene is poetic—somberly, gruesomely poetic, like the poems of Poe. Too well I know it—too often have I walked over the grass-grown path beside the reflections of black trees and tumble-down shacks and distant factory chimneys in the sluggish waters that moved so slowly, and ceased to move at all.

I shall be called mad, and I shall be a suicide. I shall take no pains to cover up my trail, or to hide the thing that I shall do. What will it matter, afterward, what they say of me? If they knew the truth—if they could vision, even dimly, the beings with whom I have consorted—if the faintest realization might be theirs of the thing I am becoming, and of the fate from which I am saving their city—then they would call me a great hero. But it does not matter what they call me, as I have said before. Let me write down the things I am about to write down, and let them be taken, as they will be taken, for the last ravings of a madman. The city will be in mourning for the thing I shall have done—but its mourning will be of no consequence beside that other fate from which I shall have saved it.

I HAVE always had a taste for nocturnal prowling. We as a race have grown too intelligent to take seriously any of the old, instinctive fears that preserved us through preceding genera-tions. Our sole remaining salvation, then, has come to be our tendency to travel in herds. We wander at night—but our objective is somewhere on the brightly lighted streets, or still somewhere where men do not go alone. When we travel far afield, it is in company. Few of my acquaintance, few in the whole city here, would care to ramble at midnight over the grass-grown path I have spoken of; not because they would fear to do so, but because such things are not being done.

Well, it is dangerous to differ individually from one's fellows. It is dangerous to wander from the beaten road. And the fears that guarded the race in the dawn of time and through the centuries were real fears, founded on reality.

A month ago, I was a stranger here. I had just taken my first position—I was graduated from college only three months before, in the spring. I was lonely, and likely to remain so for some time, for I have always been of a solitary nature, making friends slowly.

I had received one invitation out—to visit the camp of a fellow employee in the firm for which I worked, a camp which was located on the farther side of the wide river—the side across from the city and the canal, where the bank was high and steep and heavily wooded, and little tents blossomed all along the water's edge. At night, these camps were a string of sparkling lights and tiny, leaping campfires, and the tinkle of music carried faintly far across the calmly flowing water. That far bank of the river was no place for an eccentric, solitary man to love. But the near bank, which would have been an eyesore to the campers had not the river been so wide,—the near bank attracted me from my first glimpse of it.

We embarked in a motor-boat at some distance downstream, and swept up along the near bank, and then out and across the current. I turned my eyes backward. The murk of stagnant water that was the canal, the jumble of low buildings beyond it, the lonely, low-lying waste of the narrow strip of land between canal and river, the dark, scattered trees growing there—I intended to see more of these things.

That week-end bored me, but I repaid myself no later than Monday evening, the first evening when I was back in the city, alone and free. I ate a solitary dinner immediately after leaving the office. I went to my room and slept from 7 until nearly midnight. I wakened naturally, then, for my whole heart was set on exploring the alluring solitude I had discovered. I dressed, slipped out of the house and into the street, started the motor in my roadster which I had left parked at the curb, and drove through the lighted streets.

I left behind that part of town which was thick with vehicles carrying people home from their evening engagements, and began to thread my way through darker and narrower streets. Once I had to back out of a cul-de-sac, and once I had to detour around a closed block. This part of town was not alluring, even to me. It was dismal without being solitary.

But when I had parked my car on a rough, cobbled street that ran directly down into the inky waters of the canal, and crossed a narrow bridge, I was repaid. A few minutes set my feet on the old tow-path where mules had drawn river-boats up and down only a year or so ago. Across the canal now, as I walked upstream at a swinging pace, the miserable shacks where miserable people lived seemed to march with me, and then fell behind. They looked like places in which murders might be committed, every one of them.

The bridge I had crossed was near the end of the city going north, as the canal marked its western extremity. Ten minutes of walking, and the dismal shacks were quite a distance behind, the river was farther away and the strip of waste land much wider and more wooded, and tall trees across the canal marched with me as the evil-looking houses had done before. Far and faint, the sound of a bell in the city reached my ears. It was midnight.

I stopped, enjoyed the desolation around me. It had the savor I had expected and hoped for. I stood for some time looking up at the sky, watching the low drift of heavy clouds,

which were visible in the dull reflected glow from distant lights
in the heart of the city, so that they appeared to have a lurid
phosphorescence of their own. The ground under my feet,
on the contrary, was utterly devoid of light. I had felt my way
carefully, knowing the edge of the canal partly by instinct,
partly by the even more perfect blackness of the water in it, and
even holding pretty well to the path, because it was perceptibly
sunken below the ground beside it.

Now as I stood motionless in this spot, my eyes upcast, my
mind adrift with strange fancies, suddenly my feelings of satisfaction and well-being gave way to something different. Fear
was an emotion unknown to me—for those things which make
men fear, I had always loved. A graveyard at night was to me a
charming place for a stroll and meditation.

But now, the roots of my hair seemed to move upright on
my head, and along all the length of my spine I was conscious
of a prickling, tingling sensation—such as my forefathers may
have felt in the jungle when the hair on their backs stood up as
the hair of my head was doing now. Also, I was afraid to move;
and I knew that there were eyes upon me, and that that was
why I was afraid to move. I was afraid of those eyes—afraid to
see them, to look into them.

All this while, I stood perfectly still, my face uptilted toward
the sky. But after a terrible mental effort, I mastered myself.

Slowly—slowly, with an attempt to propitiate the owner
of the unseen eyes by my casual manner, I lowered my own.
I looked straight ahead—at the softly swaying silhouette of
the tree-tops across the canal as they moved gently in the cool
night wind; at the mass of blackness that was those trees, and
the opposite shore; at the shiny blackness where the reflections of the clouds glinted vaguely and disappeared, that was
the canal. And again I raised my eyes a little, for just across
the canal where the shadows massed most heavily, there was
that at which I must look more closely. And now, as I grew
accustomed to the greater blackness and my pupils expanded,

I dimly discerned the contours of an old boat or barge, half sunken in the water.

An old, abandoned canal-boat.

But was I dreaming, or was there a white-clad figure seated on the roof of the low cabin aft, a pale, heart-shaped face gleaming strangely at me from the darkness, the glow of two eyes seeming to light up the face, and to detach it from the darkness?

Surely, there could be no doubt as to the eyes. They shone as the eyes of animals shine in the dark—with a phosphorescent gleam, and a glimmer of red! Well, I had heard that some human eyes have that quality at night.

But what a place for a human being to be—a girl, too, I was sure. That daintily heart-shaped face was the face of a girl, surely —I was seeing it clearer and clearer, either because my eyes were growing more accustomed to peering into the deeper shadows, or because of that phosphorescence in the eyes that stared back at me.

I RAISED my voice softly, not to break too much the stillness of the night.

"Hello! who's there? Are you lost, or marooned, and can I help?"

There was a little pause. I was conscious of a soft lapping at my feet. A stronger night wind had sprung up, was ruffling the dark waters. I had been over-warm, and where it struck me the perspiration turned cold on my body, so that I shivered uncontrollably.

"You can stay—and talk awhile, if you will. I am lonely, but not lost—I—I live here."

I could hardly believe my ears. The voice was little more than a whisper, but it had carried clearly—a girl's voice, sure enough. And she lived *there*—in an old, abandoned canal-boat, half submerged in the stagnant water.

"You are not *alone* there?"

"No, not alone. My father lives here with me, but he is deaf—and he sleeps soundly."

Did the night wind blow still colder, as though it came to us from some unseen, frozen sea—or was there something in her tone that chilled me, even as a strange attraction drew me toward her? I wanted to draw near to her, to see closely the pale, heart-shaped face, to lose myself in the bright eyes that I had seen shining in the darkness. I wanted—I wanted to hold her in my arms, to find her mouth with mine, to kiss it——

With a start, I realized the nature of my thoughts, and for an instant lost all thought in surprize. Never in my twenty-two years had I felt love before. My fancies had been otherwise directed—a moss-grown, fallen gravestone was a dearer thing to me to contemplate than the fairest face in all the world. Yet, surely, what I felt now was love!

I took a reckless step nearer the edge of the bank.

"Could I come over to you?" I begged. "It's warm, and I don't mind a wetting. It's late, I know—but I would give a great deal to sit beside you and talk, if only for a few minutes before I go back to town. It's a lonely place here for a girl like you to live—your father should not mind if you exchange a few words with someone occasionally."

Was it the unconventionality of my request that made her next words sound like a long-drawn shudder of protest? There was a strangeness in the tones of her voice that held me wondering, every time she spoke.

"No—no. Oh, no! *You must not swim across.*"

"Then—could I come tomorrow, or some day soon, in the daytime; and would you let me come on board then—or would you come on shore and talk to me, perhaps?"

"Not in the daytime—*never* in the daytime!"

Again the intensity of her low-toned negation held me spellbound.

It was not her sense of the impropriety of the hour, then, that had dictated her manner. For surely, any girl with the slightest sense of the fitness of things would rather have a tryst by daytime than after midnight—yet there was an inference in her last words that if I came again it should be again at night.

Still feeling the spell that had enthralled me, as one does not forget the presence of a drug in the air that is stealing one's senses, even when those senses begin to wander and to busy themselves with other things, I yet spoke shortly.

"Why do you say, 'Never in the daytime?' Do you mean that I may come more than this once at night, though now you won't let me cross the canal to you at the expense of my own clothes, and you won't put down your plank or drawbridge, or whatever you come on shore with, and talk to me here for only a moment? I'll come again, if you'll let me talk to you instead of calling across the water. I'll come again, any time you will let me—day or night, I don't care. I want to come to you. But I only ask you to explain. If I came in the daytime and met your father, wouldn't that be the best thing to do? Then we could be really acquainted—we could be friends."

"In the night time, my father sleeps. In the daytime, *I* sleep. How could I talk to you, or introduce you to my father then? If you came on board this boat in the daytime, you would find my father—and you would be sorry. As for me, I would be sleeping. I could never introduce you to my father, do you see?"

"You sleep soundly, you and your father." Again there was pique in my voice.

"Yes, we sleep soundly."

"And always at different times?"

"Always at different times. We are on guard—one of us is always on guard. We have been hardly used, down there in your city. And we have taken refuge here. And we are always—always—on guard."

The resentment vanished from my breast, and I felt my heart go out to her anew. She was so pale, so pitiful in the night. My eyes were learning better and better how to pierce the darkness, they were giving me a more definite picture of my compan-

ion—if I could think of her as a companion, between myself
and whom stretched the black water.

The sadness of the lonely scene, the perfection of the solitude itself, these things contributed to her pitifulness. Then
there was that strangeness of atmosphere of which, even yet,
I had only partly taken note. There was the strange, shivering
chill, which yet did not seem like the healthful chill of a cool
evening. In fact, it did not prevent me from feeling the oppression of the night, which was unusually sultry. It was like a little
breath of deadly cold that came and went, and yet did not alter
the temperature of the air itself, as the small ripples on the surface of water do not concern the water even a foot down.

And even that was not all. There was an unwholesome smell
about the night—a dank, moldy smell that might have been the
very breath of death and decay. Even I, the connoisseur in all
things dismal and unwholesome, tried to keep my mind from
dwelling overmuch upon that smell. What it must be to live
breathing it constantly in, I could not think. But no doubt the
girl and her father were used to it; and no doubt it came from
the stagnant water of the canal and from the rotting wood of
the old, half-sunken boat that was their refuge.

My heart throbbed with pity again. Their refuge—what a
place! And my clearer vision of the girl showed me that she was
pitifully thin, even though possessed of the strange face that
drew me to her. Her clothes hung around her like old rags, but
hers was no scarecrow aspect. Although little flesh clothed her
bones, her very bones were beautiful. I was sure the little, pale,
heart-shaped face would be more beautiful still, if I could only
see it closely. I must see it closely—I must establish some claim
to consideration as a friend of the strange, lonely crew of the
half-sunken wreck.

"This is a poor place to call a refuge," I said finally. "One
might have very little money, and yet do somewhat better. Perhaps I might help you—I am sure I could. If your ill-treatment
in the city was because of poverty—I am not rich, but I could

help that. I could help you a little with money—if you would let me—or, in any case, I could find a position for you. I'm sure I could do that."

The eyes that shone fitfully toward me like two small pools of water intermittently lit by a cloud-swept sky seemed to glow more brightly. She had been half crouching, half sitting on top of the cabin; now she leaped to her feet with one quick, sinuous, abrupt motion, and took a few rapid, restless steps to and fro before she answered.

When she spoke, her voice was little more than a whisper; yet surely rage was in its shrill sibilance.

"Fool! Do you think you would be helping me, to tie me to a desk, to shut me behind doors, away from freedom, away from the delight of doing my own will, of seeking my own way? Never, never would I let you do that. Rather this old boat, rather a deserted grave under the stars, for my home!"

A boundless surprize swept over me, and a positive feeling of kinship with this strange being, whose face I had hardly seen, possessed me. So I myself might have spoken—so I had often felt, though I had never dreamed of putting my thoughts so definitely, so forcibly. My regularized daytime life was a thing I thought little of; I really lived only in my nocturnal prowlings. Why, this girl was right! All of life should be free—and spent in places that interested and attracted.

How little, how little I knew, that night, that dread forces were tugging at my soul, were finding entrance to it and easy access through the morbid weakness of my nature! How little I knew at what a cost I deviated so radically from my kind, who herd in cities and love well-lit ways and the sight of man, and sweet and wholesome places to be solitary in, when the desire for solitude comes over them!

That night it seemed to me that there was but one important thing in life—to allay the angry passion my unfortunate words had aroused in the breast of my beloved, and to win from her some answering feeling.

"I understand—much better than you think," I whispered tremulously. "What I want is to see you again, to come to know you. And to serve you in any way that I may. Surely, there must be something in which I can be of use to you. All you have to do from tonight on forever, is to command me. I swear it!"

"You swear *that*—you do swear it?"

Delighted at the eagerness of her words, I lifted my hand toward the dark heavens.

"I swear it. From this night on, forever—I swear it."

"Then listen. Tonight you may not come to me, nor I to you. I do not want you to board this boat, not tonight, not any night. And most of all, not any day. But do not look so sad. I will come to you. No, not tonight. Perhaps not for many nights—yet before very long. I will come to you there, on the bank of the canal, when the water in the canal ceases to flow."

I must have made a gesture of impatience, or of despair. It sounded like a way of saying "never"—for why should the water in the canal cease to flow? She read my thoughts in some way, for she answered them.

"You do not understand. I am speaking seriously—I am promising to meet you there on the bank, and soon. For the water within these banks is moving slower, always slower. Higher up, I have heard that the canal has been drained. Between these lower locks, the water still seeps in and drops slowly, slowly downstream. But there will come a night when it will be quite, quite stagnant—and on that night I will come to you. And when I come, I will ask of you a favor. And you will keep your oath."

IT was all the assurance I could get that night. She had come back to the side of the cabin where she had sat crouched before, and she resumed again that posture and sat still and silent, watching me. Sometimes I could see her eyes upon me, and sometimes not. But I felt that their gaze was unwavering. The little cold breeze, which I had finally forgotten while I was talking with her, was blowing again, and the unwholesome smell of decay grew heavier before the dawn.

She would not speak again, nor answer me when I spoke to her, and I grew nervous, and strangely ill at ease.

At last I went away. And in the first faint light of dawn I slipped up the stairs of my rooming-house, and into my own room.

I was deadly tired at the office next day. And day after day slipped away and I grew more and more weary. For a man can not wake day and night without suffering, especially in hot weather, and that was what I was doing. I haunted the old tow-path and waited, night after night, on the bank opposite the sunken boat. Sometimes I saw my lady of the darkness, and sometimes not. When I saw her, she spoke little; but sometimes she sat there on the top of the cabin and let me watch her till the dawn, or until the strange uneasiness that was like fright drove me from her and back to my room, where I tossed restlessly in the heat and dreamed strange dreams, half waking, till the sun shone in on my forehead and I tumbled into my clothes and down to the office again.

Once I asked her why she had made the fanciful condition that she would not come ashore to meet me until the waters of the canal had ceased to run. (How eagerly I studied those waters; how I stole away at noontime more than once, not to approach the old boat, but to watch the almost imperceptible downward drift of bubbles, bits of straw, twigs, rubbish!)

My questioning displeased her, and I asked her that no more. It was enough that she chose to be whimsical. My part was to wait.

It was more than a week later that I questioned her again, this time on a different subject. And after that, I curbed my curiosity relentlessly.

"Never speak to me of things you do not understand about me. Never again, or I will not show myself to you again.

And when I walk on the path yonder, it will not be with you."

I had asked her what form of persecution she and her father had suffered in the city, that had driven them out to this lonely place, and where in the city they had lived.

Frightened seriously lest I lose the ground I was sure I had gained with her, I was about to speak of something else. But before I could find the words, her low voice came to me again.

"It was horrible—horrible! Those little houses below the bridge, those houses along the canal—tell me, are they not worse than my boat? Life there was shut in, and furtive. I was not free as I am now—and the freedom I will soon have will make me forget the things I have not yet forgotten. The screaming, the reviling and cursing! Fear and flight! As you pass back by those houses, think how you would like to be shut in one of them, and in fear of your life. And then think of them no more—for I would forget them, and I will never speak of them again!"

I dared not answer her. I was surprized that she had vouchsafed me so much. But surely her words meant this—that before she had come to live on the decaying, water-rotted old boat, she had lived in one of those horrible houses I passed by on my way to her. Those houses, each of which looked like the predestined scene of a murder!

As I left her that night, I felt that I was very daring.

"One or two nights more and you will walk beside me," I called to her. "I have watched the water at noon, and it hardly moves at all. I threw a scrap of paper into the canal, and it whirled and swung a little where a thin skim of oil lay on the water down there—oil from the big, dirty city you are well out of. But though I watched and watched, I could not see it move downward at all. Perhaps tomorrow night, or the night after, you will walk on the bank with me. I hope it will be clear and moonlight; and I will be near enough to see you clearly—as well as you seem always to see me in darkness or moonlight, equally well. And perhaps I will kiss you—but not unless you let me."

And yet, the next day, for the first time my thoughts were definitely troubled. I had been living in a dream—I began to speculate concerning the end of the path on which my feet were set.

I had conceived, from the first, such a horror of those old houses by the canal! They were well enough to walk past, nursing gruesome thoughts for a midnight treat. But, much as I loved all that was weird and eery about the girl I was wooing so strangely, it was a little too much for my fancy that she had come from them.

By this time, I had become decidedly unpopular in my place of business. Not that I had made enemies, but that my peculiar ways had caused too much adverse comment. It would have taken very little, I think, to have made the entire office force decide that I was mad. After the events of the next twenty-four hours, and after this letter is found and read, they will be sure that they knew it all along! At this time, however, they were punctiliously polite to me, and merely let me alone as much as possible—which suited me perfectly. I dragged wearily through day after day, exhausted for lack of sleep, conscious of their speculative glances, living only for the night to come.

But on this day, I approached the man who had invited me to the camp across the river, who had unknowingly shown me the way that led to my love.

"Have you ever noticed the row of tumble-down houses along the canal on the city side?" I asked him.

He gave me an odd look. I suppose he sensed the significance of my breaking silence after so long to speak of *them*—sensed that in some way I had a deep interest in them.

"You have odd tastes, Morton," he said after a moment. "I suppose you wander into strange places sometimes—I've heard you speak of an enthusiasm for graveyards at night. But my advice to you is to keep away from those houses. They're unsavory, and their reputation is unsavory. Positively, I think you'd be in danger of your life, if you go poking around there. They have been the scene of several murders, and a dope den or two has been cleaned out of them. Why in the world you should want to investigate them——"

"I don't expect to investigate them," I said testily. "I was merely interested in them—from the outside. To tell you the truth, I'd heard a story, a rumor—never mind where. But you say there have been murders there—I suppose this rumor I heard may have had to do with an attempted one. There was a girl who lived there with her father once—and they were set upon there, or something of the sort, and had to run away. Did you ever hear *that* story?"

Barrett gave me an odd look such as one gives in speaking of a past horror so dreadful that the mere speaking of it makes it live terribly again.

"What you say reminds me of a horrible thing that was said to have happened down there once," he said. "It was in all the papers. A little child disappeared in one of those houses— and a couple of poor lodgers who lived there, a girl and her father, were accused of having made away with it. They were accused—they were accused—oh, well, I don't like to talk about such things. It was too dreadful. The child's body was found—*part* of it was found. It was mutilated, and the people in the house seemed to believe it had been mutilated in order to conceal the manner of its death—there was an ugly wound in the throat, it finally came out, and it seemed as if the child might have been bled to death. It was found in the girl's room, hidden away. The old man and his daughter escaped, before the police were called. The countryside was scoured for them—the whole country was scoured, but they were never found. Why, you must have read it in the papers, several years ago."

I nodded, with a heavy heart. I *had* read it in the papers, I remembered now. And again, a terrible questioning came over me. Who was this girl, *what* was this girl, who seemed to have my heart in her keeping?

Why did not a merciful God let me die then?

Befogged with exhaustion, bemused in a dire enchantment, my mind was incapable of thought. And yet, some soul-process akin to that which saves the sleepwalker poised at perilous heights sounded its warning now.

My mind was filled with doleful images. There were women —I had heard and read—who slew to satisfy a blood-lust. There were ghosts, specters—call them what you will, their names have been legion in the dark pages of that lore which dates back to the infancy of the races of the earth—who retained even in death this blood-lust. Vampires—they had been called that. I had read of them. Corpses by day, spirits of evil by night, roaming abroad in their own forms or in the forms of bats or unclean beasts, killing body and soul of their victims—for whoever dies of the repeated "kiss" of the vampire, which leaves its mark on the throat and draws the blood from the body, becomes a vampire also—of such beings I had read.

And, horror of horrors! In that last cursed day at the office, I remembered reading of these vampires—these undead—that in their nocturnal flights they had one limitation—*they could not cross running water*.

THAT night I went my usual nightly way with tears of weakness on my face—for my weakness was supreme, and I recognized fully at last the misery of being the victim of an enchantment stronger than my feeble will. But I went.

I approached the neighborhood of the canal-boat as the distant city clock chimed the first stroke of 12. It was the dark of the moon and the sky was overcast. Heat-lightning flickered low in the sky, seeming to come from every point of the compass and circumscribe the horizon, as if unseen fires burned behind the rim of the world. By its fitful glimmer, I saw a new thing—between the old boat and the canal bank stretched a long, slim; solid-looking shadow—a plank had been let down! In that moment, I realized that I had been playing with powers of evil which had no intent now to let me go, which were indeed about to lay hold upon me with an inexorable grasp. Why had I come tonight? Why, but that the spell of the enchantment laid upon me was a thing more potent, and far more unbreakable, than any wholesome spell of love? The creature I sought out—oh, I remembered now, with the cold perspiration beading my brow, the lore hidden away between the covers of the dark old book which I had read so many years ago and half forgotten!—until dim memories of it stirred within me, this last day and night.

My lady of the night! No woman of wholesome flesh and blood and odd perverted tastes that matched my own, but one of the undead. In that moment, I knew it, and knew that the vampires of old legends polluted still, in these latter days, the fair surface of the earth.

And on the instant, behind me in the darkness there was the crackle of a twig, and something brushed against my arm!

This, then, was the fulfilment of my dream. I knew, without turning my head, that the pale, dainty face with its glowing eyes was near my own—that I had only to stretch out my arm to touch the slender grace of the girl I had so longed to draw near. I knew, and should have felt the rapture I had anticipated. Instead, the roots of my hair prickled coldly, unendurably, as they had on the night when I had first sighted the old boat. The miasmic odors of the night, heavy and oppressive with heat and unrelieved by a breath of air, all but overcame me, and I fought with myself to prevent my teeth clicking in my head. The little waves of coldness I had felt often in this spot were chasing over my body; yet they were not from any breeze; the leaves on the trees hung down motionless, as though they were actually wilting on their branches.

With an effort, I turned my head.

Two hands caught me around my neck. The pale face was so near, that I felt the warm breath from its nostrils fanning my cheek.

And, suddenly, all that was wholesome in my perverted nature rose uppermost. I longed for the touch of the red mouth, like a dark flower opening before me in the night. I longed for it—and yet more I dreaded it. I shrank back, catching in a powerful grip the fragile wrists of the hands that strove to hold me. I must not—I must not yield to the faintness that I felt stealing languorously over me.

I was facing down the path, toward the city. A low rumble of thunder—the first—broke the torrid hush of the summer night. A glare of lightning seemed to tear the night asunder, to light up the whole universe. Overhead, the clouds were careening madly in fantastic shapes, driven by a wind that swept the upper heavens without as yet causing even a trembling in the air lower down. And far down the canal, that baleful glare seemed to play around and hover over the little row of shanties—murder-cursed, and haunted by the ghost of a dead child.

My gaze was fixed on them, while I held away from me the pallid face and fought off the embrace that sought to overcome my resisting will. And so a long moment passed. The glare faded out of the sky, and a greater darkness took the world. But there was a near, more menacing glare fastened upon my face— the glare of two eyes that watched mine, that had watched me as I, unthinking, stared down at the dark houses.

This girl—this woman who had come to me at my own importunate requests, did not love me, since I had shrunk from her. She did not love me; but it was not only that. She had watched me as I gazed down at the houses that held her dark past—and I was sure that she divined my thoughts. She knew my horror of those houses—she knew my new-born horror of *her*. And she hated me for it, hated me more malignantly than I had believed a human being could hate.

And at that point in my thoughts, I felt my skin prickle and my scalp rise again: could a *human being* cherish such hatred as I read, trembling more and more, in those glowing fires lit with what seemed to me more like the fires of hell than any light that ought to shine in a woman's eyes?

And through all this, not a word had passed between us!

So FAR I have written calmly. I wish that I could write on so, to the end. If I could do that there might be one or two of those who will regard this as the document of a maniac, who would believe the horrors of which I am about to write.

But I am only flesh and blood. At this point in the happenings of the awful night, my calmness deserted me—at this point I felt that I had been drawn into the midst of a horrible nightmare from which there was no escape, no waking! As I write, this feeling again overwhelms me, until I can hardly write at all—until, were it not for the thing which I must do, I would rush out into the street and run, screaming, until I was caught and dragged away, to be put behind strong iron bars. Perhaps I would feel safe there—perhaps!

I know that, terrified at the hate I saw confronting me in those redly gleaming eyes, I would have slunk away. The two thin hands that caught my arm again were strong enough to prevent that, however. I had been spared her kiss—I was not to escape from the oath I had taken to serve her.

"You promised—you swore," she hissed in my ear. "And tonight, you are to keep your oath."

I felt my senses reel. My oath—yes, I had an oath to keep. I had lifted my hand toward the dark heavens, and sworn to serve her in any way she chose—freely, and of my own volition, I had sworn.

I sought to evade her.

"Let me help you back to your boat," I begged. "You have no kindly feeling for me—and—you have seen it—I love you no longer. I will go back to the city—you can go back to your father, and forget that I broke your peace."

The laughter that greeted my speech I shall never forget—not in the depths under the scummy surface of the canal—not in the empty places between the worlds, where my tortured soul may wander.

"So you do not love me, and I hate you! Fool! Have I waited these weary months for the water to stop, only to go back now? After my father and I returned here and found the old boat rotting in the drained canal, and took refuge in it; when the water was turned into the canal while I slept, so that I could never escape until its flow should cease, *because of the thing that I am*—even then I dreamed of tonight.

"When the imprisonment we still shared ceased to matter to my father—come on board the deserted boat tomorrow, and see why, if you dare!—still I dreamed on, of tonight!

"I have been lonely, desolate, starving—now the whole world shall be mine! And by *your* help!"

I asked, her, somehow, what she wanted of me, and a madness overcame me so that I hardly heard her reply. Yet somehow, I knew that there was that on the opposite shore of the great river where the pleasure camps were, that she wanted to find. In the madness of my terror, she made me understand and obey her.

I must carry her in my arms across the long bridge over the river, deserted in the small hours of the night!

The way back to the city was long tonight—long, she walked behind me, and I turned my eyes neither to right nor left. Only as I passed the tumbledown houses, I saw their reflection in the canal and trembled so that I could have fallen to the ground, at the thoughts of the little child this woman had been accused of slaying there, and at the certainty I felt that she was reading my thoughts.

And now the horror that engulfed me darkened my brain.

I know that we set our feet upon the long, wide bridge that spanned the river. I know the storm broke there, so that I battled for my footing, almost for my life, it seemed, against the pelting deluge. And the horror I had invoked was in my arms, clinging to me, burying its head upon my shoulder. So increasingly dreadful had my pale-faced companion become to me, that I hardly thought of her now as a woman at all—only as a demon of the night.

The tempest raged still as she leaped down out of my arms on the other shore. And again I walked with her against my will, while the trees lashed their branches madly around me, showing the pale undersides of their leaves in the vivid frequent flashes that rent the heavens.

On and on we went, branches flying through the air and missing us by a miracle of ill fortune. Such as she and I are not slain by falling branches. The river was a welter of whitecaps, flattened down into strange shapes by the pounding rain. The clouds as we glimpsed them were like devils flying through the sky.

Past dark tent after dark tent we stole, and past a few where lights burned dimly behind their canvas walls. And at last we came to an old quarry. Into its artificial ravine she led me, and up to a crevice in the rock wall.

"Reach in your hand and pull out the loose stone you will feel," she whispered. "It closes an opening that leads into deep caverns. A human hand must remove that stone—your hand must move it!"

Why did I struggle so to disobey her? Why did I fail? It was as though I *knew*—but my failure was foreordained—I had taken oath!

IF YOU who read have believed that I have set down the truth thus far, the little that is left you will call the ravings of a madman overtaken by his madness. Yet these things happened.

I stretched out my arm, driven by a compulsion I could not resist. At arm's length in the niche in the rock, I felt something move—the loose rock, a long, narrow fragment, much larger than I had expected. Yet it moved easily, seeming to swing on a natural pivot. Outward it swung, toppling toward me—a moment more and there was a swift rush of the ponderous weight I had loosened. I leaped aside and went down, my forehead grazed by the rock.

For a brief moment I must have been unconscious. But only for a moment. My head a stabbing agony of pain, unreal lights flashing before my eyes, I yet knew the reality of the storm that beat me down as I struggled to my feet. I knew the reality of the dark, loathsome shapes that passed me in the dark, crawling out of the orifice in the rock and flapping through the wild night, along the way that led to the pleasure camps.

So the caverns I had laid open to the outer world were infested with bats. I had been inside unlit caverns, and had heard there the squeaking of the things, felt and heard the flapping of their wings—*but never in all my life before had I seen bats as large as men and women!*

Sick and dizzy from the blow on my head, and from disgust, I crept along the way they were going. If I touched one of them, I felt that I should die of horror.

Now, at last, the storm abated, and a heavy darkness made the whole world seem like the inside of a tomb.

Where the tents stood in a long row, the number of the monster bats seemed to diminish. It was as though—horrible thought!—they were creeping into the tents, with their slumbering occupants.

At last I came to a lighted tent, and paused, crouching so that the dim radiance that shone through the canvas did not touch me in the shadows. And there I waited, but not for long. There was a dark form silhouetted against the tent—a movement of the flap of the tent—a rustle and confusion, and the dark thing was again in silhouette—but with a difference in the quality of the shadow. The dark thing was *inside* the tent now, its bat wings extending across the entrance through which it had crept.

Fear held me spellbound. And as I looked the shadow

changed again—imperceptibly, so that I could not have told *how* it changed.

But now it was not the shadow of a bat, but of a woman.

"The storm—the storm! I am lost, exhausted—I crept in here, to beg for refuge until the dawn!"

That low, thrilling, sibilant voice—too well I knew it!

Within the tent I heard a murmur of acquiescent voices. At last I began to understand.

I knew the nature of the woman I had carried over the river in my arms, the woman who would not even cross the canal until the water should have ceased utterly to flow. I remembered books I had read—*Dracula*—other books, and stories. I knew they were true books and stories, now—I knew those horrors existed for me.

I had indeed kept my oath to the creature of darkness—I had brought her to her kind, under her guidance. I had let them loose in hordes upon the pleasure camps. The campers were doomed—and through them, others——

I forgot my fear. I rushed from my hiding-place up to the tent door, and there I screamed and called aloud.

"Don't take her in—don't let her stay—nor the others, that have crept into the other tents! Wake all the campers—they will sleep on to their destruction! Drive out the interlopers— drive them out quickly! *They are not human—no, and they are not bats*. Do you hear me—do you understand?"

I was fairly howling, in a voice that was strange to me.

"She is a vampire!—they are all vampires. *Vampires!*"

Inside the tent I heard a new voice. "What can be the matter with that poor man?" the voice said. It was a woman's, and gentle.

"Crazy—somebody out of his senses, dear," a man's voice answered. "Don't be frightened."

And then the voice I knew so well—so well: "I saw a falling rock strike a man on the head in the storm. He staggered away, but I suppose it crazed him."

I waited for no more. I ran away, madly, through the night and back across the bridge to the city.

Next day—today—I boarded the sunken canal-boat. It is the abode of death—no woman could have lived there—only such an one as *she*. The old man's corpse was there—he must have died long, long ago. The smell of death and of decay on the boat was dreadful.

Again, I felt that I understood. Back in those awful houses, she had committed the crime when first she became the thing she is. And he—her father—less sin-steeped, and less accursed, attempted to destroy the evidence of her crime, and fled with her, but died without becoming like her. She had said that one of those two was always on watch—did he indeed divide her vigil on the boat? What more fitting—the dead standing watch with the undead! And no wonder that she would not let me board the craft of death, even to carry her away.

And still I feel the old compulsion. I have been spared her kiss—but for a little while. Yet I will not let the power of my oath to her draw me back, till I enter the caverns with her and creep forth in the form of a bat to prey upon mankind. Before that can happen, I too will die.

The Curse of a Song

Eli Colter

"He said the damned thing was cursed." Armitage threw back his head and laughed. The laugh held as much of contempt as it did of amusement. "I wonder if he thinks anyone is superstitious enough to believe in such antediluvian stuff as curses in this hectic era?"

"Oh, you don't believe in curses, eh?" Morgenthaler tapped the coal in his pipe and fixed a speculative gaze on Armitage.

"Huh? What's that? Believe in *curses?*" Armitage sobered slightly, returning Morgenthaler's gaze with surprise for the other man's serious tone. "Certainly not! Save the kind in which I indulge when I kick my shin on the rocking-chair in the dark. The other kind are the quintessence of absurdity. Hank! Don't tell me you believe in curses!"

"I'm not telling you anything." Henry Morgenthaler drew deeply on his pipe and shrugged his shoulders, and the serious look in his eyes grew till his whole face was dark and somber with its reflection. "But I've seen things that leave me guessing—yet only to a certain extent. What I've seen and known didn't leave much room for guesswork."

"Well, I didn't mean to step on anybody's toes. If I offended some particular idea of yours, I beg pardon." Armitage settled back in his chair and lit a cigarette, his eyes still on Morgenthaler, surprised and puzzled. Morgenthaler was a hard-headed, practical sort of chap. "I've heard and read a lot of that stuff, naturally. Curses, ghosts, and all that rot. But I always grinned up my sleeve, took it at face value and let it go at that. Certainly, I never put any credence in it."

"No, I never used to, either." Morgenthaler carefully knocked the dottle from his pipe and began refilling it. "I used to believe the same way you do. But I can't believe that way now.

"You've heard me speak of Rose Wilzen. You knew I'd met her out in Portland, Oregon, that six years I spent on the coast. And you've wondered why I never want to go back to the West. Well, Rose, and her curse, are the reason. Rose's whole life was overshadowed with tragedy and curse. From the first time I heard about it I ceased scoffing. Grant Wilzen, Rose's father, was born in the East. He had a brother named Thaddeus. They called him Thad. Thad was engaged to a girl back there in the Eastern town where the Wilzen family then lived. He was three years older than Grant.

"An old barnstorming troupe came through the town with an *Uncle Tom's Cabin* show. The fellow playing the role of Simon Legree was a young man of talent, much dissatisfied with his villain's part. He's climbed. You'd be startled if I told you who he is now in the theatrical world. He had become acquainted with Grant Wilzen the year before while Grant was away at a summer resort on his vacation. When the troupe came to the town the actor looked up Grant, and so got acquainted with Thad.

"Thad didn't like him. There was no particular reason for his dislike. Just one of those peculiar things nobody can explain. He simply didn't like him. And he liked him less when circumstances forced him to introduce the actor to his fiancée. The actor showed marked interest in the girl and called on her the next afternoon. Thad was furious, but he didn't say much. The troupe's stay lengthened to two weeks, and every day the actor called on Thad's girl. And still Thad kept his mouth shut.

"The middle of the second week, Thad was sent away on business to be gone for two days. He wasn't really much concerned over the affair. He felt certain that the girl would forget all about the actor the moment the show was gone. He went on his business trip rather glad of something to help the time pass. The day he got back, he went straight to her house. There was a little latticed window opening from the parlor on to the front lawn. Thad stepped up to the window and looked through the pane, hearing the sound of the organ, and intending to surprise her. He stopped still at what he saw and heard.

"The girl was seated at the organ, playing and singing *Love's Old Sweet Song*. The actor stood by with an arm over her shoulders, and just as she finished the song he said, 'Wonderful, my darling! So shall our lives be. A continued dream of *Love's Old Sweet Song*.' And the girl answered, 'Yes, my beloved. Yes. I am thine forever!'

"The very tone of the high-flown words should have been revealing to Thad Wilzen. But he was a man of volcanic, vindictive nature—jealous, hot-headed, easily roused to an unreasoning fury. He glared at them for a moment, whirled and rushed blindly down the street, found Grant and told him what had happened. Then, in spite of Grant's efforts to prevent any hasty action on his part, he rushed madly out of town, swearing he would never come back—that none of them would ever see him again. 'His faith in women was broken, he didn't care what became of him,' and all that stuff.

"Grant went straight to the girl, demanded an explanation, and told her what had happened. She was heart-broken, and she explained to Grant that the actor was coaching her in a scene for a play that the girls of her set were going to produce after the troupe left town. She had refrained from telling Thad because she wanted to surprise him by showing him how clever she was. Those girls were just like a bunch of kids, wanting to play circus after the circus is gone. They had become inoculated with the atmosphere of the theater, and with much high glee and enthusiasm had decided to put on a show of their own. It was merely a passing whim, a regular kid trick, and the actor had good-naturedly entered into the spirit of the thing. He was secretly coaching all the girls and fellows, not only Thad's fiancée. He was a very decent chap, and he was aghast when the girl told him about Thad's misunderstanding of what he had seen, and of his rash action.

"They did everything they could to locate Thad, and the actor left the town with his troupe the next week, expressing deep and sincere regret, saying he was certain they would find Thad and everything would be all right. But they didn't find Thad. He had simply disappeared. Two years passed. The girl married another man. Grant got an opportunity to go to the West, where he had always wanted to go, and he went out to Portland, Oregon.

"At that time—it was some forty years ago—Portland was vastly different from the metropolis it is now. There were no big steel bridges over the wide Willamette River running through the center of the town. The city was still young, in its making. You had to cross the river on either the Jefferson Street or the Stark Street ferry. There was only one street-car in the town—a horse-drawn 'bob-car' running up and down Front Street along the west side of the river.

"Grant was delighted with the place. He wanted to grow up with it. He went to work, accumulated a circle of friends and set himself to carve out his future. But he thought he was missing something if he didn't see all of it. One night he went on a curiosity-impelled excursion with some boon companions into the then terrible North End. They roamed around through the joints, and rambled along through a couple of wide-open 'music halls' and saloons called by the names of the proprietors—Erickson's and Blazier's. Then they went on to the smaller dives, and in one wild place Grant ran bang-up into his brother Thad. Thad, neither drunk nor wild, was standing around watching the poor devils about him with a kind of cynical sympathy.

"After he recovered from his first astonishment, Grant went close to him, took his brother by the arm and spoke to him.

" 'Thad! Where have you been all this time?'

" 'Thad?' His brother frowned in polite and distant bewilderment. 'You must be mistaken. My name is John Rogers.'

"Grant saw instantly that Thad wasn't running any bluff. He never learned how it happened, but Thad's mind had gone God knows where, and some stranger mind was in its place. Grant tried to make him remember who he was, but failed utterly. Then he tried to make friends with him, but only partly succeeded. Thad refused to go to live with him. He hung around the North End, gambling incessantly, looking on, never drinking, but never content anywhere else.

"One night when Grant was roaming around with him, trying to win his confidence and striving to bring back something of the past to Thad's mind, they went into a stinking little hell-hole of a music hall. There was a drunkard in there, seated at a wheezy old organ in the corner, maudlinly playing and singing *Love's Old Sweet Song.* And something of what Grant had utterly failed to do was accomplished in a split second by that melody. Thad remembered. He stopped short, stared at the man, went white as a sheet and began to shake from head to foot. His stare turned into a maniacal glare; he pulled out a gun and emptied it into the body of the man at the organ.

"The place was instantly in an uproar. Some rushed to pick up the dead man, and others rushed at Thad. Grant managed to get his brother out of the place and away from the North End.

"From then on a curious thing came to pass. Concerning some things, Thad was as level-headed and cool as you could want a man to be. He knew who he was, knew Grant, and remembered most of the past. But just mention *Love's Old Sweet Song,* or let him hear a strain of it, and he was instantly a raving maniac. His insanity was so apparent that there was no talk of sending him to the gallows.

"He was immediately committed to the insane asylum, then situated in Portland on Twelfth and Hawthorne Streets. It was not at that time a state institution, but a private one kept by Dr. Hawthorne, who had built it on his own property and who ran it for the good of the state. There Thad was taken, and there Grant went often to see him, always hoping to find him improved and perhaps in time turned sane. But Thad never changed, except to grow worse. He remembered enough of the incident concerning the girl and the actor to send him into a murderous fury every time she was mentioned, or every time he thought of her or the song. Grant never mentioned either, but he couldn't keep Thad from thinking. Because Grant was with him at the time his memory partly returned, and because the song was so important a part of the shooting affair, Thad began to associate Grant with all his troubles. Every time Grant went to see him he would go into a rage and begin to curse him. He kept steadily getting worse to such an extent that Grant had to stay away.

"Then Grant got married, and for two years he didn't see Thad. And Thad went into another rage, in which he was plainly dying. They sent for Grant. Thad had cooled down in the meantime and become more lucid and calm than he had been since his incarceration in the asylum. But the moment he saw Grant he went again into a wild fury. He had been told of Grant's marriage. He cursed Grant, his wife, and all of his descendants. He swore that after he died he would come back and curse him so long as he lived, if he ever dared have that song around him or allowed it played in his house. He died repeating that curse over and over.

"Grant, of course, grieved over it. But he was humanely relieved to see Thad out of his troubles, and he paid no attention to the curse. He laughed at it, as you and I would have done, Armitage. For the next few years life moved along smoothly for him, and he about forgot Thad's curse. But he had told his wife about it, and she was just superstitious enough so that she wouldn't have the song in the house, and she wouldn't let anyone sing it or play it on their organ.

"Grant's family began to come, and he had bought himself

a place in the town of Lents—then a separate town but since a suburb of Portland. Grant prospered. Portland had grown. Three big steel bridges, the Morrison, Steel, and Burnside, had gone up over the river. Street-cars were running on both sides of the Willamette. And as the town grew, Grant grew up with it. He had got to be pretty well off, and was feeling well satisfied with life.

"The tragedy of Thad was legend in the family, but none save Grant's wife put any credence in the curse the insane man had leveled at them all. Rose, the youngest of Grant's children, a sensitive, delicate child, grew up with the shadow of that curse hanging over her. She couldn't tell why, but she had an instinctive, uncontrollable belief in it. The asylum had been taken over by the state, and the inmates moved to the state institution at Salem. But the old private asylum remained there on Hawthorne's property for a long time, on the bank of a little creek, empty and deserted. She saw it once, when she was a little kid, and it made a powerful impression on her mind.

"The other children of the family sighed in perfunctory sympathy and shrugged away from them their Uncle Thad's tragedy, although they were oddly careful to avoid any contact with that song. But Rose couldn't shake it off so easily. Nor could she ever get out of her head the inner picture of the gloomy old asylum. It grew to shadow her. She couldn't get away from it. By the time she was eighteen her entire existence was colored by a dread belief in the curse bound up in *Love's Old Sweet Song*. Whenever she would even think of it she would remember the gloomy old asylum, and shiver. The building had been torn down, the creek filled in, and concrete streets heavy with traffic now ran over its site. But to Rose it still stood, a sinister monument of the wreck of Thad's life and the curse of a song.

"When she was nineteen years old she could look back and count seven different tragical happenings that had occurred in connection with that song. Her belief in the curse was so implicit that no one could make her believe other than that to sing it or hear it was disaster.

"Then she met Murray Fielding. He was just back from the war. We were attending a party at the home of one of her friends. I had taken her there. Long since I had made my try for her affections, and lost. But, contrary to commonly accepted opinion on that subject, we remained fast friends. Well, we arrived at her friend's house, and her friend's brother and I stood in the hall talking, waiting for her. She and her friend had gone upstairs to the friend's room where she was to leave her wraps.

"I heard her voice, and turned to see her coming down the stairs arm in arm with the other girl. The girl was telling Rose about Murray Fielding, how fine-looking he was, what a nice fellow, you know—came of a splendid family, was decorated in the war, and all the things girls say about men when they want to interest another girl. I grinned up at them. They were about halfway down the stairs and they were making no effort to lower their voices.

"Just then Murray himself came into the hall, paused by the table where the punch-bowl stood, and began to ladle out a glassful of punch. Rose's friend hailed him gaily. He looked up, smiled at her, and his glance passed to Rose. Just at that precise moment three or four of the girls in the room beyond began to bang on the piano and sing *Love's Old Sweet Song*.

"I started, and shot a glance at Rose. She went white, and stopped short on the stairs, staring at Murray Fielding. Because, in that instant, she knew that Murray was the one man for whom she was intended. And she heard the wailing of that song behind him. He put down the ladle and glass he held, staring back at her, puzzled and amazed by the look on her face and the pallor, knowing also that she was the one girl for him. Rose's friend knew all about the curse, and even had a kind of romantic respect for it. But she didn't believe in it. She took Rose by the arm, drew her on down into the hall and introduced Murray Fielding to her.

"For the next three months Rose and Murray went through a strange experience. They couldn't bear to be apart, and they were miserable when they were together. Rose was frightened out of her wits. Murray was entirely at sea, bewildered and puzzled by her actions. She hadn't told him about the curse, and she had forbidden anyone else's doing so. Up to that time I had treated the whole thing as a joke, only that I deplored what I considered Rose's foolish belief in it. But now I began to be worried about the thing. I could see that Rose was wearing down under severe strain, and one night I deliberately brought up the subject, intending to try and talk her out of it.

" 'It's no use, Hank,' she told me, her face colorless and her eyes dilated with apprehension. 'I know you laugh at it, but that curse is very real. Uncle Thad hangs around me all the time. I don't know what he wants, but he intends to carry out that curse so long as any of us live.'

" 'He hangs around you?' I repeated, staring at her, wondering if she was a little bit unsettled in her mind from brooding over it. 'See here, my dear, that's all bunk. When a man's dead, he's dead.'

" 'You may think so,' she answered, shaking her head, 'but you're wrong. Twice in the last month I've seen him, but I've been afraid to tell anybody but you. They'd only laugh at me. I know you won't.'

" 'No, I won't laugh at you,' I said soberly, studying her face, noting the dark circles under her eyes and the drawn look about her mouth. 'What do you mean—you've seen him? '

" 'Why, just that.' She sank into a chair, and as I walked over to sit beside her she went white, put her hand over her mouth to stopper a scream, and pointed behind me with a shaking finger. 'He follows me, I tell you! There he is, now! '

"I wheeled and stared across the room where she pointed. For a moment I didn't see anything. Then I saw a shadow pass along the wall. It was exactly like the shadow of some person cast by the sun, on the clear blue-gray tone of the solid-colored paper. I started to say that someone must have come up on the porch, that the sun had thrown the shadow there. Then I realized with a start that the sun was shining from the other direction—that had the shadow been a normal one it would have appeared on the *opposite* wall. That stopped me.

"I stood there staring at that slowly moving shadow, telling myself that it was some ghastly hoax. A ghost in broad daylight! Nonsense. But I couldn't make myself believe it was nonsense. That damned shadow was too clearly outlined. It was the shadow of a man a little above average height, in profile, showing a lean figure, a thin mouth-line and a long hooked nose. And it was moving. When it got within four feet of Rose it stopped. A queer kind of smoky light grew around the edges of it and it began to assume rounded proportions. It took on a color of flesh, and the face became fairly clear.

"And of all the faces I ever saw! It was positively diabolical in expression. The glaring, maniacal eyes glued to Rose's face. The thin mouth twisted in a hideous sneer. It was horrible, menacing, gloating. I felt a chill go over me and the hair raised on my scalp. The whole room was filled with a dank, foul odor, as though something loathsome and putrefying had been injected into the atmosphere. The very sunlight streaming through the window seemed polluted and soiled. I was frozen. I couldn't move. Then, as quickly as he had come, he was gone.

"I got a grip on myself and turned to Rose. She was all but frightened into a faint, and I didn't for one moment try to conceal the fact that I myself was badly shaken.

" 'You saw him?' she gasped.

" 'Yes, I saw him, damn him!' I answered harshly. I took her cold hand and gripped it tightly. My own wasn't much warmer. 'Why in thunder is he following you about in that way? What's he up to?' I had no scoffing defense left. He had been there and that's all there was to it. I knew what I had seen. Then, before she could answer, my own reason explained it partly. I summed it up to Rose. 'He knows you're the only one in the family who has really taken him seriously. The very unbelief of the others held him off and rendered his power impotent. The three boys have all married and gone away without anything happening to them, you'll notice. Nothing ever happened to your father— save your mother's death, and *he* couldn't have been connected with that.'

" 'He was,' Rose interrupted, shivering and clinging to my hand. 'He was! You don't know all about this thing, Hank. Mother was getting better—and some crazy Italian came along the street playing a hand-organ. And of all things on earth he was playing that hideous song! And Mother heard it, and she cried out in a kind of terror, as if she saw something at the foot of her bed. She shrank back on her pillow and died in the instant. All of them stared toward the foot of her bed, and though they saw nothing, they remembered the curse, and they were secretly startled and shaken. But I—I saw. I saw that shadow—for the first time.'

" 'Exactly!' I put in, getting some control of my shaken faculties in my eager following out of the hypothesis I had formulated. 'You saw him! No one else did. Your very belief in him has given him power to reach you.'

" 'Yes, and his power is growing.' Rose shivered uncontrollably and clung to me like a child afraid of the dark. 'And I'm so fearful of the future that it's breaking my nerve. I don't know what to do.'

"I didn't know what to do either. I didn't know what to suggest. All my preconceived ideas of such things were knocked into a cocked hat, utterly shattered by the proof lately put before me. I couldn't shake off the feeling of dread that had descended on me. I couldn't get rid of the picture of that hideous, leering, rage-contorted face. I couldn't smell anything but that putrid, foul odor he had brought with him. I stayed around for over an hour, trying to calm her and persuade her that the problem could be worked out somehow. But I made a rather poor job of it because I was so upset myself, and I had no idea what might be ahead of her if that fiend were not stopped in some way.

"I left the house, finally, and walked the streets for another hour, trying to think, and not making much headway with that, either. There was no doubt about it. Thad had come back, all right, if he had ever left the family in the first place. And he had fastened himself on the one member of the family who was approachable by him. What he intended there was no way to hazard an opinion. But it was something ugly and horrible, and he would succeed in it all right;—if someone didn't find the means of stopping him.

"That week the crowd of young people with which Rose associated took a sudden idea into their heads to make up a party and go to Mount Hood for the week-end. Mount Hood is a magnificent snow peak, 11,225 feet in elevation, some fifty or sixty miles from Portland. All the girls of the crowd were jeering at me because I had never been even so far as Government Camp. They begged me to come along on this week-end trip, and although I didn't care to get that far away from Rose, I did feel a desire to see the place for its historic significance.

"I wanted to see the beauty of the mountain, and I had a desire to look at the monument erected there by the Sons and Daughters of Oregon Pioneers—the monument dedicated to Samuel Barlow, pioneer from Kentucky, who built the first wagon road across the Cascade Mountains, passing that spot at the base of Mount Hood somewhere in 1845 to '46, enabling other wagon-train immigrants to have direct ingress to the Willamette Valley. But though I knew how much there was to see up there, I refused to go till I found that Rose and Murray had finally agreed to trail along. Then I consented in double-quick time.

"The party was bound for a cottage, owned by one of the girls' parents, and built a little way this side of Government Camp, in the big firs. The camp was then the end of the road, or nearly so. That was long before the cement highway was built to form the loop around Hood. The girls thought it would be no end of a lark to go up there on Saturday, take a trip a little way up the mountain, and come back on Sunday.

"Well, of course we started out in fine spirits. I hadn't heard the curse-bearing song since that night of the party three months before. If it had been a favorite with the gang, it wouldn't have seemed so strange a thing for it to crop up that night. But it wasn't. The girls didn't like it. They voted it sloppy and slow. They couldn't understand what motive had impelled them to tear into it right at that moment. I know. I asked them. And why should they take a freak notion to take a bust at it at the precise instant when Rose first laid eyes on Murray Fielding? I never have believed in coincidence. I guess I was the only one in that gay crowd that Saturday evening who had the shivers under the grin I wore to mask my feelings. I was thinking of all the affairs, and mostly of Thad's appearance.

"Murray's presence had steadied Rose a great deal, and the rest of the crowd was so hilarious that they drew her into their nonsense in spite of herself. We started from Portland early, but the roads were bad, and we struck one nasty detour that forced us to crawl along at five miles in low. At Rose's request I had gone in Murray's car with him and her. He had a roadster that would barely accommodate the three of us. When we reached the detour, another party bound for the mountain drove up even with us and the cars got all mixed up. The rest of our party got away ahead of us, but Murray didn't pay any attention.

"I noticed that he was watching the side roads; a few of them showed up here and there, rutted and almost impassable, and he was keeping a careful eye on them. Finally he stopped at one of them, turned down it, and crawled along through the timber on miserable going. I wondered what he was up to, but I kept my mouth shut and attended to my own business. Murray was a fine, keen, level-headed chap, and I knew that whatever he was doing was all right. He finally drew up before a dark, remote and hidden cabin. Still, I didn't say a word. And neither did he.

And neither did Rose. He got out of the car, assisted her out and started toward the cabin with a beckoning gesture for me. Of course I followed close.

"The cabin was locked, but he took out a key, opened the door, preceded us in and struck a match to light the oil lamp sitting on the table. It had grown dusky early there in the shadow of the trees. I don't know to this day whether he simply accepted me as someone close enough to Rose to be trusted all the way, or whether he was driven so hard he didn't give a whoop who was around. At all events he turned and faced Rose, ignoring me utterly, and asked bluntly, 'Rose, just why are you afraid of me?'

"'I'm—I'm not,' she denied, but she went white as paper and I felt the cold chills go up and down my spine. In a passing car on the not distant detour I could faintly hear a band of celebrators singing Love's Old Sweet Song. And squarely behind Murray on the wall appeared that malignant shadow.

"Murray set his mouth grimly as Rose dropped into a chair, too much frightened to keep her feet, and answered with terse words, 'Rose, you can't expect me to believe that weak denial. Why, you're as white as a death's-head at the very question!'

"He was shaking with emotion, and I felt infinitely sorry for him, but I couldn't tear my eyes from that hideous shadow on the wall. It wasn't moving now—it was standing still directly behind him. He went on harshly, 'I'd swear you care as much for me as I do for you. I've seen it in your eyes, if I'm any judge of human beings at all. Yet, every time I come close to you, you shudder. You shuddered and went white the first time you ever saw me. What is it? What have I done? What do you think I've done? I swear I've never committed any act in my life of which I need be ashamed. I've not even any relative of which I need be ashamed. As a matter of fact, I've no living relative at all save a half-brother from whom I became separated during the war. I never could find him again, never expect to see him again. But he was one of the finest chaps I ever knew, and I'd give ten years of my life to find him. What is it, Rose? You've got to tell me. Your treatment of me is driving me mad!'

"*Mad*. Ugly word. Driving him mad! Rose's eyes dilated terribly as she stared at the shadow taking shape behind him, and the voices from that car crawling along the detour still faintly wafted that cursed song down to us.

"Rose half got up from her chair, driven beyond control, and cried out at him, 'Murray—listen—what do you hear?' He strained his ears for the least sound, and caught the echo of that song, as Rose finished wildly, 'Look behind you! Murray— look behind you!'

"Murray wheeled, and stared where her gaze was riveted. The shadow had completely taken form by this time, and he saw clearly, as we saw, that horrible, sinister figure, with the thin cruel mouth and the glaring mad eyes. As he looked, the thin mouth opened, twisting, writhing, and I knew Thad Wilzen was trying to speak to him. But his power hadn't grown strong enough for that yet, and no sound came from the menacing, diabolical shape. Murray stared a moment, then his face went black with anger. He thought it was a real corporeal fleshly body standing there.

" 'Get out of here!' he roared, jerking out the little automatic he habitually carried in defiance of all laws to the contrary, leveling the snub-nosed wicked weapon at the vicious figure he now faced. 'Get out of here, instantly, or I'll drill you!'

"Thad got out. But he didn't go through any fear of Murray, nor because Murray had commanded it. He did it to put the fear into Murray's heart, and he succeeded. He laughed—and we heard that. A thin, high, mocking titter. The glare in his eyes shot an ugly threat at Rose, his whole figure wavered, grew thin and vanished into the air. Oh, he went, all right. And there was no mistaking the *way* he went, either! Murray stared a moment at the blank wall, his eyes starting from his head, then he turned slowly, replacing the gun in his pocket, shifting his stare to Rose's white face.

"'Good God!' he cried hoarsely; 'what was that? Rose, what does it mean? What's back of all this?'

"'That— that song——' Rose gasped, and fainted in her chair.

"Both of us sprang toward her, but he reached her first. He picked her up in his arms, took the chair himself, and sat there rocking her in his arms like a baby, staring down into her colorless face, smoothing her forehead with one hand.

"'She'll come about all right in a moment,' I said, trying to speak calmly. 'I know the whole affair. Better let me tell you before she comes out of her faint. She's merely frightened.'

"Murray looked up at me with a start, suddenly recalled to the fact of my presence. The shock and bewilderment on his face settled a little, and he asked in a steadier voice, though still hoarse and shaken, 'You—you saw it, Hank? You smelled that vile odor? I thought at first that the cabin was just musty from being closed so long. It's our summer house, you know. The folks haven't been up since last year—the folks where I stay. They have made me one of the family. They're all the folks I have. But Rose saw it. You—did you?'

"'Certainly I saw him,' I cut in. 'I've seen him before. If you'll give me just a minute or two I'll explain to you.' And I did so, rapidly and briefly.

"He listened silently, sitting there and rocking Rose in his arms, and she looked so white and still that it gave me the shivers just to glance at her. 'I don't know how in God's name it will end,' I finished, 'but we've got to fight the thing out somehow. Rose has managed to keep it from you all along. She feared if you learned of it, and believed in it, it would give him power over you, too. But you had to know, and I'm glad it's come about this way. We've got to figure out some way of stopping him before he literally frightens her to death. I'm certain that's what he's trying to do. He's violently, unreasoningly bitter against Grant, her father. She's all Grant has left. The boys are all married, as you know, and none of them nearer than

Canada. Rose's mother is dead. You see what a keen revenge he'll have against Grant if he can bring tragedy on Rose. Rose was always her father's favorite, anyway.'

"'There's just one thing I want to know,' Murray said tensely. 'Not that it will make any difference in my fighting for her so long as there's any fight left. But I've got to know whether or not Rose cares for me. I can't stand the suspense any longer. I've got to know.'

"'She loves you better than anything in the world,' I said steadily, and I had good cause to be sure of that. 'You can feel absolutely settled about it. All you've got to do is help us plan some campaign against that ghoul that threatens her.'

"Rose stirred in his arms, and he turned his entire attention to her, swiftly, looking anxiously into her eyes as she opened them and stared up into his face.

"'Are you all right, Rose? You've got to be! Hank and I are going to see this through somehow. Can't you buck up a bit, and trust us to manage to find the way to foil him—whatever he intends doing? Just so surely as we three are here on the bank of the Salmon River, I tell you there is a way, and Hank and I will find it.'

"'If you could!' Rose shuddered and leaned wearily against his shoulder. 'I am—am so afraid! I don't feel like going on to Mount Hood.'

"'We don't need to go on,' Murray answered, glancing up at me. 'I couldn't go on myself without knowing just how matters stood between you and me. That's why I stopped off here. I intended stopping here when we started from Portland. We'll turn around and go back, if you wish.'

"'Yes—I'd rather. It's all right with you, Hank?' She looked up to catch my vehement nod of assent, and went on talking to Murray. 'I'm too much frightened to think clearly, or to bear the nonsense of the crowd tonight and tomorrow. Maybe Hank has told you—that song has spelled tragedy for me all my life.'

"Murray nodded, and she got to her feet with his aid, white and weary till it cut my heart to look at her. 'Well, there's no good going over it, then. You know. And the moment I saw you on the stairs that first time—those crazy youngsters began singing that awful song. Why, have you ever stopped to think what the initial letters of the horrible thing spell? L—o—s—s, loss! What are we going to do? He—he's getting closer. I feel him more powerful and hideous all the time.' She shuddered and stopped for sheer lack of breath.

"'I don't'—Murray started to speak, hesitated, then went on grimly—'I don't know what we're going to do. But we're going to do something, never doubt that. Rose—are you afraid to marry me with that thing hanging over?'

"'Oh——!' She started, shrank back, then stumbled on: 'Yes—I—I am. I'm afraid to do that—and I'm afraid to let you go.'

"'You're not letting me go,' Murray returned curtly. 'It can't be done. I'm yours for good, and if he stops us he's got a big job on his hands!'

"'Let's get back to Portland,' I said abruptly. 'I don't think any of us feels much like mingling with a picnic crowd.'

"Murray nodded, handed me his flashlight and motioned toward the door as he went to the table to blow out the lamp. I snapped on the flash and lit the three of us out, and none of us spoke again till we were in the car and headed back for Portland. As a matter of fact, little was said at all on the way back to town. We rode in a strained silence, too much shaken for further speech, busy with ghastly thoughts, and the remembrance of Thad's appearance in the cabin. We left Rose at her front door, and didn't drive on till we saw the lights go up inside the house. Then we drove away, and Murray asked me to spend the night with him.

"I was rather glad to accept that invitation. I knew his thoughts were the same as mine. Knew that he had the idea of our getting together with all possible haste.

"The people with whom he stayed were all abed and the house dark, and we went up to his room with as little disturbance as possible. But not to sleep. We never even removed our clothes. For a while we didn't even talk. Murray switched on the light, and we sat around and paced the room, alternately. Then suddenly Murray wheeled to face me with a queer light in his eyes.

" 'Listen here, Hank. I've got an idea. I don't know that song. Never even read it through. But one of the girls here has a book of old home and college songs that's bound to contain it. I'm going to get it.'

"He went out of the room abruptly, and I paced back and forth awaiting his return, wondering what kind of scheme he had in his head. He was back shortly, carrying the book spread open to the song.

" 'Look here, Hank. Read it,' he said, and held the book out to me.

"Neither had I ever read the song through, and I took it in my hands with a kind of grisly interest, seeing in my mind's eye again the thin malignant face of Thad Wilzen. I went through the two stanzas word by word:

> Once in the dear dead days beyond recall,
> When on the world a mist began to fall,
> Out of the dreams that rose in happy throng,
> Lo, to our hearts love sang an old, sweet song;
> And through the dusk, where fell the firelight's gleam,
> Softly it wove itself into our dream.
>
> Even today we hear love's song of yore,
> Deep in our hearts it dwells forever more,
> Footsteps may falter, weary grow the way,
> Yet we can hear it at the close of day;
> So to the end, when life's dim shadows fall,
> Love shall be found the sweetest song of all.

Chorus

Just a song at twilight, when the lights are low,
And the flick'ring shadows softly come and go;
Though the heart be weary, sad the day and long,
Still to us at twilight comes love's old song—
Comes love's old, sweet song.

"'Exquisite,' Murray breathed. 'I never realized before how lovely the old thing is, set to that haunting music. And he's trying to make of it a hideous, horror-ridden symbol of tragedy. Trying to frighten the life out of Rose through one of the most glorious melodies, written on a glorious theme. Well, I think I've discovered the way to stop him. I—damn him! Look!'

"I whirled to look toward the doorway, where Murray's gaze had flashed. There was the shadow, materializing as though it had just come through the door. And as we stared, it assumed full shape quickly, and Thad stood there pointing at the open book, glaring malevolently at Murray, mouthing furiously and striving to speak so that we could hear. But only one word could we get—the word 'Rose.' Murray hurled the book at him furiously, his face white with rage. Thad went out exactly as he had gone from the cabin. And again that high, thin, tittering laugh trailed in the air as he disappeared.

"Murray sprang across the room, picked up the book and whirled to face me. I asked him what his idea was, but he shook his head, dumb with anger and fear for Rose, with a shaking realization of what a futile-seeming battle was ahead of us, fighting a ghoul that could laugh and fade out on the wall like a shadow. He finally told me he would explain to Rose and me together, and began pacing the floor like a madman. I slumped into a chair, staring at him, and slowly it grew in my mind exactly what Thad intended. If he could frighten Rose to death and send Murray insane, he would accomplish his hideous design. He knew too well how utterly that would break Grant

Wilzen. And as though in affirmation to my thought I heard again his high, tittering laugh.

"Both Murray and I were about half mad when the night had finally worn away and the morning was late enough for us to go over to the Wilzen house. Rose let us in with a sigh of relief, and we saw from the weariness on her face that she had slept little. Murray asked after her father, and she said he had gone out for a drive with some friends up the Columbia River Highway. He had gone before she was up, surprised to find her returned when he thought she had gone out to Mount Hood. He left a note saying he wouldn't have gone if he'd known she was to be home, but he'd already given his word and didn't want to disappoint the men with whom he was going.

"Rose led us on into the living-room, and Murray followed her to the divan and sat down by her side. I dropped into a chair across from them, and he pulled from his pocket that book, and spread it open to the song. One hand on the page, he looked intently into her eyes and asked, 'Rose, how do you kill a leech?'

" 'Why'—Rose frowned, puzzled—'I—I don't know.'

" 'You stick a knife into it,' Murray answered tersely. 'Stick a knife into it and let the blood out. The thing that hangs over you is a leech, menacing, striving to sap your life of happiness till it will leave nothing but a drained husk in its wake. It—he, that crazed fiend of yours, is trying to frighten you to death and drive me mad.' I caught my breath. I hadn't thought he'd got it, too. He went on swiftly, 'He's a leech, hanging onto you like death. And we're going to stick a knife into him! You and I love each other too much to be licked by a thing like this. We're starting a line of active defense, right now! See here!'

"He lifted his hand from the page and held out the book. Rose saw the song to which the page was opened, shivered and shrank back. He got up, walked over to the piano and spread the book open on the music rack, then turned and walked back to her.

"'We're going to show him!' he said sharply, taking her hand and drawing her to her feet. 'He can't hang anything on us like that with that lovely old song. I want you to sit down there and sing it and play it from beginning to end. And we're going to keep right on singing it, and repeating it, day after day, till we drive him out of our reckoning by the very force we set up against him. For every note you play and every word you sing, Hank and I will shoot out every ounce of will we possess to make of it a blessing instead of a curse. We'll stick a knife into that damnable leech—we'll drain him of every ounce of blood-power he possesses. Play it, Rose!'

"She shrank from it in abject terror, and Murray almost had to force her to the piano. But she did get there finally, and I sat dumb in my chair, looking on. She dropped on the piano bench as though her knees had buckled under her, and managed to command her fingers as she raised them to the keys. Only the iron dominance of Murray's will drove her on.

"The melody stumbled under her hands at first, and her voice wavered over the words. But the song grew clearer as she went on, and Murray stood close to her with his arm about her shoulder. And I shivered—and thought of Thad's girl. Then I had something else to shiver about. As she began the second stanza the shadow appeared on the wall. It writhed and danced in a blast of insane fury, and speedily grew to form the figure of Thad Wilzen. Murray was watching for it, and he whirled around, dropping his arm from about Rose's shoulder.

"She knew instinctively what had happened, and Murray shouted at her, 'Don't stop, Rose! Go on! *Go on!*' And he advanced two or three steps to face Thad, keeping between him and Rose. 'Get out!' he cried. 'Get out of here and stay out!—Come on, Hank—quick! Pit your will against him with mine!—Get out of here, you devil! That song is a blessing, a psalm to the most holy and God-given emotion on earth! You can't stand against it! Get out!'

"Rose's voice stumbled, caught, and wavered on, gaining

strength as it approached the glorious close. I sprang to my feet and stood face to face with Thad, shoulder to shoulder with Murray, willing with all my might that the song should change from curse to blessing, that he should go down before it. We were two to one. The malignant, hideous face contorted and mouthed at us, and we advanced side by side toward him, striving to stare him down, to force him out of there. The closer to him we got the more revolting grew the putrid odor in our nostrils. And then, suddenly, as the song trembled to a finish, he was gone as quickly as light, leaving behind him only that horrible odor and the echo of his thin, high, tittering laugh.

"Murray wheeled around with a look of grim triumph on his white face, and Rose swayed where she sat. Murray sprang to her, and she wilted limply on the bench, drooping against him.

" 'We got him that time,' Murray exulted, throwing an arm about Rose's shoulder. 'And we'll get him every time. We'll drum that song into his ears till he's sick of the sound of it. We'll drive him so far away he can't ever come back!'

" 'Oh—I'm afraid!' Rose sat up rigidly, clinging to Murray's hand on her shoulder. 'I'm afraid! I heard him laugh. There was something triumphant in it!'

"I felt a quiver of apprehension. I'd got that, too, and I saw by the look in Murray's eyes that it hadn't escaped him, either. But he wouldn't admit it to her. He sat down by her and talked incessantly for nearly a half-hour, exulting in what he felt certain was an initial victory, trying to calm her and banish her fears. He'd about succeeded and she was growing nearly normal again, when the 'phone rang. She got up to answer it, and we could both see her from where we sat, standing in the hall opposite the open door.

"She took down the receiver and answered, made a short reply to some question, stood listening a long minute, then cried out sharply and dropped the 'phone. Murray sprang toward her as she turned to face us, her features the color of a corpse. He caught her, and I went past them to replace the receiver on the hook, then rushed back into the room where he had taken her.

"'Rose—what is it?' he was asking as I came through the door.

"'Father——' Rose gasped. 'The call was from a house on the highway. The car—went over the bank—Father was driving. One of the men heard him cry out something like—Thad—then he twisted the wheel crazily—the car went over. All but one were killed.'

"'Your father carried an identification card—saying to notify you in case of accident, didn't he?' I interrupted.

"'Y-yes,' she nodded, her face strained and her haggard eyes filling with tears. 'It—it happened about half an hour ago. Oh—I told you he—he had triumph in that horrible laugh! Murray!' She turned to him and beat her hands against his arm. 'Don't ever defy him again!'

"'I'm killing a leech!' Murray's voice was hard. 'He shan't have you! I'll drain him, and pound him and knock every ounce of power out of him! Or die in the attempt! Hank, my car's out front. You drive, will you?'

"I nodded, speechless, stunned before the swift comeback Thad had accomplished in answer to Murray's defiance. Murray helped Rose into her wraps, and we went out to get into the car and drive to the scene of the accident. Murray gave all his attention to Rose, and I drove in a kind of grim daze, but I could hear his low voice running along.

"'The fight's on, Rose. I'm going to win, if you and Hank will just stick with me.'

"I was pretty sick inside, and I wasn't at all hopeful about the tactics he was pursuing, but I had no idea myself that was any better, and I determined I was certainly going to stick with them no matter what the end might be. We got out to the Highway, and came back with another bigger car, bringing her father's body with us. Two days later he was buried. Rose went through it all in a cold, numbed state that precluded tears and

words. She took up life alone in the house, with a companion
Murray hired to stay with her, an old Irishwoman who had
sense enough to keep out of sight and sound when she wasn't
wanted.

"But Murray never gave any quarter, never relaxed an inch
in the fight he had begun. He had a professional singer render
that song at the funeral, and held Rose's head against his shoulder so that she couldn't see the figure of Thad literally dancing
in unholy triumph as the coffin was lowered into the ground.
Of course none but we three could have seen him, anyhow.
And none but we three heard his tittering laugh of triumph as
we turned away from the grave.

"After that, Murray and I both spent with Rose every hour
away from business. And every day he made her sing that song
for him. And every day we went through the same old ghastly
business of striving, to will that song into a blessing, as Thad
grimaced and threatened and filled us with a horrible fear we
couldn't name or conquer. Inside of a week we were beginning
to feel the wear of it. Murray was looking like a ghost himself,
and Rose went around like a phantom. Murray began to carry
a wild, fanatical light in his eyes, and I knew that Rose was sick
with dread. But he wouldn't give up. He kept on with his mad
campaign, and gradually I began to think I saw a change in
Thad himself. Not that he was any the less furious at us.

"He grew more violent and threatening every time he
appeared. And he appeared more quickly each time, now. The
moment she struck the first notes of that song the shadow
darkened the wall, and each time the shadow remained for less
time a shadow and took on more swiftly the full outlines of the
figure. Undoubtedly he was growing stronger. His laugh was
clearer. Now and then we could catch clearly a word or two
that he mouthed at us. And he was positively maniacal in his
fury. But—it was the fury of a man *fighting* something tangible! Of a man who realizes that *he has something to fight!*

"We all saw that, and though the strain was terrific, a look of fanatical triumph and frantic suspense began to grow in Murray's eyes. Then the climax was on us before we realized it.

"Murray worked for a lumber company, and he was given orders to go down to Astoria, a little town about a hundred miles west on the Columbia River, to inspect some trees for the company. It seemed there was a tract there of heavily timbered land, and its owner had promised the president of the company that he would give him first chance at the timber in the event that he ever decided to sell it. The timber was of exceptional value. Murray was panic-stricken to think he must leave Portland right at that time, but his position with the company was important, and he was compelled to make the trip.

"The moment he told me he was forced to go, I felt a chill of apprehension. He was to be gone for a week. My fear of Thad's ultimate victory over Rose hadn't for a minute subsided. I marveled at her ability to keep going under that strain. It was wearing Murray and me both down. But the old Irishwoman said she slept like a baby at night—Murray had insisted that the old woman was to sleep right in Rose's room—and I think that was the only thing that helped her to carry on. She was sick with fear when she learned of Murray's coming absence. And the grimmest part of it was that Murray insisted that she was to keep singing that song, every night.

"'We've got him going,' he said, and I could see from his white face that he knew we were making our last stand against the powers of darkness. 'We can't let up now, or we're lost. You'll stick, Hank?' He turned to me, and I nodded in silent assent. He knew very well I'd stick. He turned back to Rose. 'Hank will be here right with you every minute he can spare. And I want you to sing that song every evening precisely at 8 o'clock. Your watch is steady, and so is mine. We'll set them together to the fraction of a second. I'll hear your voice down there, as surely as I do here. And exactly at 8 o'clock, *wherever I am, no matter what I'm doing,* I'll stop and listen. I'll stop and set my mind with Hank's, against his. You'll—carry on, Rose?'

"I could see her shaking with fear, clear across the room, and her lips were stiff, but she was game to the core. She promised, and I knew she'd keep her promise no matter what it should cost. And Murray knew it also.

"He went to Astoria the following morning. He gave us his word to drop us a telegram every evening to let us know that he was all right, and everything was going well. The timber land was near enough to town so that he could go in on one of the man's horses.

"And that night Rose sang the song for Murray, a hundred miles away. We sat there in the living-room, she in front of the piano on the bench, I standing by her, our eyes glued to the dial of her watch, waiting for the hands to reach 8 o'clock. On the precise instant she lifted her hands to the keys. I saw her fingers tremble, and her voice wavered, but she didn't falter for a moment. She'd hardly struck the first chord when Thad followed his hideous shadow and faced me across the room, menacing and horrible. I sprang between him and her, walking slowly toward him, and stopped within four feet of him, my nostrils smarting with the foul odor surrounding him, my will battling his as I held his mad, glaring eyes.

"It seemed an eternity that I stood there, straining every ounce of will and brain against him, till the song was done, and he was gone with that tittering, mocking laugh, and Rose fainted on the bench and slipped to the floor. I sprang to pick her up, and it took me twenty frantic minutes to bring her back to consciousness. She wasn't the hysterical type, or she'd have gone completely out of her head, then. As it was, it was more than an hour before I succeeded in calming her to any extent, and I was utterly shocked to see how thin she'd grown with the wear of the battle we waged. For all I could do, I accomplished little in easing her mind. It was a telegram from Murray that did the trick there. Just a short, terse message, saying that he had accomplished quite a good deal that day. He was well. He had heard her.

"That was Monday. Tuesday, Wednesday and Thursday weren't much different. Every evening Rose, growing thinner and more like a spirit herself every hour, struggled through that song, while I stood between her and Thad and held him off. Every evening it grew more difficult for us both. And every evening Thad was more violent and harder to handle. I began to have a sick fear that ours was a ghastly, losing battle. Yet every evening we got a telegram from Murray, saying he was well. And he always added that he heard her.

"On Friday evening it seemed to me that I couldn't go on. Rose was so white and wraithlike that I shook with fear for her. I didn't see how she was going to endure much longer. I wanted to be loyal to Murray, yet I feared he was killing all three of us. He was hard as rock when he thought he was right, and he was nearer apt to be right than any fellow I ever knew. I had no defense for my own reluctance to keep up the battle he had begun for us. I couldn't see any other way out. That evening when the hands of the watch drew close to 8 o'clock, I knew that Rose was about at the end of her tether.

"There was a frightful tension in the atmosphere. I felt a terrific struggle dead ahead of us. I almost yielded to the impulse to tell her to stop, to let the ghastly song alone. But I didn't dare. We'd both given our word to Murray. Then the hands of the watch stood at 8 sharp, and she forced herself to begin playing.

"Thad burst upon us in a wild whirl, full-figured, not even preceded by the vestige of a shadow. I had to make the quickest move of my life to get between him and her. And the moment I did it, I knew his power had come down with him full-fledged. For the first time, I felt him like a body of corporeal flesh. But he was cold, hideously cold. It was like battling with a corpse. And around him rose that putrid odor so strongly that it caused me to choke. He launched himself upon me like a black fury, struggling and trying to reach her. He shouted at her, and every word was clear.

"'Stop!' he screamed. 'Stop that damnable song! I hate it! Stop it!'

"'Don't listen to him, Rose!' I shouted, from a choked throat. 'Keep on—keep on to the end. We promised Murray.'

"And Rose kept on. Her voice wavered and quivered, and her fingers shook till they stumbled over the keys, but she kept steadily on. He shrieked in utter abandonment to fury, and for the first time in my life I was glad of my six feet three and the exercise that had kept my muscles hard as nails. I've always been powerful physically, but I had my hands full then. He raged and tore, struck, bit and kicked, cursed and tried to get to my throat. It took every ounce of strength I possessed to keep him from her. And by the time she had reached the second stanza I realized that he was gaining on me.

"I roused myself to desperate effort, choking in that foul odor, beating back that cold, hideous body. But he was bearing me down. In spite of my frantic, superhuman effort to prevent his accomplishing what he strove to do, he was wearing me down, forcing me back and drawing closer to her. I threw all I had into one last mighty effort, lunging against him, just as Rose swung into the last chorus.

"And suddenly with a wild, horrible shriek, he collapsed in my grip. I staggered, finding it all I could do to keep my feet, as he fell back away from me. He mouthed and gibbered, flinging up his arms above his head like a man so maddened, so utterly overcome by fury that he had no control of himself whatever. There was a sudden flash before my eyes, like a puff of red fire, the room was filled with a rank odor entirely different from the odor that had been there before—an odor like the acrid stench of burning rubbish. Then he was gone with another wild shriek. But he didn't laugh. And abruptly the last word of the song died away, and both Rose and I went out.

"That was the first, last and only time in my life that I ever fainted. And because of my greater strength I came back to consciousness before Rose did. She lay on the floor by the piano bench, so white and still that I thought at first she was dead. But as I stared at her I saw that she was breathing, and I got to my feet and went into the kitchen for some water. I came back and bathed her face with it, and got her back to her senses again. I was weakened, worn as though I'd been through a long sick spell, and she wasn't any better. Time dragged by.

"I got her over to the divan, and she lay down there, while I sat by her side and held her hand and tried to think of something to say. But the same thought was with us both, and we couldn't put it in words. We had both looked at the clock on the wall. It was an hour past time for Murray's telegram to come. And he was punctual. I never knew any man so iron-bound in keeping his word as Murray Fielding. It was an hour past time for his telegram, and Thad's last furious shriek rang in our ears. We were both of us on the edge of insanity from suspense when a boy brought a telegram a half-hour later.

"I dragged myself to the door, got the yellow flimsy and brought it to her. She stared at it, shivering, and looked up at me with terrible eyes.

"'Murray!' she said, and her tone made me wince. 'Oh— Murray—Murray! You open it, Hank. I—can't.'

"I thought at first that I couldn't either; my fingers were cold, and even that flimsy envelope seemed to be too much for them. But at last I managed to get it opened somehow, unfolded the sheet and looked at it with fearful eyes. And at what I saw, I froze. This is what it said:

ROSE READ THIS TWICE THIS AFTERNOON THIS MAN LAWSON AND I WENT OUT TO TAKE DOWN A BIG TREE THE OFFICE TOLD ME TO FELL ONE AND EXAMINE THE GRAIN LAWSON AND I GOT IT ALMOST CUT THROUGH WHEN MRS LAWSON CALLED US IN TO DINNER AFTER DINNER LAWSON SAID WE HAD BETTER HURRY OUT AND GET IT DOWN BEFORE DARK WE GOT ALMOST TO THE TREE WHEN I THOUGHT OF THE TIME I LOOKED AT MY WATCH AND IT WAS JUST EIGHT OCLOCK I STOPPED AND STOOD

THERE WAITING FOR YOU THEN I HEARD YOU A SUDDEN
WIND CAME UP OUT OF THE CLEAR SKY AND LAWSON
EXCLAIMED ABOUT IT THEN LOOKED BACK AND ASKED
WHAT I WAS WAITING FOR I MOTIONED HIM TO BE STILL
AND HE STROLLED ON UP TO THE TREE AND STOOD
IMPATIENTLY WAITING FOR ME I HEARD YOUR VOICE
QUIVER AS THOUGH YOU WERE BADLY FRIGHTENED
I PUT ALL MY WILL TO HELPING HANK THEN JUST AS
YOU GOT INTO THE SECOND CHORUS THAT WIND KEPT
RISING WITH A PERFECT FURY AND SUDDENLY THAT
TREE SWAYED AND WENT OVER WITH A CRASH IF I HAD
NOT STOPPED TO LISTEN TO YOU I WOULD HAVE BEEN
UNDER THAT TREE MASHED TO A JELLY AS LAWSON WAS
THINK HARD ROSE WE HAVE WON HOME TOMORROW
MURRAY

"I handed the telegram to Rose, wordlessly, and she read
it with something of eagerness, having been watching the
expression of my face. And when she got to the last word she
broke down and cried. Every tear she had held back in stunned
grief at her father's death demanded its outlet then, along with
the tears of joy for Murray. And I sat there, limp with relief,
and let her cry. She literally cried herself to sleep. I got her coat
out of the hall, threw it over her, and let her sleep. I went across
the room and stretched out in an easy chair to watch by her,
and she slept there till morning. I warned the old Irishwoman
not to wake her. She had come in to say she had some breakfast
ready.

"I went out into the kitchen with her and had a bite, but I
knew sleep was the best thing Rose could have right then. She
was still asleep, four hours later, when Murray came racing up
the steps. He'd left Astoria at daybreak. I wrung his hand in
speechless gratitude for the outcome of the thing, and turned
my back when he went over to kneel by Rose and wake her.
Then I did something for which I have no reason and no excuse.
I went over to the piano, sat down on the bench, and began

to play that song. They were still, behind me, listening—as I played on to the close.

"Just a song at twilight, when the lights are low——"

"There was a slight quiver in the air just beyond me, as though something furious, maddened, but impotent, was striving to reach toward me, and could not. But that was all. The atmosphere of the room remained clear, unpolluted by that foul odor. Thad's malignant, hideous shade never came back again. Murray had won against him and all the dark powers he may have had allied with him.

"And Murray and Rose were married the next week. They had a friend of Rose's sing that song at the wedding. I came away and left them a very happy couple. They're out there in Portland, now, living as serene and untroubled a life as you could wish for your most beloved friends. In Rose's mind, in place of the gloomy picture of the old asylum, she carries a still photograph of Murray standing with his head lifted, listening for her voice a hundred miles distant, with a great tree falling—safely twenty feet away. And about the first melody she taught their two children was *Love's Old, Sweet Song*.

"You know I'm not an imaginative man, Armitage, and you know I don't spin fairy-tales. What have you got to say about curses, now?"

Morgenthaler raised his eyes to the other man's face as he knocked the dottle from his cold pipe.

"Nothing. I've said altogether too much already." Armitage leaned forward in his chair, a strange light in his eyes, and Morgenthaler noted for the first time that the other man's face had gone oddly pale. "I tried for years to find him, but I'd given up hope. I'm greatly indebted to you, Hank. I shall take the next train for Portland. I am Murray Fielding's half-brother."

Vulture Crag

Everil Worrell

WHEN Donald Chester was invited to accompany his new friend, Count Zolani, on a trip, he was surprized. Count Zolani had showed sufficient preference for Donald's company—more than Donald had been able, in the bottom of his heart, to feel for Zolani. He wouldn't have been surprized in the least at a week-end invitation on a house-party, even a yachting-party. But Count Zolani and the simple life—an unattended camp for two in one of the near-by lonely places of the world—that was the unexpected feature of the affair.

"We'll camp at a place I found on a solitary expedition," the count had said. And that added to the strangeness of things. Count Zolani, who moved surrounded by satellites, attended always by at least one good serving-man pre-eminently not of the type to be converted at a notice into a wilderness guide, to have been in the habit of making lonely trips away from civilization and its amusements and luxuries!

Until the actual moment of starting, Donald had half expected that all this was only Zolani's way of talking about his trips, and that after all the two of them would be attended by a retinue of servants. But when they set forth together in a gray dawn in midsummer—which meant that they started very early indeed—he was obliged to admit to himself that here was a Zolani with whom he was unacquainted. The languid grace, the touch of boredom, the weary sophistication—all had fallen from the count. In the beginning of this new day he was as keenly eager as any great explorer might have been before plunging into an unmapped continental interior. One might have imagined that the two men were on the verge of an adventure, instead of merely being about to camp alone for a few days in a spot on the Maryland sea-coast—a spot unfrequented, but not far at all from the beaten paths of travel.

Through the long, hot day his enthusiasm did not flag. Donald relieved him at the wheel for a few hours, at his own suggestion, knowing that Zolani was not at all weary, and believing that he would have been capable of making a nonstop drive of days and nights on end, so long as that quiet look of intensity brooded on his aquiline features. Toward sunset, they were well down into the "eastern shore" country. The macadam road stretched fair and even, with few turns and no hills, between primeval bits of forest and empty meadows. The world might have been asleep while it still was light, so deep was the sense of peacefulness that brooded over it. Only when the road was tinged with red and the shadows of the pines were blue-black across it, the count turned his low-slung roadster from the highway and headed eastward over an unmade road.

"I take it we're in reach of the end," Donald volunteered. Words had been few between the two men, all through the long day of hot high speed. The car, of necessity, went slowly now for the first time in many hours.

"In reach of the end," Zolani smiled, with a sudden flash of teeth beneath his well-kept tiny black mustaches. "I wonder—I wonder what you will think of the end, when you see—and when you know!"

Donald was not altogether surprized at the turn of his companion's sentence. It implied that there was about this journey something that lay beneath the surface. That, however, was not altogether a new thought to Donald.

"I'm expecting to see something—and maybe to know something too," he said carelessly enough. "I'll be glad to get to it, Zolani. I never thought you insisted on dragging me down here for nothing except the beauties of nature!"

For a moment, Zolani's flashing smile was turned on him again. Then the count's attention was taken by the nature of the road, which had degenerated rather suddenly after the last crossroad into a rough, rutty pair of wheel tracks with grass growing between them. From that point, also, the road became winding; at the next crossroad and at the next, Zolani turned to right and left. Turns came frequently during the next hour, while the red of sunset faded to the ashes of twilight and plunged into the blue gloom of dusk. The thought crossed Donald's mind that Zolani knew this lonely territory well, well enough to have been here not once, but many times, and that his frequent turnings were in the nature of detours, which brought him back always to a direction he might have adhered to more closely but for a desire to make the way of his going intricate and labyrinthine.

"Is it possible he's trying to lose me?" Donald wondered idly, once, and blushed at the fantastic nature of the thought.

"We're here, and soon the moon will rise and I shall show you—Vulture Crag!"

Zolani's words sounded like a shout of triumph, so silent was the night around them as the car went slowly with motor all but inaudible.

"Vulture Crag! Cheerful name!" Donald commented.

"I named it, but not without good reason," the count rejoined. "I like the name. The truth is, Chester, I'm planning to make some improvements in this part of the country; but I'm not planning to make it a popular summer resort. Not even to attract picnic parties from the countryside near by."

INTO the stillness of the summer evening a new sound had crept—a rhythmic, murmuring sound which Donald at first had hardly been conscious of. Now it was louder, nearer. The road had become sandy and heavy. It seemed almost to shake itself, so sudden was the next turn—and Donald uttered a cry of pleasure. He loved the sea, and they had come upon it so suddenly that its far, dark mystery was like an unexpected adventure. Through a break in crags they saw it, across a miniature sandy desert where rolling dunes rose toward the distant horizon. Upon that unbroken sky line blazed a tiny speck where a ship moved, and above, the sky was sown with stars.

"Ecstasy, to stand upon the shore of the trackless sea!" Count Zolani's voice showed more feeling than Donald had ever heard in it. "Ecstasy! In imagination one breaks the bonds that hold him to the shore and follows his outward gaze. Think, friend! In all the universe, I think there is possible one greater ecstasy of contemplation. What, then, is that?"

Donald gazed into his companion's face, half visible in the deepening gloom. Was he idly philosophizing, playing with an abstract fancy, or was he challenging Donald to answer a riddle which had to do with this odd trip of theirs? Donald made a sudden gesture of impatience.

"I've come along because you asked me to, Zolani, and I've gone blind for quite a while. I know there's something beneath the surface, something I hope you're going to explain, and something I hope will give motive to our journey—not that it needs one to be pleasant, but because I feel there *is* one. So I won't do any guessing at meanings; I'll just tell you I'm waiting, and getting more than a little anxious to find out what it's all about. The ecstasy of contemplation doesn't sound like an adventure; yet, somehow, you make me feel as though we're on the edge of an adventure!"

Zolani stopped the motor and leaned back in his seat, lighting a cigarette with provoking deliberation.

"The greatest ecstasy of contemplation!" he resumed slowly. "To stand, my friend, on the shore of the sea—on the shore of the world! To gaze outward across the boundless ocean—outward into more boundless space! To know that one can voyage afar upon that sea—can voyage farther, farther—farther than the farthest stars your feeble vision can detect, in the limitless sea of space. You, Chester, if you will, shall know the delirious thrill of traversing space. I promise it. Is that adventure enough for you?"

There was silence between the two men. Count Zolani's cigarette made a near-by circle of light which outshone some of those distant specks of light which were, perhaps, larger than the sun around which the earth and her sister planets revolved. Donald was caught in an odd feeling of futility. Not for a moment did he think Zolani mad, although he wondered why he did not. He felt only that space was a thing apart, a thing that did not concern mankind; he felt that his spirit had been called upon to grasp a thing beyond its conception. He could have read of such a thing between the covers of a book, and felt his imagination kindle; but personally to him like this, the very stupendousness of the idea stunned his perceptions.

The count's profile, visible in the starlight, gave a tinge of reality to the impossible statement he had made. It was not the profile of a dreamer's face. In it there was power. There might be in it, also, evil; but no touch of vagueness, of futility. Looking at it, Donald forced himself to clear thought. If he was to take Zolani's words literally, and since he could not for a moment think of Zolani as the victim of a hallucination, he was up against a tremendous opportunity—a new thing. Later, he would realize it; even now he might at least try to understand it. There were the tales of Jules Verne—the *Trip to the Moon*—Edgar Allan Poe's fanciful trip, and others....

"I suppose you're going to perfect an invention down here, and I suppose you're going to tell me you've solved the problem of making a space-ship—that will fly!" he said at last. "I can't grasp it at once; but everyone knows that the fancies of yesterday are the facts of tomorrow. So another tomorrow has come!"

Zolani turned to face him. The glow from his cigarette lit up his aquiline features, which seemed more clearly lit by his triumphant smile.

"Proud as Lucifer!" Donald found himself thinking. "And Lucifer fell through pride. But Zolani has reason enough to be the proudest man on earth, if he's solved the thing few men have dared dream of attempting!"

"Chester, my friend," Zolani began, "my invention is to be perfected here, but it's not an old dream of another man made real by myself; it is my own dream, my own thought, perhaps, if there is any new thought under the sun. It is——"

At that instant a flapping of great wings swept away the sound of his words, and a dark, ugly form blotted out the starlight and swooped low toward the side of the open car. Donald caught a glare as of red eyes in the darkness and smelled an evil smell—and then the thing was gone.

"One of the vultures—my friends!" Zolani said, with a little, twisted smile. "Look yonder!"

Donald, gazing seaward, had noticed but little the sides of the ravine through which they had approached. The structure was unusual for the eastern coast so far south as this. A low crag to the south made the end of the ravine on one side, a high crag to the north; and for the first time Donald saw that a house stood on this northern crag, built against the natural elevation of the land so that in the darkness it was easily overlooked. It seemed, however, to be a large house—an abandoned mansion. Some recluse had fancied a home in this lonely spot, and had tired of the unchanging solitude. Everything about the place spoke of utter desolation. And—final touch and most sinister—as the two men gazed, several dark forms detached themselves from the block of unlit darkness which was the deserted building, and circled against the sky, while odd, raucous, creaking cries were borne on the sweet sea breeze.

"More of our friends!" Zolani spoke again. "That old house is their roosting-place. Odd fancies, vultures have, to take to artificial shelter of four walls and a roof. The windows, mostly broken, give them easy access, however; and you and I, my friend, will camp in the open. And not too much in the open either; our tent shall have the flaps well drawn together. A man need hardly be dead, but only sleeping, to have his eyes plucked from his head by our scavenger friends, whose indefatigable zeal makes them so valuable that the state sets a fine of fifty dollars on the killing of one of them. Well! I shall explain no more of my grand plan until tomorrow. I can see that you need time for adjustment; tomorrow in the light of day what I say to you will be real; if I told you all tonight, tomorrow it would appear as a dream and require retelling.

"Only let me say that I am to rob our vultures of their happy home—I intend to make use of that building. I hope, friend Chester, for your interest—and for the loan of a little of your superabundant wealth. A short loan; with the working of my scheme, gold will flow freely to our hands. And for the rest, and to keep the curious of the countryside from showing too much interest in our affairs, I depend on our friends the vultures, who make this portion of the coast very disagreeable by their presence, and who will not go far from the home of which I dispossess them."

To THE end of his life, Donald Chester would remember the year 1928 as the most vivid of his whole manhood; at least it eclipsed utterly all the years and all the seasons which had preceded it.

It was only a few days after the memorable night when he beheld for the first time Vulture Crag, and the equally memorable morning of shining blue and silver when he listened to Count Zolani's recital of his plans and intentions, before he was back again in the city arranging a loan of several thousand dollars, which would put Zolani's scheme in the way of fruition. That scheme burned day and night in Donald's brain, with its wonderful train of adventures. Donald would make possible the realization of man's loftiest dream; he would be a pioneer in exploring the mystery of the universe; he would know the unknowable, grasp the unattainable, help Zolani to add a new and most lustrous wreath of laurel to the ever more glorious wreath of man's victories and achievements.

Then, on the top of adventure's highest pinnacle of rapture—and now it was all as real and close at hand as on that first
evening beside the sea all had been tenuous and unreal—he met
Dorothy Leigh.

Dorothy—"Gift of God!" Never was any living creature so
well named. There were stars in the depths of her blue-black
eyes, stars which beckoned as those stars in the night sky toward
which Donald never failed now to lift eager eyes in anticipation
of the nearing time of his flight of exploration toward them.
But there were other things about Dorothy, so dear that they
might well nigh hold a man to the earth. There were her little,
clinging hands, that seemed eloquent when they caressed
merely the leaves of a book or touched the steering-gear of
Donald's car; there were all her graceful, little, unstudied ways,
her fragile beauty of form and feature, and the gay daring of
her sudden laughter.

Donald had only begun to hope that he, too, by some mysterious magic, was beginning to live in Dorothy's heart, when he
found himself telling her about the great secret. And in the telling, there was an interruption; and by the interruption many
things were made clear.

"Oh, Donald—my dear!" Dorothy had cried, the pain
in her voice a heritage from time immemorial, since the first
woman watched her man go forth to adventure hand in hand
with death. "My dear, must it be you—among the first?"

For a while after that, Donald did not give the details which
had been locked in his heart for months. Neither the world nor
the universe mattered beside Dorothy's "My dear." But when
a little later Donald remembered, his spirit was more than ever
unshaken. If he had been able to dare the horror of utter emptiness through which stars and planets hurtle on their courses,
how much better able was he to dare them, now that he held
Dorothy's love locked safe within his breast, a charm against all
evil?

"You won't ask me to give up my adventure when you know

how much it means to me," he said gently to Dorothy. "When a man loves as I love you, he wants, more than ever, to prove his manhood. But after all, my darling, this adventure, while thrilling enough, has hardly enough of peril about it to prove that. In fact, when I have explained it to you as the count explained it to me on a June morning, you'll laugh at your fears."

He went on, then, to paint her the picture of Count Zolani's great project in the colors in which he himself saw it.

"You're familiar with simple chemistry, Dorothy," he began. "Well! Take one of the very simplest experiments of all—the conversion of water into its two elements, hydrogen and oxygen. Is there any doubt that hydrogen and oxygen can be brought together to form water?"

Dorothy shook her head, deeply puzzled. What a simple chemical experiment had to do with the extreme safety of the launching of a ship in space, she could not imagine. Nevertheless, because she was rather given to quiet thought than to disjointed protest, she listened after that without a word until the end of Donald's rather long explanation.

"Suppose, now, that the hydrogen and oxygen so separated and released could be given a certain rate of atomic vibration— you've heard of that, too. So that, wherever they might wander in the whole universe, they would retain a separate entity from any other atoms of hydrogen and oxygen. And now—I'm mixing my metaphors because it is necessary, because as the different laws of nature are always interactive, so to explain any complicated phenomenon of nature whether naturally or artificially—which still, of course, is naturally—produced, it is necessary to describe the various actions of the different laws involved in whatever way makes them most easily comprehended.

"To continue where I broke off to apologize. Suppose, now, that the hydrogen atoms to which you give a certain atomic vibration were to be magnetized with a certain definite magnetism, as definite as the positive and negative magnetism which everybody knows, but infinitely diversified—as diversified, in fact, as the infinite differences of wave length which can be established in a radio station, so that the etheric vibrations to which that station is attuned will be received there, out of all the other vibrations that permeate space.

"I'm afraid this is all rather deep, and quite involved, but Zolani gave it to me in far more intricate and technical terms, and I'm doing what I can to translate. In brief, Dorothy, Zolani's achievement lies rather within the field of physical chemistry than in the field of mechanics. He isn't going to launch me, with other favored souls, through space in a ship the mechanism of which *might* go wrong. He is, instead, through a triumph of chemistry and physics which involves plain chemistry, atomic vibration and magnetism all three, to change the nature of my being, and of the others, so that we, loosed from the chains of gravity and physical necessity, can travel at our own free will through space, to be drawn back quite definitely and certainly by means of his apparatus to our own bodies."

Dorothy had grown paler as she listened to the end of Donald's speech. A low cry of horror issued from her lips, at last.

"I didn't understand what you were talking about, Donald. And now that I see the application of it, it still seems vague, and horrible. Do you mean that you are going to put yourself in the hands of that man, to be altered in the inmost fibers of your being?—Oh!"

She shuddered, and the words died away on her lips. Donald shrugged his shoulders in mock despair.

"Darling, I've been telling you how very safe it is, and this is the impression you've drawn from all I've been saying!" he protested. "Well! It serves me right for unloading that scientific stuff on a girl who only dabbled in the shallowest ripples of science a finishing-school ever taught. I haven't given up making you see and understand, however. I'll tackle it next, Dorothy, from the descriptive angle. Suppose——"

Donald was off again, talking eagerly, urgently. And this

time, as he talked, Dorothy was better able to understand the picture his words painted.

Zolani, he told her, had taken the lonely house at Vulture Crag (he touched lightly on the subject of those vultures, and the desolation of the spot). In the basement, Zolani had set up a powerful apparatus, while the top of the house, renovated and repaired, had been made into a sort of hospital. In that hospital, carefully guarded, were to repose the bodies of the space-travelers, while their intelligences and certain vital elements temporarily translated out of those bodies roved freely through space. Out of that exploration would vanish the black night of ignorance; to future generations the ways and customs of the oddest denizens of the farthest stars, were any of them indeed populated, would be as freely studied as were now the habits of people living on the other side of the world.

The powerful apparatus which Zolani had set up in his basement laboratory would react upon men and women harm-lessly. Upon each space-traveler it would be set differently in certain small degrees, so that the liberated spirit might have a "vibration number" of its own. Twenty space-travelers could be taken care of at the same time, and twenty levers corre-sponded to twenty storage batteries—Donald described them so. At least, they stored the current which would draw back, when the levers were shot backward in their slots, the various twenty wandering spirits. The unconscious physical forms of the twenty, properly attached to the apparatus, would then receive the spirits, souls, intelligences—Donald rather stam-mered in his search of words, since no words previously coined exactly described what actually took place; "the released entity" suited him better than the triter forms, but he sought for a terminology which would make the things he spoke of more real to Dorothy.

"Since the portion of the man or woman who has been exploring space comprises only the intelligence, plus a certain amount of vital energy—all the vital energy not required to keep the body which remains behind from actual death," he added, "the space traveler can not have been harmed. You see there is nothing to hurt. Since Zolani's apparatus is minutely tuned, as I must express it, to each individuality, that individuality must be attracted back to its earthly habitation, so soon as he sets in action the powerful magnetic current which 'receives it.'

"I don't mean to become technical again. But this, you see, is what really happens. On October first, I, and nineteen others, will find ourselves with Count Zolani at his restored mansion beside the sea. In the building comfortable arrangements are made, so that a person might comfortably sleep and rest for— two weeks was the period he spoke of. You may picture, Dorothy, the safe orderliness of a hospital ward, if you like. Well, there our bodies will sleep, after we have spent a quiet hour in the laboratory below, and had an agreeable current passed through our bodies, like a mild, invigorating electric current, or so Zolani describes it.

"Say that the two weeks are up. Attendants will carry our sleeping forms back to the laboratory, and each man and woman will be attached to the storage battery which has the power to call him, or her, back to life. A slight effort of will will be required on the part of the wandering spirit to re-enter the body itself, but that will present no complications; should any one of us desire, for some strange, unknown, unpredictable reason, to remain free in space, it is understood that we will make our return there at a future time. Zolani has picked only honorable men and women for his great experiment—men and women who will not be subject to freaks of fancy which might embarrass him and thwart the purpose of the experiment. As for myself, beloved, returning to earth will mean returning to you; my effort of will, then, will hardly be an effort at all, since my soul will speed to you—would speed to you even if the forces of Zolani's magnetism were directed not for but against it."

Love had won where arguments might all have failed. Looking into the depths of Dorothy's eyes, Donald knew that there was to be no strife between them. And in the weeks that followed, love even displaced in his mind the thrill of anticipation that had filled his days and nights, together with his thoughts of Dorothy. Now that he knew Dorothy returned his love, everything in the world beside that magnificent fact seemed dwarfed and of no consequence. And as for Dorothy, he suspected that she almost forgot the ordeal the autumn would bring. Having spent herself in combat to no avail and yielded gracefully—although, thinking back, Donald was not sure that either combat or yielding had taken place in words—she was now feeling the unreal dreaminess about the affair which had possessed Donald in the beginning. Perhaps she believed that, after all, Zolani would be defeated; that the first of October would find him ready to give up his fantastic scheme. Perhaps she only felt that life and love and the world on which the sun shone were real, and that the vast emptiness which encircled these things was not, and could not actually become so, to herself or to Donald or to anyone.

THE summer had come in on rose-flung wings of anticipation; it came to its height of beauty on a high-pitched ecstasy that seemed, perhaps, too beautiful to last. The perfection of summer, the full sweetness of love, have about them something of the evanescent shimmer of the wings of a dragon-fly, which is a thing of beauty doomed to live full and vibrantly, but never long. Summer had, then, to die, and its passing was sorrowful, wind-torn and rain-weary. Toward the end of September heavy rains set in, but they were not as dismal as the slow falling of inward tears which takes the place of the tears a man may not shed.

It had been inevitable that Dorothy should meet Zolani, with whom Donald had associated in a social way before the two men became identified with the same venture. The meeting had taken place on a hotel roof garden, and the stars Donald had all but worshiped through the summer in his eagerness to explore them seemed to be watching in a shining surprize, as Dorothy gave to Zolani the deep, sweet look Donald had never seen her give to anyone but him.

After that, Dorothy had seen Donald often, but not so often as before, although their engagement was not broken. She had, however, seen Zolani at least as often, while he was in town, and, what was worst of all, Donald knew that he was not wrong when he felt that Dorothy's deepest interest hung upon Zolani's slightest word. Never a word was spoken now of her concern for Donald in the coming adventure; and while Donald did not want Dorothy to be distressed, it cut him cruelly to know that the reason for her ceasing to worry was, simply, that she had ceased to care. Donald's journey among distant stars and planets? It had become more real to Dorothy since her meeting with Zolani, and since certain long talks which she had had with him alone. Donald knew that, but he knew, too, that she wasted no alarms now. Let the first of October come; it brought no slightest uneasiness with it, so far as Donald could see. He himself was not uneasy, but he knew that Dorothy, in the natural course of events, should now be deeply worried.

And the last week of September brought in the delayed equinoctial storm, and the weeping skies opened their fountains yet unemptied, and the winds tore the sodden, clinging leaves from the trees. And on the last day of the month, Donald drove four men over the road that led to Zolani's restored mansion, followed by two other cars, each carrying five. Zolani had driven down the day before. Not since the evening before that day had Donald seen Dorothy; she had suggested then that she wish him luck, and say good-bye—thus hastening needlessly the time of their parting.

Dusk on this thirtieth of September was dull and heavy, and fell early. It was dark night, and the rain-wet wind from the sea howled like seven demons, when the party under Donald's convoy reached Vulture Crag. Even in the blackness, Donald had a consciousness of black wings upborne on the raging wind. He was glad to step inside the square lighted hallway of the building Count Zolani had restored, and conscious of a sense of hurrying drama as he stood waiting there with his four companions. It was as though a long-awaited hour at last had struck.

The count came to them after a short delay.

"I shall take our newcomers with me into the laboratory," he smiled with the flash of white teeth Donald had come to dislike, since he had so often seen its glitter turned upon Dorothy. "For you, Chester my friend, I have a great surprize. Wait here. Ah!"

The door through which the count had entered swung slowly open again. Donald, following his gaze, saw the last face he would have expected to behold here, of any in the world which he, perhaps, might be leaving forever, in spite of the confidence he had felt stedfastly for months. It was the face of Dorothy.

The count bowed low, his eyes on the deep blue ones turned to him. His voice when he spoke again was a caress.

"My dear, you had better explain to our friend Chester, who does not understand."

Once more the white teeth flashed. The count was bowing the four men who were to join in his experiment through another doorway. A moment more, and they were alone— Donald and Dorothy, with the sound of Zolani's "My dear" ringing in Donald's ears. So Dorothy had first revealed her love for Donald—in just those two words. But Zolani must have had full confidence that his love was returned, to use those words to Dorothy in the presence of others; in the presence of Donald, whose engagement to Dorothy had not been definitely broken.

It was Dorothy who broke the silence.

"You see, Chester—Zolani considers that we are engaged," she offered timidly.

And then Donald's wrath broke the bounds that had held it.

"As I have still considered that you and I——" he began.

Looking back later, he could not remember all that he said then to Dorothy, though he never forgot the stricken look in her eyes as she listened. At last she held up her hand with a gesture which stopped him.

"Donald, I thought I could go through with it, but I can't," she said with a little moan. "I had steeled myself to endure your hurt. But I find that I can't. To let you believe that I am honest with Zolani—that would have been safer for both of us, dear. Since I can't, I will explain. There is no time to lose."

A little flame of hope springing up in Donald's heart seemed to change the universe from a barren waste back to the old paradise, as Dorothy continued.

"Donald, I was determined to share in this experiment. To go with you—wherever you go—to become as you become—not to be parted from you, whatever may be your destiny. I knew there was no hope of persuading you to let me go. I knew, too, that, so long as Zolani was your friend and I nothing to Zolani, he would probably accede to your wishes if the matter were put up to him. So—I let him fall in love with me, Donald. Perhaps I made him. Certainly, I willed him to. I'm sorry, but it was the only way to accomplish the thing I was determined to accomplish—that I should not be parted from you. When this is over, when we are safely back on earth in the bodies our spirits inhabit, I shall explain to Zolani. I hope he will forgive me. Surely, he can understand the feeling that drove me to make him serve my purpose.

"At least, that was the way I have felt about it until lately. Of late, I have come to doubt his forgiveness, and to feel that I can do without it. Because, Donald, I do not trust Zolani. I have come to feel that he is evil; and if he knew, or dreamed, or guessed that my love is unalterably yours——"

She was leaning toward him now. In the brilliantly lit entrance hall, Donald could see deeply into her blue-black eyes, could mark every shade of expression in their tender depths. Never had she been more adorable than with the expression of anxiety softening them, as she thought of Zolani with regret and foreboding. With a sudden motion, Donald drew her into his arms, where he had thought never to hold her again. Their lips met——

"Zolani!"

Donald cried the name out like a challenge, as the count's dark, hawklike face appeared suddenly in the doorway. There was again the flash of the count's white teeth—Donald had come to dread that ordinary phenomenon.

"I smile—because a man must be as you would say, a good sport!" Zolani said in light, but slightly strained tones. "So a love is not so easily changed, and my promised bride is still *your* promised bride—and her wandering heart returns to its allegiance, as her wandering spirit will return *at my command* to the lovely form which enshrines it. Well! Perhaps, friend Chester, her heart never wandered at all. Never has she looked at me as she looked at you, and she has withheld her lips. Perhaps it was all a game—to make me consent to experiment upon so lovely a victim, so that she could accompany you on your flight through space."

There was a heavy silence in the little room, except for the beating of the wind outside—could the beating of wings be heard as well? Donald and Dorothy had given one startled glance, each at the other. Had Zolani heard everything, or had he guessed? Now they stood silently, with eyes downcast. Dorothy, Donald knew, was both frightened and ashamed. As for himself, he was conscious of a heavy depression which he could not analyze.

After a little, Zolani spoke again.

"Perhaps it will be as well to speak no more of this unhappy affair—unhappy for me, however fortunate for my friend.

Although I have smiled, my heart is breaking. Now, however, I am ready to forget myself, and to show to my two most honored guests what I have done, and what will take place tomorrow. It is my suggestion that you, Chester, and Miss Leigh, behold with me the beginning of my experiment upon the others. After that, it will be the turn of you two. And, in the meantime, I shall give myself the honor of showing you over the place—my dormuary."

"Dormuary?"

Dorothy's lips parted as Donald repeated the word. It had an ugly sound. Donald was sure that it had put both of them in mind of the same other word, "mortuary," which it greatly resembled. The count smiled back at them serenely.

"Don't like the sound of it? Think it sounds like 'mortuary'?" he said coolly. "I created it from that word, of course. Pardon me if my humor is a little grim, but a man who works his brain as hard as I work mine requires the relief of humor, and his humor should suit his fancy. My fancies have always, I am afraid, been a little grim. You see, this place I have equipped is a reposing-place for the sleeping, as a mortuary is for the dead. I put away the sleeping, as I shall show you, to remain asleep for the period I shall choose, as a mortician puts away the dead, to be dead forever. I, then, am a dormician. But I must show you these sleeping-places."

DURING the hour that followed, Dorothy clung close to Donald's arm. It was a rather horrible hour.

Zolani had prepared his house to accommodate more than twenty, although he was not completely equipped as to laboratory apparatus to handle more than twenty now. Donald had spoken of the upper regions of this building as a sort of hospital; they did, in fact, much more resemble the corridors of a morgue.

There were no beds, in the ordinary sense of the word, to accommodate the tenantless, sleeping bodies. It was well, perhaps, that the others who had already retired had not been shown over the place at all, and were to see only the laboratory. Donald marveled at the calmness with which they accepted their ignorance, until he remembered that they were spending this night crowded together in several large, comfortable bedrooms containing various beds and couches, and that they probably pictured these very rooms as their abiding-place for Zolani's period of two weeks, during which only their bodies were to remain on earth. As a matter of fact, instead of beds and rooms, the sleepers were to occupy lockers very much like the lockers of a well-equipped morgue, except that comfortable mattresses had been installed.

Gruesome, indeed, were the rows of empty, yawning lockers. Gruesome, and suggestive of either a morgue or a mausoleum. Certainly, Zolani in his efficiency had had no regard for esthetics.

"They're safer in lockers, you know!" Zolani answered Donald's thought with his usual uncanny intuition. "A lever in the laboratory controls all the doors of these lockers at once. Ordinarily, I don't think it will be necessary to have them closed. But in case of any accident or disturbance, I should close them immediately. Should there be even so much as a broken window, I should close the lockers, for otherwise the dispossessed vultures, returning, might make a meal——

"I beg your pardon!" Zolani broke off abruptly, his eyes on Dorothy's face, who looked as though she might be about to faint. "I forget, where we are all daring adventurers, that one of us is yet a delicate girl who should be shielded from too much of the gruesome. But let me continue, taking care not to offend again."

With a long forefinger, he pointed within the nearest white-enameled locker.

"My device for pumping air through all the lockers, should it be necessary to close the doors," he explained. "You see, although these sleeping bodies will hardly seem to breathe, yet breathe they will a little, and must."

The pipe he had designated had openings through which the air would pass. Another pipe beside it, however, had none.

Donald questioned him as to the use of this pipe. "It looks like——"

He broke off as Zolani had done a moment before, mindful of Dorothy.

"It is. You see, I thought some day I might wish to use this place for the other thing which it resembles. My scheme is safe enough, but it might break down. The government might object to my sending its citizens so far abroad without passports—anything might happen. Then I had a scheme for using the refrigeration plant"—Zolani approached his mouth to Chester's ear—"making a sure enough morgue of the joint, you see, and keeping people here preserved by cold without embalmment for a while, while I tried to resuscitate them. No, I'm not the wizard of the ages; I can't restore life, and I have no hope of doing that. But I could pull in some money while making the attempt."

Before Donald's horrified stare, the count showed some slight uneasiness.

"Well, perhaps I'm letting you see and know too much. But you needn't assume an air of superior virtue. Most people resort to various methods of gaining their ends. Perhaps if you knew *everything* I have in mind at this moment, you would be even more shocked. Your fiancée tricked me quite thoroughly and well. And you know many men in your own world who have founded fortunes by putting something over on the right person at the right time, or even cheating thousands out of their just dues. No! I wouldn't presume to look down on me, if I were you. Life is short—too short for indulgence in snobbery."

They had returned at last to the outer hall, and Zolani pressed an electric button.

"Show the gentleman and the lady to their respective rooms. They have a hard day ahead tomorrow," the count said to a herculean colored man who appeared.

They passed the door of Dorothy's room before they reached the one which was Donald's. Talking together, Dorothy and Donald did not address the giant serving-man. It was only at the door of his own room that Donald discovered that the negro could hear but not speak. He pointed to his mouth in explanation and Donald, looking, saw that his tongue was shriveled almost to the root.

As he fell asleep, the sight of that shriveled tongue was with him like a nightmare horror.

"Born like that? Maybe. But Zolani wouldn't have to *cut* a tongue out. He'd know a way—some chemical, some devilish compound—that would produce an effect like that without being telltale." That was his last conscious thought.

ZOLONI had selected the hour of dawn for his great experiment. Seeing the group of men who reported at that zero hour in the little waiting-room off his basement laboratory, Donald marveled. Bank presidents, statesmen, college professors—these were among others at whose identity Donald could only guess. Truly, this affair was to make Zolani famous immediately, and rich almost as soon. There could be no claiming that a fraud had been practised upon one or two insignificant or unbalanced dupes. Zolani had assured Donald that he had set free and recalled the spirits of one or two individuals who "did not greatly matter." Perhaps the servitor with the withered tongue was one of these. At any rate, the count was marvelously sure of himself.

In spite of himself, Donald sickened as he watched this experiment proceed—so far as one could watch a thing, the salient feature of which was invisible. He saw eighteen men lie back in comfortable reclining-chairs and suffer Zolani to hook them up by means of wires to a great, humming dynamo in the center of the room; so far, it was unpleasantly like the preparation for an electrocution. There were dials which Zolani watched, delicate manipulations which he performed. Over

the top of the dynamo was a great flask in which a watery bubbling liquid alternately clouded and cleared. Before each man
was a smaller globe which seemed to duplicate the reaction of
the large one; and, as Donald observed that the men leaning
back in their chairs appeared one by one to drowse and doze,
he observed the liquid in each man's respective globe change
color from white to rose. A little later a white flame appeared
to shine within the center of the fluid, which was now brilliant
in color and quite clear, and no longer bubbling at all; and as
this phenomenon appeared, each man drew a long sigh and
appeared to sink into deep slumber. Donald, watching the
nearest man—the one who was president of one of the large
eastern universities—observed an expression of peace upon his
face, which seemed a moment later to grow sharp of feature
and livid of complexion, so that Donald felt as though he were
indeed gazing upon a corpse. He would have cried out, then,
and called upon Zolani, perhaps, to bring the hovering spirit
back to the habitation in which God had placed it for the span
of an earthly lifetime; but in that moment the light disappeared
from the rose-colored, liquid-filled globe, as though it had been
snuffed out, and the liquid itself suffered a change, becoming
leaden gray, with an over-tinge of green. This, for some reason,
was more horrible to Donald than all the other features of the
transformation: it spoke so clearly of the withdrawing of life to
a far distant place. Even the carting away of the limp figures one
by one, in the arms of Zolani's withered-tongued assistant, to
be stored in their respective locker spaces like so many carcasses,
was no worse than that sickly changing of the bright-colored
liquid in the glass.

Donald turned to Zolani now, prepared to fight out a thing
upon which he had determined.

"Miss Leigh can't be allowed to take part in this, however
safe, however sure," he said firmly. "Women were never meant
to pioneer among new dangers and new horrors. They are to
be cherished, safeguarded. You have loved Miss Leigh; perhaps

you still love her. I love her, too, and, since I am to be her husband, I must protect her. I have no doubt that you will agree
with me—that you will forbid at the last minute that to which
you have already consented."

Zolani's smile cut whitely across his dark face like a menace.

"My friend, you are too late!" he cried softly. Beckoning
Donald, he led him to a near-by doorway and bade him look
through it. Incredulous, Donald saw the deeply slumbering
form of Dorothy Leigh stretched upon a couch in the room
beyond.

"This is the chair in which she reclined, and this the glass
globe filled with the essence into which her spirit was withdrawn, before it took its farther flight in space."

As Donald looked upon these things, his heart sank sickly,
while the pounding of his pulse was like the beating of a drum.
Oh, he had believed in the safety of Zolani's experiment!—but
then he had trusted Zolani. What had Dorothy said? "I have
come to feel that he is evil." Donald, too, had come to feel that
the count was evil.

"You will want to follow her swiftly," the count was contin-
uing. "See, you may have this last place—the one next Dorothy
Leigh's. You will wish to hasten?"

Donald was about to follow the count's instructions. What
instinct he had indeed prompted him to share as rapidly as possible Dorothy's fate. He should follow her out into the great
unknown, even though he did not trust Zolani, because it was
the only thing he knew which he could do.

And then a little thing occurred.

Donald was possessed of keen powers of observation. Now,
just before he seated himself in the reclining-chair, he noticed
a tiny green bulb, apparently an ordinary electric light, which
burned upon the baseboard that supported the individual
smallish globes of liquid. This light was burning beside none
of the other globes—only beside his own. Donald was sure
that during the experiment which had been completed on the

others—completed in its first stage, at least—this light had not been lit. And now, stooping suddenly, he was able to read the letters of an abbreviated word, small and almost invisible on the black baseboard underneath the green light: "Refrig."

He started back, more than half expecting to be instantly engaged in a fight for his life. The doors of the room were closed—probably locked. There was no escape, and besides, the helpless, sleeping, deathlike form of Dorothy Leigh lay in the adjoining room, dependent upon Count Zolani's whim if it were to be restored ever to life and consciousness. To challenge Zolani would do little good, but perhaps it was as well to have all of the cards on the table.

"Zolani!" Donald cried as these thoughts coursed through his brain. "I'll stay in my own body, please; and I'll see that you take good care of that helpless girl in there. I'm not blind, nor a fool."

He pointed to the green light with its all but invisible labeling.

"You had the refrigeration current turned on for *me*—only for me, Zolani," he continued. "You would have locked me into my locker and let me freeze—killed my body while my soul was absent, so that I could never come back to claim Dorothy—to protect her!"

For several minutes, the two men stared into each other's eyes. At last Zolani shrugged his shoulders, though now his white-toothed smile was absent.

"Well, it is true you are not the fool I thought you!" he said, slowly. "So, while you may perhaps surmise that your future is a brief one, you may as well see a little drama which will deeply interest you. Dorothy Leigh sleeps only for a brief interval— only for the space of one hour. Already that hour is near its end. And I shall let you see the restoration. One warning, first.

"It is not my will that you leave this place alive. So much you have already divined. But since I choose to let you take with you the bitter memory of that which you are to behold, remember this: only *I* can restore the absent soul of Dorothy Leigh. And, whatever you see me do, if you interrupt me it shall not be restored. It shall wander, homeless and friendless in outer space, until the normal time of the termination of her life upon this earth—a period of some fifty years, no doubt. If you interrupt me, you will have condemned her whom you love to the most horrible exile the mind of man can imagine. Do you agree—do you swear—*to hold your hand, not to interrupt me under any circumstances?"*

Donald took the oath which Zolani commanded. He watched then, while Zolani brought the deathlike body of Dorothy Leigh and laid it in the reclining-chair which awaited it. The horrible apparatus which had reminded him of the electric connections essential to a death chair was put in correct arrangement. Zolani showed him the irreversible switch marked "time," which he had set for one hour, and which in a few minutes would have its period of operation fulfilled. He showed him the other switch which was to be operated by the throwing of a lever—and when this switch was thrown in, the returning spirit of Dorothy would appear as a bright flame in the glass globe. Then, and then only, the element of will-power entered into consideration: Dorothy must will herself back from the rosy fluid into her waiting body.

"No trouble there—she'll come to me! She'll come to me!" Donald thought, trying to forget that soon after her coming she would in all probability find herself mourning Donald's death by murder at the hands of Zolani or his dumb assistant.

IT SEEMED a long time, but was probably in reality only minutes, before the leaden-colored liquid began to quiver and change within its glass walls. Donald's heart leaped high; then suddenly a soft brightness like the glow of a sunrise made the globe beautiful, and in another instant a pure flame like the fire of a star bathed in dawnlight appeared—the soul of Dorothy Leigh imprisoned in the globe, needing only an effort of her pure will to re-enter the waiting body, which now seemed to stir a little and to breathe visibly.

"Dorothy!" Donald's soul was on his lips. But Zolani suddenly stooped over the girl, reminding Donald of the swooping flight of one of the vultures whose home this desolate place had been. His arms encircled the plastic waist of the girl, his lips were laid upon her fluttering lips. Donald cried out again, this time in horror. For a moment only, Zolani turned to him.

"She makes her choice!" he cried triumphantly. "Either her exiled spirit refuses to re-enter her body, and is condemned to the horrible fate I have described—or she comes back, not only to herself, but—to me—to my arms, my lips! My spirit strives with hers. If Dorothy Leigh is now restored to life, never can her spirit shake off mine—never can she be free of me, or free to love any but her master! Fool! I could almost let you live, in your harmlessness—almost!"

In the next moments, Donald lived an eternity of anguish. What fate to pray for, for the girl he loved, he did not know. Horrible, that long disembodied exile—horrible beyond words! But equally horrible, the slavery Zolani hinted at—the slavery which would begin by forcing Dorothy, who loathed Zolani, to return to consciousness in his arms, never again to be far from them or free of him.

Once more, Zolani's embrace clasped the girl more closely. Once more his avid lips sought hers. And suddenly, a splintering crash, which was again and again repeated, broke the spell which seemed to hold them all immovable. Zolani sprang to his feet, a pale horror on his countenance:

"In spite of all precautions, I am discovered!" he cried. "In spite of my silencing all those who have helped, in spite of all—surely, men are battering in the windows of the house upstairs—the windows of my dormuary——"

Undecided, he looked at the body of Dorothy Leigh. But to Donald, nothing but Dorothy mattered—nothing else in the world. For him there was no fatal moment of vacillation. Even as Zolani spoke, he had rushed to her, drawn her into his arms, kissed her warming lips—and felt the ecstasy of their return kiss.

He turned, then, to Zolani. Before either man could speak, another crash and clatter made the building shake, and he could hear the screaming of voices through the thick walls, and the screaming of other things—could they be the angry souls of the eighteen sleepers who had been mysteriously attacked and could not return to their dwelling-places?

"One of my men must have gotten away—and managed to communicate with the nearest town, which is only ten miles from here!" Zolani hissed. "You know what the ignorant mob mind is capable of—fanatics and fools! They have heard a tale of my putting men to sleep and incarcerating their bodies in my dormuary above. They have made of it a tale of whole-sale murder, and come to wreak revenge. Explain to them, convince them? It would be hard to do as much to a body of savants, unprepared for my stupendous discoveries—impossible to a herd of yokels. No! One thing there is that terrifies me, as some men are stricken out of themselves with horror by great heights, or fire, or water. The thing that makes me less than a man with fear, is—a mob! Once I suffered at the hands of a mob——"

He covered his face with his shaking hands. Then, leaping forward, Donald strove to tear those hands from the count's face, seeing that in the palm of one was held a small vial full of a black fluid, which, even as Donald stared in horror, disappeared down the throat of the count. Zolani dropped his hands, then, and stared blankly at Donald, with a horrid, empty smile. His body, Donald knew, was tenantless, before it crumpled slowly to the floor, and to it there would be no returning of the banished spirit, for the very lips were blackened and burned with the poison which had brought instant and strangely painless death.

An overpowering impulse seized then upon Donald—an

impulse to catch up Dorothy in his arms and make his escape with her—to get her away from this room of death, and away from the confusion and rioting which he could hear from above stairs and from without. Zolani had been right—there were shouts of men mingled with sounds of violence, and again that other shrieking which seemed to touch Donald's heart with a strange horror. He turned hastily to Dorothy now, but made no move to touch her; before he had the right to take her away, there was work to be done. To his relief, her eyes were open, and she smiled.

"Don't be afraid, my darling—I will be back at once," he reassured her. "Can you wait alone here for just a little while?"

The girl nodded. Her eyes seemed full of a strange dream, but they were clear and calm.

Donald rushed through the door which, after all, Zolani had not thought it necessary to lock, and up a winding stairway. As he burst into the entrance hall of the building, he heard the crackling of flames: the building had been fired by a thrown torch, so that the upper portion was burning before the lower part took fire. And now those eery screeches were no longer mystery, but horrible fact. Around the gloomy mansion the vultures were wheeling; in and out through broken window-panes they flew, and one bore in his talons something at which Donald could not look. . . .

HE FLUNG open the outer door and faced the mob. A shower of missiles seemed about to descend around him; the mob, after the manner of mobs, had gone berserk, and the light in the eyes of its leaders was not the light of reason. And yet, by some miracle of perils escaped and vital need, Donald made them listen—made them believe.

"The man you came to find is dead," he shouted above the din, and they heard him. "The man who rebuilt this house— the man who filled it with corpses, as you think. *Men!* That man was about to murder me—I escaped death at his hands because you came. Now there is barely time to avert—to *try* to avert—a horrible tragedy. I can explain later, not now. The bodies you thought were dead bodies are about to be burnt here, as though this whole house were a funeral pyre. Worse still, these horrible birds——"

Donald felt a responsive shudder run through the crowd.

"It is worse than you think. These men——"

He stopped suddenly. He had been about to tell them that these men were not dead, but sleeping. But to say such a thing to these farmers and small shopkeepers would be to brand himself as a madman. Moreover, even if Count Zolani's apparatus could yet be saved from the flames, he was not sure that he knew how to operate it. And if it could not be operated, the sleepers would sleep on. He wondered, miserably, just when that sleep would become grim, literal death. And, even as he wondered, he flung out his hands in a gesture of entreaty. He dared not identify himself with the count's great experiment, if he were to preserve a hope of attempting to complete it.

"Carry out the bodies! Save them!" he begged.

He rushed back, then, to rescue Dorothy. There were enough of those others to carry the eighteen helpless bodies of men out of the lockers of the "dormuary," which had become more sinister than its name, borrowed from the name of an abode of death. There were enough, and they were responding to his appeal. Would there be time? And could the basement laboratory be saved?

When he fought his way back through suffocating fumes to the open air, one of the leaders of the mob whose face bore the recent mark of an angry burn, sought him humbly.

"We have added horror to horror," he confessed, sadly. "We made our way inside—we found that dreadful locker room, like the locker room of a morgue. *What has been going on here?* Well, though the foreigner we heard of who conducted this establishment is dead, we may solve that problem later. But—I can not tell you of the condition in which we found those bodies. Before the flames drove them away, the vultures——"

He covered his face with his hands. And in that moment, the very air seemed shattered, and a burst of flame and smoke belched from the broken, yawning windows. Already the structure was falling.

On the grass there lay the body of one man. Donald had caught sight of it—it seemed the only one the men had carried out.

"The flames were getting to them, and it seemed *better to leave them,*" the man beside him said then with a shudder. *"This* one was in much better condition than any of the others."

Looking, Donald saw that vultures first attack the eyes of an unconscious victim. Even though they had not finished their work, never, as long as he should live, would he be able to look upon a vulture without the dreadful feeling of nausea creeping over him which overcame him now. In that moment, he abandoned all hope of saving the laboratory. Even knowing what *he* knew, he agreed with the villager who had said "better to leave them."

DOROTHY and Donald were cared for in the village. There was an investigation, and later another, for all of the eighteen had been important men. The story the two survivors had finally to tell was converted by scientists who walk in beaten paths, into other terms. Zolani had been making hypnotic experiments, and most of his victims, or dupes, had died. That was the version which was accepted.

Terrors outlived together bind closer the ties of love and affection, and Donald and Dorothy were married before they left the village. And not until then did Donald question Dorothy as to the things which had befallen her absent spirit, during the brief hour of its wandering.

"I had thought that I, like the others, was to be left without my body for two weeks," she said musingly. "And it was such a little while—only an hour you say, Donald. Well! Perhaps that is why I have so little to tell, because the time was so short—and yet that hour, though empty, seemed an eternity. It seemed as though there is no time to a disembodied spirit—as though in one instant there is eternity. Besides that feeling, there was another—of great emptiness, of space, I suppose, and a feeling of being alone there, as a star is alone in space. And really, Donald—that is all. I think there will be more than that, in the life that comes after death. God has given me a body here on earth, and eyes to see with, and ears to hear with. Since my spirit is indestructible, I think some day He will give me another, perhaps not like this one which we know, you and I, but still a way of expressing that which I am, of comprehending in a greater or a less degree those things which are about me.

"As to the count's experiment—well, as I said, it was only an hour. But it left me with two feelings—one that of my indestructibility, and the other, a consciousness of eternity. And it left me with a conviction that though men should learn to synthesize both body and soul, only God can make them live, as He sees fit."

The Rays of the Moon

Everil Worrell

For hours I had lain hidden behind the gravestone. I was a medical student—and I needed a cadaver.

My pal and I had always been different from our classmates. We would have departed from the ways of other doctors, too, had we gone on to practise our profession. In our class there were men who have given their lives in the service of humanity—but we would have made humanity serve us. We aspired to fame, to the making of spectacular discoveries, perhaps— and we would have stopped not for fear or mercy. How quickly we would have been expelled from the college in which we were enrolled, had our standards of conduct been made known to our fellow students and instructors!

Well, it would not matter now if we had been expelled. Better for us if we had been. My pal died of septicemia—the revenge, perhaps, of the corpse he was working on in the close-shuttered basement of his house when his knife slipped and infected his hand. For that corpse had been walking on two feet only a week before, the healthy body of a charwoman who worked in the medical school building, and whose naturally appointed time to die had not yet come.

Ah, well! The charwoman's disappearance created hardly a ripple of interest, and Browne's death not much more.

And now I lay hidden through hours of darkness in a large, well-filled cemetery not far from the outskirts of a city. The city was not the one in which I lived and pursued my studies. For caution's sake, I had driven more than forty miles. Yet I was familiar with the countryside, for six months before I had passed this way often, on my way to the home of a girl to whom I was engaged. I had loved this girl until I became sure of her affection, and then I tired of her. Besides, I had given my allegiance to morphia, and had become unsocial. After I wearied of her it became a monotonous thing to know that she loved me, and so I broke my engagement. A few months later her brother called on me, begging that I go to see his sister, if only once more. She was a delicate, sensitive, high-strung girl, not very strong. My treatment of her, he said, had broken her heart, and her family actually believed her to be dying of grief. Her brother was not very courteous to me, for he had gotten the idea that a little kindness from me might save his sister's life.

"You may not be a murderer, but you have the heart of a murderer," he said to me.

I laughed at him, and never went near the girl again. That sort of thing is ridiculous! No girl with any sense pines away and dies of disillusionment and lost love in this day and age, as I told him. I had no time to waste in considering her feelings. And a girl who would have so little pride as to do such an unreasonable thing would be better dead, in any case. I told him that, too; and he went away and left me alone, and I never again traveled that road until I went to tear from a new-made grave its quiet tenant.

I had gone there in the early evening, in order to reconnoiter. It was a cloudy night, and although the moon was full, it would be hard to locate the fresh grave I hoped to find, after dark. I might have carried a flashlight, but I had not the nerve for that. A moving light in a graveyard at night is more likely to attract the curious than to terrify chance passers-by and send them hurrying away, as would have been the case a century ago.

Driving slowly past, I got the lie of the land, and then drove on. I had seen what I wanted to see—a mound of fresh earth, far in from the road. I parked the car a little way down in a side road and walked back, climbed the low fence and crept to my

place of vigil, and waited. I wanted the road empty and deserted, but I wanted to leave myself plenty of time to rearrange
the despoiled grave before dawn, and to get the heavy burden I
expected to take away with me safely hidden in the bottom of
my car. I did not care very much what kind of body I would
find in the new-made grave. Man, woman or child—I was
going to use the brain for some experimental work, and the
brain of one was as good as the brain of another.

While I waited, I had added a new mark to the many tiny
puncture marks my pocket hypodermic had left upon my arm.
With a strong shot of morphine in my veins, time had gone
pleasantly and fast.

As I started to dig, the clouds thinned overhead, and a faint,
ghostly light shone down upon me. Accustomed as my eyes
were to the darkness, I could do without the light, and I did not
like it. True, it was hardly strong enough to make me visible,
even from a short distance. But it had an unwholesome, sickly
quality that preyed upon my spirits. To me a corpse was just
a corpse—but why is it that ghosts are always said to be seen
by the light of the moon? For every ghost-story in which the
moon is not mentioned, there are a thousand in which it is.
Digging into this grave in the darkness, I had experienced no
more emotion than, in my boyhood, I had felt on digging into
a hill of potatoes. We had needed potatoes for dinner, and I had
taken a spade and dug into a hill after them. I needed a body,
and I was digging into its hill after it. But with the coming of
this unwelcome, eery half-light, I began to feel a chill creep up
my spine.

I tried to laugh it off, to see my adventure again in its true
perspective. I needed a corpse, and here, beneath my spade,
was one that was going to waste. It was dead enough. It would
not be annoyed, and the people who had placed it here in the
heart of the cemetery could adorn the grave with flowers just
the same, thinking there was that beneath them which perhaps
occupied, in part, various alcohol-pickle jars.

I caught myself up with a shudder. My bravado was going too far. Instead of reassuring myself, I would unbalance my nerves.

Just then my spade struck something hard, and I breathed a sigh of relief. Now to get it over! Since I had gotten myself into this uneasy, shivery state, the quicker I proceeded the better. I had brought tools to force the coffin lid. I meant to replace the coffin, and throw in the dirt. I had brought a bundle of gunny sack to wrap the body in. It would be a serious enough thing for me if I were observed carrying my burden to the car, but better wrapped than unwrapped. A curious observer might possibly give me the benefit of the doubt in the first case, and pass on speculating.

I worked hard, now, the perspiration standing out all over my body from my efforts and my excitement.

I DUG out the coffin, and, straining every muscle, lifted it out. And just here an actual physical giddiness seized me. I had a sudden feeling as though the yawning hole at my feet were infinitely deep—as though I stood precariously upon the earth, and might slip from my footing and fall endlessly into some horrible abyss. I was overcome by the feeling of *space*—though why this should be, as I looked down into the hole I had dug, I can not say.

I knelt by the coffin and with shaking hand attacked the lid with my tools. Prying, wrenching, hurrying more and more, I threw the lid aside, at last, with a muffled clang. The dim light of the cloud-covered moon faded at this moment, and it was as dark as I could wish. Little comforted, however, I made no attempt to inspect my prize. I could see that it was a woman, who had been buried in a white dress. The face was no more than a white blur, but I had—I, the cold-blooded, intellectual resurrectionist—I had a feeling as though it *saw* me. Hastily snatching one of the gunny sacks I had at hand, I wrapped it around the head, shrinking a little from the clammy touch of lifeless hair and flesh where my bare hand came in contact with them.

I had time to wonder at the strength of my nervous revulsion of feeling—only for a moment. Only for a moment, and then the clouds parted, as if at a signal, and the moon shone out. God, what a sight met my horrified eyes!

It was midnight, for the moon was full, and it stood in the exact zenith of the sky. It shone directly down on me, and on the pitiful figure of the dead that I had torn from its last earthly refuge. It shone into the yawning grave, and seemed to gather there in a pool, to fill it as it filled the vast dome of the sky. There seemed to be no bottom to the grave, and this was so strange a thing that I reeled and would have fallen to the ground, overcome again by the dizziness I had felt before. Suppose the feeling of fixed attachment to the earth should fail you—that the bonds of gravity should not seem to hold you firmly—and you can imagine something of the physical sensations that beset me. But you can form no image of the mental agony, the mental horror—for I have not told you all.

I say I *would* have fallen to the ground. I did not, for even as the desperate dizziness assailed me, a greater horror assailed me also, and I could not fall. It seemed to me that the pale but brilliant rays of the moon had taken hold of me, as the invisible power of a magnet takes hold upon a piece of steel. As the sickening feeling struck me that the earth was, somehow, letting me slip away—fall away into the hollow ether—so, a second later, it seemed to me that I was upborne by a force to which I did not willingly submit. I could not fall, because the moon was directly overhead, and because it held me, drew me, as the tide draws the sea.

Who can explain the mysteries of matter? The sea follows the moon; why not, then, our corporeal bodies, which are made up largely of water? Are there not tides within us which we should feel? On this night, the moon was drawing *me,* with a resistless, inexorable attraction. I was being drawn upward, so that I could not fall. I was being drawn upward, so that I felt less and less the pressure of my feet upon the earth—more and more that horrible dizziness, the dizziness of space. I was being drawn upward as a mote is drawn into a vacuum.

And surely, that were enough—but it was not all, nor was it the worst. For the still figure lying at my feet;—the white-clad figure with the gunny sack incongruously wrapped around its head and face—that figure, too, was being drawn upward. It was rising slowly from the ground, swinging a little, almost imperceptibly, into an upright position. In I know not how long a time, while I stood motionless as though frozen into stone, watching its stiff gyration through the air, it assumed, finally, an upright posture, and stood facing me—facing me, with the horrible, gunny-shrouded head opposite mine, as though it were peering out, perhaps, through some thin spot in the coarse fabric.

Suddenly my own voice pierced the night in a frantic shriek that seemed to echo among the low white stones and massive monuments. I had screamed out in a nightmarish feeling that what was happening could not be real. And then I clapped my hand over my mouth in a very ecstasy of terror. For all around me, a doleful moaning proceeded from the graves. And above every grave in the vast acreage gorged with the rotting corpses of the dead, the sod was billowing—swelling outward, as though a mighty struggle took place beneath the surface of the earth.

There is a passage in the Scriptures, in which the evil-doer implores the hills to fall upon him. Maddened by my frantic terror, this passage flashed into my mind. I wanted to take refuge from the unnatural horrors surrounding me; from the merciless, pale light that displayed them to me, and—horrible thought!—that exposed me to them. Another moment, I thought, and the dead will leap out from their tombs and fall upon me in vengeance for desecrating the city belonging to the dead. And still I had the desperate feeling that the rays of the moon exercised a potent attraction upon my body, as though I were about to be swept entirely off my feet by them, and drawn upward into space.

The open grave before me appeared in that awful moment as a refuge. But between me and it swayed that upright figure—the figure of the corpse I had dragged out of it, with its head swathed in the coarse bag I had drawn over it. I leaped madly forward, my hands out-thrust to push that figure aside, to hurl it to the ground—and as I leaped, I felt that I was rushing *upward*. The cemetery with its long rows of mounds and grave-stones fell away from me. Around me I was conscious of nothing but the misty flood of moonlight, and the horrible figure I had sought to thrust from me—the rigid body of the dead woman, which still confronted me with its faceless, bundled head. Then I plunged into unconsciousness.

As ONE recovering from a swoon, I felt the powers of thought and feeling return to me. Slowly and wearily they came back. I knew, before I remembered the horrors of which I have just written, that they were no kindly gift. Better an eternity of unconsciousness; I did not want to think and feel again.

Heavily, impelled by an urge that could not be longer denied, I lifted the lids from my aching eyes. And for a merciful moment, I thought I was alone.

Where? I was not, thank God, in the cemetery. Those count-less heaving mounds of earth that should have lain quietly over their decaying contents were not around me now. But *where* I was, and in what manner of place, was quite beyond me.

Imagine a desert of white sand, hemmed in by mountains white, but not of the sparkling whiteness of snow—of the whiteness, rather, of bare, bleached bone; and yet this desert was not of sand, for instead of tiny particles, the floor of the plain on which I lay was rather like bare, bleached bone, too. There was a deathliness about the very substance of which plain and near-by mountains were formed, which is indescribable. There was a deathliness in the silence of the place. There was a deathliness in the absence of motion, in the absence of color; even the sky was colorless, although it was dead black. But there were glaring lights hung in that black sky—not stars! Surely, no stars shone down on any part of the earth's globe, as these lights shone.

Somehow, they terrified me, those glaring, tiny points of light, thick-strewn against the blackness, varying in the colors of their flames, distant yet overpowering in the intensity of the rays they hurled against my retinas.

Has it ever occurred to you to think of the panic into which you would be thrown if the consistency of a single law of nature failed you? Imagine, for instance, that your optic nerve suddenly forgot to register perspective in transmitting images to your brain, as it has been trained from boyhood to do. Imagine your terror at the growing immensity of a housefly, darting toward your eyes, blotting out the world with its black body and spreading wings. So it was that the strangeness of those awful stars, shining down on me, terrified me.

As I turned my head so that I could see more of the heavens—my arm, lying across my face, had shown me but a small sector of them before, although I had been able to see my nearer surroundings by looking beneath it—a sight burst upon my vision which I can never forget. If I were to live through indescribable tortures for a thousand years, even then the wonder of it would not fade from my memory.

In the midst of the heavens hung two glorious orbs: the one, the first glimpses of which all but blinded me, a blazing mass of flame; the other, a beautiful disk shining with a softer light, on which there was a faint tracery which reminded me of the schoolroom globe on which, years ago, I had studied the oceans and continents. The rim of this disk had a softened, slightly blurred appearance, which added to its beauty. And the whole disk was large—perhaps some four or five times larger than the full moon is.

And now, my mind and vision began to correlate my observations. Those burning stars and that ball of flame that glared upon me, as though the softening veil of air had been withdrawn from between them and my eyes; the familiar, maplike tracery of that enormous sphere, with the softer outline which set it apart from everything else within the range of my vision; those baldly glaring peaks towering around me on every side— their glaring outlines sharply cut against the dead, black sky— their contours wild, fantastic, like the shapes of the mountains of the moon——

I uttered a wild shriek, and fell upon my face. I was panting madly. An unbelievably awful conviction had swept over me. That dreadful, drawing feeling which the moon's rays had exercised upon me—my swooning memory of slipping from the earth——

I was not on the earth. The earth hung there, beautiful as a lost paradise, in the sky above me. I was on the moon, among the desolate, dead mountains of the moon. The veil of air had indeed vanished from before the faces of the stars, for the moon was as airless as it was lifeless. There was no air for me to breathe—no air for me to breathe! That thought in that moment eclipsed all other thoughts. Prostrate, I groveled, I gasped, I threw out my arms. My lungs seemed laboring madly, my chest expanded as though it would burst.

Then something touched me, from which, even in that desperate moment, I shrank away. And there came to my ears a sort of soundless voice—no voice such as we of earth know voices, yet some impulse which seemed to impinge tonelessly upon my eardrums, and which my brain translated into words.

"*This* distress is needless," said the voice. "You are suffering from an idea. A disembodied spirit—an astral body—needs no air to breathe."

Relieved of my instant physical terror, I was at once the victim of a more subtle, more excruciating anguish. I need not fear to die! No; for this—*this was death!*

I had been in the moonlit graveyard in the hour when the dead wake, and ghosts "walk." And I had become one of that dread company. My body, not swooning, but lifeless, lay in the cemetery—perhaps it had fallen into the grave toward which I had leaped. But I, unknowing, had parted from it and from the fair earth, and had fallen under other bonds.

I got to my feet; turned in that direction from which it seemed to me those words had proceeded; raised my head—and dropped it lower, not to see.

Not to see! For in the lifeless desolation around me, I had one companion—the rigid figure of the dead woman with the shrouded head!

Twice, then, I sought to flee; and twice the grisly Thing confronted me.

At last I sank down in a hopeless, ultimate despair.

If this were death, and I a spirit, moving in an astral body—I had heard of such things, and had laughed quite merrily at them—then this companionship in death seemed to be ordained. For the present, there was no escape from it. And so, for a while, time passed, while I sat motionless, brooding, in an inaction which, it seemed, might endure for all eternity. And while the radiant vision that was the earth with its teeming nations of living men, turning the passing instants to good or evil, showed a changing face—for the faint traceries of continents slipped aside and another hemisphere began to appear—that other figure waited.

AT LAST I summoned all my fortitude and spoke to it. Better the emptiness of a dead planet than its company, and yet—it had occurred to me that I might learn of it, since it seemed, after its brief tenancy of the grave, more versed than I in the way of death.

I shrank anew from the sound of my own voice, which sounded toneless as that other voice had sounded. But somehow I asked where were the other dead.

"*Space* is the pit into which the souls of dead men fall," was the pitiless answer. "By God's mercy, some are saved—but you, standing at midnight by the open grave from which you dragged my unwilling body, are not a candidate for God's mercy, in your present state.

"I—I may be one, perhaps. I am on a mission, now. And even you—since it is for your sake that I was sent on it, there may be hope for you. Later I shall speak of that.

"The dead who are lost in space are drawn to the moon, which exerts a compelling power upon their astral bodies. That is why spirits sometimes appear to living men in the pallid light of the encircling satellite. When the light of the moon is turned from the earth, the dead can not easily revisit it; but when it bathes the earth in its radiance, they are sometimes able to follow the rays of moonlight to the planet that was their home. So they sometimes reanimate their abandoned physical bodies—the graves in the cemetery tonight were disturbed by the efforts of bodies and souls to reunite."

Suddenly I was seized with a desire to know more. Even my terror was held in abeyance by my longing to understand more of the mysteries of death.

"There should be other dead around us, then," I said. "Why do I not see all of them, as well as you?"

"The sight would unseat your reason, and you have still a chance to undo some of the evil you have done," came the reply. "Besides, few of the dead concern you. To the dead who wander here, only the evil they have done is real. *Look!*"

Obedient to the pointing finger, I turned.

There, before me now, appeared the shadowy form of my pal—of Browne, who had kidnaped and murdered the old charwoman, and had died of septicemia. And beside him, ghastly with a cruel hole in the head, was the woman.

I shrank away, and as Browne held out his hands to me in pleading, I made a threatening gesture which repelled him. Slowly the vision faded, and again my only companion in the desolate place was the figure with the shrouded head.

"That was not well done, nor was it well-omened," said the monotonous voice. "You would not have seen him, but for the fact that you encouraged him along his evil way. True, you were ignorant of the murder until it was accomplished. Yet I tell you that but for your influence upon his life on earth, it would never have been committed. It was not well done to cast him from you. He is not evil incarnate, but only the lost soul of an evil-doer, and little worse than you."

Once more I was the victim of an unreasoning terror. During my whole life I had refused to hold myself accountable to any law, human or divine. I had made my rules of life, and succeeded in "getting away with them." Now there was a deadliness of import in the words I had just listened to, which I did not understand; they implied that in some awful way I was at last to be brought to book—confronted with a terrible reckoning. Perhaps an eternity of this——

I was desperate, and in my despair I grew bold.

"Unloose that covering from your head," I cried. "It is horrible to me. I can not stand to see it. I would rather see your face!"

Somehow, I felt the unseen gaze that greeted my outburst. I felt the approach of a horror, unseen, unknown.

"The time is not yet. Your hands put this covering upon my head, and over my dead face; roughly they put it there, to hide your wrongdoing from the eyes of men. Your hands shall remove it—but the time is not yet.

"And be not surprized if the sight of my face is more terrible to you than this that hides it from you."

I held my hands before my eyes, and sank again upon the ground. And again it seemed as though eternity were passing, without life or motion, with nothing to look forward to but the dread reality of death.

Yet it could not have been long before I felt again the unwelcome touch upon my shoulder. For when I drew back from it and leaped to my feet, the continent that had been slipping away toward the rim of the earth was still visible. On that part of it which had been my mortal home, the moon was setting. Longingly I strained my eyes upward.

Oh, to know again the joy of a sunrise on the earth! The wholesomeness of things that lived—of things that had their lives to turn to good account! To be again a living man among my fellows, with the right to *hope*— to spend my days in worthy things, and to hope that at the end of them I might have earned the right to another fate than this upon which I had fallen!

Once more the specter approached me.

"Come, it is time to go, before that open grave has turned away from the moon. We are to go back there, you and I together. I told you, there is yet a chance for you! We are to go back, and you have yet more time to spend on earth. See that you use each moment to good account, for perhaps the first few moments of your return may decide eternity for you. Come, you must go back with me, into the grave."

Into the grave!

I could not have prevented my shudder at that, if that alone had cost me my salvation.

"I told you, you should not have shrunk from Browne. It will be better now, not to shrink from me. You dragged me from the grave into which they put me—why should you not take me back there? Who are you, a soul steeped in sin, that you should spurn the company of the stolen, lifeless body you would have violated in your laboratory? You would have dissected it—severed bone and thew and sinew. Instead, it is a part of your reparation to resume your earth life in that grave—with me."

I had no time to question farther. The deadly, sickening dizziness of space had seized upon me. In some mysterious manner, or by some dispensation, we were to be borne back on the rays of the moon that had swept me from my living body, as the tide is lifted above the barriers that hold the sea at ebb.

And the Thing from which I had shrunk since that moment in which I felt the earth slipping from me—the Thing for which I had developed an unspeakable repulsion—that Thing was with me, pressing close beside me, turning its hateful hidden face toward me, as my senses swam and faded into unconsciousness.

IN MY mind there was, at first, little more than a confusion of memories. I seemed to have looked down upon my own body, lying in the bottom of the grave which I myself had opened, in a sickly glimmer that might have been reflected from the long beams of the sinking moon, or might have been a phosphorescence of the damp earth. In that open grave, partly resting on my body, there was another that bore it down—a gruesome thing of death between me and the open air.

I seemed to have seen this, but in a second instant, it became rather *feeling,* than seeing.

I lay heavily pressed against the damp ground that was the bottom of the grave. The horrible thing was with me there; a fold of that gunny sack I had used to hide its face when first I dragged it from its coffin lay across my mouth and nostrils. I seemed to inhale the very air of death and of decay.

I was weak, and my first struggles were futile. Only one thing in the world could have been more appalling—to be buried alive. I seemed, even, to taste of the horror of that. Somehow my arms were pinioned beneath me, so that for long moments I could not even free my face. I began to think that I would die, here, in the open tomb with this dead body, and that someone might come and hastily throw down the dirt and sod upon us both.

Spurred by this unreasoning terror, my strength began to return. I raised myself to a sitting posture. I breathed freely. I began to prepare for the effort of climbing out of the grave.

But what awful sound assailed my ears?

Surely, the quiet form that lay at my feet was waking too.

The occupant of the grave, that had lain there many hours before my coming, was doing that most horrible, unnatural thing—returning to life after its burial.

And I, alone, nerve-shattered, horror-stricken—I was the sole witness of the dread sight.

The bosom of the dead girl moved beneath the folds of her burial gown. The whole form stirred. Long sighs and deep groans burst from the unseen lips.

I gathered all my energies for flight.

Let life reanimate the corpse before me—I would not stay to see the awful drama. I *dared* not stay. It would be ruinous to be found here, to be known as the violator of the grave. If I lingered, someone would come. If I lingered and this returning life were not transient, then the corpse itself could condemn me. True, I would have been the unwitting means of giving it a second chance at life—but it would surely be known in what manner I came to have done so. The dead woman who was agonizing her way back to life might not even thank me for my part in her return; her suffering seemed dreadful, now, and, since she had once passed the portals of the grave, this reawakening might be as unwelcome to her as it was to me.

I was clambering to my feet, when I felt a clammy, damp, yet unbelievably strong hand close upon my ankle. I tripped and stumbled, and could not get away.

Helping itself by clinging to me with both hands, now, the body of the woman who had been dead rose slowly to a sitting posture.

A smothered, stumbling, thick-tongued speech greeted my unwilling ear.

"So this was why—was why—my last request, not to be embalmed. I knew. I must have known. Something told me, that I must come back. Yet I did not want to come back! You—you—ah, why is the grave open? It was you opened it—but not for my sake. *Morton!*"

Spellbound, I waited. The voice was changing, becoming

more lifelike. As it spoke my name in accents of dread import, it was familiar. *This woman who was buried yesterday knew me!*

Suddenly, a shriek pierced the still air of dawn. "Oh, I am afraid, I am afraid! I died, unhappy to the end, longing for one last glimpse of your face. I wake here in my own grave—and you are here. But you are as hard now as you were then. You came—you came—oh, I remember how you told me once, that some day you would rob a grave. I thought it was a horrid jest—I thought you meant to frighten me. It was true—*it was true, and you came to rob my grave!* Oh, I am afraid to be here alone, alone in a grave. You shall stay with me—I will scream until someone hears me, and you shall stay here until they come. No, I will not let you go. I am afraid to be alone. You shall stay, and I will tell what you have done—I will tell, and you shall be punished for *that*——"

Frantically I strove to free myself from the grip of those clinging hands.

It was in vain to plead, to threaten, to reason. I snatched the gunny sacking, at last, from the head of the girl who knelt at my feet. But it was dreadful to look upon the face of this girl who had loved me. It was dreadful that we should have met thus; a thing unspeakably dreadful, a thing outside all human experience.

God! Why should it have been *her* grave?

And in her eyes, I read that she was on the verge of madness.

No arguments would serve; she would not listen. No appeals to her old love for me could move her; waking within the narrow limits of her grave, there was room in her brain, room in her heart, for but two things—fear and vengeance.

Outside, the light was growing. Soon people would be passing along the road. They would see from afar the open grave with the coffin lying beside it, and the heaped-up earth. They would enter—and hear the things she was saying.

What they would do to me, I did not know. At the very least, my life would be ruined. I could never practise my profession. I could never occupy my place in the world again.

And suddenly, the girl at my feet began to scream.

THERE was but one thing to do, and I did it. Dead she had been, dead she should be again. I seized the slender throat in my hands. . . .

Although she had seemed so strong, the life so newly returned was easily banished. Almost at once, I felt her grow limp in my grip.

There was not time to rearrange the grave. There was only time to fly.

Of course, there was a great mystery about it. A grave had been opened, presumably by body-snatchers, and the body of the girl who had been buried there the day before was found lying in the bottom of it, while the open coffin rested on the ground outside. Strangest of all, the corpse had not been taken away, but it showed signs of violence, marks upon the throat that had not been there before.

I have saved myself from disgrace, but I have given up my profession. Death frightens me too much. I can not endure the presence of the dead or dying.

I have changed. Surely I have changed! After my headlong flight from the cemetery, I remembered the things that had happened to me. I had fallen, fainting, into the grave, dragging down with me the corpse. That is, my physical body had fallen into the grave—but something that was I had been drawn upward, beyond the limits of the earth, into the realm of death.

Never do I see the full moon shining from the midheavens without a shudder. I hide away from its rays. It is as horrible to me as a corpse.

Was it fantasy—a nightmarish hallucination that visited my brain between swooning and waking? I should say so, for I was to be a doctor. The profession I was not fit to practise would agree that it was so, for they would seize upon a natural explanation.

I managed, prompted by a ghastly curiosity, to verify the words of the reanimated corpse with regard to its embalmment. The girl who had died of a broken heart had had a horror of embalmment—she had indeed made the unusual request that her body be buried without it. I could, then, assume that she might have been buried alive; that her departed spirit had not journeyed from the earth with mine its unwilling companion, but that she had been buried and laid in the grave in a state of coma.

This would explain it all—explain it naturally. And then, there was the shot of morphine I had taken in the evening, which might have overcome my senses and inflicted a wild vision upon my inflamed brain. Then, too, there is a moon-madness that is known to the tropics. Perhaps some might say that the rays of the moon shining more strongly than is their wont in our temperate clime had maddened me.

But the horror that lives on with me is too real. The memory is too vivid. Too well do I remember certain doom-laden words: "The first few moments of your return may decide eternity for you."

I know that for the space of that night, two lifeless bodies lay in that open grave. I know my memory of that night is no fantasy, but the awful truth, and that in driving forth by violence the returning spirit from that other body, I made an eternal choice.

I, who had been told that I had the heart of a murderer, have become that most awful thing—a murderer!

I wait for death, which will come some day to me, with a dread beyond description. I no longer believe, as once I believed, that death is the end. I believe it is the beginning—*the beginning, for the evil-doer, of an eternity of the horror of death.*

The Gray Killer

Everil Worrell

Narrative and Diary of Marion Wheaton, Patient in R——— Hospital from November 15 to November 28, 1928.

Such terrible things are happening here that I feel the need to set them down, as I dare not speak to anyone of my thoughts and of my fears. I will go back and begin at the beginning, a few nights ago. Later, if there is more to be written—God grant there may not be!—I will continue this narrative as a diary.

It began three nights ago—and this is the twenty-sixth of November. The red light in the corridor outside my door burned like an eye lit with an ugly menace. In the dead of night bells sounded intermittently—the shrill ringing of the telephone, or the rasping buzzer that could mean so many things. Cold, and the need to borrow strength to spread a blanket within fingertip reach. Night loneliness and night terrors; fear of the known and of the unknown; fear of a stabbing agony called life and of a veiled release called death. Terror of pain. And in the shut-in private rooms and in the bare, orderly wards, that hydra-headed horror of a hospital—pain itself.

I, too, was in pain. A rusty nail had gone through the thin sole of my slipper and torn a gash in my foot which nearly ended in blood poisoning. And on the night of November twenty-third I lay tossing in my hot bed, feeling the burning lances of flame shoot upward from the horribly swollen foot.

Lying so, I had the horrors, rather. I was not out of the woods, not by a long shot. My foot might mend rapidly, or it might yet take a sudden turn for the worse, in which case I should leave this narrow room only for a narrower one. The woman across the hall, who had had her fourth operation for cancer, would be leaving so, perhaps, and would, I believed, be glad to go. Her broken moans had seemed to tell me that. And there was a man down the corridor who groaned. . . .

Well, I wished it were over and I were well, and safely out of the place. And in the meantime the bedcovers were too heavy and were burning me up, adding needlessly to my tortures.

I rang my bell, and listened to its dull, rasping sound in the distance. In some hospitals only a light flashed on a signal board and over your door—better arrangement, I'd say.

I waited for Miss Larcom or Miss Wurt. Miss Larcom would seem glad to see me—she would make me feel better and think of little extra things to do for me. Miss Wurt would snap at me, cross at having had to put down her novel. And she would do as little as she could, and very likely drag the covers roughly over that fiendish foot of mine. But if Miss Wurt were on the floor tonight, I should likely have to ring again.

I waited. It didn't do to ring again too soon. Then Miss Wurt would be certain to let those covers saw across my foot—or was that one of those sick, invalid fancies of which one hears? Still, all nurses aren't alike, and they aren't all angels.

I waited, and heard an unfamiliar footstep, that seemed to slide a little—not to shuffle but to slide, as a serpent would slide on hard ground or on a hard floor. Why did a coldness strike me then, that made me draw closer the covers that had irked me? And why did a sudden vivid conscious love of life and of the earth on which my days were spent sweep over me? I was afraid of the *emptiness* outside this world I knew; a realization of the vacant chasm of space swept my soul. Was it death I feared in that moment, or had I an instinctive prescience of strange Things—real, but unknown?

Sick terrors of a hospital night! I fixed my gaze unwaveringly on the doorway. Mustn't let Miss Wurt catch me looking or acting goofy. It would be fun for her to recommend me to the psychopathic ward. (No, of course I didn't think that seriously; of course I was just being an imaginative sick person.)

At any rate, my whole attention was on the dim-lit oblong of my door. The footsteps that sounded, somehow, so unusual, paused before a figure was framed there; not, however, before one of the feet that made the sliding sound was visible. There it was, for a few moments, alone: the end of a shoe that seemed enormously long. Then the figure caught up with the foot—not Miss Wurt or Miss Larcom, but a man.

A man dressed in gray. A man whose *face* (in the half-light, at least) was gray. Whose face, whose form, whose way of walking, I—didn't like. My fingers sought the bell cord.

Before they found it, however, the room was flooded with light. That seemed reassuring, somehow, and I was ashamed of my panic—my flightiness I ought perhaps to call it.

In a hospital you get used to people going and coming, surprizing you when you're awake, surprizing you when you're asleep. Strange nurses with thermometers happen in every day; strange house doctors now and then. I didn't need his statement now to fit him in.

"I'm Dr. Zingler, the new house doctor. Haven't seen you before. I have heard you had a hard time with your foot. I came because I heard your bell, and the nurse did not answer. Miss Wurt—I will send her, though I am afraid she moves slowly. In the meantime, if it is pain, I can help you."

In a reaction from the fantastic fear that had laid hold on me, I smiled warmly up at the strangely pallid face. Grayish skin, sunken cheeks, hollow, *hungry* eyes, and a strange, deathly immobility of feature—if an attractive personality was necessary to success the new house doctor was foredoomed to failure. Yet his professional manner was good enough, though somehow rather strange, too. Suave and smooth, but—indescribably queer.

I smiled, with an effort.

"Pain—yes, my foot hurts," I answered him, trying to make light of it. "But I rang for Miss Wurt merely to have her turn back the top coverings, to cool my foot, especially. I feel as though it were roasting over red-hot coals."

The ill-favored face looking down on me seemed to attempt a smile of sympathy.

"Miss Wurt will be able to make you more comfortable, no doubt," it promised. "But I think I can do more—I think I can insure you sleep for the remainder of the night. I'll just give you a hypodermic."

A wave of gratitude swept over me. I'd had a few brief intervals of forgetfulness when the pain was greatest, by the administration of a hypo; lately these had been discontinued. Complete oblivion for a few hours would be welcome now.

I watched Dr. Zingler as he busied himself with a small box and its contents, which he took from a pocket; did the man carry hypodermics and opiates always like this, ready for instant use? Generally the doctors rang for a nurse. . . .

THE hypodermic, held in a bony, long-fingered hand of the same unholy color as Dr. Zingler's face, moved toward me. I glanced at it, idly, baring my arm for the merciful prick. It was near my face as I looked at it. Heavens, how strange! Or was it due to fever that every little happening of this night took on a grotesque significance? Be that as it may, the appearance of the liquid in the hollow glass tube was violently repulsive to me: a viscid, slimy-looking, yellowish white, with an overtone of that same gray color that made the hand holding it look like the hand of a corpse. At the same moment an odor assailed my nostrils: a putrescent aroma of decay; the very essence of death embodied in a smell.

The needle was approaching my arm when I drew away from it—hurled myself from it, rather, forgetful of my foot, crouching in the far corner of my narrow hospital bed like a trapped animal at bay.

"No, no!" I cried, my voice rising queerly. "I won't take it, I'm not in pain, I need nothing! I'll ring, I'll scream! I'll arouse the whole floor!" The gray doctor—so I thought of him and shall always think of him—withdrew his hand, an expression of extreme contempt stamping his immobile features.

"Of course, if you prefer to bear your pain!" he shrugged. "Though it hardly needed such vehemence. There's a ward for patients like you where the walls are thicker. As to arousing *this* floor, I think you've succeeded in your humane endeavor. Listen!"

I listened. God forgive me, I had succeeded. The woman with the cancer was moaning pitiably—but for the opiates given her so heavily she would doubtless be shrieking. Down the hall the man with the grievous hurt was groaning, delirious too:

"Mary, you've come at last! Oh, no, nurse, it's only you! She died in the accident—I remember," he wailed. And then, again: "Oh, Mary, at last!"

Also the little boy who had had a tonsillectomy done yesterday was screaming down the hall, hoarse, half-intelligible words.

I buried my head beneath the covers in an agony of shame as I heard the sliding step of the doctor withdrawing. Through my door it passed and across the hall, and I heard the familiar hinge of the cancer patient's door creak. Well, perhaps he could quiet her, the new doctor. What had been the matter with me, anyway? Had I been mad?

Another footstep approached my door, a well-known footstep. Miss Wurt's healthy, round, red face appealed like an unamiable harvest moon. She fixed my covers, not so roughly as I had feared, and stood ready to depart. "That all?" she suggested hopefully.

"Almost," I said, detaining her with an urgent gesture. "But tell me—is Dr. Zingler often on the floor at night? He's—a queer-looking man, is he not?"

The red of Miss Wurt's face deepened to a mild purple. Some attraction between her and the new doctor, on her side at least, that was certain. Then my remark had been undiplomatic.

It had.

"I've never heard any of the patients comment on Dr. Zingler's personal appearance," she said in icy reproof.

I was glad to drop the subject. Next morning, however, I had a real surprize.

Miss Edgeworth, my day nurse, was a friendly girl, who had fallen into a habit of gossiping with me about the people and happenings around the hospital. After the night I hailed her coming with relief. I'd even dare tell her if I chose, I thought, that the new house doctor gave me the horrors.

"Have you seen Dr. Zingler?" I began tentatively as she wet my wash cloth, preparatory to washing my face.

"Dr. Zingler?" she answered with a quick look of pleasure and what appeared to be a blush. "He's the kind that makes the grind go easier. Handsome, too, isn't he? Or have you seen him?"

"Yes——" I hesitated. "I've seen him."

I said no more. Surely he must hypnotize the nurses. That gray pallor, those mask-like features—handsome! I turned my face to the wall and lay brooding. My foot was better today. I had leisure to wonder if I need feel graver concern for my mind. Last night was a nightmare, and the new "handsome" doctor a hideous ghoul! No, no—what was I thinking? Things that weren't possible! Had I fallen victim to an obsession, a hallucination?

THE greater part of the morning I brooded. And then I heard something that made me forget myself.

The house doctor whom I was accustomed to see on his daily rounds, Dr. Rountree, called a little after 3. Like Nurse Edgeworth, he occasionally stayed for a short chat. Today, however, I knew at once that he had something important on his mind—something, perhaps, which he hesitated to speak of.

"Have you heard the news about that cancer patient you've been grieving so over?" he began.

"The cancer case!"

I think there was horror in my voice. In my mind was a picture of a gray figure stalking, *sliding* in at the door behind which those hopeless moans were uttered. I think I was prepared for something gruesome, something incredibly awful, certainly not for Dr. Rountree's next words.

"It's something like a miracle, it seems," he said. "You know, we don't talk about these things, but this case was really hopeless. There couldn't have been another operation; and the thing still was gnawing at her vitals. Well! It was a case for increasing opiates until the end, with the opiates losing their power to alleviate. You've heard her moaning in spite of them. But today! Have you heard her? Listen!"

I listened. No, it was true, I had not heard her. The man down the corridor still groaned. The little boy who had lost his tonsils did not cry so much. The cancer patient had been silent all the morning, as she was now.

Again I felt a recurrence of my first horror.

"Not—dead!" The word one hates even to think in a hospital.

But Dr. Rountree shook his head and made a quick gesture with his hand that he used in moments of great enthusiasm.

"Oh, no, no!" he said quickly. "So much better that we've discontinued all opiates. Fully conscious and out of pain. A miracle, positively. She had an opiate last night, she says, though it isn't down on her chart. She was semi-conscious and didn't know who gave it to her, but she had that one—and hasn't needed one since. And she's stronger, too; the mere cessation of pain, I suppose, has given her the will to live. If it goes on this way her wound will heal and she'll go out in two weeks time, a well woman. I've never heard of such a thing!"

"Dr. Zingler went into her room. He had wanted to give me an opiate and must have given her hers," I said. "He's—rather hard to look at, isn't he?"

Dr. Rountree's face showed puzzlement.

"Didn't know Zingler was on last night, but he'd leave the opiates to the nurses, I should think," he said shortly. "He'll have the patients expecting the doctors to wash their faces for them next. As to looks, you're the first girl I've heard express a contrary opinion. Most of the nurses seem to think he's an Atlantic City beauty."

I tried during the rest of the long day to be glad of my neighbor's good fortune. I could not. I could only think with a kind of shrinking dread of the "handsome" Dr. Zingler slipping in at her door in the dead of night.

Of course it was only coincidence that the gray doctor had administered the woman's last opiate, and that the next day she had been so miraculously better. Only coincidence. Nevertheless, I inconsistently told myself that I would rather die than be miraculously cured by Dr. Zingler.

LIGHT came.

Again the red light in the darkened hall loomed sinister, ominous, and the shadows it gave were macabre. My foot was better tonight—still a tortured thing of fire and anguish, yet definitely better. If I had rung for a sedative which I had had upon request several times, I might have slept. But I didn't want to sleep, though I knew that sleep was necessary to my recovery. I had a horror of sleeping and waking to see a long, narrow foot pressing the threshold of my door—to see a gray figure creeping in at that door.

I would have given worlds to be able to lock my door on the inside. Since that was impossible I had it left open as usual, and kept my eye on the dull red oblong of light.

Hour after hour. The man down the hall was groaning, now—groaning in delirium, raving of the accident that brought him here. Not an auto smash, but a derailed train. I'd read of it. Only a few passengers hurt, but this man's wife, Mary, had been killed. He was crying her name out loud again, calling to her.

His groans—they hurt. Hospital nights! Awfulness of pain. Oh, why didn't someone hear and go to him? Miss Wurt on duty again, of course, and reading in whatever quiet corner she spent her nights. If she heard the groans, she didn't care. Oh, *why didn't someone go?*

And then I knew someone was going. For I heard footsteps, and they were the slow, sliding steps of Dr. Zingler. A door opened and shut. After a little, the groaning was cut off suddenly, as though a sound-proof wall had intervened.

Then I lay listening, till, after a long time, those sliding footsteps crept into the corridor. No sound, now, from the man who had groaned, as they retreated—going in the opposite direction from my door, thank God!

And still not another sound from the man who had groaned. The sufferer might have had his throat cut.

Next morning, however:

"You'd never imagine the things that are going on in this hospital!" Miss Edgeworth cried as she brought my morning thermometer. "Too bad *you* haven't come in for a miracle. You're mending, but slowly. Not like the case across the hall, I mean, or the railroad accident."

"The man from the railroad wreck—oh, what became of him?" My voice was sharp with anxiety, and Miss Edgeworth showed surprize and a little disapproval.

"You're guessing wrong, when you ask what's 'become of' him in *that* tone!" she said. "What's 'become of' him is that an almost hopeless spine condition is miraculously improved. He is out of pain. He can move his legs under the covers and we thought they'd always be like fallen logs. That's what's 'become of' him!"

I turned my face to the wall, because I couldn't smile,

couldn't show the decent human emotion of pleasure at another's merciful reprieve. Why couldn't I? Because my mind could image just one thing: the sound of those horrible, sliding footsteps last night, the picture I had visualized then of a lanky form and a gray death's-head creeping in at the delirious man's door—creeping out, leaving silence behind him.

What kind of opiate did the new doctor dispense, that not only alleviated pain, but cured everything from cancer to an injured back? Well, of course there was no connection; if there were, I should be honoring the gray doctor as a worker of miracles. But I didn't. I felt a greater horror of him than ever—and that horror extended itself now to the two who had so strangely recovered after his midnight visits.

Not for all the gold in the mint would I have entered the room of the cancer patient, or the room of the man who had been in the railroad wreck.

THE next two nights I slept heavily. My foot was improving more rapidly, and I was worn out with pain and with night vigils. True, I closed my eyes with a sense of surrounding peril of some queer, undreamable kind, but I closed them nevertheless, and opened them only as the winter dawn crept in at my windows. And on the second morning I think I must have given Miss Edgeworth a real shock.

She had merely mentioned the little boy who had had his tonsils out.

"Rodney Penning—the little tonsillectomy case——" she began.

I caught her arm in a grip that must have hurt.

"Has *he* had a sudden strange improvement?" I asked in a tone that rang unpleasantly in my own ears.

Miss Edgeworth drew her arm away from me and passed the fingers of her other hand speculatively over her sleeve.

"I think you've bruised me, Miss Wheaton," she said reprovingly; "I must speak to the head nurse about a sedative for you.

I don't know why you should be so dreadfully nervous, now your foot's doing so well. As for little Rodney Penning—I don't understand your question. Of course he's improved. Many children leave the hospital on the day of a tonsillectomy. Little Rodney is going home tomorrow."

I CAN hardly write of the horror of that tomorrow. I can hear yet the screams of little Rodney's mother—when little Rodney went home.

The little lad had cried pitifully after the operation on his throat. That wound had been agony for a child to bear. But the making of it was merciful: *that* cutting had been done under anesthesia. There was no anesthetic when the little boy's newly healed throat was neatly cut from the outside, so that his head was nearly severed from the trunk, and a great pool of blood had washed with red, as though a careless painter had smeared his paints, the skylight over the operating-room. The skylight? Yes, that was where the body was found, a shapeless black blob against the wan-starred sky of early dawn.

But the worst thing of all I have not yet written down. The worst thing of all was also the thing in which lay the greatest mystery.

Surely little Rodney Penning had been done to death by a mad fiend, for his body was transfixed with a needle-shaped bar of iron, bearing on the pointed end a barb suggestive of the barb of a fish-hook. And to the blunter end of the bar appended a fine but strong steel cord. It was as if some maniac obsessed with the harmless sport of fishing had played at using human bait. Only, if so, scarce half a mile from the hospital pounded the surf of the Atlantic. So why did he choose the hospital roof to carry out his grim travesty?

Writing this has turned me quite sick. If it had not been for this horror, I would soon be able to leave the hospital— and to tell the truth, I have conceived a horror of the whole place. The condition of my foot now permits me to get around on crutches. But they say, and my doctor says, that I am too nearly in a state of nervous collapse to permit of my discharge. And besides, an eruption has appeared on my body which has resulted from my near approach to blood poisoning, and which they say requires observation. I am on a special diet, and everyone is particularly thoughtful and considerate—even Miss Wurt. But I do not see how I can get better with this horror clutching at my heart.

They didn't mean to tell me, of course. But I had heard the screams of little Rodney's mother, and wormed the truth out of black Hannah, who brings the patients' trays. I was hysterical then, and from something the house doctor who is my friend, Dr. Rountree, said to me, I must have said some terrible things about Dr. Zingler. Dr. Rountree's eyes are dark and very deep, and can be very kindly and pitiful, and I know that he meant me to take what he said very seriously.

"Don't speak of your feeling about Dr. Zingler, Miss Wheaton, to *anyone*. Much better yet, never speak of Dr. Zingler at all."

I wish I had friends in this city. I wish I could be moved at once to another hospital. I don't seem quite able to arrange such a thing from inside. I spoke of it to my doctor, who is a great specialist, and so of course very impersonal. His eyes narrowed as he answered me, and I knew that he was studying me—regarding me as a case, and not as a human being.

"I can't order all my patients out of the hospital because of the most awful occurrence that has given you the horrors, Miss Wheaton, for I don't attribute it to any negligence on the part of the hospital officials. None of the other patients know of this thing. You gossip too much, ask too many questions for your own good, inquire too much into the goings on around the hospital. Then I must add to that an unfortunate tendency on your part to take personal dislikes, and most unreasonable ones. Not, for instance, that it injures Dr. Zingler to have you conceive an abhorrence for him—not, even, that it discredits

him that you should accuse him in a hysterical fit and utterly
without reason, of being the fiend killer. No, it only does *you
harm.*"

The lecture went on. I turned my face to the wall. When
the head nurse came in, a person who seems to have considerable authority, I said meekly that I would like to be moved to
another hospital. She said only:

"There, there! Dr. Smythe-Burns wants you to stay here.
We'll have you feeling more like yourself before long. And Dr.
Smythe-Burns orders your nightly sedative continued. We'll
have no more midnight blues."

Tuesday, November 26.
For all that, I had a nightmare last night.

I dreamed, most realistically, that I lay in the half stupor
which bridges, under a heavy sedative, the awful chasm between
"Visitors out" and the dawn light. And as I lay so, a figure came
creeping in at my door—creeping on long, strangely sliding
feet, and carrying in a gray, bony hand a hypodermic. The
figure came close to my bed, and by a supreme miracle of will I
opened my mouth and gasped my lungs full of air for a scream
that would have roused the floor, if not the whole hospital—
while my heavy hand moved spasmodically to grasp the bell-
cord. For a while my eyes locked with the deep-set eyes in the
gray face bent above me. Those eyes into which I looked were
cold as the eyes of a serpent—utterly inhuman, I thought.

After awhile the eyes changed in expression. The lean, gray
figure shrugged its shoulders and drew away. Then—thank
God!—it left me. But I had a sort of knowledge that it meant to
wait until a time when I would fail to wake.

I sounded out Miss Edgeworth about the strength of the sedative I am getting. She says it is enough to hold me, most likely,
in a deep sleep all night. If I dared tell her about *last* night—but
somehow I don't, after Dr. Rountree's warning. I asked my
doctor, when he came, to reduce the strength of the sedative,

saying I did not like to sleep so heavily it would take a great deal to waken me. He shook his head, and said I'd get over my nervous fancies, and assured me that all entrances and exits and fire escapes are being patrolled. I doubt that. It costs money to set a patrol, and I don't think it's done in a place where a single crime has occurred. In cases of *repeated* horrors——

I mustn't let myself think of the things that may be *going to* happen. But—I doubt, anyway, if any ordinary patrol could catch the gray doctor.

Wednesday, November 27.
I MADE a last attempt today, and failed.

I don't know why I had hesitated to ask Dr. Rountree's intervention. Perhaps because I like him so much. When you feel yourself sinking in a horrible morass of dread and terror, there isn't much time or energy to spare for ignoring real things. Vincent Rountree has come to be a sort of symbol to me—a symbol of all that is sound and normal, humanly healthy, pityingly tender and strong. I think he likes me too; I have been studying myself in a hand mirror at times, wondering why he should—for the dark blue of my eyes looks too sad with the dark blue circles worry has set beneath them. My hair is silky still and softly brown, but the natural curl has been all dragged out of it by fever and tossing, and although the eruption is not on my face, my face is white and drawn-looking.

It was late this afternoon when he stopped in for the two minutes' chat I look forward to, and the sunlight slanting in at my window had already the hazy tinge of an early winter sunset.

"Could *you* do anything, Dr. Rountree—in your capacity of house doctor——" I began.

His answer put an end to my last hope.

"Miss Wheaton, I've already tried. I suggested to your doctor—much more strongly than etiquette permits—well, the situation is delicate. He is afraid of offending the hospital authorities with no reason. If you discharged him and called another doctor, the situation would be much the same. I hope you'll try to take it as calmly as you can, for really all the patients in this hospital should be very safe now. It is true that special precautions are being taken, with regard to seeing visitors out, and the like."

I did not answer. The hazy yellow sunlight was fading fast—and with it my hopes. All at once a thought had definitely formed itself in my mind: that I should not leave the hospital at all—not living. I wished that I had died of blood poisoning. That is not so dreadful—not nearly so dreadful as some other things.

Vincent Rountree bridged the dark chasm of my thoughts, speaking almost shyly.

"I gained just one point—permission to take you out some evening soon in my car, in case you should consent to go. It would rest and refresh you——"

How grimly wrong he was in *that* surmise!

Thursday, November 28.

ANOTHER weary night has passed and morning come—a morning of driving rain and wind that howled around the hospital's corners like a banshee. It was a fit day for a culmination of horrors—though no day could be evil enough for the gruesome discoveries this day has brought forth.

At 7 in the morning, the hour when the day nurses relieve the night shift, I heard one of the girls crying bitterly. There was a good deal of running around, then voices raised and lowered quickly.

After half an hour or so of this, there was a silence. Such a silence as I hope never again to hear. It was like the sudden stalking of death itself into the midst of a group of agitated, sentient beings.

My heart was beating heavily as I listened alone in my room. And then I heard sounds of sobbing—of more than one person sobbing.

But a little later, I beheld an agony of grief that called to mind Gethsemane.

One of the night nurses had come to the end of the corridor where my room was—to get away from the others, I suppose. She did not see that my door was open—did not even look at it. She leaned against the wall, shaking from head to foot, making no attempt to cover her face. Her arms hung down limply, as though there was no life in them. From one hand dangled her nurse's cap. Her face was so drawn and contorted with anguish that her own mother would not have known her, and her wide eyes seemed to stare as at a specter. No tears came to ease her soundless, shattering sobbing.

When I could not stand it any longer, I called to the girl, and she came as though she were walking in her sleep, and stood in my door.

"Won't you please—please tell me what has happened?" I begged.

Still in that sleep-walking manner, she answered me, her words sounding like the words of a thing that has been learned by heart:

"I am—I *was*—in charge of the night nursery—the little, new babies you know. Last night after the last feeding I fell asleep. Somehow I overslept, and so no one knew what has happened until the day shift came on."

"And—what has happened?" I prompted her in spite of myself, my tongue sticking to the roof of my mouth.

"One of the babies—the youngest little baby—a little baby two days old——"

Suddenly a realization seemed to strike the girl. I was a patient. She was a nurse. She had said too much to stop now—but she mustn't tell me anything too dreadful.

"A baby was kidnaped last night," she ended lamely.

Kidnaped! It is a terrible, dreadful thing for a little baby to be kidnaped—to disappear. But I think I know—oh, yes, *I know* what blacker horror the word covered.

I have not forgotten little Rodney Penning.

Afternoon.

ONE of the unfortunate nurse's friends came hunting for her
and took her away. And all the weary, dreary day of driving
rain, gloom was like an evil fog in the hospital. This time, no
one can forget the tragedy for a moment. The nurses seldom
talk together and if they do they seem half afraid of the sound
of their own voices.

One selfish thought came to give me relief—that *now,*
perhaps Dr. Smythe-Burns would sanction my removal. Perhaps—and yet, perhaps not! The web of hospital and professional etiquette is too deep for me to fathom, as it has proved
too strong for me to break. In any case, Dr. Smythe-Burns has
not been in today, and I shall have to wait for his next visit.
Another curious thing about hospital etiquette is that you can't
telephone your doctor from the hospital. Anything he needs to
know about you, someone else will tell him—perhaps. At any
rate, *you* can't.

As I write, there is a congregation of doctors and nurses
outside the closed door of the cancer patient across the way. A
while ago I heard them gathered outside another door down
the corridor. I wonder what can have happened to excite
them—for I am sure they seem excited. At least the woman
who had cancer has not disappeared, nor has she had a recurrence of pain. I saw her through her half-opened door this
morning, eating a hearty breakfast.

Those worried faces outside her door grow graver and
graver. Surely this one day can bear no heavier burden of evil
than it has already disclosed.

I can't hear the voices across the hall. I am glad. I don't want
to hear them. Those faces are too much to have seen, in their
worry and—yes, *horror and fear again*. If any more black mis-
haps are to be known, I want to be spared them. I have almost
reached the point where I can endure no more.

Now they are talking louder. I am afraid I shall hear—*something I don't want to hear*.

"Dr. Fritz, we didn't dare pronounce in so grave a matter until we had *your* opinion——"

"And at the same time the patient in 26—the railroad accident case——"

"Both had made miraculous recoveries—pitiful, to end in this!"

"But, the coincidence!"

"Her husband will be heart-broken. Hard to tell him—but there's no possible course but immediate isolation."

"I hardly think before tomorrow——"

"They can be sent away tomorrow. There's a small colony—"

"Could a cancer disappearing suddenly, then, take *this* form?"

"Nurse, you'd make a very imaginative research scientist. Certainly not! And in *his* case, it was merely a railroad accident."

"But for both of them to have——"

★ ★ ★ ★ ★

Before writing the word that must come next, I fainted.

I had written, not everything that I heard said, but as much as I had time for. At the end I fainted—I don't know how long I have been unconscious here alone. But now I must finish— must write that horrible word:

Leprosy!

The gray doctor. The hypodermic filled with a strange, filthy-smelling stuff—which he intended to shoot into *my* veins, too. Dr. Zingler, the gray doctor, the gray fiend! And I mustn't speak of these horrors; of the things I am thinking— not to anyone. . . .

My hand is shaking so that I can hardly write, and I am

sobbing—dry, tearing sobs like those of the nurse this morning. But mine are not soundless as hers were—I must put this
book away, for I am losing all control of myself—someone is
coming. . . .

Chart of patient Marion Wheaton, November 28, 1929.

DELIRIOUS as result of recent catastrophes in hospital. Shows
mental aberration as well, however, accusing one of the house
doctors of horrible and fantastic crimes. Ordered detained for
observation a short while, then, failing improvement, transfer
to a psychopathic institution. The house doctor who is the
subject of the patient's hallucination has been kept from her
presence. Dr. Rountree is given permission to take the patient
out in his car when the weather permits.

Diary of Marion Wheaton, November 29, 10 p.m.

I AM keeping this small notebook always in the pocket of my
dressing-gown now. I have a feeling that it may some day furnish important evidence—perhaps after I have been locked up
in an insane asylum, or perhaps after I am dead. The latter seems
to be most likely. More and more as the moments pass, I feel
that my life while I stay here is hanging by a thread. Removal,
even to the hospital for the insane, would be merciful; I doubt
if I shall live to know that mercy.

This evening Dr. Rountree took me for the ride which was
to have calmed my nerves. Thank God, he at least knows that
my mind is not unhinged. He even talks to me freely of the
things which are supposed to be kept from me—and that goes
far to restore my mental balance and self-confidence.

"I can't understand your feeling about Zingler," he said.
"I find him a likable chap. However—just try again, try still
harder, not to refer to that feeling.

"And I know there's no reason for all this whispering behind your back. Today, for instance—you've heard them talking all day over some new excitement, I know. As a matter of fact, it's leaked out; everyone in the hospital has heard of it. It's this. Those two patients in 19 and 26 have developed leprosy in an unheard-of manner—as though a noxious plant were to strike root in soil where it had not been sown, and to grow to maturity in the passing of a night. An unheard-of change in human tissues!

"However, today's *new* mystery is merely this: the man in 26 has been removed to a leper colony; the woman in 19, however, has—disappeared."

I gave a sudden, startled cry.

"'No—no!" he reassured me, quickly. "Not another murder tragedy—simply and really a disappearance. Her husband seems completely mystified; but somehow, someone has saved her from incarceration, I suppose. A pity too, since leprosy may now often be cured."

I leaned back in my seat. The sea wind was in my face—I felt relaxed for the first time in days. But of course—I couldn't forget the things in both our minds.

"I don't want any horrible details," I said. "But about the—the little baby who was—kidnaped—was there, that time, any clue at all?"

Vincent Rountree nodded. "One clue, pointing to the hypothesis that the maniac may be a religious fanatic," he said shortly. "On a flat part of the roof, a sort of altar——"

I wondered. Would a doctor of medicine be likely to be a religious fanatic? Could I, after all, be wrong?

I felt myself shaking, and he felt it too as his arm touched mine.

"Try to forget!" he urged. "There are, after all, other things—things of beauty. Night—stars—the sea"—his last word was shaped soundlessly rather than spoken; I thought that it was—"you!"

He parked the car near the beach. I am able to walk with

a cane now, and so I took his arm and we walked along the
sand.

God! We walked along the sand!

It was I who saw first, caught against one of the dry rocks of
a jetty above the level of high tide—something. Something—a
hank of white fuzz in the starlight. No, not exactly fuzz. A
hank, grayish white, of something like human hair.

A hank of gray-white hair, roughly or carelessly torn from a
woman's head.

It was Vincent, then, who saw how the sand was tumbled
and rough and uneven, in an irregular patch some six feet long
and two or three feet wide. Six feet by two or three!

Both of us felt that it was necessary—a duty, at least—to
make sure, to investigate—*to find out if there were anything hidden
beneath that oblong of tumbled sand.*

I waited alone at a little distance with my back turned. Vincent came to me very soon. His face was livid in the starlight,
and he looked ill.

"I am a doctor, and I've seen things——" he began. Then he
pulled himself together. "We'll both be called as witnesses of
this, but you must come away. It—was very near the surface.
It—was the woman who had cancer—who had leprosy. Her
disappearance was—not an escape."

Back at the hospital, I was taken directly to my room and
prepared for the night, with the usual sedative—unless, perhaps, they may have strengthened it in view of the experience I
have just passed through. I have written this in bed, and will slip
the book into the handkerchief pocket of the crepe de chine
gown I am wearing.

The hour for "Visitors out" has passed. The hall lights are
out, except the dim light from the far end of the hall and the
nearer, lurid red light that I have always disliked, as though I
knew somehow that *sometime* I was to see by that light a thing
that would terrify me—live through, in its glare, something
more dreadful than all that has come, so far, to me myself. Is

tonight the night? More than ever, I am afraid. That red light! The light of morning shining through the bloodstained skylight over the operating-room on the morning when Rodney Penning lay murdered there, must have been of such a color.

I wish that I could stay awake—tonight of all nights.

I wish by some happy miracle I could know that for this one night that gray figure was outside the hospital walls. Does a house doctor always "sleep in"?

I feel that tonight I *must* keep awake. But can I?

I can not. I—am going . . .

Last entry in Marion Wheaton's hospital diary. Written between midnight and 2 a.m., November 28.

IN THE little time *he* has been gone, I have been praying for mercy. I can not feel that my prayers will be answered. Was there mercy for little Rodney Penning? For the new-born baby taken from the nursery? Was there mercy for the woman who had cancer?

There is a chance that he may overlook the small diary notebook and pencil tucked in the pocket of my nightgown with my handkerchief. In that unlikely event, this will serve as evidence.

I must hurry. At any moment he will return. He is on the roof by the skylight, and I can hear him mumbling—a sort of chant. He *has,* then, a religious mania. But the fiend is—Dr. Zingler.

I waked to find him bending over me, and I waked too late. He crammed a large handkerchief into my mouth before terror had struggled through my stupor. But tonight, he had no hypodermic.

"A large bait—*It* must want a larger sacrifice," he was saying. And his eyes—I swear they were not human, somehow. They were as ruthlessly cruel as the eyes of a serpent.

Pressing the handkerchief down my throat so that I was half

strangled, he dragged me from my bed and carried me down the hall. And Miss Wurt saw us—she passed by the stairs just as he started to mount them, and she saw us, and started back in horror. But she made no move to help me, only shrank away. Nor has she given any alarm, for—God pity me!—I have been strapped to the operating-table by ankles and body for fully half an hour, waiting for his return with that sharp knife he chose before he went out and somehow reached the roof and began puttering about up there—and chanting.

By turns he called me a "bait" and a "sacrifice." Yes, the gray doctor is a fiend—a mad fiend! He will butcher me here, and I shall die trying to scream, with this gag in my mouth; I shall die in agony and terror unspeakable—and he will merely be locked up somewhere afterward.

His voice is rising as he chants. Soon, now———

★   ★   ★   ★   ★

He is worse than a fiend and a maniac. He is in league with supernal powers of evil.

As he chanted, I saw for a little while, through the sky-light—a *Thing*. I can think of no word for it. It seemed to swoop down suddenly, as from a great distance—as though a monster had emerged from the cold abyss between the stars. And it was monster-size, so that I saw only a little part of it— and that was a sort of huge, pulsing projection which seemed to press against the skylight—and in which there was something that might have been either eye or mouth—I believe it to be both. A mouth that sees; an eye that may devour.

The gray doctor must not have expected his celestial visitant quite so soon; for I heard running feet on the roof—and now I hear him outside the door of the operating-room, fumbling with the lock. He had locked it after him. It will take but an instant———

May God—Who surely reigns supreme somewhere beyond

such foul blasphemies as haunt space—have mercy on my soul!

And if this testimony is accepted, do not treat Dr. Zingler as an ordinary maniac. He is——

Excerpt from the testimony of Nurse Wurt, following her confession.

OF COURSE I knew that "the gray doctor" was not Dr. Zingler, though I was on night duty and Dr. Zingler was seldom on the floor at night.

This stranger appeared—I didn't know how. He made love to me. I had never been noticed in that way before. Some women never are. The other nurses had affairs—I never.

I let him frequent my floor against the regulations. When the first crime occurred—I did not believe it was he. A little later, I would not believe it. Still later, I was afraid—afraid of him, and afraid to confess that at such a time I had been allowing the presence on my floor at night of a man utterly unknown to me—to anyone.

When he carried Miss Wheaton up the stairs, I knew—I feared—but I was afraid *then* to cry out.

Statement of Dr. Rountree made before the Hospital Committee of Investigation.

I AM laying before the committee the confession of the Gray Killer, as he has come to be called—or "The Gray Doctor", as Miss Wheaton called him—poor girl, when to peril of her life the hospital authorities saw fit to add the peril of being judged insane. It will be remembered that no confession could be forced from the Killer by the police; that I alone was able to obtain his remarkable statement, spurred by my anxiety to substantiate the statements made in those lines written in Miss Wheaton's diary on the operating-table. Those lines have been called "ravings". And out of the regard I had come to have for

Miss Wheaton while she was a patient here and out of the deep confidence I felt in her judgment, I determined to seek corroboration for those very statements which must naturally appear the most insupportable.

Her confusion of the Killer, whose confession is appended below, with Dr. Zingler, is most natural. She had never seen Dr. Zingler, and after she had encountered and conceived a horror of the Killer, Dr. Zingler was kept from her room. She naturally felt assured that Miss Wurt would have known of the habitual presence of any stranger, and so accepted the Killer's statement as to his identity.

Out of the depths of my anxiety to substantiate Miss Wheaton's story, I have done a difficult thing—approached the Killer in the guise of a friend. I obtained—a confession. And before this confession is judged to be utterly beyond the bounds of possibility, I will ask urgently that two things be explained away—*the feet of the Killer*—*and his manner of cheating the law*.

The Confession

NEVER again shall I return home, and it is all in vain. Nevertheless, easily can I escape the pit into which I have dug my way. There is always the ultimate way out.

Even to me, who can regard all of the race of Earth as so many stupid cattle, the enmity that surrounds me now grows heavy to bear. Also, why should one suffer punishment and death at the hands of inferiors? But before I enter the great oblivion I will give my story to Dr. Rountree, who alone has dealt with me as with a man of knowledge, and not a crazy man whose wits have gone astray.

Know, then, that my home is not upon Earth, but rather on Horil, satellite which circles a sun that burns beyond the narrow limits of this galaxy. Is the planet Earth then unknown to the dwellers of Horil? No, for the astronomers of Horil compare with those of Earth as Earth's greatest astronomer might compare with a child with an opera glass.

On Horil, I was for eleven centuries high priest to the Devil-God of Space. (I approximate terms familiar to men of Earth.) We of Horil believe that a great Power of Good has created all things, and that He is opposed by a lesser Power of Evil. But we worship at no shrine to an Unknown God on Horil—and the Devil-God of Space is very real, and one of the most dreaded of those strange beings that infest the trackless ether.

Its characteristics? As to form of worship, a love of human sacrifice. To many an altar on Horil It has descended, to snatch thence living food.

Its form and nature?

The biologists of Horil are far in advance of those of Earth, as you shall see. Yet even they do not understand the nature of the great denizens of Space. They may breathe ether—they may be forms of vibral energy, and know no need to breathe, being electro-chemical in their nature. But—whether or not the Devil-God breathes—It *eats*.

As to form—here is a coincidence for the philosophers of Earth to ponder, parallel to that phenomenon by which unrelated races of the Earth find for the same things names built on similar phonetic principles. The form of the Devil-God of Horil and of Space resembles that of the monster of the deep which men on Earth have named the devil-fish. Miss Wheaton described truly the appearance of one of its monster tentacles, and she was right in her surmise that the orifice on the end serves both as mouth and eye.

So. My deity was a being of definite power and substance, of knowledge of the far corners of the universe, and of great evil. To Horil It may have been drawn by the psychic nature of our people. We have grown mighty in knowledge while retaining habits common on Earth only to the most primitive races. Cannibalism is practised universally on Horil. The Devil-God loves human sacrifice and the slaying of men and women. Hence the

Devil-God came to haunt the altars of Horil, its temples and the hearts of its men and women. You of Earth would say that evil attracts evil.

And for eleven centuries I was Its high priest. On Horil the only death comes by way of cannibalism, or an occasional suicide, since we have done away with accidental death. Yet, sooner or later, men on Horil die. It is one's turn to furnish food for others, or life grows weary—so does life equalize itself among those who might otherwise become immortal; balancing knowledge and character of destructive traits, perhaps, that the eternal plan of the great Unknown be not thwarted. . . .

But this is not to the point.

At last I offended the Devil-God. I stole from his altar— well, she was beautiful, and the gray pallor of her skin was like the early dawn-light. Love is rare on Horil—but it had me in its grip.

After I had loosed her from the altar we dared not go into the City—she would have been returned to the altar, and I should have furnished a feast for the royal family. We fled into the barren places. And the Devil-God, returning to Its altar, saw us and overtook us in a great, empty, stony field. There *she,* the beloved, was seized and devoured before my eyes. And I——

No such mercy was intended for the faithless high priest of the altar of human sacrifice. I was caught up—gently—in one of the monster tentacles. The wide, barren plain lit by the cold stars fell away beneath me—shrunk to the size of a handker-chief. An entire hemisphere of Horil lay like a saucer holding the sky—then shrank too, and fell away. My senses left me, and the breath of my nostrils. Then——

I was lying in a field on the planet Earth, which I soon rec-ognized by the customs and types of its inhabitants, from my knowledge of schoolroom astronomy. How did I survive the journey through space? Who knows? Ask of the Devil-God, Which has—perhaps—no words for all Its knowledge.

I would not starve—I, an eater of human flesh. But here another thing must be explained. On Horil we prepare human flesh for consumption. Countless centuries ago our epicures evolved a taste for the flesh of leprous persons. Through constant usage, we have come to eat no other flesh—and by some physiological idiosyncrasy, our stomachs became unadapted to other flesh. I can eat nonleprous flesh—but it inflicts on me fearful pangs of nausea.

Our biologists, then, developed a specific which implants a swift-growing culture of leprosy in any flesh into which it is injected—and which at the same time cures and restores all bodily tissues suffering from any other injury. So our health is safe-guarded. And hence the cure of the man in 26, and the woman in 19, who had cancer. Hence the sudden development of leprosy in these patients. For they were to give me needed food.

Hence, the buried and mutilated body in the sand. I was starving, famished.

The sacrifices on the roof altar, on the other hand, were sacrifices of propitiation; but the improvised "fish-hooks"——

I madly hoped to snare the Devil-God I served—as men on Earth of primitive tribes, so I have heard, turn upside down the images of their saints to force them to their bidding. But I dared more—hoping literally to hook the monster with steel barb and cable.

Two sacrifices It scorned.

Driven by hunger, I had prepared my necessary feast. The girl with deep blue eyes that grew sad and terrified as they gazed on me was my first selection. Obedient to a true instinct, however, she shunned me. So I prepared the man and woman for myself—and sacrificed the children.

Then a new thought came to me. My sacrifices had been too small. They should have matched my own necessity. I determined to raise once more an altar on the roof, and to fasten to it the slain body of the girl with the sad terrified eyes.

I crept upon her as she slept at last a sleep so deep that the sense of my nearness failed to rouse her, as it had done before. I gagged her and carried her from her room, half smothering her as her sad eyes implored. Even to me, she was pitifully beautiful; the better to allure the Monster-God of Space.

I conveyed her—as she wrote down—to the operating-room, and strapped her to the table—leaving free her hands, since she had little strength and could not loose herself with her body fastened flat to the table, and I had need to hasten.

I offered up my prayers upon the roof—the prayers I had made before the altars of Horil through eleven centuries.

The Being—the Monster—swooped down out of the "empty" skies—the "empty" skies that teem with the Unseen and the Unknowable.

I hastened back from the roof, to the operating-room. I threw myself, knife in hand, upon the operating-table—

And I was seized from behind!

Miss Wurt at last had dared to give the alarm. No sacrifice was made upon the roof again. And I was taken captive—though soon I shall escape.

Comment by the Superintendent of R—— Hospital, signed before witnesses at the request of Dr. Rountree and Marian Wheaton.

THE "Confession" of the unknown man captured almost in the act of murdering Miss Wheaton upon an operating-table in our hospital is beyond credence.

Nevertheless, I hereby testify to two things. The Killer's entrances and exits were made through unnoticed back windows which were not near stairs or fire escapes. This was possible, because he *scaled* the walls of the building—not climbing them, but *walking up them*. When his shoes were removed, his feet appeared as long segments of the bodies of serpents—and they could grip and scale any kind of wall. His feet, he said, were as the feet of all "human" beings on Horil; and "on Earth" his shoes were made specially, and his feet were coiled within these shoes!

Likewise the manner of his suicide is beyond explanation. He had been searched and was guarded carefully, of course, and he died—simply by holding his breath. No living thing on Earth has been known to do this thing, since at a certain degree of weakness the will is replaced by automatic functions.

To the physiologic norm of no known species of Earth could the Killer conform.

The Black Stone Statue

Mary Elizabeth Counselman

DIRECTORS,
Museum of Fine Arts,
Boston, Mass.

Gentlemen:

Today I have just received aboard the *S. S. Madrigal* your most kind cable, praising my work and asking—humbly, as one might ask it of a true genius!—if I would do a statue of myself to be placed among the great in your illustrious museum. Ah, gentlemen, that cablegram was to me the last turn of the screw!

I despise myself for what I have done in the name of art. Greed for money and acclaim, weariness with poverty and the contempt of my inferiors, hatred for a world that refused to see any merit in my work: these things have driven me to commit a series of strange and terrible crimes.

In these days I have thought often of suicide as a way out—a coward's way, leaving me the fame I do not deserve. But since receiving your cablegram, lauding me for what I am not and never could be, I am determined to write this letter for the world to read. It will explain everything. And having written it, I shall then atone for my sin in (to you, perhaps) a horribly ironic manner but (to me) one that is most fitting.

Let me go back to that miserable sleet-lashed afternoon as I came into the hall of Mrs. Bates's rooming-house—a crawling, filthy hovel for the poverty-stricken, like myself, who were too proud to go on relief. When I stumbled in, drenched and dizzy with hunger, our landlady's ample figure was blocking the hallway. She was arguing with a tall, shabbily dressed young man whose face I was certain I had seen somewhere before.

"Just a week," his deep, pleasant voice was beseeching the old harridan. "I'll pay you double at the end of that time, just as soon as I can put over a deal I have in mind."

I paused, staring at him covertly while I shook the sleet from my hat-brim. Fine gray eyes met mine across the landlady's head—haggard now, and overbright with suppressed excitement. There was strength, character, in that face under its stubble of mahogany-brown beard. There was, too, a firm set to the man's shoulders and beautifully formed head. Here, I told myself, was someone who had lived all his life with dangerous adventure, someone whose clean-cut features, even under that growth of beard, seemed vaguely familiar to my sculptor's-eye for detail.

"Not one day, no sirree!" Mrs. Bates had folded her arms stubbornly. "A week's rent in advance, or ye don't step foot into one o' *my* rooms!"

On impulse I moved forward, digging into my pocket. I smiled at the young man and thrust almost my last two dollars into the landlady's hand. Smirking, she bobbed off and left me alone with the stranger.

"You shouldn't have done that," he sighed, and gripped my hand hard. "Thanks, old man. I'll repay you next week, though. Next week," he whispered, and his eyes took on a glow of anticipation, "I'll write you a check for a thousand dollars. Two thousand!"

He laughed delightedly at my quizzical expression and plunged out into the storm again, whistling.

In that moment his identity struck me like a blow. Paul Kennicott—the young aviator whose picture had been on the front page of every newspaper in the country a few months ago! His plane had crashed somewhere in the Brazilian wilds, and the nation mourned him and his co-pilot for dead. Why was he sneaking back into New York like a criminal—penniless, almost hysterical with excitement, with an air of secrecy about him—to hide himself here in the slum district?

I CLIMBED the rickety stairs to my shabby room and was plying the chisel half-heartedly on my *Dancing Group,* when suddenly I became aware of a peculiar buzzing sound, like an angry bee shut up in a jar. I slapped my ears several times, annoyed, believing the noise to be in my own head. But it kept on, growing louder by the moment.

It seemed to come from the hall; and simultaneously I heard the stair-steps creak just outside my room.

Striding to the door, I jerked it open—to see Paul Kennicott tiptoeing up the stairs in stealthy haste. He started violently at sight of me and attempted to hide under his coat an odd black box he was carrying.

But it was too large: almost two feet square, roughly fashioned of wood and the canvas off an airplane wing. But this was not immediately apparent, for the whole thing seemed to be covered with a coat of shiny black enamel. When it bumped against the balustrade, however, it gave a solid metallic sound, unlike cloth-covered wood. That humming noise, I was sharply aware, came from inside the box.

I stepped out into the hall and stood blocking the passage rather grimly.

"Look here," I snapped, "I know who you are, Kennicott, but I don't know why you're hiding out like this. What's it all about? You'll tell me, or I'll turn you over to the police!"

Panic leaped into his eyes. They pleaded with me silently for an instant, and then we heard the plodding footsteps of Mrs. Bates come upstairs.

"Who's got that raddio?" her querulous voice preceded her. "I hear it hummin'! Get it right out of here if you don't wanta pay me extry for the 'lectricity it's burnin'."

"Oh, ye gods!" Kennicott groaned frantically. "Stall her! Don't let that gabby old fool find out about this—it'll ruin everything! Help me, and I'll tell you the whole story."

He darted past me without waiting for my answer and slammed the door after him. The droning noise subsided and then was swiftly muffled so that it was no longer audible.

Mrs. Bates puffed up the stairs and eyed me accusingly. "So it's you that's got that raddio? I told you the day you come—"

"All right," I said, pretending annoyance. "I've turned it off, and anyhow it goes out tomorrow. I was just keeping it for a friend."

"Eh? Well——" She eyed me sourly, then sniffed and went on back downstairs, muttering under her breath.

I strode to Kennicott's door and rapped softly. A key grated in the lock and I was admitted by my wild-eyed neighbor. On the bed, muffled by pillows, lay the black box humming softly on a shrill note.

"*I n—n n—ng—ng!*" it went, exactly like a radio tuned to a station that is temporarily off the air.

Curiosity was gnawing at my vitals. Impatiently I watched Kennicott striding up and down the little attic room, striking one fist against the other palm.

"Well?" I demanded.

And with obvious reluctance, in a voice jerky with excitement, he began to unfold the secret of the thing inside that onyx-like box. I sat on the bed beside it, my eyes riveted on Kennicott's face, spellbound by what he was saying.

"*Our* plane," he began, "was demolished. We made a forced landing in the center of a dense jungle. If you know Brazil at all, you'll know what it was like. Trees, trees, trees! Crawling insects as big as your fist. A hot sickening smell of rotting vegetation, and now and then the screech of some animal or bird eery enough to make your hair stand on end. We cracked up right in the middle of nowhere.

"I crawled out of the wreckage with only a sprained wrist and a few minor cuts, but McCrea—my co-pilot, you know—got a broken leg and a couple of bashed ribs. He was in a bad way, poor devil! Fat little guy, bald, scared of women, and always cracking wise about something. A swell sport."

The aviator's face convulsed briefly, and he stared at the box on the bed beside me with a peculiar expression of loathing.

"McCrea's dead, then?" I prompted.

Kennicott nodded his head dully, and shrugged. "God only knows! I guess you'd call it death. But let me get on with it.

"We slashed and sweated our way through an almost impenetrable wall of undergrowth for two days, carrying what food and cigarettes we had in that makeshift box there."

A thumb-jerk indicated the square black thing beside me, droning softly without a break on the same high note.

"McCrea was running a fever, though, so we made camp and I struck out to find water. When I came back——"

Kennicott choked. I stared at him, waiting until his hoarse voice went on doggedly:

"When I came back, McCrea was gone. I called and called. No answer. Then, thinking he might have wandered away delirious, I picked out his trail and followed it into the jungle. It wasn't hard to do, because he had to break a path through that wall of undergrowth, and now and then I'd find blood on a bramble or maybe a scrap of torn cloth from his khaki shirt.

"Not more than a hundred yards south of our camp I suddenly became aware of a queer humming sound in my ears. Positive that this had drawn McCrea, I followed it. It got louder and louder, like the drone of a powerful dynamo. It seemed to fill the air and set all the trees to quivering. My teeth were on edge with the monotony of it, but I kept on, and unexpectedly found myself walking into a patch of jungle that was *all black!* Not burnt in a forest fire, as I first thought, but dead-black in every detail. Not a spot of color anywhere; and in that jungle with all its vivid foliage, the effect really slapped you in the face! It was as though somebody had turned out the lights and yet you could still distinguish the formation of every object around you. It was uncanny!

"There was black sand on the ground as far as I could see. Not soft jungle-soil, damp and fertile. This stuff was as hard and dry as emery, and it glittered like soft coal. All the trees were black and shiny like anthracite, and not a leaf stirred anywhere, not an insect crawled. I almost fainted as I realized why.

"It was a petrified forest!

"Those trees, leaves and all, had turned into a shiny black kind of stone that looked like coal but was much harder. It wouldn't chip when I struck it with a fallen limb of the same stuff. It wouldn't bend; I simply had to squeeze through holes in underbrush more rigid than cast iron. And all black, mind you—a jungle of fuliginous rock like something out of Dante's *Inferno*.

"Once I stumbled over an object and stopped to pick it up. It was McCrea's canteen—the only thing in sight, besides myself, that was not made of that queer black stone. He had come this way, then. Relieved, I started shouting his name again, but the sound of my voice frightened me. The silence of that place fairly pressed against my eardrums, broken only by that steady droning sound. But, you see, I'd become so used to it, like the constant ticking of a clock, that I hardly heard it.

"Panic swept over me all at once, an unreasonable fear, as the sound of my own voice banged against the trees and came back in a thousand echoes, borne on that humming sound that never changed its tone. I don't know why; maybe it was the grinding monotony of it and the unrelieved black of that stone forest. But my nerve snapped and I bolted back along the way I had come, sobbing like a kid.

"I must have run in a circle, though, tripping and cutting myself on that rock-underbrush. In my terror I forgot the direction of our camp. I was lost—abruptly I realized it—lost in that hell of coal-black stone, without food or any chance of getting it, with McCrea's empty canteen in my hand and no idea where he had wandered in his fever.

"For hours I plunged on, forgetting to back-track, and cursing aloud because McCrea wouldn't answer me. That humming noise had got on my nerves now, droning on that one shrill note until I thought I would go mad. Exhausted, I sank down on that emery-sand, crouched against the trunk of a black stone tree. McCrea had deserted me, I thought crazily. Someone had rescued him and he had left me here to die— which should give you an idea of my state of mind.

"I huddled there, letting my eyes rove in a sort of helpless stupor. On the sand beside me was a tiny rock that resembled a butterfly delicately carved out of onyx. I picked it up dazedly, staring at its hard little legs and feelers like wire that would neither bend nor break off. And then my gaze started wandering again.

"It fastened on something a few dozen paces to my right:— and I was sure then that I had gone mad. At first it seemed to be a stump of that same dark mineral. But it wasn't a stump. I crawled over to it and sat there, gaping at it with my senses reeling, while that humming noise rang louder and louder in my ears.

It was a black stone statue of McCrea, perfect in every detail!

"He was depicted stooping over, with one hand holding out his automatic gripped by the barrel. His stocky figure, aviator's helmet, his makeshift crutch, and even the splints on his broken leg were shiny black stone. And his face, to the last hair of his eyelashes, was a perfect mask of black rock set in an expression of puzzled curiosity.

"I GOT to my feet and walked around the figure, then gave it a push. It toppled over, just like a statue, and the sound of its fall was deafening in that silent forest. Hefting it, I was amazed to find that it weighed less than twenty pounds. I hacked at it with a file we had brought from the plane in lieu of a machete, but only succeeded in snapping the tool in half. Not a chip flew off the statue. Not a dent appeared in its polished surface.

"The thing was so unspeakably weird that I did not even try to explain it to myself, but started calling McCrea again. If it was a gag of some kind, he could explain it. But there was no answer to my shouts other than the monotonous hum of that unseen dynamo.

"Instead of frightening me more, this weird discovery seemed to jerk me up short. Collecting my scattered wits, I started back-trailing myself to the camp, thinking McCrea might have returned in my absence. The droning noise was so loud now, it pained my eardrums unless I kept my hands over my ears. This I did, stumbling along with my eyes glued to my own footprints in the hard dry sand.

"And suddenly I brought up short. Directly ahead of me, under a black stone bush, lay something that made me gape with my mouth ajar.

"I can't describe it—no one could. It resembled nothing so much as a star-shaped blob of transparent jelly that shimmered and changed color like an opal. It appeared to be some lower form of animal, one-celled, not large, only about a foot in circumference when it stretched those feelers out to full length. It oozed along over the sand like a snail, groping its way with those star-points—*and it hummed!*

"The droning noise ringing in my ears issued from this nightmare creature!

"It was nauseating to watch, and yet beautiful, too, with all those iridescent colors gleaming against that setting of dead-black stone. I approached within a pace of it, started to nudge it with my foot, but couldn't quite bring myself to touch the squashy thing. And I've thanked my stars ever since for being so squeamish!

"Instead, I took off my flying-helmet and tossed the goggles directly in the path of the creature. It did not pause or turn aside, but merely reached out one of those sickening feelers and brushed the goggles very lightly.

"*And they turned to stone!*

"Just that! God be my witness that those leather and glass goggles grew black before my starting eyes. In less than a minute they were petrified into hard fuliginous rock like everything else around me.

"In one hideous moment I realized the meaning of that weirdly life-like statue of McCrea. I knew what he had done. He had prodded this jelly-like Thing with his automatic, and it had turned him—and everything in contact with him—into shiny dark stone.

"Nausea overcame me. I wanted to run, to escape the sight of that oozing horror, but reason came to my rescue. I reminded myself that I was Paul Kennicott, intrepid explorer. Through a horrible experience McCrea and I had stumbled upon something in the Brazilian wilds which would revolutionize the civilized world. McCrea was dead, or in some ghastly suspended form of life, through his efforts to solve the mystery. I owed it to him and to myself not to lose my head now.

"For the practical possibilities of the Thing struck me like a blow. That black stone the creature's touch created from any earth-substance—by rays from its body, by a secretion of its glands, by God knows what strange metamorphosis—was indestructible! Bridges, houses, buildings, roads, could be built of ordinary material and then petrified by the touch of this jelly-like Thing which had surely tumbled from some planet with life-forces diametrically opposed to our own.

"Millions of dollars squandered on construction each year could be diverted to other phases of life, for no cyclone or flood could damage a city built of this hard black rock.

"I said a little prayer for my martyred co-pilot, and then and there resolved to take the creature back to civilization with me.

"It could be trapped, I was sure—though the prospect appealed to me far less than that of caging a hungry leopard! I did not venture to try it until I had studied the problem from every angle, however, and made certain deductions through experiment.

"I found that any substance already petrified was insulated against the thing's power. I tossed my belt on it, saw it freeze into black rock, then put my wrist-watch in contact with the rock belt. My watch remained as it was. Another phenomenon I discovered was that petrifaction also occurred in things in *direct contact* with something the creature touched, if that something was not already petrified.

"Dropping my glove fastened to my signet ring, I let the creature touch only the glove. But both objects were petrified. I tried it again with a chain of three objects, and discovered that the touched object and the one in contact with it turned into black rock, while the third on the chain remained unaffected.

"It took me about three days to trap the thing, although it gave no more actual resistance, of course, than a large snail. McCrea, poor devil, had blundered into the business; but I went at it in a scientific manner, knowing what danger I faced from the creature. I found my way again to our camp and brought back our provision box—yes, the one there on the bed beside you. When the thing's touch had turned it into a perfect stone cage for itself, I scooped it inside with petrified branches. But, Lord! How the sweat stood out on my face at the prospect of a slip that might make me touch the horrible little organism!

"The trip out of that jungle was a nightmare. I spent almost all I had, hiring scared natives to guide me a mile or so before they'd bolt with terror of my humming box. On board a tramp steamer bound for the States, I nearly lost my captive. The first mate thought it was an infernal machine and tried to throw it overboard. My last cent went to shut him up; so I landed in New York flat broke."

Paul Kennicott laughed and spread his hands. "But here I

am. I don't dare go to anyone I know just yet. Reporters will run me ragged, and I want plenty of time to make the right contacts. Do you realize what's in that box?" He grinned with boyish delight. "Fame and fortune, that's what! McCrea's family will never know want again. Science will remember our names along with Edison and Bell and all the rest. We've discovered a new force that will rock the world with its possibilities. That's why," he explained, "I've sneaked into the country like an alien. If the wrong people heard of this first, my life wouldn't be worth a dime, understand? There are millions involved in this thing. Billions! Don't you see?"

He stopped, eyeing me anxiously. I stared at him and rose slowly from the bed. Thoughts were seething in my mind—dark ugly thoughts, ebbing and flowing to the sound of that *"i—n n—n n g—n n g!"* that filled the shabby room.

For I did see the possibilities of that jelly-like thing's power to turn any object into black stone. But I was thinking as a sculptor. What do I care for roads or buildings? Sculpture is my whole life! To my mind's eye rose the picture of copilot McCrea as Kennicott had described him—a figure, perfect to the last detail, done in black stone.

Kennicott was still eyeing me anxiously—perhaps reading the ugly thoughts that flitted like shadows behind my eyes.

"You'll keep mum?" he begged. "Do that for me, old boy, and I'll set you up in a studio beyond your wildest dreams. I'll build up your fame as—what are you?"

His gray eyes fastened on my dirty smock.

"Some kind of an artist? I'll show you how much I appreciate your help. Are you with me?"

Some kind of an artist! Perhaps if he had not said that, flaying my crushed pride and ambition to the quick, I would never have done the awful thing I did. But black jealousy rose in my soul—jealousy of this eager young man who could walk out into the streets now with his achievement and make the world bow at his feet, while I in my own field was no more to the public than what he had called me: "some kind of an artist." At that moment I knew precisely what I wanted to do.

I did not meet his frank gray eyes. Instead, I pinned my gaze on that droning black box as my voice rasped harshly:

"No! Do you really imagine that I believe this idiotic story of yours? You're insane! I'm going to call the police—they'll find out what really happened to McCrea out there in the jungle! There's nothing in that box. It's just a trick."

Kennicott's mouth fell open, then closed in an angry line. The next moment he shrugged and laughed.

"Of course you don't believe me," he nodded. "Who could?—unless they had seen what I've seen with my own eyes. Here," he said briskly, "I'll take this book and drop it in the box for you. You'll see the creature, and you'll see this book turned into black stone."

I stepped back, heart pounding, eyes narrowed. Kennicott leaned over the bed, unfastened the box gingerly with a wary expression on his face, and motioned me to approach. Briefly I glanced over his shoulder as he dropped the book inside the open box.

I saw horror—a jelly-like, opalescent thing like a five-pointed star. It pulsed and quivered for an instant, and the room fairly rocked to the unmuffled sound of that vibrant humming.

I also saw the small cloth-bound book Kennicott had dropped inside. It lay half on top of the squirming creature—a book carved out of black stone.

"There! You see?" Kennicott pointed. And those were the last words he ever uttered.

Remembering what he had said about the power of the creature being unable to penetrate to a third object, I snatched at Kennicott's sleeve-covered arm, gave him a violent shove, and saw his muscular hand plunge for an instant deep into the black box. The sleeve hardened beneath my fingers.

I cowered back, sickened at what I had done.

Paul Kennicott, his arms thrown out and horror stamped

on his fine young face, had frozen into a statue of black shiny stone!

Then footsteps were clumping up the stairs again. I realized that Mrs. Bates would surely have heard the violent droning that issued from the open box. I shut it swiftly, muffled it, and shoved it under the bed.

I was at my own doorway when the landlady came puffing up the stairs. My face was calm, my voice contained, and no one but me could hear the furious pounding of my heart.

"Now, you look a-here!" Mrs. Bates burst out. "I told you to turn that raddio off. You take it right out of my room this minute! Runnin' up my bill for 'lectricity!"

I apologized meekly and with a great show carried out a tool-case of mine, saying it was the portable radio I had been testing for a friend. It satisfied her for the moment, but later, as I was carrying the black stone figure of Paul Kennicott to my own room, she caught me at it.

"Why," the old snoop exclaimed. "If that ain't the spittin' image of our new roomer! Friend of yours, is he?"

I thought swiftly and lied jauntily. "A model of mine. I've been working on this statue at night, the reason you haven't seen him going in and out. I thought I would have to rent a room for him here, but as the statue is finished now, it won't be necessary after all. You may keep the rent money, though," I added. "And get me a taxi to haul my masterpiece to the express station. I am ready to submit it to the Museum of Fine Arts."

And that is my story, gentlemen. The black stone statue which, ironically, I chose to call *Fear of the Unknown,* is not a product of my skill. (Small wonder several people have noticed its resemblance to the "lost explorer," Paul Kennicott!) Nor did I do the group of soldiers commissioned by the Anti-War Association. None of my so-called *Symphonies in Black* were wrought by my hand—but I can tell you what became of the models who were unfortunate enough to pose for me!

My real work is perhaps no better than that of a rank novice, although up to that fatal afternoon I had honestly believed myself capable of great work as a sculptor some day.

But I am an impostor. You want a statue of me, you say in your cablegram, done in the mysterious black stone which has made me so famous? Ah, gentlemen, you shall have that statue!

I am writing this confession aboard the *S. S. Madrigal,* and I shall leave it with a steward to be mailed to you at our next port of call.

Tonight I shall take out of my stateroom the hideous thing in its black box which has never left my side. Such a creature, contrary to all nature on this earth of ours, should be exterminated. As soon as darkness falls I shall stand on deck and balance the box on the rail so that it will fall into the sea after my hand has touched what is inside.

I wonder if the process of being turned into that black rock is painful, or if it is accompanied only by a feeling of lethargy? And McCrea, Paul Kennicott, and those unfortunate models whom I have passed off as "my work"—are they dead, as we know death, or are their statues sentient and possessed of nerves? How does that jelly creature feel to the touch? Does it impart a violent electrical shock or a subtle emanation of some force beyond our ken, changing the atom-structure of the flesh it turns into stone?

Many such questions have occurred to me often in the small hours when I lie awake, tortured by remorse for what I have done.

But tonight, gentlemen, I shall know all the answers.

The Web of Silence

Mary Elizabeth Counselman

THE thing was supposed to have started around noon, April the 11th. As a matter of scientific record, that is when it did start.

But to Jeff Haverty, editor of the *News,* to Mayor Tom Seeley, and the little valley town of Blankville (which name will serve in lieu of the real one), there was a prelude. It came a full week before the eleventh, April the 3rd to be exact, when Mayor Seeley waved away his breakfast orange and opened the first letter in his stack of morning mail.

The shape of it caught his attention at once, as the sender doubtless intended. An odd-looking letter, it was only a single sheet of paper written on one side, folded into a three-cornered envelope, and sealed with the stamp. The handwriting was angular and had, as the mayor remarked, a slightly foreign aspect, as if the writer were more accustomed to the script of another language.

Scrupulously formal and precise, it might have been any ordinary business letter, except for its triangular envelope— and its outrageous content:

Mayor Thomas Seeley
Covington Arms
Blankville,—

Dear Sir:—
    Please oblige me by placing two hundred and fifty thousand dollars ($250,000) *in new twenties and fifties in an ordinary oil-can painted*

a bright yellow. Drop this can, sealed with paraffin and containing the correct amount, from the river bridge facing upstream, no later than April 10th at midnight.

In the event that you choose to regard this as an idle threat and refuse to comply with my request, I must warn you that the entire city of Blankville will straightway find itself in the grip of an unusual phenomenon.

Business, educational and civic affairs will be brought to a standstill—at a cost to your charming city somewhat in excess of the amount mentioned above. Ordinary living will be paralyzed completely. Accidents, painful and perhaps fatal, will undoubtedly occur to many of your populace.

I trust that these measures will not be forced upon me by your refusal to comply with my request. It would be most unwise, I assure you.

Very truly yours,
"DR. UBIQUE."

There was no other signature, simply "Doctor Everywhere;" and the postmark was a local one.

But Mayor Seeley, like every public figure great or small, had received dozens of crank-letters in his career. At a glance, this was merely another one of those. The vague threat, the demand for money, the melodramatic signature—all were characteristic. With a snort Blankville's mayor tossed it aside and opened his next letter.

That same day, April the 3rd, Jeff Haverty received a similar note, mentioning the demand from Mayor Seeley and urging him to publicize the matter. Haverty read it with a brief grin, he passed it on to one of his staff as a possible feature story, and promptly forgot it.

That was the real beginning—but it was not until a week later, that memorable Sunday of April the 11th, that either of the two men realized it.

SUNDAY. About twenty minutes to twelve.

It was a pleasant spring day, clear and a bit over-warm due to

an unseasonable dry spell. Blankville—with its 30,000 inhabitants, two movies, six drug stores, and four public schools—is
a religious town. Approximately two-thirds of its population,
therefore, was in church that Sabbath morning in late spring.
What happened in Jeff Haverty's church, as he describes it, was
in fine what was happening all over town.

Haverty himself, he confides, was dozing a bit in his
family pew, lulled by the soporific boom of the sermon. He
had a headache—as, it developed later, had every person in
Blankville that morning—just a dull throbbing, not worthy of
comment, which had been bothering him ever since he got up.
It was pleasant to sit there in church, listening to the rise and fall
of the pastor's voice. A clear voice, vibrant and oratorical. . . .

It was the abrupt cessation of it, Haverty says, which woke
him with a start.

Blinking, he looked toward the pulpit and fumbled for his
hymnal, believing the sermon was over. But suddenly he saw
that the Reverend Doctor Hobbs had stopped talking in the
middle of a sentence. Even now his lips still moved, but no
words came out.

The pastor stood for a moment, flushed with embarrassment
and clutching at his neck. Then, with an apologetic grin at
his congregation, he gestured for the presiding elder to take
over—by signs indicating that something was the matter with
his larynx.

The elder, bald-headed and pompous, bustled forward,
thumbing the pages of a hymn-book. Nodding for the organist
to start the next hymn scheduled, he stepped up on the dais to
announce the page and title. Beaming, hand raised for attention, he opened his mouth . . . opened it—and shut it slowly.
Color rose to his round face as he, too, clutched at his throat—
with a wild look at the pastor, who was eyeing this exhibition
of mimicry without amusement.

The choir rose. The organist, struggling with a desire to
giggle, bore down on her keys. But no sound issued from the

instrument—no sound from the open mouths of the choir who gaped at each other, blank-faced with astonishment and growing alarm.

By this time pandemonium had swept over the members of the congregation, who were discovering things for themselves.

An old lady leaped to her feet, dropping an umbrella—but no clatter accompanied its fall to the floor. A child in its mother's lap, sensing a disturbance it could not understand, opened its mouth in a lusty wail—inaudible even to the mother who, frightened, clutched the baby to her breast. Everywhere people were opening and closing their mouths like stranded fish. Cupped ears strained to catch even the faintest reassuring sound.

In a panic, now, the congregation made a concerted rush for the exits, driven by a feeling of claustrophobia that sudden quiet often induces.

But outside it was worse.

A tomb-like silence had fallen over Blankville. Nowhere was there so much as in echo of sound to alleviate the painful stillness.

After that first surge of panic, however, Haverty says, people began to grin and gesture at one another. Young Ralston, the bank teller, nudged him as he stood in front of the church, and passed a note scribbled hastily on an old envelope.

What's causing it? Ralston had written.

Damned if I know!!! Haverty scrawled in answer. *Certainly is spooky, isn't it?*

Sure is! Wonder how long it will last? the teller wrote.

Haverty held up five fingers, then ten. He shrugged, grinned. The teller nodded agreement, and strolled away to his parked car. Haverty, chuckling at the gyrations of everyone he met, made a bee-line for his newspaper office, composing mental headlines as he went.

STROLLING through the streets of Blankville must have been like stepping, alive, into a silent movie. Cars thundered by, as quiet as shadows. Dogs barked, without making a whisper of noise. Children yelled and shouted at one another, whistled, clapped their hands—but they might have been figures in a dream. There was an eery, unreal quality about the familiar streets, Haverty says. It grew oppressive as the expected "five-or-ten-minute" hush lengthened like the held breath of a scared diver. It made you want to loosen your collar and gulp in a lungful of fresh air. It pressed against your face like a soft pillow, deadly, insidious, something you could not fight.

As he reached the *News* building, Haverty was composing an editorial in which the horrors of Devil's Island and solitary confinement formed a keynote. It was borne upon him that weird Sunday, he says, why men have gone mad under the weight of mere silence.

He had unlocked the office door before realizing, with a curse, that he could not summon his staff by telephone. When they did turn up (they would eventually, to cover such a story), the extra he planned would have to be got out by sign language and written direction and leg-work. An extra? If it went to press by the next day, it would require all manner of ingenuity!

Haverty fumed. And only then did he recall that tri-cornered letter with its polite demand and its mysterious warning. His face must have been a study as he stood there, key in hand, gazing up and down a busy traffic-tangled street more silent than the inside of a pyramid. "An unusual phenomenon . . . ordinary living paralyzed," phrases recurred to him. . . .

Haverty snorted, without sound. It was fantastic, absolutely incredible. No; that crank-letter had no connection with this eery silence. It was nothing more than a coincidence, and the people of Blankville, he decided, must not be further frightened by such an idea.

Stubbornly, then and there, he dismissed the sinister possibility and went about the lunatic business of getting out an extra with a deaf and dumb staff.

IT WAS on the streets by nightfall—a feat that speaks well for Haverty's resourcefulness. For it must have been a prodigious job getting that story together without the use of phones, with the reporters running helter-skelter all over the little city out of touch with the rewrite man, and with the office staff unable to exchange the slightest remark unless they wrote it down.

It was Haverty's idea, too, that the newsboys carry torches and large printed banners, in lieu of yelling:

"Extra! Extra! All about the Weird Silence!"

And those papers were a sell-out. The first page was given over to probable explanations of the bizarre phenomenon.

"Atmospheric disturbances are causing the destruction of sound waves in this valley"—advanced by a local know-it-all who had an answer to every question.

"Result of falling meteors," declared another—someone having found a hot meteorite in a cornfield outside the town.

"A change in the earth's speed of revolution is causing sound to operate on a frequency not attuned to the human ear. It will not last overnight!" from the local radio-station manager, frantic at the prospect of losing hundreds of dollars worth of advertising.

For radios were reduced to the value of cumbersome furniture in Blankville. Telephones were useless. The fact—stumbled upon by a switchboard girl—that Blankville voices could be heard over wire and wireless by persons outside the valley, only maddened everyone all the more, adding to the unsolved riddle. However, as everyone agreed, it could not last.

But it did last. At dawn the next day, the town of Blankville was still in the grip of that dead silence. More stories trickled in and were duly passed around, via the *News*.

On Maple Street a small child had been locked in a closet for sixteen hours, unable to make its frantic parents hear its knocks and cries.

On Argyle Circle, a visiting prima donna, practising her scales that memorable Sunday morning, had fainted dead away when her famous voice went silent in the middle of a high C.

At the intersection of Fifth and Chestnut Streets, a man on a bicycle was killed by a truck whose warning horn could not be heard as it sped out of a side street.

An illiterate Negro worker was arrested Sunday night for stealing and torturing a pedigreed dog—which, he was finally able to convey by drawing a crude picture on the jail wall, he had merely found injured in an alley and was trying to return to its owner.

At the Blankville fire station, eight firemen, in silent concentration over a game of checkers, could not hear a box signal set off at the corner of Eighth and Shadowlawn—a duplex garage, which burnt to the ground in the silent dawn of Monday the 12th.

There was, too, the newly-wed couple, quarreling heatedly in their bungalow on Beech Street—so frightened by the abrupt cessation of both their voices that they fell into each other's arms, terrified into forgiveness.

And there was the story from Mercy Hospital: at noon Sunday a surgeon in the midst of a mastoid operation called twice for an instrument which the sterile nurse, of course, did not hand him, unable to hear or see his lips move under the gauze mask. Perspiring, snatching at it himself, the surgeon dropped it on the floor—a delay that almost cost the patient's life.

These were incidents, and relatively unimportant. But by Monday noon, with the weird silence still crouching over Blankville, Haverty began to realize its growing power.

All the stores, except the serve-yourself ones, were closed. There was a rush sale of paper and pencils, but very little else, it being too difficult to make the clerks understand what one wanted.

At the courthouse and city hall, all trials and public meetings were canceled. The three theatres were closed; no one cared to see a movie without sound to make it intelligible. All civic club

meetings were postponed, indefinitely, because no one knew
how long the silence would last. Schools, too, were closed;
and the children who were Scouts were much in demand as
instructors in code and semaphore. It was indeed exactly as
that tri-cornered note had said it would be: the whole process
of normal living, for 30,000 bewildered people, had to be re-
adjusted as completely as though the town of Blankville had
been whisked away and set down on another planet.

Tourists began to pour in by Monday noon. These—with
the steady stream of Blankville natives who went hourly
beyond the "sound limit" for the sheer pleasure of hearing
noise again—made life a nightmare for the highway patrol. For,
outside the valley, noises went on as usual. Passing back and
forth across the "silence boundary" gave one a sharp headache,
it was noted; but no one could offer a plausible reason why.

Inside the valley, within a radius of some five miles, quiet
rested like a pall over everything. Silence that pressed down like
a tangible force, smothering, nerve-racking, had the town by
the throat. Like a helpless fly, Blankville was caught in a spider
web of utter stillness from which there was no escape.

MONDAY passed. Tuesday. And then, Wednesday morning,
Mayor Seeley received another three-cornered letter.

There it was in his morning mail, dated April the 14th, post-
marked locally like the first—and equally polite, detached, and
outrageous:

Dear Sir:—

*I trust you are convinced by this time that the first letter to you was
not an idle threat. The price remains the same, $250,000, to be sealed in
a yellow oil-can and thrown from the river bridge, facing upstream, at
midnight as directed. Any deviation from these directions will inconvenience me, so I beg you to comply in detail.*

*A copy of this letter will be sent to the editor of your local newspaper.
If he does not make it public, I shall use other methods. When the good*

inhabitants of Blankville hear of your failure to protect their interests, I hesitate to predict your political future.

Borrow the above-mentioned sum at once as a civic loan, and pay it back by bond issue, donation, or sales tax. That is no concern of mine. But $250,000 is a mere pittance compared with what your merchants, lawyers, theatre managers, etc., have already lost. And let me assure you that the phenomenon will remain as it is until you comply with my request. . . .

Very truly yours,

"Dr. Ubique."

Mayor Seeley reread the letter and, mopping his florid brow, sent post-haste for Jeff Haverty—who had indeed received a similar note, and was frowning over it with a growing wonder.

One can imagine that conference: two wordy, excitable men, accustomed to yelling orders, closeted together in the mayor's inner sanctum without any means of verbal communication. Their pencils must have scratched frantically. Notes flew back and forth like snowflakes.

And that night, the whole Blankville police force, assisted by the National Guard and the highway patrol, threw a secret cordon around the entire city. They were looking, it leaked out, for an infernal machine of some sort. Several arrests were made. One young man, experimenting with television in the cellar of his home, spent a bad four hours of explaining at headquarters, in a little room reserved for such matters. But nothing else was found.

That same evening the *News* came out with a four-column cut of the two letters received by Mayor Seeley. The accompanying article, written by Haverty himself, was light and amused at the idea of a "mad scientist" hidden in their midst. But there was an undercurrent of gravity in the article, presenting the problem squarely to the harassed citizens of a town of silence.

Were they, in truth, the victims of a fantastic extortion plot?

After all, as Haverty pointed out, no one else had predicted any "unusual phenomenon" for April the 11th. If the letters had been written *after* the silence began, it might have been the work of a nervy opportunist. But that first letter had threatened them with a paralysis of normal living a full week in advance. And the threat had been weirdly carried out. No one could deny that.

THE inhabitants of Blankville read those pictured letters with growing awe. Nerves drawn taut by the strain under which they were living, they seized on this new explanation with excitement not unmixed with terror.

A madman in their midst! A clever, ruthless extortioner who, by some uncanny means, had destroyed all sound in their busy valley—as effective a monkey-wrench as was ever thrown into the machinery of an average American town!

"Doctor Everywhere!" The name was on every tongue— with various attempts at the Latin "Ubique." It was sinister, melodramatic. It caught at the imagination, and caused prickles of fear to run up and down the spine. Doors were locked. Children were not allowed out after dark. The police station was flooded with messages that a prowler had been seen lurking in alleys all over town. Every stranger was a suspect.

For, what was the monster like? Was he gaunt and cadaverous, like Dracula? Fat and suavely cold-blooded? Or, as some suggested, could "Doctor Ubique" possibly be a woman? Was he a stranger, or someone they all knew and trusted?

His mysterious power of silence caused even more conjecture. How did he cause it? Chemicals? Electricity? A ray-gun of some kind, its projector located far from the city that was his prey? Everyone had a different opinion; anyone could be right, for no one knew.

And the net of silence tightened unbearably with the added idea that it was man-made and therefore could be stopped . . . for a price.

Thursday morning, letters began to pour into the *News*

office. At last a delegation called upon Mayor Tom Seeley, perspiring and ill at ease without the glib oratory of his profession.
Sternly he was rebuked—in the written proclamation handed
him by the silent foreman—for keeping that first threat-letter
a secret. And, flatly, he was ordered to act, and act in a hurry.

Pay the ransom: that was the opinion of an overwhelming
majority. If the weird silence continued, said the proclamation,
Blankville would become in truth the ghost-town it seemed.
For everyone was deciding to move out of the eery little valley
Property was one thing. Living in ghostly quiet, day in, day
out, and rearing one's children to be deaf-mutes: that was
something else. Besides, it was costing everyone a fortune to
carry on work in such an unnatural manner. A few businesses,
which depended entirely on sound, would be ruined.

The silence, said Blankville, must go—or they would. And
if the release could be effected by the payment of a quarter-
million dollars, it must be done at once. At any rate, there was
no harm in trying—to which even the cautious Mayor Seeley
agreed.

And so, Thursday night, April the 15th, was chosen. The
Farmer's Trust and the First National banks combined to make
the loan, in new twenties and fifties. And every filling-station
proprietor in Blankville importantly came forward with an
oil-drum painted a brilliant yellow to be used as the sealed container.

THURSDAY night. Four days after the silence first occurred.
Four of the strangest days an ordinary American town ever
spent.

Thursday night. Everyone was ordered to stay indoors
during the hour agreed upon. And so, at eleven-thirty, everyone turned out in a body to watch Mayor Seeley stand on the
Municipal Bridge that joined west and east Blankville, staring
down at the dark river below. Authorities blustered, herded,
shooed, perspired—but they might have known they could

not keep Blankville in bed while their civic leader handed over a small fortune to a shadowy figure who, even now, moved among them at will.

The population turned out in full force, lining up along the river banks and peering over one another's heads with a kind of shivery enjoyment. It was like a parade or a dedication, except that in all that milling, shoving crowd there was not a whisper of sound. No cheering. No whistling. No shuffle of feet or murmur of many voices. Like a congregation of ghosts, visible now and then as lightning flickered over the cloudy sky, they stared up at the cement bridge, white against the darkness. Blocked off by uniformed police at either end, it spanned the river. In its center, with two uniformed men carrying the yellow can, Mayor Seeley peered over the railing and waved solemnly.

By the dim light of the clouded moon, he balanced the yellow can, its precious contents sealed inside, on the rail for a moment. It must have been impressive, that soundless pantomime. Haverty—who was one of that eagerly watching crowd—says he will never forget it. A can containing a quarter-million dollars, being dropped into the swirling current of a muddy river, and from there to . . . where? No one could dive into a river, in plain sight of 30,000 people, and drag out a heavy cumbersome object like a weighted oil-can! Suppose it sank, bedded deep in river ooze where no one could find it. . . .

Mayor Seeley waved. Then, solemnly, he gave the balanced can a shove. It fell with a silent splash, went under, stayed under.

Everyone stared, spell-bound, for twenty-odd minutes, watching the ripples spread out from the spot where it fell. Bridge lights shimmered on the widening circles. Lightning, flickering across the sky, lighted each wondering face. A few drops of rain spattered down, unnoticed.

There was nothing to see; no hand clad in white samite which reached up out of the water, brandishing a handful of currency, as Haverty remarked. Nothing but silence, dense and oppressive, as the rain—the first in several weeks—pelted down upon that tense deaf-mute throng, drenched but still unwilling to leave and seek shelter from the downpour.

And then . . . someone coughed. An *audible* cough.

For a full minute the significance of it did not strike those who heard. Then, like a cackling of geese, voices suddenly broke into an excited babble. A cheer went up, deafening and full of pent-up nerves.

"He's done it! He's taken it away!" everyone was yelling. "The silence is gone!"

A wave of sound rose, the impact of it battering against ears so long attuned to stillness. As mysteriously as it had come, the web of silence was lifted, and Blankville was once more a busy ordinary little American city—minus a quarter-million of its capital. "Doctor Ubique" had fulfilled his weird contract to the letter, and now his fee lay somewhere at the bottom of the river. No hidden boat shot out to retrieve it. No supernatural force parted the waters to reveal its hiding-place. Shivering there in the rainy darkness, the people of Blankville wavered between comfort and a gnawing curiosity.

"Where is he?" awed murmurs ebbed and flowed about Haverty.

"Why doesn't he get it? Afraid he'll be caught in the act, eh?"

"How can he get it? It's sunk now. He'll have to drag the river for it. . . ."

"Maybe they've caught him already. . . ."

And then someone shouted. Other voices took up the cry. Fingers pointed. Those in back jostled those along the bank, craning their necks to see. A hundred flashlights trained their beams on the river, where something yellow and cylindrical was bobbing along heavily on the current.

"The can! It's the money! Get it! Go get it, somebody!" shouts rose in chorus.

Before anyone else could make a move, two uniformed

police, in an outboard motor concealed and ready for such an emergency, shot out into midstream and towed the floating object ashore. The yellow oil-can it was, sealed tight with paraffin. People crowded close, ordered back by the police, as the top was pried loose. Then, as the heavy container was upended, a murmur of awe swept over the throng.

For the yellow can was empty, quite empty, save for a single copper penny that rattled and rolled on the bottom.

THAT was all Haverty was waiting for.

Juggling mental headlines, he elbowed his way through the crowd, making another bee-line for his newspaper. His staff was waiting, with the story half written, when he reached the *News* office. Silence that had cloaked the big news room for four strange days was replaced by the familiar click of typewriter and teletype.

He had been seated at his desk, scrawling headlines, for perhaps ten minutes when his phone rang. It was Mayor Seeley, phoning en route home from his ceremony on the bridge. The plump mayor sounded furious and ineffectual.

"Jeff," he growled, "they'll want my scalp for this. A quarter of a million dollars, gone ... where? I wish I had that—that fellow by the neck, whoever he is! A wholesale hold-up, think of it! I was so sure we'd catch him when he—I'll have somebody's badge for this!" He calmed down with an effort, adding wearily: "Come over to my office. You can swing public opinion my way; make them see I was helpless in the hands of this—this lunatic, this scientific bandit!"

Haverty drove to the courthouse in record time—blowing his horn at intervals, he admits sheepishly, for the sheer pleasure of hearing noise again. Mayor Seeley was waiting for him on the steps, mopping the rain from his face and muttering under his breath. Their footsteps echoed hollowly as they strode down the hall, and Seeley fumbled for the key to his office.

"There's this about it," the mayor growled. "If this Doctor

Ubique, as he calls himself, can do it once, he'll do it again! What town will be his next victim?"

"Yes," Haverty was saying with a scowl of gravity. "A weapon like that, wielded against an entire town! It's far and away the boldest extortion plot I ever——"

Under Seeley's hand the light clicked on—and whatever Haverty was going to say hung suspended in midair. The *News* editor's mouth hung open.

There on his desk, muddy and dripping with river slime, sat a yellow oil-can sealed with paraffin, an exact duplicate of the one hauled from the river by the two police.

Haverty leaped forward. But he knew, somehow, before he pried open the lid that it contained $250,000 in new twenties and fifties. They were all there, carefully wrapped in a rubber bag where Seeley had put them in case the sealed top leaked.

And beside the yellow oil-can lay a tri-cornered letter, unstamped, addressed merely: *"To Whom It May Concern."*

Without a word, Jeff Haverty ripped open that letter and read it aloud, his voice echoing eerily in the quiet building:

To Whom It May Concern:

I hope the good people of Blankville will forgive my little whimsy at their expense. Truly I had no wish to harm or to inconvenience anyone, and certainly not to rob them of their honest gain.

I am a scientist, an astronomer of some note in my own country (which is, I may add, halfway across the world from your charming city, in case you have any plans for legal reprisal). In my private observatory, somewhat larger than the largest now in public use, I study the heavenly bodies and make certain calculations which I shall publicize at my death.

These calculations, based on years of research, led to my discovery of an interesting new star in the constellation Aquila—a nova gaining in brightness, due to some internal outburst of which I have not been able to determine the cause. Its increase in brightness over a four-day interval promised to be about 60,000 fold.

Quite by accident, I made a remarkable discovery about this star. A certain mineral, similar to pitchblende, is so susceptible to its magnified rays that a sharp vibration is set up shortly after contact. Only when the mineral is thoroughly wetted does this vibration cease—an inaudible humming, so alien to the human make-up that it renders the eardrum useless.

My nova was increasing in brightness, so I hurriedly made inquiries as to the location of spots on our planet where this mineral deposit was plentiful. Several were given me as a choice, but unfortunately it had rained at all of these localities save one, your small valley of Blankville here in the American states. As it was rich in this peculiar metal—and as my nova was steadily increasing its brightness and power—I hurried to Blankville to witness the effect when the rays from this star reached full power to impregnate the metal without being magnified.

I came to your city for the sole purpose of observing this contact. That was all. But in mingling with your people (a rather stodgy unimaginative lot, who place more value on money than on truth), it occurred to me to play a little prank on the entire city. Hence my first letter to your excellent mayor, demanding a large sum of money and threatening the town with an "unusual phenomenon."

My "silence"! (Actually, I had no way of knowing it would work out!) But I have had many a quiet chuckle at your expense, reading the learned explanations offered in your local paper concerning the "mysterious destruction of sound waves," etc. You comprehend? The ray from this star simply impregnated the metal in this valley (parched by a long dry spell), with some sort of electric charge, causing the atmosphere to vibrate in a peculiar way. The human ear, unused to such vibrations, rebelled.

Therefore, Blankville was not a city of silence. It was merely a city of the deaf. Sounds went on as before, but no one exposed to those vibrations could hear them.

I was annoyed that my first letter to your mayor had no effect; so I wrote another, saying, in fine: "I told you so!" Your reception of it has afforded me great amusement and delight—especially the way my foolish little trick of legerdemain with the two oil-cans baffled you. What I did, *of course, was drop a duplicate can into the river to draw your attention from the real one, which I later drew ashore in the sunken net placed to catch it.*

At no time did I harbor any intention of keeping the money for my own use, although by your standards I am not a rich man. He who has truth at his fingertips has little regard for material things, however, as I believe my small prank has taught you.

Had one of you known what I knew, you would not have been the victims of my "extortion plot."

For, as you now are aware, I did not control the "silence" as a super-natural weapon. I could no more have caused it than I could have stopped it. A very obliging rain abetted me in my little whimsy, dampening the dry atmosphere and relieving the pressure on everyone's eardrums—at the psychological moment. If it had not rained, Blankville would still be caught in my web of silence. Likewise, if your good mayor had waited another night to pay the "ransom," my "fiendish power" would have been destroyed.

So now, I must bid you all farewell and return to my work. I herewith return the $250,000 (you may also keep the penny in the other yellow can!) Since it has been collected for civic betterment, I hope that you will use it for the common good—may I suggest building a public observatory in which your good people may study the heavens (!)

Happiness to you all, and I hope you will forgive my little joke.

                                                            "DR. UBIQUE."

In the quiet office Mayor Tom Seeley looked at Jeff Haverty. The editor looked at the mayor.

Haverty's lip twitched. Seeley choked.

And then, in chorus, they burst out laughing—clung to each other, shaking with laughter that echoed and re-echoed later, over the little valley town of Blankville when Haverty made public the true nature of their web of silence.

The Deadly Theory

Greye La Spina

"Palingenesis?" said the man standing next to me at the bar, as he turned to face me. "What do you think *you* know about it? Scientists say it's a mythical theory based on that legendary tale of a rose reduced to ashes and then restored magically to living loveliness by some olden Mage for a queen of Sweden."

I thought to myself that scientists had other theories but that after all nothing in the cosmos is ever lost; things merely change their unessential qualities and become other things. At any rate, it wasn't palingenesis I wanted to discuss; what I wanted was to draw out that man until he forgot his lofty reserve. I wanted to make sure—well—

"You'll have to pardon me," said I aloud, "but you have such a striking resemblance to my old friend, the artist Julian Crosse who enlisted in the French Foreign Legion about 1914 and was later reported dead, that I was attempting to account for it by palingenesis. Jestingly, of course. I was his agent," I explained.

"Oh?" said the man and ordered another gin-and-tonic.

He sipped his drink with obvious appreciation.

I kept watching, careful not to let him see how amazed I was at what appeared to me not a resemblance but Julian redivivus, only it couldn't be, for Julian would have known and greeted me. This man had done neither; he had indifferently suffered my presence and my attempts at conversation until I had jestingly uttered that open-sesame word, palingenesis. Then he abruptly turned to me with that scornful query as to what *I* knew about palingenesis.

I finished my Scotch-and-soda; beckoned the bartender to bring me another drink and a fresh pack of cigarettes. I had a feeling that my vis-a-vis was about to spill something interesting, so I lighted a cigarette and waited with outward patience that belied my inward state, for the likeness to Julian Crosse was rather more than I had observed at first glance. It is true that this man had an unruly shock of hair even if it was iron-gray while Julian's had been warm brown. The man had no last joint on the fourth finger of his left hand; Julian had once caught and mashed that joint and it had been amputated. This man's skin was an even pallor while Julian's face had always glowed with the warm tan of the outdoor man. Yet there was, in the very manner the chap spoke, something that brought Julian vividly to mind; I mean, his assumption of esoteric knowledge that Julian always pretended but did not possess as far as my experience with him had brought out. No matter what branch of occultism we discussed, he had always touched upon it as the mystery of today and the scientific fact of tomorrow. So I waited, sure that I would shortly be given a dissertation upon palingenesis, the phoenix-like rebirth from its ashes of what had once been a living entity. That was how sure I was that the stranger was Julian and that the discussion, whether as a workable theory or as a survival of superstition, would be couched in such magical phrases that no one could listen without being caught in the trailing fringes of enthusiasm.

"I had an experience with palingenesis," said the man, holding up his glass and twirling it so that the clear contents purled against the edges. "It might interest you, if you are open-minded."

He hesitated and then said slowly, his piercing blue eyes full on mine, transfixing me much as the Ancient Mariner transfixed the Wedding Guest: "My profession took me to Maine. I was doing a lot of painting those days."

A strong conviction grew within me but the potency of that gaze restrained my mind from forming a conclusion and my tongue from uttering my thoughts. I rubbed out my half-smoked cigarette and nervously lighted another.

"Yes?" said I non-committally.

An expression that I interpreted as satisfaction flickered over the man's face. He took another sip of gin-and-tonic and mercifully lowered his hypnotic eyes from my face.

I wanted to clap him on the back and shout, "You weren't killed. You are Julian Crosse." But I was morally certain that he would have replied with chilling gravity that Julian Crosse was dead. So I confined myself to observing his every movement while I thought of many things, all closely connected with my old friend.

THE art world knows his work well. The character of his brilliant canvases, drenched with golden sunshine in the portrayal of which no other contemporary artist could equal or surpass him, told its own story of the young man's joyous attitude toward life. Up to 1912 he had painted nothing but trees; individual trees, groups of trees, vistas of forest glades in their virgin loveliness, pierced by those miraculous shafts of amber light which he knew how to paint with such sumptuous technique. The work he produced in the early part of the following year was of such entirely different character that I found it difficult to accept as his, for in spite of its undoubted qualities his gifted brush had made an entirely new departure.

As soon as collectors discovered that in these new pictures Julian had intensified the qualities that had made his wild, sun-drenched woods so distinctive and different, they began to buy up the new paintings at a rate which kept me frantically begging for canvases, more canvases, and yet more canvases. These new pictures featured a single model, a charming young girl; slender, supple, dark hair and eyes. Julian painted her in innumerable poses that built up a fairly representative picture of her life. The interpretation of that series formed the continuous life of a simple country girl whose existence was bounded by the

narrow horizon of humble duties. Julian injected an enchantment, a charm, into those homely tasks that threw a glamorous
haze about the girl so that the loveliness of her utter simplicity,
the quiet acceptance of her apparently uneventful life, became
things of spiritual beauty almost too great for words. Julian's
"Girl Peeling Potatoes," for instance (now one of the valued
modern acquisitions of the New York Metropolitan Museum
of Art), is something more than its name signifies; it is a vision
of innate beauty underlying the humblest duties that are
accepted with spiritual insight as symbols of higher things.

Throughout 1912, then, Julian painted his Maine model
assiduously. But there were two distinct periods in that year.
It was not until the second period canvases had been on sale for
some time that one art critic discovered that in these later canvases the girl's face was never depicted, that her hidden hands
were idle, her figure always drooping, half concealed in volu-
minous draperies. This fact met with a certain amount of speculative interpretation. These last pictures did not sell as did the
earlier ones; they possessed a peculiar morbidness to the point
of blocking an assault on the public imagination that might
have inspired the passion of ownership. Despite my protests,
Julian continued to ship me those sodden canvases unanimated
by the spiritual qualities that had made the earlier portraits so
noble. People would look at them, shudder, walk away with
corrugated brows and narrowed eyes. They could not help
feeling, as I felt, a strange quality emanating from them; a powerful, undeniable impression of something unhealthy, morbid,
far from sane.

Then some newspaper fellow got it into his head to ferret
out the artist. He made a big feature article for his Sunday paper
out of what he thought he'd dug up. He said Julian had fallen
in love with one of two sisters, of whom the younger died and
the one he loved had gone completely out of her mind and run
away. Julian and the girl's guardian had found her in Bangor,
dying of consumption, and had brought her body home. The

reporter had it that Julian had painted the first portraits when the girl was herself and the others after she'd begun to fail mentally. This account satisfied the public's curiosity more or less and Julian told me he didn't care enough about what was being said to affirm or deny the story; he said there were things in life of such vast inner import that their outward and often misleading manifestations mean nothing to the human being who experiences them.

Julian's last paintings were a drug on the market and all at once he must have stopped his work entirely for I got no more from him. He came to see me in New York and when I remonstrated, he replied that he was sailing for France and intended to join the Foreign Legion. He told me that the woman he loved had died horribly and he himself could only wish for death now. I have to say that he went to his death as a bridegroom to his wedding morning, welcoming it as a door that would open a wider, happier existence. I add this last because some fool reporter had the impudence or temerity to suggest that Julian must have been a drug victim to have put into his work the weird and bizarre qualities such as emanated from it during his last painting period.

At this point in my reminiscences, the stranger (or was he?) confronting me at the bar broke in upon my rambling thoughts and began to talk in a low, intense but unhurried voice, every intonation of which strengthened that incredible conviction which grew and grew within me as I listened.

"I met a girl up in the Maine woods," said he. "Her name was Marzha. She lived with her younger sister Idell in a log shack, put up in the wilderness by her uncle Elisha Moffatt so that he might study without human interruptions the occult subjects to which he had devoted himself. Her father, a sea-captain, had gone down with his ship and her mother, a passionately-loving Persian woman, had not long survived him. Elisha had taken his orphaned nieces into his home and they had been brought up in his own fashion, which meant that he had taught them a smattering of mathematics and their ABCs and had then let them seek their own education from the books in his library, mostly comprised of occult volumes.

"I felt that in Marzha I had met everything man could desire in woman, so accompanied her to the log cabin to meet her uncle. Elisha was a remarkable man. Black smocked, heavy black hair in wavy masses; shaggy black brows over deep-set black eyes, rich black beard parted in the middle like old pictures of Moses, he impressed me as a being whom it would be a privilege to know better, especially as I soon learned from sixteen-year-old Idell that he was always carrying on some obscure occult experiment in his completely equipped laboratory. To my astonishment, Elisha welcomed me into the family circle as a guest, with a disregard of conventions that made me like him the more. As our acquaintance ripened into warm intimacy, I realized that he had hoped for just what happened, the growing attachment between Marzha and myself.

"There was, however, what at first seemed to me a silly situation to deal with; Idell imagined herself in love with me. She had inherited a tempestuous temperament and at sixteen was more highly sexed than Marzha at nineteen. She entertained a raging jealousy of her sister that tore at her soul. My devotion to my betrothed, my depiction of her in my canvases, brought the wild girl's passion to such a point that she determined to usurp her sister's place at any cost. Her simpler arts of feminine seduction degenerated into sheer, open, abject pleading for a love she ardently desired with every fiber of her wild being. She found me deaf, dumb and blind to anything but Marzha.

"Early one morning I went with Elisha to Bangor; he needed certain herbs that were not procurable in his woods and I wanted several tubes of color. We returned in the late afternoon. Marzha did not come to meet us, although I kept my eyes on the open doorway hungrily from the moment the loghouse came in sight. It was Idell who burst out and ran toward us. Her appearance was alarming. Her hair tumbled in wild confusion about her shoulders; her face was a pallid white; her eyes were wide and staring. She screamed at us over and over as she half ran, half stumbled, toward us.

"'Marzha is dead! Marzha is dead!'

"Elisha groaned in stupefied incredulity and I knew then what I had suspected—that Marzha was his best loved niece.

"Our flying feet carried us into the log-house but we were too late. Marzha's head rested on her outstretched arms on the table; her flesh was cold and stiff. Already her body showed the dreadful signs of reaction from the poisoned mushrooms that Idell declared her sister had inadvertently included in those prepared for lunch. I held to my almost stilled heart the distorted, terrible, discoloring face of my dear dead, trying to hide its horror in my bosom.

"Idell cried out to her uncle that he knew well her own aversion to fungi. Elisha replied, with a slow restrained speech more terrible than any emotional outpouring, that Marzha must have been strangely bespelled to have picked a poisonous genus after her long years of familiarity with the innocuous fungi. From this veiled innuendo Idell did not defend herself but she withdrew from the log-house as if she could not meet our eyes.

"Palingenesis, you said, didn't you? Well, paligenesis is what Elisha Moffatt said to me. I was to help him; he had spent much study on it; it could be done; I need not mourn. We need only build a funeral pyre and cremate Marzha's body, preserving the ashes.

"The idea of cremation met my approval. I could not bear to put her body in the earth while the hateful poison still tore at her so relentlessly. At the same time I feared lest Elisha's mind had become unhinged by the disaster. I told him that I intended to scatter the purified ashes upon the running water of the clear brook that murmured near the log-house. At this he protested hysterically, declaring that I would be a madman to block his plan. Have her back, he said, he would. He *knew* how the process worked and believed he could bring Marzha back, warmly pulsing with life.

"I told him defiantly that he was certainly mad and that I would not have her ashes desecrated by his unholy experiments. He swore to me in turn by the Ark of the Covenant that held the seven mysteries of creation that he would not permit my stupidity to stand in his way. When I in turn swore to keep Marzha from him, he laughed.

"He bade me note how easily he could wrest her body from me, and lifted his arm until I felt so numbed from head to foot with my impotent struggle against an unseen but potent power he wielded so easily that I was obliged, against my will, to bow reluctantly to his wishes.

"I told myself that fire purified that which it consumed and was it not better than the worm? I tried to believe that the pure element of flame would clarify the poison's dire work, returning Marzha to my arms alive and lovely as Elisha declared."

The bartender paused significantly before the narrator and me, his eyes bent upon our drained glasses.

"Will you accept a drink?" I asked my vis-a-vis.

"Gin-and-tonic," replied he indifferently.

"Give me another Scotch-and-soda," I ordered.

For a few moments the man and I sipped our drinks and puffed at our cigarettes. He had accepted a cigarette from me, rolling it slightly between his fingers as Julian had used to do, so that it got so soft it only lasted for a few puffs. I was full of impatience and kept wondering when the moment would arrive to clap the man on the shoulder and cry joyfully that he was Julian Crosse and I'd known it all along. After three or four puffs he rubbed out the cigarette and took up the burden of his discourse.

"We made up a pile of wood," went on the man, "and reverently laid on that rude pyre the stiffened, hideous travesty of what had been a gracious living creature. About this pyre Elisha paced with priestly solemnity, chanting strange words in an unknown tongue. As his signal I lighted the pyre with a torch he had hastily prepared. The red flames leaped avidly until naught was left but a pile of powdery gray ash. This Elisha carefully gathered to the finest particle, putting it into a great urn against the time of the experiment, for the performance of which his consuming anxiety betrayed itself in almost feverish word and gesture. He had also, he explained, to make certain alterations in the incantations because of extraneous matter from the pyre itself.

"Meantime Idell fumed and fretted but kept well away from her uncle's accusing eyes, for she had reason to believe in his more than ordinary powers. Me, also, she left alone.

"The morning after the episode of the funeral pyre, Elisha told me that I must let him have a small quantity of blood from my median vein. It was an ingredient in what he called the elixir Primum Ens Sanguinis. He put this blood into a bottle, adding by twice its weight a certain alcahest of which fortunately he had just sufficient. He sealed the bottle and arranged for it to be maintained at blood warmth in the laboratory for fourteen days.

"If you chance, my friend," said the man (I almost spoke out my secret thoughts when he called me that) as he sipped his drink, "to have curiosity as to the nature of the alcahest, you will find it in any accredited magical book by Paracelsus, Eliphus Levi, Trithemius, even Agrippa. Suffice it that after fourteen days Elisha filtered the flashing, ruby-clear liquid that had risen to the top of the bottle. The elixir was carefully decanted into a chemically clean container and put to one side where it would be safe until needed.

"I insisted upon being present at the ceremony, which meant Idell's presence, as this particular rite depended upon a unity or a triad. Idell was admitted between the outer and inner circles her uncle had traced upon the laboratory floor, and was bidden to feed the lamps that at stated distances sent up clouds of pungent, perfumed smoke. The great urn stood in the center of the inner circle, where Elisha and I were also, surrounded by that ring of oil lamps that sent up clouds of choking smoke from their tiny wicks. My skin stung into gooseflesh with vaguely intangible intuitions of something portentous, amazing, hovering at the exact point of revelation. So we stood, the uncle, the lover, and the slayer of the dead girl, in unholy combination to rob Death.

"With my own eyes," said the man (and bent them upon me until responsive goose-flesh pricked upon the surface of my body while I listened in a kind of trance to the eerie tale), "I *saw* that palingenesis. My ears tingled with the strange combinations of syllables Elisha chanted. At last the lid of the urn stirred slowly as if pushed upward by some as yet unharnessed but potent power. I cannot express in words the terror that struck me at that sluggish movement as of something horrible beyond words, for beneath that cover I knew there was nothing but gray ash, the final chemical resolution into nothingness of a human body. Yet the cover did move, despite my bristling hair and goosefleshed skin. It moved—it tilted upward—fell back as if that which impelled it were not yet strong enough to concentrate upon pushing it aside.

"Then from that urn where reposed the ashes of the dead there puffed an occasional darkish mist. Horror tore at me and I could hardly control the agonized retching that began to shake my body.

"Again that Something lifted the lid of the urn. Elisha cried his charms the louder, chanting a barbaric strain the words of which throbbed within my brain as if even they, each individual word, was possessed of strange occult significance and living power.

"Did you ever stop to consider," the man digressed thoughtfully, "the amazing magical powers that lie within two or three tiny words, rightly used?"

He did not pause for my comment but continued.

"I watched the urn. Finally the lid was pushed perceptibly to one side. It trembled there upon the edge of the urn. I gazed with a fixed stare for I could see nothing below it but empty air hazy with clouds of pungent smoke. All at once the cover flew off and crashed upon the floor, shattering into a thousand fragments as if the power that lifted and flung it were almost too tremendous yet to control or direct itself.

"The voice of the adept became a shouting triumph even if an undertow of something tremulous within his being betrayed to me a human shrinking at this fearful thing he was doing. I realized too late that something obscene and unholy was taking place. When my staring eyes could no longer doubt that they were in reality seeing the actual recall into life of what had become an appalling horror, I sickened so that I could no longer look upon it. Retching, I turned my back upon what I could not bring myself to credit although my eyes had told me it was only too true.

"From that urn where had reposed the sacred ashes of the dead there arose a tenuous vapor that slowly and undeniably was taking a woman's shape. It was darkly purple, horribly suggestive of the grave and decay. As I had looked, this slowly materializing Thing drifted downward from the open top of the great urn and came to a rest upon the floor beside me. The glassy, unseeing eyes had no intelligence in them, yet were they in horrid manner the eyes of Marzha. The awful purple face, the writhing features that shaped more and more into familiar, beloved semblance, yet so loathly were in their suggestions of rotten decomposition that I went down upon the floor at that horrid phantom's feet, unconscious.

"Palingenesis! The Thing Elisha Moffatt had resurrected from Marzha's ashes was her body *as it had gone from life,* disfigured by purple and black discolorations due to the poison's rapid action; ghastly, too, because of the unwholesome, suggestive puffiness of gas-inflated flesh that had decomposed so rapidly. This Thing neither ate, drank, spoke nor breathed, as far as we could perceive. It walked among the haunted three in that log-house, affecting each in different fashion by its loathly presence.

"Idell frankly feared the Thing's clumsy approach and would fling herself abjectly upon me, begging for protection. To Elisha it represented at once his occult triumph and the sad evidence that a little knowledge is a dangerous thing; yet his horror was transcended by his scientific enthusiasm at his experiment's success. If he had a regret, it was that he had not foreseen that he could not raise up a body to the beauty it had possessed before Death had defaced it so horribly. It was I who suffered most poignantly. The resurrected Thing was obviously soulless and this seemed the ultimate desecration. I could hardly bear to look upon it, so unutterably repulsive and loathsome did I feel it to be. I begged Elisha to reverse, if he could, the spell that bound the Thing to earth, that it might crumble into ashes and those ashes be given decent interment. At first he would not acquiesce for the evidence of his ghastly success was as yet too precious for what he bitterly termed my mania of wanton destruction. So I began secretly to plot for its removal. I remembered that when It had first appeared from the urn the adept had sprayed it with a dilution of that ruby elixir he had distilled from the alcahest and my blood. I noted later that three drops of the elixir in distilled water were given daily to the ghastly Thing that not only offended the eye with its appalling appearance of death and decay but only too well attacked the sense of smell so that at its approach nausea would invariably seize upon me.

"Each day Elisha took the elixir from the safe in order to feed and spray the Thing. I saw that the ruby liquid was diminishing in quantity day by day and asked him what he planned to do when it was gone. Make more, he had replied. I told him I would refuse to give my blood and that Idell certainly would not be complaisant about hers. This must have filled him with despair since it seemed the adept could not use his own life

fluid. The liquid grew less. Then Idell took a hand. She said that
as she saw it, the Thing had not been sprayed sufficiently and
that if her uncle were to be more generous the following day,
the Thing might in turn throw off its horrid mantle of decay
and become Marzha in all her beauty. For this I thanked her, as
Elisha agreed to think over the situation from my standpoint if
this further experiment did not succeed.

"Despite the dwindling supply of the elixir, Elisha was more
generous with the spray the following morning and his attempt
was, in a strange way, successful. The lips of the Thing opened;
the puffed eyelids lifted a crack to show the gleam of intelligence. No words came from the Thing but the dry, blackened
lips mouthed inaudibly. The Thing sank supinely upon the
floor as if exhausted by that small effort, and Elisha sprayed it
again, while I begged that he let it droll away into nothingness.
He pushed me aside and shouted with triumph as the Thing
began to revive slowly. It raised to a sitting posture. It began
to alter subtly, the frightful evidence of decomposition fading
and the skin glowing with new life. The dark eyes opened
under normal lids. What had been a loathsome Thing became
Marzha, beautiful as before. Elisha, in wild excitement, sprayed
the reviving body recklessly with the Primum Ens. Pulsing
blood reddened pale cheeks; puffy paws became white, delicate
hands.

"While Elisha started for his desk to consult a notable tome
on palingenesis, I received in my welcoming arms the miraculously revived beauty and life that was Marzha; sweet and
wholesome to the touch, fragrant with fair health, incredibly
thrilling as her mouth fixed upon mine in a long, hungry
kiss. At just that moment Elisha checked his rush, standing as
if frozen. He called me to throw her from my arms and look
upon something lying behind the table at his feet.

"Marzha's arms clung, her voice caressed with passionate
words of love, so fiery with ardor that I could hardly credit
her lips with having uttered them. Prescience of unutterable

calamity overwhelmed me as I tore myself from her embrace and followed Elisha, to stand staring like a lack-wit at that which lay behind the table."

"Make it a Scotch-and-soda for me," said I to the approaching bartender. "On second thought, better make it a double one. I need it."

"Another gin-and-tonic," said the narrator impatiently. He fixed me again with that hypnotic gaze which I did not heed, for I could not have left him with the tale still untold and the hoped-for disclosure still a secret.

"The revenant pursued me," said the man, after the bartender had set our drinks on the counter and lingered a moment to wipe up the rings left by our last drinks. "She called me her life, her love. She begged me not to look upon what her uncle wished me to see. She promised that if I would only love her she would be a thousand women for me and could grant untold gratifications if she chose.

"SHE was too late to deceive me. On the floor behind the table lay the still warm body of Idell, an ironical smile of evil triumph on her lips. Beside her on the floor a labeled bottle told the story.

"I could not understand until Elisha cried in fury that she had done it purposely that her soul might inhabit and renovate Marzha's body. To me this was the supreme, unpardonable desecration. The dead body of my sweet love was obviously animated now by the passionate fire and wicked intelligence of the tempestuous Idell, who again approached me with the sinuous litheness of an enamoured tigress. I hesitated, for the woman approaching me was to all appearances the woman I had loved and lost; I wondered if perhaps this were not some further spell of Elisha's.

"Then the woman cried out, 'Oh, my beloved, can you deny our love? Look, could any other woman be as desirable as I?' and she tore from her gleaming white body the homespun garment and smiled with such allure that Elisha must have trembled for me. She said, as she neared me, that she had learned to create such delights as no man had ever yet been permitted to enjoy....

"As she approached, I withdrew, for never could I have believed that this tempestuous, abandoned creature was the finely reserved woman I had worshiped. I bade her let me alone, saying harshly that I did not care to traffic with Marzha's murderess.

"Idell must have read in my voice the doom of all she had dared for; she turned upon me in fury and despair. From her delicate lips—the lips that had been Marzha's—words poured telling the hideous story of a perverted passion, a hatred too deep not to have seized upon the opportunity to rid herself of an envied rival.

"In the midst of this tirade I realized what the withdrawal of the Primum Ens Sanguinis might mean to this unwelcome revenant.

"I snatched up the bottle, lifted it high in the air, then crashed it purposefully to the floor where it burst into fragments that flicked the ruby drops of sparkling life-essence seeping into the cracks, every drop lost forever.

"Elisha shouted a protest that changed to a moan of resignation. Idell sank upon the floor and, face in hands, wept with tumultous sobs that shook Marzha's body.

"That was the beginning of the end. Fearful were the days that came and went. Elisha and I were determined that the going, whatever it might be, should be in our presence for we feared lest Idell might have learned somewhat that would enable her to maintain Marzha's body and transport it from our sphere of influence; to what evil she might, by her knowledge and wicked will, have devoted it we dared not think. With the passing of each day the body that had been Marzha's became more attenuated, more subtle in essence. At moments Idell would throw herself at my feet and beg me to give my blood

again to Elisha for the prolongation of her life. Although it was
agony to see Marzha's body perishing before my eyes, I braced
myself to watch her die.

"A day came when the misty body subsided like a thin layer
of gray ash upon the floor.

"As it sank, I heard—or thought I heard—a thin, threadlike
sigh in my ears. I breathed a prayer; not for Marzha who did
not need it but for the unhappy Idell, and may God pardon me
if I did wrong. Upon the surface of the brook's running waters
I scattered the gray dust that it might be too widely separated
ever again to be subject to palingenesis."

The narrator stopped abruptly and addressed himself to his
half-empty tumbler of gin-and-tonic. His obvious attitude was
that he had gone to considerable trouble to clarify palingenesis
to me, even to the point of furnishing an example of its work-
out in everyday life.

I waited in trepidation to hear what I hoped for but the man
said no more; he sipped his drink in silence.

"You painted both the girls, didn't you?" I ventured finally.

"Yes," he said, and sipped again.

"Marzha first and Idell in Marzha's body afterward?"

"Yes," he said.

"Then you are Julian Crosse," said I and would have clapped
him on the shoulder but that he incomprehensibly removed
himself by rising and starting to leave the bar.

"Julian Crosse died in 1915," he said. "Also, it isn't expedient
for the dead to return," he threw back over his shoulder.

"Dead men don't drink gin-and-tonic," I muttered.

He was still looking at me and he smiled. "No?" he said.

The swinging-door flapped and a man in perhaps his early
seventies came into the bar. "Oh, here you are," he said. He
was a remarkable man with shaggy white hair, shaggy white
eyebrows, shaggy white beard divided in the middle like the
pictures of Moses. "You forgot your drops," he said, and gave
the other man a small bottle that sparkled redly.

"I suppose I ought to thank you," returned my man resignedly.

He turned a sadly whimsical smile upon me as he opened the outside door.

"How some human beings cling to the evidence of their past successes," he said, and went out, followed by the ancient.

I said to the bartender, "Put the bottle of Scotch on the counter. I think I want to get drunk."

Great Pan Is Here

Greye La Spina

LYING at the edge of the asphalt road just outside the gutter and far enough back so that passing car wheels could not crush it, lay a seven-reed pandean pipe. Incredible anachronism on a modern highway; I could hardly believe my eyes. It might have been dropped just before our car swung around the corner by my garden; I had an eerie feeling that the owner had dodged out of sight in the thicket of shrubbery a fraction of a minute before.

I said quickly to Cecily: "Did you see that syrinx?"

Cecily insinuated delicately that I had had one cocktail too many. Although it lay on her side of the road, she had seen nothing.

First time I'd known her to miss anything out of the ordinary.

Aunt Kate was muttering vexedly from the rear seat. I'd been of half a mind to go back and pick up that shepherd's flute just to prove to Cecily that five cocktails were well within my limit, but although I couldn't distinguish a word I knew what Aunt Kate was saying. She doesn't approve of late arrival at symphony concerts. I did hint loudly that I'd like to pick up the unusual object but she promptly blew the man down with a loud snort, adding that she didn't intend to lose the first movement of the symphony just because I'd imagined something that, having no business to be there, couldn't have been there, consequently wasn't there.

Cecily said she thought this was fairly conclusive reasoning, so between them I was dissuaded from returning. What

240

I didn't realize then was that neither Aunt Kate, who usually drove from the back seat directing our course for every bump or puddle in the road, hadn't seen that glaring anachronism. Nor had Cecily—Cecily, who rarely misses seeing the wariest pheasant or the smallest couchant cottontail. I only, of the three of us, had seen those pipes. So we drove on, leaving the syrinx lying by the roadside. The symphony concert was, as usual, magnificent. One of the encores held undue significance for me that night; it was the piping entrance of the little fauns. It carried me completely out of myself and back to that object I had seen lying on the gravel at the turn in the road. I promised myself to watch for it and salvage it on the way home. I had a burning curiosity to handle it and an overpowering desire to lay it against my lips and sound its shrill, sweet notes.

But either the headlights—or the opposite side of the road when we returned—did not pick it out or it had already been seen and appropriated by someone else. Cecily insisted that my imagination was working overtime but I was so positive of that Pan-pipe's reality that I even remembered a fine cord attached to it, as if it had but recently hung about some little faun's sun-browned neck. That last touch was too much for Cecily. She told me shortly that she thought it rather silly on my part to attempt embroidering a story that was obviously only a fabrication of my too-vivid imagination. We had what is euphemistically termed "words" and Cecily flounced into the house with Aunt Kate, disdaining to complete our tentative plans for a sail next morning in the *Sprite*.

I PUT up the car and followed Aunt Kate and my charming cousin into the house, hoping that Cecily had relented and that we would have a cigarette together before retiring for the night, but the house was as still as if a chatty old lady and a lively young girl had not preceded me five minutes before my own entrance. I went to the kitchen to see if they had gone there for sandwiches and drinks but it was deserted. Those "words" had cooked my

goose as far as a half-hour alone with Cecily was concerned. I
sometimes feared that my aunt's strict, old-fashioned ideas had
made Cecily too reserved, too cold. I had long wished ardently
that something would rouse her to understand that a man in
love cannot be held forever at a chilling distance.

I took some ice cubes to the library, mixed a highball, lighted
a cigarette and went to the screened bay-window overlooking
my sunken garden. There was a tender crescent moon hanging
low in the sky with no cloud to dim the broad expanse of
twinkling, starry attendants. I longed to share that beauty
with Cecily. There was just enough light to make the garden
an enchanted spot, highlighted here and there against the deep
shadows of the pine grove at the rear, beyond which boomed
the sea. The nymph fountain I had brought from Italy sprinkled
sparkling pearly spray against a background of shrubbery and
farther down the graveled path I could see the sun-dial on its
marble pedestal surrounded by the sheen of white flowers
whose heavy fragrance hung on the night air. Aunt Kate dearly
loves a white garden because it is so lovely at night and when
she took over the management of my household after my
parents' death, I had the white garden planted to please her.

I was just on the point of snuffing out my cigarette and
going up to bed when I thought I detected a movement at the
rear of the garden. I say a movement, because what I really saw
I didn't actually see. I mean, what I glimpsed was an apparent
disappearance of the sun-dial on its gleaming marble pedestal.
It was as if some obscuring shadow had passed between it and
me, blotting it momentarily from sight. I was startled because
I knew neither Aunt Kate nor Cecily would be strolling out
there alone. By midnight, too, the servants were abed snoring
comfortably, as we rarely kept anyone up on symphony nights
because it was far more fun to raid refrigerator and pantry than
to call a sleepy butler or dopy-eyed maid to fetch sandwiches
and drinks. Moreover, the intruder in the garden could not
have been Aunt Kate or Cecily; their dresses would have shown

up in the starlight. Aunt Kate had worn a light gray silk and Cecily had been in frilly dotted muslin, white as an October hoar frost, a charming cool frock for a hot summer night. Who the deuce, thought I, has taken the liberty of promenading in our garden at midnight without so much as a by-your-leave?

I took a last puff at my cigarette, crushed it out on an ashtray, and went down the room to the French doors. Of course they were locked; Ashby would have seen to that on his nightly rounds. I unlocked them and went out on the bricked terrace and stood there quietly under the myriad stars. I sensed an inner suspense, as if something notable were about to happen. I listened, feeling that I must surely hear the sound of feet on the shifting gravel of the path but while I watched, the sundial again performed its disappearing act, unaccompanied by the merest whisper of sound. It was uncanny. I wanted to call, "Who's there?" but knew that if I did I'd have my aunt out in the hall, Cecily at her window, Ashby prancing about in pajamas and quite probably cook and the maids uttering shrieks from the back stairs. So I held my peace.

A MOMENT later I was glad I had. There came a whispered stirring of shrubbery somewhere in the garden. I couldn't locate the sound but I heard it distinctly. It was an irregular rustle quite unlike the gentle urge of a night breeze. Then borne on the sweet night air sounded a series of distinct, if pianissimo, flute-like notes. As they fell upon my straining, grateful ears I stood stock-still, amazed and intrigued by what somehow seemed a mystical sequence to the syrinx lying by the roadside, the symphonic encore featuring the piping of the little fauns, the mysterious behavior of the sun-dial. The night silence pressed in upon me with a significance out of all proportion to its simple normality and in the midst of that heightened stillness, as if all Nature listened with me, I heard the notes again like drops of liquid gold and knew them for what they were. Someone had picked up that lost Pan-pipe and was trying the reeds one by one, under the magical young moon in my enchanted sunken garden.

My first sensation was one of outrage. I had wanted those pipes myself, as if they had been meant to fall into my hands. I felt that an unauthorized intruder had robbed me of something so much my own that he must have sensed it to be adding insult to injury by playing on those shepherd pipes in my garden. I was so angry that I threw aside my previous caution. I dashed down the steps from the terrace, my feet crunching over the gravel straight to the pedestal where the dial stood. Of course, as I might have realized in my noisy advance, there would be no one there when I arrived. I did imagine for a moment that the shrubbery, in the spot where it was so thickly interlaced that it seemed a tangled wildwood, stirred ever so slightly as I approached. But when I rushed up, it had already stopped its swaying and I heard no sound save the rising murmur of a night breeze that might have caused that slight agitation of the leafy branches.

I stood perfectly still and listened intently. There was not an unfriendly sound drifting on the sweet fragrance of the air. There was only the faint incessant chirping of crickets and once a birdling uttered a small smothered twitter from its nest in the crotch of one of the pines bordering the garden. I told myself I must have imagined the whole thing, conjured it up out of the enchantment of the night. Yet returning slowly to the house I wheeled about twice and faced back, for I could have sworn that someone or something was following closely behind with noiseless, airy footsteps. I was uncomfortably conscious of faint, amused disdain impingeing on my consciousness as if someone were sardonically aware of my unease and enjoyed my discomfiture.

I closed and locked the French door so quickly upon my own wary entrance that not even an invisible entity could very well have followed me inside. Then I went out to the kitchen, got more ice cubes and back in the library I fixed a whopper of a highball. I needed a bracer. I felt strongly that I had happily escaped from something faintly, but none the less obviously, inimical. Also I could not persuade myself that I had imagined those flute-like, golden notes that had fallen out of the starlit night upon my astonished, ravished ears.

By next morning Cecily had apparently forgotten her vexation. She came to breakfast looking like a rather withdrawn young goddess in that paucity of attire girls assume for sports wear. Of course she was as beautiful as the sun, moon and stars, and I told her so. She looked at me and smiled and I knew, as I always had when she smiled at me, that even if she wanted my heart to trample, it was hers for the asking. After breakfast we strolled down to the beach with a packed luncheon basket. I keep a rowboat with an outboard motor at our private wharf near the bathing pavilions.

Cecily protested, as I started the motor: "Don't be in such a rush, Craig. Isn't that Tommy Leatherman coming down the beach?"

I'd seen him. That was why I wanted to be off. I presume I must have looked sulky for Cecily pointed one finger at me derisively, wrinkling her nice straight nose.

"Etta's in New York for the week-end and Tommy's simply forlorn, Craig. Be humane and ask him along."

"But I don't want him along," I objected. "You act as if you didn't want to be alone with me, Cecily. I like to have you to myself once in a while. Your mother's such a strict duenna, and now you want Tommy to chaperone us."

Cecily tried to look offended but failed. Her lips drew into a smile. She looked at me from under curling lashes and I was lost and she knew it.

I hailed Tom none too pleasantly. Of course he wanted to go along. Men always wanted to go along with Cecily. So that was the end of my plan for a day alone with my cousin. We climbed aboard the *Sprite* and I tied the small boat to her stern. Cecily disposed herself picturesquely where she needn't move until it was time to open the luncheon hamper. Tom sat beside her. That left me to sail the boat. Ordinarily I wouldn't have cared, for I love the wild abandon of the *Sprite* when she takes the wind in her sails and fairly flies. Aunt Kate once said that if the *Sprite* had been a girl, she would have been of the type considered "fast." I was busy with the boat and paid no attention to my passengers until I caught a few words that made me prick up my ears and almost stop what I was doing.

Tom said: "—so I went back and picked it up and it was a curious little reed instrument hanging on a brown string. It was the sort of thing nymphs and fauns used to play on, you know."

"Well!" I heard Cecily exclaim in an amazed undertone. She turned her face to me and said sweetly, "Sorry, Craig! My error."

Tom stared, brow puzzled into a scowl, but I knew she was apologizing for not having believed me when I'd told her about the Pan-pipe by the side of the road. Now she was hearing from Tom that it had been there and that he'd picked it up himself.

A strange resentment rose in me. The thing had little or no intrinsic value but it had impressed me as something closely associated with myself.

I said disgustedly: "So it was you piping in our garden last night. Rather a childish performance, Tom. You might have come in for a drink before slipping away as you did."

Tom said he didn't know what I was getting at.

"What I'm getting at is this," said I, growing a little angry at his evasion. "What possessed you to come piping in my garden on those ridiculous reeds at midnight? I heard you, Tom. Every time you paraded past the sun-dial I knew it, too."

"I was sound asleep in bed before midnight last night, Craig."

I said, "Oh, yeah?" and let it go at that. I didn't intend to get into an argument with him before Cecily; I had a feeling that she might side with him as she had with Aunt Kate the previous night.

Then she took the wind out of my sails by declaring: "But I heard the piping, Tom. If it wasn't you, who could it have been? It was you who found the syrinx."

Tom stared at her, speechless. So did I.

"It was a very disturbing sound. It reached way inside me," said she in a troubled voice. "I thought it was you, Craig."

"It wasn't I. It was someone who had no business in my garden. Sure you're not a somnambulist?" I asked Tom drily.

He snapped rather disagreeably that he had already told me he was home, asleep in bed, before midnight. "I certainly wasn't making an ass of myself, prancing about your garden tootling on a silly, childish toy," he growled.

"Of course you wouldn't do anything like that," agreed Cecily warmly.

I thought, "Drat the gal," until I caught the sparkle of a sly twinkle in her eyes.

"I would like to know who was serenading," she went on, her gray eyes dark with secret thoughts. "There was something eerie about those fragile, flute-like notes. They allured and frightened me. I wanted to follow the player and yet I was so terrified that the blood ran cold in my veins. Those notes were strangely haunting."

I thought myself that they had seemed most unusual for a broken series of unlinked musical notes that carried no particular motif; they were at once plaintive and searching. It was as if someone had tried one reed after the other, moving the pipes slowly across his lips without actually playing the instrument. It was the golden quality of those notes that had made such a strong impression on me. There had been something almost magical about them as they fell with clarity on the night air. I had felt as if night and Nature had awaited those lovely sounds; that the silence had hushed to a deeper degree of summer stillness for their reception. It had sounded like the prelude to an enchanted musical rite. Magical. That was the proper word for these notes.

★

I ASKED Tom abruptly if he had any plans for the syrinx. He stared at me almost unpleasantly and then observed significantly that they weren't going out of his hands.

"They seem to be in demand, Craig. What with one Panpipe lost by the highway, and a midnight musician tuning up on another under Cecily's window at midnight, it—there's something distinctly off about the whole situation and I don't like it, if you ask me."

Cecily flicked me a warning look. She knew I was about to retort that nobody was going to ask him. I withheld my goading comment. But for the rest of the day there wasn't a moment I didn't think about that shepherd's flute and wish I'd gone back to pick it up. Cecily herself brought up the subject after we'd left Tom on the beach later that afternoon. We swung up through the back of the garden, the hamper in my right hand and Cecily's arm twined about my left arm. I got a faint impression that she was glad she was with me, and I dared to say so boldly in the absence of her usual aloofness and reserve.

Her fingers tightened on my arm. "I'm always happiest when I'm with you, Craig. Even if we're quarreling," she admitted impishly. "But I'm especially glad not to be alone today. In the garden," she explained oddly.

"Why the garden?" I quizzed, intrigued.

"Because something is here now that wasn't here yesterday, Craig. I can feel it and it terrifies me. I feel all panicky and I don't know why. Silly, isn't it?"

I didn't want her troubled, so gave a short dry laugh of incredulity.

"Oh, it isn't imagination, Craig. Truly it isn't. It is something very frightening. It came last night. After that piping. I feel it doesn't really mean to hurt—but if it has to, it won't even realize it's hurting. It will have its way at any cost to—well, to lesser creatures."

I said teasingly, "The hot sun must have affected you, darling."

She pinched my arm until I yelped at the sharp pain.

"Don't be horrid, Craig, or I'll never tell you my innermost thoughts again."

"That being a dire penalty," said I, "I'll not be horrid, for I felt something strange in the garden last night, myself. Although I must say I don't feel it in broad daylight."

And then we both stopped short where we stood at the opening of the shrubbery that gave upon the graveled path leading to the fountain; I with amazed resentment, Cecily with a sharp indrawing of breath and a pressure of her trembling body against me.

A strange, foreign looking man, who seemed at once like a seafaring person and a countryman from the back mountains, stood lean and angular between us and the sun-dial, his peaked brown face under the slouch hat complacently upon us as if he had known to the minute just when we would emerge to confront him. His jutting jaw bore a scanty, ragged beard like a he-goat's scraggly chin-whiskers. Strangely vivid eyes peered at us from under bushy brows as might canny wood creatures from their shrubby hiding-places, missing nothing—piercing my startled discomposure and Cecily's trembling apprehension as if their gaze penetrated flesh and entered unobstructedly the inner recesses of our minds. His widely curving, full-lipped mouth shaped a flickering, half-mocking smile. A kind of dark shawl draped in romantic fashion across his shoulders concealed his entire body; the fringes, trailing over the ground, covered even his feet.

CECILY shrank against me, clutching feverishly at my arm as she whispered in a shaky voice: "Craig, I'm afraid. I don't know why, but I'm awfully scared. Something's terribly wrong here. That man—" she shuddered.

I pressed her clinging hand against my side with my arm and turned so that she was partly behind me.

I said sharply, "What are you doing here? Don't you know you're trespassing?"

The stranger spoke to me but his eyes were on Cecily's slender body clad in shorts and bra. "The maiden is fair," he gloated.

I shook Cecily's hand from my arm, set down the luncheon hamper, doubled up my fists and advanced toward him.

"Get out of here!" I grated, feeling my face whiten with repressed fury at his impudence.

He responded with a question. "Is this garden yours, youth?"

"The garden is mine and I'll thank you to clear out of it."

His flickering, mocking smile deepened into a more ingratiating expression. "Has your garden no welcome for its lord and master, Pan?" he inquired.

A warning tingle quivered down my spinal column at that sublime self-confidence. I heard my voice weakly echoing, "Pan?"

"I have spoken, youth. I am seeking quiet gardens in this New World where perchance a few still survive who know my name and will not fear to harken to the pipes of Pan, to the lilting notes that burn away the dross of human convention and open joyous paths of natural impulse. My groves in the Old World have been destroyed.

"Dryads and nymphs fear to follow the sound of my pipes for there is no more night since you mad, deluded human creatures began to fling Jove's thunder-bolts and lightnings over the world. This garden you call yours has its good points; not every garden borders upon Neptune's domain. I need your garden, youth."

Sudden unreasoning, unwelcome panic seized upon me. I felt gooseflesh pricking my skin. Was the man mad? Or was I? His words seemed to mingle the vaporings of a deluded lunatic and the reasonable expression of sanity.

The stranger continued after a brief pause, his piercing eyes still upon Cecily.

"Be not afraid, youth. You and this maiden have come part way to my worship, since you do not cover your bodies with the ugly garments I have seen in your cities. Give me, then, the freedom of this fair garden and the word of release for my dancing nymph."

One long hairy arm pushed out from under the clumsy drapery and a finger pointed.

Cecily and I exchanged a quick glance of wary puzzlement. That finger drew our eyes to the marble fountain we had had so much trouble bringing back with us from Italy on our last trip there before the global war.

We knew it had been dug up from the foundations of an ancient temple near Girgenti in Sicily. Had the Italian authorities known this, we could not have brought the marble to America, hence it had been billed to us by the finder as a copy only. Perhaps because it had cost us so much trouble, as well as because of its beauty, I valued my nymph fountain greatly.

It was a lovely thing in the trailing shadow of that late afternoon, but at night it was the center of my sunken garden's enchantment. The nymph's delicate figure was exposed where scant drapery did not swirl from one shoulder to dimpled knees. Above flying locks she held a large scallop-shell into which splashed sparkling jets of crystal clear spring water from an opening in the rugged marble rock behind her. The water splashed from the shell over her body so that at times the flowing radiance created an illusion of movement as if the laughing girl were alive.

Said the strange being confronting us: "More than once she had danced down from her pedestal when I piped in the temple grove at Girgenti. Too long has she lain under the earth. It is time she danced again."

His vibrant voice was so akin to the soughing of early night breezes, twittering of sleepy birds, chuckles and squeaks of wee woodland creatures, that I was obliged to admit that I was in the presence of something alien to modern human experience, something about which my flying conjectures could tell me nothing as yet.

"Give me the freedom of your garden, good youth. You shall not regret it. Pan knows what your soul desires and will grant your wish."

"And if I refuse?" I muttered, unable to free myself from the spell of that potent personality.

"I have the power to summon this maid if I so choose. You would not like that," he said knowingly.

Cecily's hand clutched at my shirt from where she stood behind me. I sensed her panicky terror and apprehension, and summoned my courage and good-sense; or so I thought it for the moment.

"The maiden," I said boldly, "is mine. As is that nymph. Now will you kindly get off my property? I don't know who you are and I like neither your silly masquerade nor your words and attitude."

THE brown face with its wispy beard lowered upon me. The narrowed eyes seemed to emit fiery sparks. In that moment *he* made me know. . . . There was indeed something in my garden and it was not a purely impersonal power. If I attempted to thwart that strange being's designs, he would crush me and my abortively launched obstacles ruthlessly. I knew deep within myself, suddenly, that he was tentatively, not actively, inimical, but that his power was far beyond my wildest imaginings.

"So the nymph is yours, youth, because to one who could never have owned her you gave your stupid gold? Have you paid gold for this maiden you call yours?" His full-lipped smile deepened. "I can offer more than a mortal's gold, youth. A god can offer his worshippers far more than they can dream. Your maiden may prefer a god to a mortal. Ask *her;* she knows."

That long finger pointed again to the marble nymph. I cursed my too-vivid imagination that made me seem to see her laughing lips curl mockingly.

"In America we do not buy maids with gold," I cried angrily in an outburst of daring.

"With what did you buy your maid, that you can call her yours?"

"I—we exchanged our love," I muttered. "Then we belong to each other."

PAN regarded me with what I felt was a kindly expression, for the blaze left his eyes and a momentary tenderness lurked within them.

"That is well," he said. "I like that in the New World. It is indeed very well. So the maiden has given you her love?" he probed with sly interest.

I felt misgivings. As yet I had not dared tell Cecily of my love in so many words and I feared that the bold declaration I had just made might tempt her into feminine contradiction. There was silence for a moment; then Cecily's voice murmured from behind me.

"Yes," it said softly. "Oh, yes!"

I turned and whipped her into my arms. "Darling," I whispered.

Something very human flickered over my strange visitor's face and I knew that he understood perfectly that Cecily and I had never before plighted our troth but that he was permitting us to believe we had fooled him.

"Tonight is Midsummer Eve, youth," he said abruptly.

From Cecily's golden head that rested against my heart I turned my uncomprehending gaze although his words brought vague recollections of childhood tales and superstitions.

"I marvel that your silly doctrines have not taught you that on this night all hidden powers above and below are loosened, youth. Alas, to be so ignorant and so blind!"

I remembered then that the morrow was Midsummer Day, the 23rd of June.

"Because I am in a strange new land where hitherto the gods have not foregathered because no worshippers called them, I must take advantage of every favorable circumstance, youth. Tonight I may best do this, in all the year. Here also have I found my playmate nymph in your sunken garden. I have found here wide spreads of grassy sward and a sheltered pine grove for my dryads. Here, too, I have found tranquil peace under the same stars that lighted my old world, that world now closed by diabolic Man to the spirits of the woods and seas and gardens."

I listened, amazed and understanding. Cecily clung to me and I knew that all I wanted was the knowledge of her security in my arms.

"You fear lest an olden god take your maid from you, youth? Give me your sunken garden and your green lawns and your pine grove, and my lonely nymph, and the maid remains yours if such is her choice."

Cecily's trembling body pressed closer to me. "Give him anything," she breathed, "but do not let him call me on his pipes for I fear him greatly. Nature can be relentlessly cruel, Craig, and Pan is the god of Nature."

"Although by now you must have admitted my identity, I offer yet further credentials than those in your own heart," offered the stranger and lifted the slouch hat from his straggling black locks, that tumbled over his forehead in wild confusion. His eyes never left mine as his hand brushed away that concealing hair from the small, polished black horns they had hidden. The incredulous truth gripped me with power beyond my will to believe.

"Name me!" said the brown man, his lips parting in a smile that mocked elfishly.

He moved ever so slightly. The fringes trailing about his feet parted; I saw that which was not a human foot. One hand half drew from his bosom the very syrinx, I could have sworn, that I had seen and Tom Leatherman had salvaged; it hung suspended by a brown cord from his neck.

I said hoarsely, "So you found the syrinx. Pan! You are Pan!"

"You believe?"

"I believe," I groaned unwillingly for my head spun with the tremendous truth.

"Bid the maiden leave us," he commanded.

In obedience to my urgent whisper, Cecily left the refuge of my arms and fled up the garden path to the house. I watched her go in at one of the French doors.

I could no longer refuse to believe the evidence of my senses that an Immortal deigned to visit my garden, incredible though it might seem. I might be unwilling, but I knew I dared not refuse to an Immortal whatsoever he asked. Resentment gnawed at me as I humbly waited for Pan to state his demands.

"The garden will be yours under the sun, youth, but at night it must be mine alone until such time as I may find another better suited to my purpose. Tonight my brother gods will lend me their aid and I shall pipe to those dryads and nymphs in the Old World who loved me best and they shall come tonight to the New World to people the pine grove with little fauns and to worship Pan once more as in days agone. The nymph you have called yours shall live again under the stars tonight. And if perchance your newly-betrothed maiden dares share her rapturous moments with a god, she may enter my garden unafraid. As may you, youth, if you can worship Pan."

I said in a choked voice that henceforth the garden would be closed to everyone at night.

With a lift of busy eyebrows and a sly quirk of full red lips Pan said, "Save to the maid, if she regret her present choice."

HE THREW back his head, laughed, and nimbly stepped past me to the thick shrubbery and there in broad daylight he went out to it as it went out to him. He had gone into nothingness while I stared stupidly at the spot where he had melted before my eyes.

I ran up to the house, thankful to get away from my now haunted garden. Cecily met me as I reached the terrace.

"Craig, who and what is he? He is no common man. He is god-like and diabolical at once. He allures and terrifies me."

I was glad that the telephone interrupted at this moment and

I went inside to answer it. Tom Leatherman's voice asked me brusquely if I'd been to his house; he'd missed the syrinx. I said the owner had seen it and taken it. Then I hung up on Tom's questionings.

"The owner?" asked Cecily pointedly.

I took her in my arms and told her what I had seen and heard and promised and believed in spite of myself.

"I knew it, Craig. It does sound incredible, but I knew he was not a real man. A god in our garden! Incredible."

"Cecily, our visitor *is* a god from the Old World. I have to believe it. I don't want to, and I don't like the situation, but I have to believe it or consider myself quite mad. Look, darling, he can do things. . . . Do you realize that I've been trying for months to get up courage to tell you I loved you? He made me say it."

I shook her gently and held her from me that I might search her face. Had she feigned her confession of love?

"Cecily, did you really mean that you love me?"

She came back into my arms with a naturalness that I had never quite hoped to see from her, in whom spontaneous impulse had been so carefully pruned away by her mother's prim ideas.

"Craig, Mother has always told me I mustn't act on impulse. I've always been afraid to let myself go," she admitted. "But I couldn't pretend before *him.*"

I said to myself, Pan was indeed a potent god. In his presence Cecily's inherited and carefully nourished ideas of prudery had died and her heart wakened to simple, natural impulse. My heart cried "Evohe, Pan!" as intuition told me my *recognition* of Pan's power was worship and that I was helping establish himself in America by my very gratitude. I held Cecily so that her heart beat against mine. Let it be worship, I told myself joyfully.

We agreed that we would watch the garden in secret that very night. As in most psychic experience, we needed more convincing evidence than we had already received. Aunt Kate was to be told nothing; she would not have believed had we told her. She might even consider us deranged, and forbid the engagement we planned to announce that night at dinner. It was a bit of good fortune that Aunt Kate's room was in an opposite wing from the sunken garden, although whether or not her stodgy materialism would enable her to see, hear, or even sense, anything unusual was questionable.

Ashby opened champagne by my special order after dinner. Aunt Kate seemed well pleased at the announcement of Cecily's engagement to me and even gave Cecily permission to stroll in the garden in my company without chaperonage. We did not take advantage of this rare liberty but retired to a corner of the living room by ourselves after dinner. Aunt Kate played solitaire until almost midnight, when to our vast relief she yawned widely, shuffled the cards into a neat pile and put them in the case.

She said as she rose, that even engaged young people should not be sitting around alone and bade Cecily say good night to me in ten minutes. Cecily looked at me archly and laughed softly, and the moment her mother disappeared from the room, the two of us hid behind the heavy velvet drapes at one of the library windows where we could observe what went on in the garden without ourselves being seen. We sat close together, hand in hand, and waited.

THE night was still with that country quiet so full of sound. Crickets and sleepy birds and an owlet's mournful hoo-hoo-hooing made a normal background that yet held something of strange magic on that mystic Midsummer Night's Eve. I was conscious of these small night sounds without actually hearing them. The luminous hands of the library clock marked midnight and the bells chimed the hour. As they ceased, Cecily and I were so aware suddenly that something had changed, that something more than simple nature—above it, beyond it, yet containing it in some mysterious way—had come into the garden, that our hands tightened involuntarily.

A low, sweet note swung out upon the waiting night, to be followed by others that dropped into a silence hollowed to receive them. Nature, become receptive, withheld those night sounds that had filled space, and drew into her yearning heart all the golden beauty that dropped generously from the pipes of Pan. Her patron god was abroad that night and well my garden knew it.

Cecily whispered, "Craig, I am not afraid any more. Pan calls tonight for love and laughter."

I clung to her hand then, for it was I who was afraid, not for myself but for her.

"Craig! The marble nymph! Look!" The delicate notes followed each other like individual entities into the waiting silence like fays sporting from flowering spray to spray. Cecily stood up so that I must stand with her, since our fingers were tightly interlaced. She was listening with her head tilted to one side, exactly as the nymph had stood beneath the crystal spray of the fountain. I followed her gaze as she listened with almost painful intensity and I could not smother a low exclamation at what I saw.

The nymph no longer held the scalloped shell above her head; the shell lay on the base of the pedestal. The nymph was dancing down the garden like a wild woman in a Bacchic orgy. The gleaming snowy marble of her body moved with the freedom of living flesh. Her scanty drapery drifted in the air where she held it high above her head like a triumphal banner as she drifted, rather than danced, across the shadowy lawn under the stars.

A series of brief notes with strange intervals lilted upward to my ears. Cecily jerked her fingers from mine. I had felt the pull of that bold theme as well as she but I tried to restrain her, fearing as I did that Immortal who waited without.

"Let me go, Craig, my dearest. Do you hear that call? I

am going to dance all night on the soft green grass. Are you coming? Come, come! If you do not, I must dance with *him*. Oh, dance with me, dearest!"

Ecstasy tingled in every passionate intonation of her joyous voice. I tried to seize her but she evaded me, laughing. As she ran, I followed, but she reached the French doors, which she flung wide before I could reach her side. I followed along a trail of draperies she discarded as she ran, and flung one way and the other carelessly. Before me, far lovelier than my wildest dreams could have imagined, Cecily's gleaming arms and throat shone like silver under the soft rays of the moon.

"Evohe, Pan, great Pan!" her voice floated back to me as she flitted past the strange god who stood piping before the sun-dial, no more disguised as an ordinary mortal.

The brown torso rose from hairy hips and thighs. His narrow dark face with wisp-like beard never left off following the two white figures dancing with abandon under the moon. Once, after a long roulade of thrilling enchantment, he dropped the syrinx from his lips, threw back his head and rocked with silent laughter. For all his alert attention, he was never still for a moment. Those goat-feet tripped lightly to and fro in time to the underlying rhythm of his piping and the unruly black hair tossed above pointed ears and little polished horns.

I approached that strange god without fear, sensing no antagonism toward me. As I approached, he took the reed-pipe from his red lips and called in friendly fashion.

"You leave your maiden to dance alone, youth? Do you not see that for the first time in her poor mortal experience she has become her natural self, uninhibited by silly conventions and prudish teachings? Go, fool. Dance with her. Else must she dance with a god and be lost to you forever."

Thereupon the piping became eldritch and maddening. I found myself leaping across the greensward in great bounds, and I sprang to Cecily's side, seizing upon the hand she extended. "Evohe, Pan!" I shouted madly as we danced and played across the lawn, while the clear moon and twinkling stars poured their rays full of the vital laughter of life upon our bodies abandoned to the ecstasy of that mad dance.

The music of the Pan-pipes went on and on and on and it seemed that our dance need never come to an end. The garden was full of piping sound, chanting voices, soft laughter. Mysterious Others joined us, as if the dryads and nymphs of the Old World were drifting into my sunken garden in joyous groups. We swung across the grass in long lines, hand in hand, to the melodious magic of Pan's weird music.

Then . . . a sudden, abrupt silence. The golden notes were still. Only the dark pine grove seemed alive as it never had been before, endued with a livingness akin to, but apart from, the trees. Across the lawn the marble nymph flitted. I saw her spring lightly to the pedestal of the fountain and lean over to pick up the scallop-shell. She flung her disheveled garment carelessly across her shoulder. No shaggy-thighed Immortal tripped nimbly to and fro on cloven hoofs before the sun-dial, piping unendurably alluring enchantments.

Cecily's grasp on my fingers relaxed. Her body slipped down at my feet. The faint, luminous dawn touched her skin with rosy highlights. With the amazed mortification overcoming me as one who in a nightmare finds himself unclothed on a busy city street, I had a sensation as if I stood naked under the retiring stars. I knelt beside the girl who had danced with me since midnight with such mad abandon; her heart beat steadily but lightly. I knew she should be inside the house and safe in bed.

I lifted her in my arms and carried her there, kissing her lips as I laid her down and drew the silken sheet over her beautiful body. Then I slipped away, lest her mother waken and find me in Cecily's room, and throw upon my sweetheart the vile suspicions of a so-called pure mind.

I WONDERED what conflict would arise in Cecily in the morning, between inherited and tutored tendencies, and the simplicity and naturalness of her behavior under the influence of Pan's piping. I wondered how I could spare her blushes and, to speak truth, my own. But at breakfast that midsummer morn Cecily met my eyes across the table with an entire absence of self-consciousness. I felt almost regretful, because it seemed that she must have thought last night a dream known only to herself, and I—I cherished the memory.

Aunt Kate remarked, as she poured my coffee, that Ashby had reported a change in the posture of the marble nymph. "This being utterly absurd," said she, "I felt that he must have had something to drink. When I accused him, he was most resentful. He said the statue's scarf, or whatever it is she seems to wear so raffishly, is hanging half off her shoulder."

"Isn't half a scarf better than none?" Cecily asked demurely and her eyes met mine dear and sweet, although the loveliest of blushes tinged her cheeks.

"I am still of the opinion that it is ridiculous for Ashby to insist that a marble statue has changed in any way," Aunt Kate retorted. "I'll take a look myself after breakfast."

A tightness about her lips told me that Ashby would be in for a bawling-out if Aunt Kate noticed nothing different and scraped up the first excuse that occurred to me since I felt one must be made sooner or later.

"I sold the marble nymph," said I. "She cost too much and I got a fat profit on the deal. I had a plastic copy made. They tell me the plastic is affected by moonlight," I explained. "It will probably seem to change slightly from time to time. Interesting, isn't it?"

Aunt Kate looked a trifle blank but Cecily broke into a gale of laughter.

I thought I heard a delicate roulade of echoing laughter drift to my ears from the sunken garden.

The Antimacassar

Greye La Spina

"She didn't last very long," said Mrs. Renner's resentful voice.

Lucy Butterfield turned her head on the pillow so that she might hear better the whisperings outside her bedroom door. She was not loath to eavesdrop in that house of secret happenings, if by listening she might find some clue to Cora Kent's mysterious disappearance.

"Because she was not a well woman, missus. It was just too much for her. You should've knowed it, if Kathy didn't."

That, Lucy knew, was the voice of Aaron Gross, the ancient pauper whom her landlady explained she had taken from the county poor-farm to do her outdoor chores. It was a high, cackling voice quite in character with the dried-up little man to whom it belonged.

"Sh-sh-sh! Want to wake her up?"

Lucy sat upright in bed, by now keenly attuned to those low voices in the corridor outside her room. The knowledge that she was not supposed to hear what her landlady and the hired man were discussing lent a certain allure—half mischievous, half serious—to her almost involuntary eavesdropping.

"Kathy had to be fed," said Mrs. Renner's sharp whisper. "Listen at her now! How'm I going to put her off? Tell me that!"

Lucy, too, listened. From one of the locked rooms along the corridor she heard a soft moaning and knew that what she had been hearing for several nights was not a dream. Twelve-year-old Kathy Renner, confined to her bed with rheumatic fever and denied the solace of sympathetic company for fear the excitement might bring on a heart attack, was wailing softly.

"Mom! I'm hungry! Mom! I'm hungry!"

Why, the poor kid! Lying there alone all day with no one to talk to, and crying all night with hunger. Lucy's gorge rose against the hard efficiency of Mrs. Renner. How could a mother bear hearing that pitiful pleading? As if some relentless intuition pushed her into explanation, Mrs. Renner's voice came huskily.

"Listen at her! Oh, my little Kathy! I just can't bear it. I can't get at them tonight but tomorrow I'm going to take out that honeysuckle!"

Lucy's gray eyes roved across the room to rest with puzzlement upon a tall vase of yellow-blossomed honeysuckle dimly seen in the half light on one shelf of the old bureau between the two south windows. She had thought it pleasant that her landlady brought them in fresh daily, for their high perfume was sweet and they seemed part of the country life to which she had given herself for a two-week vacation from her new and responsible buyer's position in the linen department of Munger Brothers in Philadelphia.

"Don't do it, missus. You'll just be sorry if you do. Don't do it!" Sharp protest in old Aaron's querulous voice. "You know what happened with that other gal. You can't keep that up, missus. If this one goes, it won't be like the first one and then you'll have double trouble, missus, mark my words. Don't do it! Accidents are one thing; on purpose is another. Let me get a sharp stake, missus—?"

"Hush! Get back to bed, Aaron. Leave this to me. After all, I'm Kathy's mother. You're not going to stop me. I'm not going to let her go hungry. Get back to bed, I tell you."

"Well, her door's locked and there's honeysuckle inside. You can't do anything tonight," grudgingly acceded Aaron.

Footsteps receded softly down the corridor. The old Pennsylvania Dutch farmhouse out in the Haycock sank into silence, save only for that plaintive moaning from the child's room.

"Mom! I'm hungry! Mom!"

LUCY lay long awake. She could not compose herself to sleep while that unhappy whimper continued. Against its eerie background her thoughts went to the reason for her stay at Mrs. Renner's out-of-the-way farmhouse in Bucks County. It had begun with the non-appearance of Cora Kent, Lucy's immediate superior in Munger Brothers' linen department. Cora had not returned to work at the expiration of her vacation period and inquiries only emphasized the fact of her disappearance. She had left for the country in her coupe, taking a small table loom and boxes of colored thread.

Lucy had liked Miss Kent as a business associate and felt reluctant at taking over her job. Somebody had had to assume the responsibility and Lucy stood next in line. Her vacation had come three weeks after Miss Kent's and she had insisted upon taking it as a partial preparation for taking over the job. In her heart she determined to scout about the countryside to see if she could find some clue to Cora Kent's mysterious disappearance. She felt that Cora would not have gone far afield and so she took up her headquarters in Doylestown, county seat of Bucks, while she carried on her self-imposed detective work.

In the Haycock region outside Quakertown, where many isolated farms were located, she came upon a clue. She had learned at the Doylestown Museum the names of weavers and inquiries had taken her to Mrs. Renner's farm. On the third day of her vacation Lucy had come to an agreement with Mrs. Renner for a week's board and weaving lessons. In the upstairs front room that was to be hers, Lucy exclaimed with enthusiasm over the coverlet on the old spool bed, at the runners on the wash-stand and the antique bureau with its tall shelves and drawers on either side of the high mirror. A stuffed chair upholstered in material that Mrs. Renner said was woven by herself caught Lucy's attention and the antimacassar pinned on the back caught her eye particularly. Mrs. Renner said with a certain uneasiness that she hadn't woven it herself and her eyes evaded Lucy's shiftily. Lucy offered to buy it and Mrs. Renner at once unpinned it.

She said shortly: "Take it. I never did like it. Glad to be shut of it."

When Lucy went back to Doylestown to pick up her belongings, she wrote a brief note to Stan's mother and enclosed the weaving. She gave her prospective mother-in-law Mrs. Renner's address. Lucy knew that Stan's mother, with whom she was on exceptionally good terms, would be pleased with the odd bit of weaving and was sure it would be shown to Stan when he came home over the week-end from his senior medical course studies.

The antimacassar wasn't as crazy-looking as she had at first imagined. It was a neat piece of work, even if the central design was loosely haphazard. The decorative blocks at corners and center top and bottom weren't so poorly designed and the irregular markings through the center were amusing; they looked like some kind of ancient symbols. Mrs. Brunner would be charmed to receive an authentic piece of obviously original weaving. Lucy promised herself to find out about the weaver, once she had gained her landlady's confidence.

She had asked Mrs. Renner outright if ever a Miss Cora Kent had been at the Renner place and her landlady had eyed her strangely and denied ever having heard the name, even. On Friday morning, her second day on the Renner farm, Aaron Gross brought Lucy a package from the Doylestown laundry, where she had left lingerie. He acted so suspicious and fearful that she was puzzled. When she stripped the covering from the package, he took it and crumpled it as if he were afraid some-one would know she had given her address freely before going to the farm. Lucy counted the small pieces; there were eleven instead of ten. There was an extra handkerchief and it was initialed. It was then that Lucy received the first impact of ominous intuition. The handkerchief carried the initials "C. K." Cora Kent must have lived somewhere in the vicinity.

There was a penciled note from the laundry. The handkerchief had been mistakenly delivered to another customer and was now being returned apologetically to its owner's address. Cora Kent had been to the Renner farm. Mrs. Renner had lied deliberately when she said she had never heard the name.

Lucy looked up at the sound of a rustling starched skirt, to find Mrs. Renner staring down at Cora's handkerchief, sallow brow furrowed, lips a straight line, black eyes narrowed. Mrs. Renner said nothing; she only stared. Then she turned suddenly on her heel and marched into the house. Lucy was disturbed without actually knowing why, yet Mrs. Renner's deliberate lie was in itself a puzzle.

THIS was only one of the small things that began to trouble her, like the locked door that confined Kathy Renner. Mrs. Renner had said definitely that she didn't want people barging in on Kathy, perhaps getting her all excited, what with the danger of heart trouble on account of the rheumatic fever. Kathy, it would appear, slept all day for Lucy was asked to be very quiet about the house in daytime. At night noise didn't disturb the little sick girl because then she would be awake anyway.

Lucy sat up in bed now and listened to the child's whining complaint. Why didn't Kathy's mother give the poor child something to eat? Surely starvation was not included in a regimen for rheumatic fever? There was the faint sound of a door opening and the wails subsided. Lucy lay down then and slipped comfortably off to sleep, feeling that Kathy's needs had been met.

Mrs. Renner's enigmatic remarks and Aaron's peevish disapproval of his employer's behavior on some former occasion dimmed as sleep stilled Lucy's active mind. It was not until afternoon of the following day that Lucy, entering her room to get her scissors so that she might use them when weaving, noticed with sudden sharp recollection of her landlady's whispered words of the previous night that the vase of honeysuckle was conspicuous by its absence. She asked herself vainly what connection had honeysuckle to do with Kathy's wailing cry of hunger? Or, for that matter, with herself?

With the vague idea of blocking Mrs. Renner's contemplated design hinted to Aaron Friday night, Lucy managed to pluck several sprays of lilac and honeysuckle from her open window, smartly avoiding carrying them through the house. She put them into the heavy stoneware tooth-mug that stood on the washstand. To remove these flowers, Mrs. Renner must come out into the open and explain her reason for taking them away, thought Lucy mischievously.

In the big downstairs living-room where Mrs. Renner's enormous lofty loom occupied space, the landlady had cleared a table and upon it stood a small loom about fifteen inches wide. Lucy examined this with interest for she recognized it at once as a model carried in the store where she worked. She said nothing of this but eyed Mrs. Renner surreptitiously when that lady explained that it was an old machine given her years ago by a former student who had no need for it. There was a white warp threaded in twill, for a plain weave, Mrs. Renner explained.

"What kind of weaving can you do on twill?" Lucy queried, thinking of the antimacassar she had sent to Stan's mother, the piece with the queer little hand inlaid figures woven into it.

"All manner of things," Mrs. Renner said. "On a twill, you can do almost anything, Miss. Mostly hand work." She manipulated the levers in illustration as she talked. "You'd better stick to plain weaving at first. Hand work isn't so easy and takes a heap more time."

"That antimacassar you let me have is hand work, isn't it?" Lucy probed.

Mrs. Renner flung her an oddly veiled look.

"Tomorrow you can weave a white cotton towel with colored borders," she said abruptly. "No use starting tonight. Hard to work with kerosene lamps."

Lucy opined that she could hardly wait. It seemed incredible that she was actually to manufacture the fabric of a towel with her own hands and within the brief limits of a day. She went up to her room fairly early and, as she had done from the first, locked her door, a habit acquired from living in city boarding houses. From deep sleep she stirred once into half waking at the sound of a cautious turning of the doorknob and retreating foot-steps and the moaning plaint of the little sick girl's "Mom, I'm hungry!" which seemed so close that for a moment she could have believed the child to be standing closely without her locked door. She thought she heard the child say, "Mom, I can't get in! I can't get in!"

Mrs. Renner was obviously feeling far from well the following morning. Her eyes were ringed by dark circles and she wore a loosely knotted kerchief about her neck, although the sweltering heat would have seemed sufficient to have made her discard rather than wear any superfluous article of clothing. When Lucy was seated at the loom, she showed her how to change the sheds and throw the shuttle for a plain weave, then left her working there while she went upstairs to tidy her guest's room. When she came down a few moments later, she walked up to Lucy, her face dark and grim, her lips a hard uncompromising line.

"Did you put those flowers up in your room?" she demanded.

Lucy stopped weaving and turned her face to Mrs. Renner in feigned surprise but her intuition told her that there was more to the inquiry than was apparent on the surface.

"I love flowers so much," she murmured, deprecatorily.

"Not in a room at night," snapped Mrs. Renner. "They're unhealthy at night. That's why I took out the others. I don't want flowers in my bedrooms at night."

The tone was that of an order and Lucy's natural resentment, as well as her heightened curiosity, made her rebel.

"I'm not afraid of having flowers in my room at night, Mrs. Renner," she persisted stubbornly.

"Well, I won't have it," said her landlady with determined voice and air.

Lucy raised her eyebrows.

"I see no good reason to make an issue of a few flowers, Mrs. Renner."

"I've thrown those flowers out, Miss. You needn't bring any more, for I'll just throw them out, too. If you want to stay in my house, you'll have to get along without flowers in your room."

"If you feel so strongly about it, of course I won't bring flowers inside. But I must say frankly that it sounds silly to me, their being unhealthful."

Mrs. Renner stalked away. She appeared satisfied at the assertion of her authority as hostess and the balance of Sunday was spent initiating Lucy into the intricacies of decorative twill weaves, to such good effect that by the time evening came Lucy had completed a small towel in white cotton with striped twill borders in color.

Lucy fell half asleep in the hammock that evening. The fresh country air and the lavish supply of good country food combined to bring early drowsiness to her eyes. She came awake when a small mongrel dog she had seen from time to time in and out of the Renner barn began to dig furiously around the roots of a nearby shrub, unearthing eventually a small blue bottle half filled with white tablets. She pushed the dog away and picked up the bottle. She looked at it curiously. A shiver of apprehension went over her body. She had seen just such a container on Cora Kent's office desk and Cora had said something about garlic being good for tubercular-inclined people. Lucy unscrewed the bottle cap and sniffed at the contents. The odor was unmistakable. She quickly slipped the bottle inside her blouse. She knew now beyond the shadow of a doubt that Cora Kent had preceded her as a guest in the Renner household. She knew now that the small loom must have been Cora's. The initialed handkerchief was yet another silent witness.

Lucy crept up to her room and again locked the door. She slipped the back of a chair under the knob as a further precaution. For the first time, she began to sense some threat to her own safety. Her thoughts flew to the flowers Mrs. Renner had tossed from the window. Why should her landlady take such a stand? Why had she told old Aaron that she was going to "take out the honeysuckle?" What was there about honeysuckle that made Mrs. Renner wish to remove it from her guest's room, as if it had something to do with Kathy Renner's plaintive, "Mom, I'm hungry!"

Lucy could not fit the pieces of the puzzle together properly. But the outstanding mention of honeysuckle determined her to pull several more sprays from the vine clambering up the wall outside her window. If Mrs. Renner did not want them in the room, then Lucy was determined to have them there. She removed the screen quietly and leaned out. It struck her with a shock. Every spray of flowering honeysuckle within reaching distance had been rudely broken off and dropped to the ground below. Somebody had foreseen her reaction. She replaced the screen and sat down on the edge of her bed, puzzled and disturbed. If Mrs. Renner was entertaining nefarious designs that mysteriously involved the absence of honeysuckle, then Lucy knew she would be unable to meet the situation suitably.

It might have been amusing in broad daylight. She could just walk away to the shed where her car was garaged. Even if "they" had done something to it, Lucy figured that she could walk or run until she reached the main road where there ought to be trucks and passenger cars; not the solitude of the secluded Renner farm, hidden behind thickly wooded slopes.

She told herself sharply that she was just being an imaginative goose, just being silly and over-suspicious. What could honeysuckle have to do with her personal security? She got ready for bed, resolutely turned out the kerosene lamp. Drowsiness overcame her and she sank into heavy sleep.

She did not hear Mrs. Renner's sibilant whisper: "Sh-sh-sh! Kathy! You can come now, Kathy. She's sound asleep. Mother took out the honeysuckle. You can get in now. Sh-sh-sh!"

She did not hear old Aaron's querulous protest: "You can't do this, missus. Let me get the stake, missus. It'd be better that way, Missus . . ."

To Lucy, soundly sleeping within her locked room, no sound penetrated. Her dreams were strangely vivid and when she finally wakened Monday morning she lay languidly recalling that final dream wherein a white-clad child had approached her bed timidly, had crept in beside her until her arms had embraced the small, shy intruder. The child had put small warm lips against her throat in what Lucy felt was a kiss, but a kiss such as she had never in her life experienced. It stung cruelly. But when she yielded to the child's caress, a complete relaxation of mind and muscle fell upon her and it was as if all of herself were being drawn up to meet those childish lips that clung close to her neck. It was a disturbing dream and even the memory of it held something of mingled antipathy and allure.

LUCY knew it was time to rise and she sat up, feeling tired, almost weak, and somehow disinclined to make the slightest physical effort. It was as if something had gone out of her, she thought exhaustedly. She lifted one hand involuntarily to her neck. Her fingers sensed a small roughness, like two pin pricks, where the dream child had kissed her so strangely, so poignantly. Lucy got out of bed then and went to the mirror. Clear on her neck were those two marks, as if a great beetle had clipped the soft flesh with sharp mandibles. She cried out softly at the sight of those ruddy punctures.

That there was something wrong, she was now convinced. That it also concerned herself, she felt certain. She was unable to analyze the precise nature of the wrongness but knew that it held something inimical in the very atmosphere of the Renner farmhouse and unreasoning terror mounted within her. Could she get to her car and escape? *Escape . . . ?* She stared at her neck in the mirrored reflection and fingered the red marks gingerly. Her thoughts could not be marshalled into coherence and she found herself thinking of but one thing—flight. She could not have put into words just what it was from which she ought to flee but that she must leave the Renner farmhouse at the earliest possible moment became a stronger conviction with every passing moment. In her mind one ugly, incontrovertible fact stood out only too clearly: Cora Kent had visited the Renner farm and had not been seen since.

Lucy dressed hastily and managed to slip out of the house without encountering her landlady. She found her car under the shed at the rear of the barn, where she had left it. It looked all right but when she got closer, she saw to her dismay that it had two flats. She had, as was usual, but one spare tire. She did not know how to take off or put on even that one spare tire, let alone manage to repair the second flat. She would be unable to drive away from the Renner farm in her car. She stood staring in dismay at the useless vehicle.

Aaron Gross's whining voice came softly to her ear. She whirled to confront him accusingly.

"What happened to my car? Who—?"

"You can't be using it right away, miss, with them two tires flat," Aaron volunteered, whiningly. "Want I should take them down to a service station for you?"

She cried with relief: "That would be splendid, Aaron. But I don't know how to get them off."

"Neither do I, miss. I dunno nothing about machines."

Impatience and apprehension mingled in the girl's voice. She threw open the luggage compartment and began to pull out the tools.

"I think I can jack up the car, Aaron. I've never done it

before, but I do want the car so that I can get to town. Shopping," she added quickly, trying to smile carelessly.

Aaron made no comment. He stood at the end of the shed watching her as she managed to get the jack under the rear axle and began to pump the car off the ground.

"I'll need a box to hold this up when I put the jack under that other tire," she suggested.

Aaron shuffled away.

Lucy managed to pry off the hub cap but with all her feverish attempts at the nuts and bolts, she could stir nothing. She stopped in despair, waiting for Aaron to return with the box. She thought she might get him to have a mechanic come up from town. Panting and disheveled, she walked out of the shed to look for him. As she emerged, Mrs. Renner confronted her, grim-lipped, narrow-eyed.

"Anything wrong?" inquired Mrs. Renner, both fat hands smoothing down blue checkered apron over ample hips.

"My car has two flats! I can't understand why," blurted Lucy.

Mrs. Renner's face remained impassive. She stated rather than asked, "You don't need to go into town. Aaron can do your errands."

"Oh, but I do want to get to town," insisted Lucy with vehemence.

"You don't need your car until you're leaving here," said Mrs. Renner coldly. She regarded Lucy with impassive face, then turned her back and walked toward the house without another word.

Lucy called: "Mrs. Renner! Mrs. Renner! I'd like to have Aaron take these two wheels into town to be repaired but I can't get them off."

Mrs. Renner continued on her way and disappeared into the house without turning or giving the least sign that she had heard a word.

From the interior of the barn Aaron's querulous voice issued cautiously.

"Miss, want I should ask the mechanic to come out here?"

"Oh, Aaron, that would be wonderful! I'd be glad to pay him—and you;—well. Tell him I just can't get those tires off by myself."

THAT would do it, she told herself. Once the mechanic was there, she would bring down her suitcase and manage to get into town and have him send someone to bring out her car when the tires were repaired. She would manage to leave before night. While Aaron was away, she would work on the loom that she was convinced had been Cora Kent's property. That might disarm Mrs. Renner's suspicions.

She walked slowly back to the house. She was thankful that Mrs. Renner was upstairs tidying the bedroom; Lucy could hear her steps as she walked from one side to the other of the big bed. Lucy sat down at the loom and began to experiment with a colored thread, to see if she would make an ornamental border like that of the antimacassar she had sent to Stan's mother. It was not as difficult as she had thought it might be and went faster than she believed possible; it was almost as if other fingers laid the threads in place for her. She began to build up the border emblems with growing excitement. The corner inserts looked for all the world like curving serpents standing upright on their tails and the center one was like a snake with its tail in its mouth. Time passed. The weaving grew under what she felt were guided fingers.

"Why," she said aloud, amazed at what she had woven in so short a time. "It looks like S-O-S!"

"So?" hissed Mrs. Renner significantly.

She was standing directly behind Lucy, staring at the woven symbols with narrowed eyes and grim mouth. She picked up the scissors lying on the table and slashed across the weaving with deliberate intent. In a moment it had been utterly destroyed.

"So!" she said with dark finality.

Lucy's hands had flown to her mouth to shut off horrified protest. She could not for a moment utter a word. The significance of that action was all too clear. She knew suddenly who had woven the antimacassar. She knew why the adaptable serpents had been chosen for decor. She looked at Mrs. Renner, all this knowledge clear on her startled face and met the grim determination with all the opposing courage and strength of purpose she could muster.

"What happened to Cora Kent?" she demanded point blank, her head high, her eyes wide with horror. "She was here. I know she was here. What did you do to her?" As if the words had been thrust upon her, she continued: "Did you take the honeysuckle from *her* room?"

AMAZINGLY, Mrs. Renner seemed to be breaking down. She began to wring her hands with futile gestures of despair. Her air of indomitable determination dissipated as she bent her body from one side to the other like an automaton.

"She didn't last long, did she?" Lucy pursued with cruel relentlessness, as the recollection of that overheard conversation pushed to the foreground of her thoughts.

Mrs. Renner stumbled backward and fell crumpled shapelessly into a chair.

"How did you know that?" she whispered hoarsely. And then, "I didn't know she was sick. I had to feed Kathy, didn't I? I thought—"

"You thought she'd last longer, missus, didn't you? You didn't really mean to let Kathy kill her, did you?"

Aaron was standing in the kitchen doorway. One gnarled hand held a stout stick, whittled into a sharp point at one end. A heavy wooden mallet weighed down his other hand.

Mrs. Renner's eyes fastened on the pointed stick. She cried out weakly.

Aaron shuffled back into the kitchen and Lucy heard his footsteps going up the stairs.

Mrs. Renner was sobbing and crying frantically: "No! No!"

She seemed entirely bereft of physical stamina, unable to lift herself from the chair into which her body had sunk weakly.

She only continued to cry out pitifully in protest against something which Lucy's dizzy surmises could not shape into tangibility.

A door opened upstairs. Aaron's footsteps paused. For a long terrible moment silence prevailed. Even Mrs. Renner's cries ceased. It was as if the house and all in it were awaiting an irrevocable event.

Then there sailed out upon that sea of silence a long quavering shriek of tormented, protesting agony that died away in spreading ripples of sound, ebbing into the finality of deep stillness as if the silence had absorbed them.

Mrs. Renner slipped unconscious to the floor. She said one word only as her body went from chair to floor. "Kathy!" Her lips pushed apart sluggishly to permit the escape of that sound.

Lucy stood without moving beside the loom with its slashed and ruined web. It was as if she were unable to initiate the next scene in the drama and were obliged to await her cue. It came with the sound of wheels and a brake and a voice that repeatedly called her name.

"Lucy! Lucy!"

Why, it was Stan. How was it that Stan had come to her? How was it that his arms were about her shelteringly? She found her own voice then.

"Aaron has killed Kathy with a sharp stick and a mallet," she accused sickly.

Stan's voice was full of quiet reassurance.

"Aaron hasn't killed Kathy. Kathy has been dead for many weeks."

"Impossible," whispered Lucy. "I've heard her calling for food, night after night."

"Food, Lucy? All Kathy wanted was blood. Her mother tried to satisfy her and couldn't, so Kathy took what Cora Kent could give and Cora couldn't stand the drain."

"Mrs. Renner said Cora didn't last long—"

Stan held her closer, comfortingly safe within his man's protective strength.

"Lucy, did she—?"

Lucy touched her neck. Incomprehensibly, the red points had smoothed away.

She said uncertainly: "I think she came, once, Stan. But I thought it was a dream. Now the red marks are gone."

"For that you can thank Aaron's action, Lucy. He has put an end to Kathy's vampirism."

He bent over the prostrate woman. "Nothing but a faint," he said briefly.

"Aaron—?"

"He's perfectly sane and he won't hurt anybody, Lucy. What he's done won't be understood by the authorities but I doubt if they do more than call him insane, for an examination will prove that Kathy was long dead before he drove that wooden stake into her heart."

"How did you know about her, Stan?"

"From the antimascassar you sent Mother."

"With the S-O-S worked into the border?" Lucy ventured.

"So you found that, too, Lucy? Did you know that poor girl had woven shorthand symbols all over the piece? As soon as I realized that they stood for 'Vampire, danger, death, Cora Kent', I came for you."

"What will happen to Mrs. Renner, Stan?"

"That's hard to say. But she may be charged with murder if they ever find Cora's body."

Lucy shuddered.

"The likelihood is that she is mentally unsound, dear. She

probably never realized that Kathy was dead. Her punishment may not be too severe.

"But come on, Lucy, and pack up your things. You're going back to town with me and we'll inform the authorities of what's happened."

Meet the Women Who Pioneered Horror and Speculative Fiction!

Monster, She Wrote

The Women Who Pioneered Horror & Speculative Fiction

BY LISA KRÖGER AND MELANIE R. ANDERSON

2019 BRAM STOKER AWARD® WINNER FOR SUPERIOR ACHIEVEMENT IN NON-FICTION

2020 LOCUS AWARD WINNER FOR NON-FICTION

"I was elated when Monster, She Wrote arrived in my mailbox. It is a book I have been waiting to read for a long time . . . Lisa Kröger and Melanie R. Anderson deserve a standing ovation."

—Danielle Trussoni for
The New York Times Book Review

Available wherever books are sold!
Visit QuirkBooks.com for more information.

CPSIA information can be obtained
at www.ICGtesting.com
Printed in the USA
LVHW091536230921
698574LV00001B/111

9 781948 405751